THE MAKE-BELIEVE

Marriage

CHAPTER 1

London, England
September 1825

CAPTAIN OCTAVIAN THORNE'S head was pounding as he lay prone on the damp grass while trying to restore his senses after falling off the roof of Sir Henry Maxwell's townhouse in London's elegant Mayfair. It was dark, well after midnight on this rainy night, and he had taken the plunge while trying to stop Lady Sydney Harcourt from breaking into Sir Henry's bedchamber to steal her father's debt vouchers. Syd, who was fast becoming the bane of his existence, was now by his side, her bosom grazing his chest as she leaned over him to run her hands along his big, brutish body. "Leave me alone, Syd."

"Don't move, you big ox. I'm just making certain you haven't broken any bones. I did not mean to push you off the roof. I thought you were one of Sir Henry's men trying to stop me. You might have said something before I shoved you. What are you doing here?"

"Me? What in blazes are you doing here?"

"Trying to find my father's vowels and destroy them. Don't move yet," she said with urgency when he attempted to sit up. "Please, Octavian. You might have broken bones."

"And you might have been caught by Sir Henry," he grumbled back, angry enough to throttle her. "What do you think he would have done to you if he had found you skulking in his bedchamber?"

"Nothing I care to think about," she admitted, placing a soft hand upon his neck to run her fingers lightly across the nape before sliding her hands down his chest and leaving a fiery trail wherever she touched. "I saw him go out earlier. I knew he would not be home. Nor is he likely to return for at least another hour. He frequents those debauched gentlemen's clubs. Look at you, what a mess you are. You ought to know better than to climb onto those rain-slicked tiles."

"Stop lecturing me and stop touching me. I came here to rescue *you*. Sir Henry does not keep his business papers in his bedchamber, something I could have told you if you had bothered to ask me."

"He doesn't? How do you know this?"

"I have my sources," he shot back, his irritation growing along with his discomfort. He was wet, bruised, and still on fire because Syd's body was practically atop his and she would not take her hands off him.

"Is the Admiralty investigating him?"

"None of your business."

She said nothing more as she cupped one of his hands in hers and ordered him to wriggle his fingers. "Good, they're all moving." She then ordered him to do the same with the other.

"I haven't broken any bones." He had merely fallen off the low roof and landed in dense shrubbery before rolling onto the wet grass. It had been raining until a few minutes ago which was why both he and Syd were soaking wet. As for his injuries, they were minor. Only a small bump to his head acquired when his skull came in contact with a protruding tree branch.

"Octavian, do you think you can walk? Let me try to find us a hack and–"

"No, my carriage is around the corner. You're coming with me to the Thorne residence. I dare not deliver you back home. If you are desperate enough to sneak into Sir Henry's home, this can only mean your father intends to do something foolish involving you." He inhaled sharply, feeling a twinge to his ribs that he ignored since any bruises incurred would fade within a day or two. "Syd, is he threatening to betroth you to Sir Henry? Why did you not come to me as soon as you learned of his plan?"

She gently brushed a stray lock of hair off his brow. "You are a good friend, Octavian. How can I toss you into my father's messes? As for your question, the answer is no. There is no betrothal planned."

"No betrothal?" There was something in the soft release of Syd's breath that had Octavian sitting up and grasping her hand. "Is he going to marry you off straight away then? No betrothal contract or banns read? Tell me the truth, Syd. Is this what he plans to do to save his own hide?"

She finally broke down and allowed her tears to fall. "Tomorrow is the big horse auction at Tattersalls, so Sir Henry will be attending that all day. I'm to marry him the day after tomorrow unless I can get my hands on my father's vowels and destroy them. The wedding is to take place at St. Andrew's Church. The plan is for Sir Henry to purchase the license, my father consents, and the ceremony occurs straight afterward. No more than ten minutes, start to finish. Everything a girl dreams of."

Octavian caressed her cheek. Sir Henry Maxwell, the lecherous old goat, had already buried two young wives. He had no intention of allowing Syd to be the third ill-fated wife, although why he should bother was beyond him. He had survived major battles with less injuries than incurred while rescuing this hazardous hoyden from her numerous scrapes. "So, he has no license yet?"

"None yet." She shook her head. "But what does it matter? He and my father have it all arranged. And I cannot find some hapless clot to marry me because I am not yet of age and need my father's consent."

"Hapless clot?" Octavian could not believe what he was about to offer. Syd was the most infuriating young woman it was ever his misfortune to know, but he had somehow taken her under his wing and sworn he would always protect her.

Yes, he had merely sworn this to himself and never actually

made that vow to Syd. However, a vow was a vow. It made no difference who knew of it. She was in trouble and he was determined to save her. One thing for certain, life would never be dull with her. He rolled to his feet with care and drew her up along with him. "Come, you little nuisance. We had better leave before we're spotted."

He gave her no chance to protest, quietly lifting her over Sir Henry's gate and climbing over it next. He caught hold of her hand again, refusing to let go of her until they were safely back at his residence because he did not trust her to stay put.

To his surprise, she did not try to fight him. Instead, she cried fresh tears the moment they were safely in his carriage and underway, making rapid time as the conveyance clattered through the London streets that were fairly empty at this hour.

Seeing her so beaten down was far worse than seeing her angry.

Octavian drew her close and wrapped his arm around her shoulders, wishing she would get that blaze back in her eyes and rail at him again.

Seeing her scared and vulnerable completely destroyed him.

The rain had renewed by the time they reached the Thorne townhouse he shared with his brothers. Ambrose, who was the eldest of the Thornes, was Duke of Huntsford and owned the house. Octavian and their youngest brother, Julius, both of them bachelors and not often in London other than on business, shared the home with Ambrose. That would soon have to change since Ambrose was married to Adela, one of Syd's best friends, and they were busy starting a family.

But for now, they were one big, happy family residing together.

Octavian was the only Thorne in London at the moment. Ambrose and Adela were in Devonshire excavating more fossils while Julius was in York attending to family business matters. Octavian was due to travel north to Glasgow and Greenock on behalf of the Royal Navy at the end of the week, an assignment he could not refuse while still actively commissioned.

An idea sprang to mind, but he was not going to discuss it with

Syd until they had changed out of their wet clothes and got warm liquids into them.

He took her straight inside as soon as the carriage drew up to the Thorne front gate. "Thank you, Hastings," he said to the driver. "I'll have no further need of the carriage tonight."

"Very good, Captain," the man replied with a nod, obviously relieved to be getting out of the rain himself.

Syd said nothing as they walked inside, but held him back when he was about to lead her upstairs. Her eyes widened in surprise. Well, not surprise so much as shock and horror once the import of what being alone with him meant. "Octavian, do you expect me to spend the night here with you? I–"

"Not another word, Syd. What difference does it make? The best thing that could happen is for word of your indiscretion to get out and cause Sir Henry to refuse to marry you."

She did not appear to like the idea at all. "But then he will hurt my father."

"Your father is a little weasel who will manage to slip out of his punishment somehow." Octavian tried to suppress his anger but could not and it resounded in his voice. "Besides, it might do him some good to get knocked about."

"Octavian!"

"The man obviously needs sense pounded into him. Why are you so considerate of him when he has never spared a thought for you or your mother? He's burned away the Harcourt assets at the gaming tables or on fanciful business schemes, and does not give a fig about having you bear the punishment for his actions."

Since he was still holding onto Syd's hand, he felt the ripples of shame flow through her. "Sorry, Syd. Falling off a roof in the pouring rain tends to put me in bad humor."

"My father is an awful scoundrel," she said with aching sadness. "I cannot blame you for despising him. But he has been a loving father to me. He does not mean to do the things he does. He keeps thinking his luck will turn with the next roll of the dice or the next ridiculous business venture."

"That does not excuse him." He led her upstairs to his bedchamber and lit a fire in the hearth. The wood had already been stacked neatly in the grate, so it took him little time to get a healthy blaze going. While it was not a cold night, dampness filled the air and Syd was shivering.

Octavian raked a hand through his hair.

What was he to do with her?

She was desperate for help and too ashamed ever to ask for it. Her heart was so battered, she did not even comment when he strode to her side and removed her coat and cap.

Octavian studied her by the golden firelight that illuminated his bedchamber.

She had donned boys clothes that were a few sizes too big for her. Cap, shirt and jacket, breeches, and sturdy boots. Tendrils of wet hair were pasted to her cheeks, and her glorious mass of ginger-blonde hair was barely held up by the few pins that had not yet fallen out.

She was soaked, bedraggled, and looked achingly beautiful.

"I'll fetch you a nightgown and robe from Adela's armoire," he said with a rasp to his voice. "Dry yourself off as best as you can. I won't be gone long."

"Do you expect me to sleep in here?" Her eyes, as she now gazed at him, were an ensorcelling green, as translucent as the crystal lochs one encountered in the Scottish highlands. They were also filled with pain and humiliation.

"Yes. But we are not going to share the bed, if this is what has you concerned. I am not going to touch you, Syd. You have my word of honor. Let me get those dry garments for you and we'll figure out the rest of it once we have both dried off."

He left before she could object.

It took only a moment for Octavian to dig through Adela's things and pull out a sturdy, cotton nightgown and light woolen robe. He would leave Syd to go through the rest of Adela's belongings tomorrow and pull out whatever gowns and unmentionables she needed for their journey.

What else could he do but take her to Scotland with him? It was the only way to keep her out of Sir Henry's clutches. He had planned to leave at the end of the week, but there was nothing to stop him from leaving tomorrow instead.

All he needed to do was keep weapons out of Syd's reach when he told her what he intended to do. No discussion. She was coming with him.

And he was going to marry her.

"Oh, you're back already." Syd had done little more than pull out the pins in her hair by the time he returned to his bedchamber. It was a large, well-appointed room with a big, canopied bed, a desk, several comfortable chairs, a thick, oriental rug, and an ornate Chinese screen that he had received as a gift from the Admiralty in advance of an upcoming promotion.

Syd could easily change behind the screen.

"Here, Syd. Take off your clothes and put these on. I'll turn around while you do."

Octavian could not see over the screen since it was taller than even his impressive height, but wanted to give her that extra margin of comfort and turn away. Besides, he needed to get out of his own sopping wet clothes.

She hesitated, but nodded and dipped behind the screen.

He tossed a towel over it. "Use this to dry yourself off."

"Stop giving me orders, Octavian. I know what to do."

"That's what I'm afraid of," he muttered under his breath, sincerely concerned about her state of mind. Lady Sydney Harcourt, albeit his dream woman – Lord, help him, what a disaster – was just as often the bane of his existence. Stubborn. Reckless. Too smart for her own good.

Too soft for her own good.

Unless he stopped her, she was going to sacrifice herself to save her undeserving father, the Earl of Harcourt, and Octavian had no intention of allowing this to happen. He tried to keep his heart from exploding within his chest as she tossed over each item she had been wearing until she had nothing left to toss and was now naked behind the screen.

Lord, help him.

His heart was not the only body part he could not seem to control.

He had just flung off his jacket, waistcoat, and shirt when she tipped her head around the screen and huffed. "It is not your place to rescue me from my father's mistakes."

He turned fully to face her and strode closer, wanting to grab her by the shoulders and shake sense into her. But he dared not touch her in his current state of arousal. How did this girl manage to turn him upside down? Most times, he did not even like her. "It is not your place to sacrifice yourself on the funeral pyre he created. I do not care what devil's pact your father signed onto. Sir Henry is a blood-sucking leech and you are not going to marry him."

Syd reached out and smacked him lightly on the shoulder. "Octavian! You haven't the right to tell me what to do."

He had every right because he was going to marry her whether she liked it or not. By heaven, he was going to protect her even if it killed him, which it probably would because this girl did not know how to stay out of trouble.

Since she was frowning at him, he suspected she was not going to be happy with his edict. Not that he cared. Someone had to inject sense into this situation.

Not that he was sensible in the least just now.

In leaning over to swat him, Syd had unwittingly given him a glimpse of a bare breast peeking out from under her tumble of hair. He took a step back before he knocked the screen aside and tossed her naked onto his bed.

"I am not discussing this with you," he said with a growl and strode to the fireplace to stare into the flames while struggling to cool the heat pulsing through his loins. After a moment, he spoke again. "You are coming to Scotland with me. Your father will have no obligation to Sir Henry once his vowels are paid, is that right?"

"Yes." Syd fumbled behind the screen to don her borrowed nightgown and robe. "Why are you asking me this? Octavian, do not be so foolish as to consider paying off Sir Henry."

He had stripped out of all but his wet breeches, and thought it safest to keep them on for now. He needed that cold water at his loins because he refused to embarrass himself in front of Syd. She did not love him. He did not love her…that is, what he felt could not possibly be love since half the time he wanted to throttle her.

And yet, he responded to her like a bull in heat. "How great is the debt?"

It could not have been too extravagant since her father had cleared all his past debts only last year after sacrificing his niece to his then largest creditor, a surly but otherwise honest Scot. By chance, the pair fell in love.

Syd would have no such luck.

Sir Henry was repulsive in every way.

Yes, the better plan was to grab Syd and haul her off to safety, her father be damned. Afterward, they would work out the details of a debt repayment and agree to some sort of betrothal arrangement or marriage settlement. Yes, it had to be a marriage settlement. He did not want Syd continuing to be at risk because she was merely betrothed to him. Her father would never honor that betrothal, nor even suffer a pang of conscience before stealing Syd and marrying her off to that repugnant oaf, Sir Henry, or another of his creditors. "We can marry in Scotland without your father's consent."

"I am going to beat you about the head if you repeat that suggestion. You must let me go to Sir Henry," Syd said, her voice tight with despair. "*Please.* My father's debt to him exceeds five thousand pounds. I cannot ask you to pay off such a vast sum. So you see, his life is at risk unless my marriage to Sir Henry goes through."

"And what of your life? Save your breath, Syd. I am not allowing him to sell you into bondage for his mistakes. You are not a commodity to be traded in this fashion."

"I know you mean well, but–"

"Be quiet." Octavian knew he could be a rude arse at times, but did this occasion not warrant it? "You are not talking your way out of this."

"And what exactly is *this*? What gives you the right to interfere?" She was standing beside him now, clad in a nightgown buttoned up to her throat and a soft pink robe.

She gazed up at him with her luminescent green eyes. "Octavian," she whispered brokenly and put a hand on his shoulder. "What about your life? Your happiness?"

How could he ever be happy if she was miserable? "We'll

work out the terms of our arrangement, I promise. Something to suit us both. I could not live with myself if ever you were hurt."

She pressed her lips to his shoulder. "Why do you have to be so nice to me, you big ox? I have been nothing but trouble for you."

Yes, all she said was true. Why he should bother with her at all was beyond him.

As the son of a duke, and now brother to the current Duke of Huntsford, in addition to being a Royal Navy captain wealthy in his own right, he was used to women fluttering around him, willing to hop into bed with him at his mere nod.

They were easy women.

Uncomplicated.

Demanding nothing of him beyond the pleasure of his body.

So why was he determined to marry Syd, this hoyden who would make it her life's ambition to irritate and rile him?

He saw her shiver lightly as he stared at her.

The girl was scared, but too proud ever to admit it.

So typical of her.

"Gad, you are an idiot," she whispered.

He laughed. "I know."

"Octavian, are you serious about marrying me?"

"Yes, Syd." He stared once more into the flames, afraid to look at her beautiful face for fear he might decide he actually loved her. He wanted affection left out of their union entirely. Syd was already too hard to handle. She would be impossible if she sensed how deeply he cared for her.

Her father needed to suffer a little for his callous behavior and Sir Henry needed to find himself another wife...one who was *not* Syd. In truth, he was doing both men a favor. First, teaching her father there were dire consequences to his foolhardy actions. Second, relieving Sir Henry of the misery Syd would put him through.

This girl was simply not biddable.

"Octavian, if you are going to be stubborn about taking me to Scotland, then you had better know everything. My father has gambled through my dowry and the trust funds my grandmother left me. I went to the bank yesterday and…" Her voice hitched. "The account has been closed. The manager advised me the last of the funds were withdrawn last week. I don't even have the means to run away with you."

"Oh, Syd," he said with a wrenching groan. "You are under my protection now and not going to pay for anything."

"But I would bring nothing to our marriage." She appeared sincerely distressed by something that truly meant nothing to him.

His brother had impressive wealth as Duke of Huntsford, but Octavian had acquired his own fortune on the high seas and never required his brother's largesse to survive in the style to which he had become accustomed. "I don't need your dowry. The decision to marry you has nothing to do with any fortune you might bring with you."

"Which is none."

He wiped a tear off her cheek.

Oh, Lord.

This girl was definitely too proud for her own good.

"We'll figure this out," he said, hoping to console her. He could not bear to see her cry. "I promise you, Syd. You know I would never hurt you."

"I know." She buried her face in her hands. "Oh, why do you insist on saving me? I had numbed myself to the misery of marrying Sir Henry. I was ready."

"You will never be ready for what Sir Henry has in mind for you. Get some sleep now. We have a long journey ahead of us."

She looked up at him. "A fake betrothal might work. Then you would not have to give up your happiness for me."

"A fake betrothal will never work. You know I am right, Syd. Your father would never honor it, even if he were inclined to give his consent, which he is not."

"A fake marriage it is then," she said with a reluctant nod. "Thank you. I will try to be as unobtrusive as possible."

He suppressed a burst of laughter.

Syd did not know the meaning of unobtrusive.

"I'm not sure how one fakes a marriage," she mused. "Once vows are exchanged, the marriage is presumed done. Once it is consummated, there is no turning back."

She paused to reflect on this a moment longer, then her eyes widened. "Oh, I see. We do not consummate it. Is this what you have in mind? That is an excellent idea. You give me the protection of your name in marriage, but we can always undo it at a later date if it proves necessary. I will turn twenty-one in nine months time. Then I will be free of my father's control...and you have only to say the word to be free of me. I will grant you the annulment if you wish it. I expect such a thing is easily accomplished in Scotland since they are quite lax about this sort of thing, right? Quick ceremony. No bother about being of age. Quietly undone within the year. Thank you, Octavian. Yes, I will marry you. I wish we were on the road already. Nine months," she repeated softly. "I don't even have nine minutes to spare."

"We'll leave tomorrow morning and stop off at Gretna Green before making our way to the Greenock shipyards." He had won this round, but why did he feel like the loser? It would not be a true marriage. She would leave him in nine months time. Would they lead separate lives all the while?

"How are we to travel north?" she asked, now smiling as they made their plans.

"In one of the Huntsford carriages. Do you think I travel by mail coach?"

She gave a soft trill of laughter. "No, I don't suppose you do." But her mirth quickly faded. "Octavian..."

"What, Syd?"

She clasped her hands in front of her and would not look him in the eye as she spoke. "What *arrangements* are we to have on the way up?"

Bed. Naked. Wild, wanton sex.

But that was just his aching loins having a say, and the last thing Syd needed to hear. "The thing of it is," he said, trying to sound logical so as not to scare her off, "I cannot leave you in a room on your own. Your father and Sir Henry will quickly figure out you have run off and might pick up our trail. It is safest if we share a room. I can make a pallet for myself on the floor wherever we stay. In any event, no reputable inn will allow an unmarried lady as young and pretty as you to sign in on her own. You'll have to pretend to be my wife, just for the week it takes us to cross into Scotland. We'll travel fast. Marry the moment we cross the border. Then you will be my wife in truth."

She stared up at him with those ensorcelling eyes of hers. "So, just to be clear…in that time, what will you expect of me?"

"On the trip to Scotland? Nothing of *that* sort, Syd. I will not touch you without your willingness. But what I will expect is for you to behave, to actually look like a newlywed in love, to not run off on your own as though you answer to nobody, or punch some poor wretch because he uttered a remark not to your liking. Can you do this?"

"Of course, I can. Do you have so little faith in me?"

"I have every faith you are going to make me regret this undertaking."

"Octavian!"

He ignored her indignant huff.

There was more to discuss, but he was tired and still a bit achy from that fall. He wanted to check out the lump on his head which was merely the size of a tiny goose egg and had not broken skin, but one could not be too careful about such things. Then he wanted to sleep. There would be time tomorrow to think about their marriage plans. She believed an unconsummated marriage was something easy to annul. In truth, it was not. There needed to be more grounds than the bride remained a virgin.

Both of them would have to come to terms with this being a permanent marriage if an annulment was impossible. Divorce was out of the question for him. He had a career in the Royal Navy. He would soon be made an Admiral of the Fleet.

All would be lost if they divorced.

Even a quiet annulment might ruin his standing.

"Syd, if the fake marriage cannot be undone, can you be my wife in truth?"

She looked up at him again. "Share your bed? Bear your children? Is this what you are demanding?"

"I am only trying to think of all possibilities."

"I see. It is not an easy answer, but something we must

consider before taking another step. I have never even kissed you."

"That is something easily remedied."

"I suppose." She nodded, reaching out and lightly running her finger across his lips. "In truth, I have never kissed anyone before."

This was not surprising, for Syd, as beautiful as she was, tended to scare off men. She was very smart. In fact, he considered her brilliant. Easily smarter than him when it came to book knowledge. "Then I'll be gentle."

Her eyes grew wide again. "You will?"

Octavian nodded. "I will always be gentle with you. You need never worry that I will hurt you."

"It never crossed my mind. Truly, Octavian. I know you are big and can appear quite daunting when you scowl, which you seem to do a lot around me. But I have always trusted you. You are the most honorable man I know. Well, same can be said for your brothers. Your father raised excellent sons."

He breathed a sigh of relief, for was this not a major step toward a good marriage? They had no chance at a decent union if there was no trust between them. It also helped if the wife was not deathly afraid of the husband.

He did not think Syd was afraid of anything.

Well, having to marry Sir Henry Maxwell had her gravely concerned.

Octavian tipped her chin up so that their gazes met. "I am going to kiss you now, Syd. All right?"

She nodded.

"Close your eyes and put all thoughts out of your head. Kisses are about pleasure. No ploys or stratagems required."

"I will try. But I am very tense right now. Not merely because I am about to be kissed by you, which is an unexpected turn of events, but a welcome one, if I am to be truthful about it. But I have so much on my mind, and now I have to worry about letting you down."

"You will not let me down." He took her hands and placed them lightly on his shoulders.

"How can I not? I am a novice at this and…oh, you've wrapped your arms around me."

"Keep yours on my shoulders. Close your eyes and stop talking."

"Well, that is not very romantic of you."

"Sorry. I do not want you talking yourself into a state of fretting. Kisses are about feelings, Syd. How does it feel for you to be in my arms?"

"Unexpected, actually." She reached up and nuzzled his neck. "Is that bergamot?"

He nodded.

"The scent is nice on you. Your skin is warm. Your body is surprisingly nice. Well, not very surprising. It's just…you have no shirt on and I am touching your skin. I've seen naked cadavers, of course. But this is not at all the same thing. Would we do this in the marriage?"

"What? Me holding you in my arms? If you like."

"Octavian, you are being remarkably cooperative."

He stifled his laughter, knowing she was already tense and would run off at his slightest misstep. "It is what husbands and wives do in a good marriage."

She nestled against his chest. "My parents have a horrible marriage. The only thing I learned from them was never to do what they did. Please don't be angry with me if I make mistakes. Starting with kisses. My parents never kiss each other."

"Then this is important, Syd. If you don't like my kisses, we had better rethink the situation."

"I'll consider it carefully. I promise."

This is what he liked about Syd, her natural honesty.

She was not a schemer or a manipulator. You always got the truth from her. Perhaps this is why he felt confident she would give him an honest answer about their kiss, even if it did set her plans back to square one.

She tilted her head up to give him unimpeded access to her lips.

He closed his mouth over hers, pressing down gently at first, and then sinking his mouth deeper onto hers until he felt her fingers curl upon his shoulders and heard a soft moan escape her lips.

He held her in his arms as though she were delicate and precious, which she was…although perhaps not really delicate. He liked that she was brave and spirited, and especially liked that she was now kissing him back with innocent ardor.

Blessed saints!

What was he doing?

Had this kiss just sealed his fate?

He ended the kiss and awaited her response.

She stared at him for the longest time, then burst into tears.

This is why Syd was the most frustrating young woman it was ever his misfortune to know. Could she not even test out a kiss without twisting his heart in knots? "Syd, stop crying. Are you going to marry me or not?"

CHAPTER 2

"NOT," SHE REPLIED, ignoring Octavian's muffled curse as he stepped away from her and began to pace. All she saw through her tears was his gorgeous body and all its perfect musculature, which was the very reason she could not get too close to this devastatingly handsome man or she would lose her heart to him.

Was she not in dire enough straits?

He stopped pacing and paused in front of her. "Are you suggesting you did not like the kiss? I want the truth, Syd. Do not give me hogwash."

She let out the breath she had been holding, which was a mistake because she breathed him in again. The scent of his skin was intoxicating. Hot. Male. Bergamot that blended so beautifully with his warm skin. "I liked the kiss."

He raked a hand through his neatly cropped head of dark hair as his tension appeared to ease. "Then where is the problem?"

"What if I fall in love with you and it turns out you do not want me?" In fact, she could not understand why he had developed this protective attitude toward her. This man could have any woman he wanted and did not need to be burdened with her. Her heart had died a little when rumors began to circulate of his courting the Duke of Renfield's daughter, Lady Clementine.

Nothing had come of those rumors...yet.

If his feelings for Lady Clementine were true, then how could he ever grow to love *her*?

It was not going to happen.

Syd knew enough about Octavian to understand he was a one-woman man.

Besides, men did not fall in love with her. She chased men away because she was too outspoken, too independent, too smart, and too much of everything a man did not want in a wife. At some point over the course of their nine months as husband and wife, she knew Octavian would grow disillusioned and rue his mistake.

Was it not better to make the inevitable break now?

But that kiss…her very first.

It was everything splendid she hoped it would be, a wonderful and exquisite kiss filled with promise, but one she knew would never be fulfilled because of who she was.

"Syd, do you really think you could fall in love with me?" He was staring at her quite intently as he wiped the tears off her cheeks with his thumbs, and now gently cupped her face in his hands so that she could not turn away from him as she answered.

She stared into those deep, silver-gray eyes of his that seemed to draw her into the mists of time. "I don't know, Octavian. I don't even know what love is because I was not raised in a happy marriage. Oh, I've seen how good it can be now that Adela and your brother, Ambrose, are married. They are so kind and loving toward each other and yet maintain the essence of themselves. The same for Marigold and Leo, and how devoted they are to each other while still allowing the other to shine. How do I achieve this? Do I dare? What happens when you decide I am a huge mistake and cannot bear to be around me any longer?"

"Syd, you are thinking too hard about it. Let's just take it one step at a time, the first step being getting us up to Gretna Green. You'll have a full week in my company–"

"And you'll have a full week in mine," she said with a nod, for he was right. This plan they were devising was not carved in stone. It could change over the course of the next few days. No matter what happened, Octavian would not abandon her penniless in the wilds of Scotland. If anything, he would be generous with her and ensure her safe return to London.

Why was she so worried?

This protective nature of his was the essence of who he was. Strong, compassionate, always going to look out for her whether he cared for her or not.

"What's your decision, Syd?" He still held her face cupped in his big hands while awaiting her answer, obviously hoping she had changed her mind. Why he should care was beyond her, but if he was willing then so was she.

Well, she was willing for now.

She would get a better sense of the situation as they traveled up to Scotland. She released a soft breath and nodded. "Yes, it is a good plan. May I send notes to Lady Withnall and Lady Dayne letting them know I am safe and will be traveling with you? I would also like to let Marigold and Gory know. I don't want them to worry about me."

"Of course," he said, releasing her to rub a hand across the nape of his neck as the impact of what he had proposed and she had accepted now fully hit him. "I'll leave word here for Ambrose and Julius. I don't want my brothers worrying about you, either. We can write our missives before we retire. But I am sleeping in here with you, Syd. I want to be clear on this. You do not leave my sight from now until the end of our journey."

"Whatever that end may be," she muttered.

He strode to the fireplace, turning his back to her as he warmed his hands by the fire. She skittered over to join him, for her insides were still chilled. More than that, she was not used to having anyone take care of her as Octavian had been doing ever since they met, and she quite liked it.

She enjoyed being near him.

Perhaps one day she would admit it to him.

He wasn't overbearing, just went about the business of protecting her. Why could her family not be like this? Instead, they all used her. She had a mother who did nothing but moan and complain about her lot, always seeking pity but never doing anything to help herself, and a father who was reckless, foolish, and kept repeating the same mistakes.

She fervently hoped she would not turn into them as she grew older. In truth, she wasn't sure how she had been born to them, for she was nothing like them. For one thing, she adored books and learning. The medical research she and Gory conducted at the Huntsford Academy was a dream come true for her. Had she been a man, there was no doubt she would have studied medicine at some distinguished college of higher learning and contributed to advancements in medicine for the greater good.

But her parents disapproved of her volunteering at the Huntsford Academy and would have stopped her from pursuing all academic endeavors if not for the fact that they were distracted with their own problems. Of course, it appalled them that an earl's daughter should be devoting all her efforts to gaining forensic knowledge, but they got around what they perceived as a scandal by telling friends and acquaintances that she was a devoted and tireless fossil hunter.

Apparently, hunting for dead bones was all right.

Studying cadavers was not.

What right did they have to judge her? Her parents never read and did not seem to ever learn anything from their life experiences. At times, she believed she was a faerie changeling because she could not understand what she had in common with her own family.

In truth, she was ashamed of them.

What good was a vaunted title and fancy homes when her father was constantly running from his creditors? Their elegant life was all a facade. None of the supposed privileges of being an earl's daughter had ever felt real to her. Nor did it strike her as fair that her father escaped most of his creditors because he was an earl and those creditors could not touch his entailment.

"Syd, you are lost in your thoughts again."

She turned to Octavian as the deep rumble of his voice invaded her musings. "Sorry, I was just thinking of my parents."

He frowned. "Are you afraid they will worry about you? We cannot tell them what we are doing or else your father and Sir Henry will try to stop us."

"I know. I would not be so foolish as to write him a note and alert him. He thinks I am spending the night with Lady Withnall at her residence. He'll know the truth by tomorrow, but it will be too late by then. As for Gory and Marigold, they know better than to tell him anything beyond that I am safe. Octavian..."

He turned to her. "What is it, Syd?"

She threw her arms around his waist and hugged him fiercely. "I don't know how to thank you."

He closed his arms around her, obviously surprised by this show of affection because she held herself back so often. "This is thanks enough."

His hold was light, allowing her to draw away whenever she was ready. In truth, it was uncanny how well this big man seemed to know her. She smiled up at him when she did finally step back. "Shall we write our letters now?"

He cast her a devastating smile in return. "Yes, we had better get them done and then try to get as much rest as possible. I want to leave at first light tomorrow."

She watched him stride to his writing desk and take out paper, ink pot, quill pen, blotter and sand. "Octavian, I think you ought to sleep in your bed. I'll take the pallet on the floor."

He removed the stopper off the ink pot and turned to her. "No, Syd. You take the bed. I'll be fine."

"But–"

"It will be like being on board my ship, only more comfortable because I'll have a fine, thick carpet beneath me and a fire to warm me." He pulled out the chair by his writing desk and motioned for her to take a seat.

"All right, but we'll take turns with the bed when we are on the road and sleeping in coaching inns." She sank onto the chair and took the quill in her hand.

She was about to dip it into the ink to start her first note when Octavian cleared his throat. She turned to him with a questioning arch of her eyebrow.

"I would like to make a rule," he said.

"Besides the first rule of always keeping me in your sight?"

He cast her a boyishly endearing smile, although he was no boy but a dangerously handsome man. "All right, rule number two is that we take it one day at a time. Stop thinking ahead and trying to account for every detail. We'll make our decisions as they come upon us."

She pursed her lips. "Shouldn't we plan a little ahead? We cannot wait for things to just spring on us."

"We'll plan out the important details," he conceded. "But these little matters are not anything we need to fret about. Are you hungry? Or thirsty? Shall I have tea and a light repast brought up here for you now?"

And have the entire Huntsford staff aware she was sleeping in his bed?

She would never live down the humiliation.

"No, Octavian. That would require waking your staff. It can hold off until the morning." She set down her quill pen. "They won't understand how it is between us. I couldn't bear to have them see me here tonight. Come morning, they'll know I shared your quarters. That is bad enough. But by that time, we will be ready to leave and I will only have to endure their disapproving looks for a short while."

Once again, he rubbed a hand across the back of his neck as he regarded her. "This cannot be helped. I'm sorry, Syd. Truly. Even if you were in a room down the opposite end of the hall, they would still believe we spent the night together. But we will soon be married and no one will think less of you when you return as my wife. Besides, they will take their cues from me. If I treat you with respect, they will do the same."

Assuming she returned as his wife.

But she was not going to bring up this issue again.

Octavian was right.

One day at a time.

As she sat down to write her letters, Octavian went behind the screen to change out of his wet trousers and don a clean pair of dry ones. He then took one of the pillows off his massive bed and a blanket stored in his wardrobe to make a pallet for himself in front of the fireplace.

His makeshift bed looked rather inviting by the time he was done.

Since her hair was still damp when she finished writing her letters and they had exchanged places, she borrowed his comb and sat beside the fire to brush out her hair. Octavian glanced over a time or two, but she merely smiled at him and made no comment.

This silence between them felt perfect.

There was no tension, just acceptance of their plan to travel to Scotland, and the comfort of being in a safe place for the evening.

Her hair was dry by the time he finished writing explanations to his brothers. She watched as he stacked all of their letters in a neat pile and then pursed his lips in thought. "Is something wrong, Octavian?"

He shook his head. "I was just wondering whether we ought to pack tonight rather than wait until the morning."

Syd was exhausted and eager for bed. "May we hold off until tomorrow? It would not be right for me to just take whatever I wanted from Adela's wardrobe. Her maid ought to be the one to assist me with that and I could not face her now. Besides, it is very late and I can hardly keep my eyes open."

He nodded, watching her as she practically dove into his bed. "I'll wake you at dawn, Syd. We'll take care of packing then. The staff will be up and about, so they can attend to most of the task while we have our breakfast. Sweet dreams."

"Sweet dreams, Octavian. Thank you for everything."

He stretched out on the pallet and casually folded his hands behind his head. "My pleasure, Syd."

She wrapped her arms around her pillow and fought to hold back her tears. What a useless thing these tears were. In truth, she had cried so much while growing up but they never made anything better. Why did she feel like crying when she felt truly safe and happy for the first time in as long as she could remember?

Being with Octavian gave her such a feeling of contentment.

She cherished this moment and reveled in it, for she knew their friendship would not last. They were both too strong-headed.

How long before they got on the road and were at each other's throats?

Oh, how lovely it would be if they weren't.

But she knew herself too well.

She would do something to rile him. The only question was, how long before she had him boiling mad and retracting his offer of their make-believe marriage?

CHAPTER 3

FOR ALL SYD'S forward thinking bluster and supposed independence, Octavian could see she was appalled to be found in his bedchamber by his staff the following morning. There was no help for it now. A select few had to be told since he was not going to have her don those boy's clothes she was wearing last night and try to sneak her out pretending she was a lad. She needed proper gowns to wear once they were on the road, and the Huntsford housekeeper would immediately notice if the so-called *lad* started pulling out gowns from Adela's wardrobe.

Nor did Octavian intend to drag Syd in front of a blacksmith and ask the man to marry them while she was garbed as a boy. She needed a pretty gown for her wedding day. As for her shame, she would be returning as his wife and her supposedly scandalous behavior would quickly be forgotten.

That she took it so hard surprised him.

Syd was tough, but he was seeing this very feminine side of her now, this traditional and genteel side she usually took great pains to hide. He liked it very much, but it also made him ache for her because she now felt so much shame in spending the night with him.

He was a dolt for not thinking twice about it last night.

But what could he have done differently?

No one was going to protect her as ably as he could. Nor did he trust her to stay put and not run back to her father, which was the reason he had insisted on their sharing quarters in the first place.

"Syd," he said quietly, "you know you can always rely on me. I will protect you from anyone and anything." This is what he kept assuring her in the hope she did not decide to cast aside their plans and run back to her father.

Or she might simply decide to run off on her own.

Syd on the loose was a dangerous thing.

"I am fine," she insisted, holding herself so stiffly Octavian was certain she would crack. "You needn't worry that I will suddenly disappear. I've agreed to our make-believe marriage."

"Good, because everything will be all right. I promise you." He requested the assistance of the housekeeper in packing a few of Adela's clothes for Syd. The housekeeper, Mrs. Quinn, was an efficient woman with decades of experience in the role. She next brought in Adela's personal maid to assist her, as expected.

Adela's maid chose well, he decided when Syd met him in the hall after washing and dressing in the duchess quarters while he did the same for himself in his own bedchamber. The soft rose color of her travel attire suited her complexion, although she was still too wan for his liking.

The gown molded delightfully to her body, but he tried his best not to gawk. It was not as though he could see much of her soft skin since the gown had a matching jacket that Syd had now buttoned to her throat. "You look lovely, by the way."

"Thank you, Octavian." She was obviously surprised, and also unsettled as the housekeeper and Adela's maid looked on while he spoke to her.

She was still suffering doubts about everything, he realized.

Was this the same brash, confident girl who had pushed him off the roof last night?

To his mind, that midnight excursion of hers was far more perilous than being caught in his bedchamber. Was it not clear to his valet and anyone else who poked their head in that the bed had been occupied by only one person? The pallet was still on the floor by the fireplace and he had left it there on purpose in order to leave no doubt in anyone's mind that they had not shared the bed.

Well, Syd always was that odd mix of independent firebrand and conventional lady. One never knew which side would come out in any given situation, but it was usually the firebrand. Why was that hotheaded girl missing today?

Perhaps he was the one who was clueless about women, having himself been raised in a family of all males. He had only courted a few young ladies and only halfheartedly at that before losing interest. His latest had been Lady Clementine Renfield, daughter of the Duke of Renfield, a beautiful debutante with an angel's smile but a devil's scheming heart.

Quietly extricating himself from that arrangement had proved thorny despite the passage of months, for Clementine was prideful and vengeful. He hoped his time in Scotland would give her the opportunity to move on and find someone else to marry.

Nor did he care if the gossip rags reported she had rejected him, which they would report because the vain girl was not going to let him walk away without dishing out a dose of humiliation.

Whatever it took to escape her clutches was worth it.

Syd also had her pride, but it was different. There was not a mean bone in her body. In truth, she was too loyal, too compassionate, and too eager to sacrifice everything for those she loved.

In their own way, both young ladies were hard to handle. For this reason, Octavian satisfied himself with casual dalliances where no commitments were required.

Not that any of it mattered now.

Once he married Syd, there would be no cheating on his part.

"Come have a bite, Syd." He was eager to grab a little sustenance before they got on the road.

Syd stared in dismay at the tray the housekeeper had just brought in and set atop his desk. "I'm not sure I can hold anything down."

"We're not going to stop along the way, Syd. You had better eat something. How about tea? And a little bread with honey."

"All right. You are quite the mother hen, did you know that?" she teased when he cut her a slice and began to pour honey on it for her.

"Never a mother hen." He grinned back at her. "I am a man, therefore I am considered manly and protective."

They shared a light breakfast while the Huntsford footmen loaded their bags onto his carriage. However, he had given more thought about their planned travel to Scotland and decided to send the coach and driver back to London once they reached Oxford. Upon arriving at that thriving town, he would make new arrangements with one of the local coaching companies to take them the rest of the way to Scotland in an unmarked conveyance.

Keeping his carriage or riding in one from Ambrose's selection would have been too conspicuous while they made their way north, especially with the Huntsford crest emblazoned on the door.

He could not risk them being so easily noticed.

A gentleman and his pretty wife signing in as Captain and Mrs. Thorne would not be nearly as conspicuous as Captain Octavian Thorne, brother of the Duke of Huntsford, traveling with a companion he claims to be his wife but why had no one heard of his marriage?

By the time he and Syd were ready to depart, they had been seen by just about everyone in the household save for the cook and scullery maids. Since Syd's presence was no longer a secret, Octavian summoned the entire staff. "Lady Sydney is here and under my protection because her life is in danger," he said, his tone quite serious. "If anyone comes around asking questions, you must tell them that you have not seen her. Her life depends on your silence. I cannot stress this enough. She was never here. Am I understood?"

They all nodded.

Syd's face was so pale, it served to confirm the peril of her situation.

That she stood silently beside him also helped convey the direness of it. He hoped she would remain meek and quiet until they were on their way. He did not need her mouthing off with false bravado and diminishing the importance of the warning he was conveying to the Huntsford staff.

"Captain Thorne," the head butler said, clearing his throat as he stepped forward.

"Yes, Greeves?"

The man appeared confused as he glanced at Syd before returning his attention to Octavian. "Are we to say nothing even if it is her family asking?"

"Especially her family." He now handed over the letters he and Syd had written last night. "These are to go out immediately to Lady Withnall, Lady Dayne, and Lady Gregoria Easton. This next one also goes immediately to Lady Muir or her husband, the Marquess of Muir. Either one will do. I trust them both."

In truth, he hoped Marigold, Lady Muir, would report the news immediately to her husband. The marquess, Leo, was smart and tough. He would look after the two dowagers, as well as Gregoria and Marigold, in the event Syd's father or Sir Henry sought to apply any pressure on them. Indeed, Leo was as fierce as a lion, as his name indicated, and would rip those scoundrels apart if they dared intimidate any of those ladies.

Octavian now held out one final letter. "This last one remains here and is to be handed over immediately to whichever brother of mine returns first."

The head butler took this last one from him, too. "I will hold this one safe and attend to these others at once, Captain Thorne."

Octavian nodded and dismissed the rest of the staff save for the Huntsford head butler and housekeeper. "If my brothers should ask, we are headed to Greenock and will return in about a month." He glanced at Syd, trying to get an indication of whether she would marry him or not. They had agreed upon their plan last night, but Syd was such a skittish thing, and she was so lost in her misery that she was not even looking at him.

So be it.

He said nothing about their marital intentions since he had no idea what would happen within the next hour, much less the full week it would take them to reach their destination.

Let his staff speculate, if they wished.

He would clarify the situation upon his return.

It was not quite seven o'clock in the morning by the time their bags were loaded onto the carriage. He helped Syd climb in and then did the same, settling in the seat opposite hers. He did not mind having to look at her lovely face the entire journey to Scotland, although he hoped to see her smile on occasion as they put distance between them and London.

She turned to stare out the window once they were off and making their way through the relatively quiet streets of London that would be bustling within the hour when many of the shops and businesses began to open. She remained staring out the window, ignoring his presence as the carriage clattered toward the outskirts of town.

Octavian glanced at her from time to time, his lips pursed in thought. Is this what their marriage would be? Her turned away from him and completely withdrawn?

What in blazes was he doing?

Syd suddenly gasped and drew back, trying to burrow into the fine leather of her seat. "That was Sir Henry's carriage. What is he doing out at this hour? He should have been home hours ago. And that is not the way to his home or my family's home. Where is he going? Do you think he knows? Is he looking for me? What if he is headed to your residence?"

"First of all, the Huntsford townhouse is one of the last places he will look. Did you not tell your family you were staying with Lady Withnall last evening? He will go to her first, and I can assure you, that tough, old bird will keep him waiting until proper visiting hours and then tell him nothing."

"All he has to do is question her staff and they will tell him I am not there."

"Perhaps, but Lady Withnall has probably trained them well by now. It is just as likely they will give out no information whatsoever."

"That is wishful thinking on your part, Octavian. Oh, dear. What if the cur is there when your messenger arrives with my letter?" Her eyes widened. "What if he steals that letter? I told her everything about our destination and our plan to marry."

"Syd, you are allowing your fear to get the better of you. Her butler will not allow him to touch her letters, nor will Sir Henry think to do so since he is going there because he believes you are sleeping over at Lady Withnall's home. So why would you write her a letter if you are already there?"

She let out a breath. "I see your point. But will he grab it once he knows I never showed up at her home? Her head butler must be over one hundred years old and will fall over if anyone merely blows on him."

"Syd, he is elderly but still has his faculties. You are grasping for reasons to alarm yourself. Lady Withnall has footmen who are young and strong enough to haul even me out of her house if she bade them. Sir Henry does not know you are with me and probably has yet to realize you are leaving London, so just calm yourself."

She leaned forward and grabbed his hands. "Octavian, if he does come after us...if he catches us and draws a weapon on you, then do not fight him. You must promise me this. He is vicious and will shoot you."

Gad, did she not get it yet?

He was going to protect her even at the risk to his own life.

He arched an eyebrow and regarded her with a look of boredom. "Fine, I will save my own hide and let him carry you off."

Her mouth formed a little "O" of surprise. "You will?"

He snorted. "Of course not. He can follow you into the bowels of hell with an army and I will be there ready to fight them to the last man."

"All of a hundred men?"

"Sir Henry is not going to travel with an army. Nor are we marching into the bowels of hell. We are only going to Gretna Green and then on to Greenock so I can complete my work on behalf of the Admiralty. You may have noticed I am wearing my uniform. It is because I am on official naval duty."

She emitted a breathy sigh. "You look splendid in it."

"Thank you, but that isn't my point. At best, Sir Henry will bring along five or six men, but no more. It becomes too unwieldy to move fast with many more men, not to mention the expense of feeding them all and difficulty in finding lodgings for them without advance planning."

"He will hire cheats and scoundrels, men no doubt used to being on the run. They can set up camp anywhere."

"Those men might, but Sir Henry is not going to sleep in a meadow, wash up in an icy stream, or dine around a campfire. He is used to his luxuries. But that raises a good point. We may have to abandon this carriage and our belongings and go on the run if Sir Henry catches up to us before we reach Gretna Green. Can you manage sleeping under the stars or eating whatever we can scavenge?"

"Sleeping outdoors? Eating...what exactly is scavenged food? But I'm sure I can." She leaned forward and gave his hands a light squeeze to emphasize her point. "I will manage. You'll just have to tell me what to do."

He sighed. "So, you've never camped out before?"

A blush stole up her cheeks. "I've gone hungry a time or two when my father had us running from creditors, but never for more than a day, and we always had a decent roof over our heads when we slept."

"So that's a *no* to all of it. All right. We'll come up with something if and when the situation arises."

She pursed her lips and frowned at him. "Should we not plan ahead for this eventuality? Especially since I am inexperienced in this matter."

"No. Besides, for a smart girl, you are inexperienced in many ways." Some more important than simply going on the run. He was thinking of the bedchamber, but quickly abandoned the thought because Syd would not appreciate that discussion. "I will show you what to do if ever we have to rough it outdoors. Stop looking for reasons to fret. This is not likely ever to come to pass. I'm sending this carriage back to London once we reach Oxford. We'll ride the rest of the way to Scotland in a hired coach."

"Is that supposed to make us less obvious?"

"Yes. I'll also use other stratagems to keep him off our trail."

"I hope they work," she muttered. "Sir Henry is quite dogged."

"I've noticed he seems to have developed an unhealthy fascination for you. Even so, he will have to get through me in order to get to you. He may be a dog, but I am a big ox and he will never get past me." Since she had yet to release her light hold on his hands, he traced a thumb across one of her small hands in the hope of soothing her. "Syd, whatever happens between here and Greenock, know that I will be with you."

She nodded unconvincingly, so he kept talking. "My first priority is to keep us out of sight as much as possible."

"That won't always be possible, especially if we are stopping at coaching inns."

"True, but I am never going to let down my guard. What we do in the unlikely event he finds us will depend on the circumstances. My battle training has prepared me for any eventuality. I'll use whatever resources available to protect you. The terrain, the weather, the proximity to friends who can hide us if Sir Henry manages to catch up to us before we are married. There is nothing to concern ourselves about right now. So, will you please stop fretting?"

She let out a soft breath. "All right. I'm sorry. It's just that I am so torn about whether I am doing the right thing. I'm putting you and my father in danger."

He emitted a soft growl. "We are both grown men. Don't you dare place blame on yourself for a situation completely of your father's own making. As for me, I volunteered. You did not coerce me. Nor could you have forced me to do anything I did not wish to do."

He stretched out on his seat bench when she released his hands, and tried to settle his large frame as comfortably as possible upon the soft leather. "I plan to catch up on my sleep since we got very little of it last night," he said, folding his arms across his chest and closing his eyes. "I suggest you do the same. You look exhausted, Syd."

She also looked achingly beautiful, but he preferred not to mention this because they were already in too close quarters and his thoughts continually strayed toward the impolite things he wished to do to her.

Oh, the things he could teach her.

Well, perhaps once they were married.

He watched her through hooded lids, pleased when she curled

up on the opposite seat. "Octavian, I slept quite soundly once I was in your bed."

"Good, Syd," he muttered.

"It is a very nice bed and the scent on your sheets was quite pleasing. I think it was your scent, bergamot. Well, the point is that I felt safe and my sleep was delightful because I knew you were near me."

He stifled his yawn, for he did not want to discourage Syd from talking to him. "I'm glad. This is why I intend to stay near you during our ride north."

"You really have a very comfortable bed. But I am still quite spent from all the tension of this situation." She paused a moment and nibbled her lip. "I don't mean that your offering me a rescue plan is the reason for my tension. It does calm me to a point, but now I find myself worried about your getting hurt."

There was only one way he would get hurt and that was if Syd ended up not caring for him. Again, he intended to keep that thought to himself.

She was not ready to hear anything of a romantic nature.

Nor did he understand why he liked her as much as he did.

"What keeps me tense is my father and his foolish investments," she said, apparently not yet finished chattering at him, "not to mention his gambling, and Sir Henry being such an ogre. These are what have me so worried. I want to help my father, but I shudder to think what would happen if I married Sir Henry to settle my father's debt and then learned my father ran up more debts. Do you think Sir Henry would help him out with those new obligations?"

"Syd, surely you know the answer. He will let your father rot because Sir Henry has no incentive to help him once he has you. In fact, he will laugh at your father when this happens. Is there a doubt? How many times does it bear repeating? All you will accomplish by shackling yourself to that despicable man is gain a life of misery for yourself. Meanwhile, your father will continue his foolish ways, continue to run up debts, and get himself in trouble again within a year."

"You may have to keep reminding me. I am in so much agony

right now."

"Because your loyalty is misplaced. Yes, he is your father and you love him. But it is he who made the mistakes and must own up to them. Even so, I will do what I can once we are married." He had been viewing her through hooded lids, but now opened his eyes fully and met her gaze. "Let me sleep, Syd. We will discuss this again later if you insist on it."

"I'm sorry. I did not mean to keep you awake. It could not have been very comfortable for you to sleep on your floor."

"It was fine."

"You are only saying this to be kind. You come across as cross and gruff, but you are quite a fine gentleman. I wish my father was more like you. I used to think he was so charming, but I know better now. Well, he is charming and affable, but quite selfish and scatterbrained. I would add forgetful, too. How does one ignore one's own mistakes and repeat them not even a few weeks later? He is so much like a child."

"And you are not his mother," Octavian warned.

"But I am his daughter."

"That's right. His daughter. Not his cattle to be sold at auction." Is this what married life was going to be with Syd? Constant talk? Constant reassurance that she was doing the right thing? Perhaps he was the one who would need the reassurance once they crossed into Scotland and were about to wed. "Are you going to keep me awake the entire ride to Oxford?"

"My, but you are a grumpy fellow." But one look at her big eyes and the soft smile she now cast him removed any doubts he might have about marrying her. This girl needed him and he felt bloody good about it.

Perhaps he needed her, too.

He had not figured out why yet.

Octavian realized he must have drifted off to sleep for at least an hour. When he woke up, they were well outside of London and making good time. If the weather held and this Huntsford carriage was exchanged for a plain passenger coach without delay once they reached Oxford, it was possible to get a good distance beyond Oxford before nightfall.

He would need to arrange for the safe return of his carriage to the Huntsford townhouse. Hopefully that would not take too long, either. Hastings was an experienced driver and knew how to care for the carriage and horses.

Most of all, Octavian hoped the weather would remain clear so they could put more distance between them and Sir Henry before the old bounder realized Syd was no longer in London.

As for sleeping arrangements, he decided they were better served by veering off the main coaching roads as night approached and finding a quiet, reputable inn within one of the smaller market towns. It was safest to remain slightly off the path rather than seek rooms in the larger cities or popular coaching inns situated along the well traveled routes.

Yes, he thought it best especially to avoid the larger cities since they were more likely to encounter other members of the *ton* there and easily be recognized. Settling Syd in a seedier part of whichever city they reached was a possibility, but held no appeal for him.

They would attract too much notice with him in his navy uniform and her in her elegant gown. Every cutpurse in the area would come after them.

Syd was no weak maiden, but he had no intention of placing her in added danger. Besides, he wanted to spoil her. Give her the best.

Again, this feeling baffled him.

What was it about Syd that made him want to give her the world?

The rest of the day passed uneventfully, although Octavian did not yet feel comfortable enough to take his eyes off her. They were not far enough away from London and Syd was unpredictable.

She could easily have a change of heart and run back to her father.

It was with much relief that she was still with him when they stopped at an inn just south of Chipping Campden for the evening. As the carriage rolled up to the Burford Inn's courtyard, Octavian turned to Syd. "All right, here we go. Our first test as lovebirds. Do you think you can act like a besotted newlywed?"

She arched an eyebrow. "Can you?"

He laughed. "Yes, so long as you do not rile me."

She cast him a playfully offended look. "You can be just as impossible, you know. Do not rile *me* and we shall be just fine. Oh, the innkeeper is scurrying toward us. What shall we say if he asks us questions?"

"About our marriage? That we were wed two days ago. A quiet ceremony in a local London church. Actually, describe Ambrose and Adela's wedding. Same details, just ours was two days ago. You are now Lady Thorne. No, make that Mrs. Thorne. Better to keep things simple."

"Wonderful," she said wryly. "How did you propose to me?"

"Same way Ambrose proposed to Adela."

She laughed. "Impossible. He insisted on marrying her because of a perceived scandal. I will not allow myself to be considered ruined and in need of your saving. Scandal is out of the question. You are in love with me, so quick...how did you propose?"

"At Lady Withnall's supper party a month ago. You looked radiant and I was transported." He groaned. "Enough, Syd. No one is going to ask us these questions. If you are at a loss, just bat your eyes at me and let me do the talking."

"You? You are going to make a mess of it."

He threw his head back and laughed again. "There's my Syd. Glad to have your insolent self back."

She winced. "I am not insolent, just–"

The carriage door was thrown open as the innkeeper and his staff hurried forward to attend to them. Octavian registered them as Captain and Mrs. Thorne, and requested their finest room.

Syd pinched his hand but he ignored her.

They were off the beaten path.

No one was going to find them tonight or follow their trail here anytime later. So why not indulge in the best for themselves?

"Yes, Captain. You are in luck. Our largest guest quarters happen to be available."

"Good," Syd said, obviously believing the innkeeper's reference to his largest quarters indicated a bedroom and a private salon – and therefore a sofa – which it probably did not have. "My husband is a big man and needs space to walk around after being cramped in a carriage all day. Would you kindly send up light refreshments for us? Dearest, would you like a bottle of scotch sent up as well?"

Octavian tried to hold back a chuckle.

Dearest?

In truth, the endearment sounded nice coming from Syd, but she must have struggled to keep from choking on it. "No, my love. A pot of tea will do for me."

The innkeeper smiled broadly. "Ah, a love match. Ye look like a pair of newlyweds."

Syd nodded. "We are, Mr. Hutchins. Married all of two days now."

The innkeeper's eyes brightened. "I knew it. Yer husband cannot take his eyes off you."

Syd turned to Octavian with an impish grin and batted her eyelashes. "Yes, he is quite besotted with me. It was love at first sight for him. Goodness, he was quite ardent in courting me. Of course, I took a bit longer to return his feelings because a gently bred young lady must be cautious in the man she chooses, don't you think? You must admit, he does look quite a bit rakish. But he has proven himself to be loyal and true. Clings to me like a little, lost lamb."

Octavian was going to throttle her if she did not stop talking. "Indeed, I cannot get enough of my new wife. If you will excuse us, we would like to retire to our chamber now. We intend to be back on the road at first light." He ordered breakfast to be sent up at the crack of dawn.

The room turned out to be quite pleasant, larger and more elegantly furnished than Octavian expected, but it was only the one room and it contained a big bed in the center of it. However, as elegant as this guest chamber was supposed to be, it had no decent carpeting. The room had small rugs the size of mats on either side of the bed so that their feet would not touch cold wood when getting out of bed, but those would not even accommodate the breadth of his shoulders if he attempted to sleep on them.

The bare wooden floor was going to be a problem.

He was not looking forward to spending the night on it after already spending last night sleeping on his carpet and then part of today sprawled uncomfortably on the narrow seat bench of their hired carriage.

His back would go out if he continued to sleep awkwardly along the journey.

Well, he had asked for this.

If he wanted a comfortable night's rest, he could have left Syd hidden somewhere in London and gone to Greenock on his own to attend to the Admiralty assignment. But those blasted protective instincts of his would never allow him to leave her behind.

Not knowing what was happening to her would eat his guts raw.

Syd was now making herself comfortable and had removed the matching jacket to her travel gown. Since it was actually Adela's gown, the fit was a bit tight and pushed up Syd's bosom so that an enticing bit of cleavage and swell of her nicely formed breasts showed.

She bent forward to retrieve something out of her travel pouch.

He needed a drink.

Perhaps he would ask for that bottle of scotch and get himself a little drunk. Better yet, he could get Syd drunk. He knew he could coax his way into that bed with her once she was feeling warm and tingly.

Well, no.

He was never going to take advantage of her in this fashion.

"Syd," he said, once the proprietor had left them and they were alone in their chamber, "need I review all the things you did wrong down there?"

"No, Octavian. I am quite aware of what I said and did. I am not in need of your lecture."

"Then why run off at the mouth, telling him how I courted you and followed you around like a lovesick lamb? Seriously?" He shook his head and sank onto the mattress. "You cannot spread lies wherever we stop. At some point, you will forget which lies you told to whom, and then we will be found out. It is your reputation at stake, not mine."

"You are right, but I needed something to ease my tension. I did not mean to irritate you. It was just gentle teasing. You and I both know you never looked at me with adoring eyes or ever followed me around other than to keep me out of tavern brawls. But we seem to have a bigger problem that I am sure you have noticed. This is a cold, hard floor. And there is a breeze coming through the door and window cracks. You cannot sleep on that floor or you will catch an ague."

"What do you propose? I am not letting you sleep there, so do not bother to mention it."

"I shall ignore the stupid remark. I can be ill and it won't matter. But you have to stay healthy and strong to protect me."

He eased back on the bed, propping his hands behind his head as he rested atop the pile of pillows. "You are not sleeping on that floor. And do not point out that I am already stretched out on the bed. It is just a temporary relaxation to ease my coiled muscles."

"Precisely the reason why you need the bed and I do not."

"Out of the question."

She sighed. "What if we asked for an adjoining room? We could tell the innkeeper your snoring seems particularly bad today and I–"

"No. I am not letting you out of my sight."

"Why? Don't you trust me?" She looked hurt. "I would never lie to you or steal from you. You know I am trustworthy."

"Syd, must I say it? Here's what I trust you will do. I trust that you will thwart me at every turn. I trust that you will run off without warning and do as you please. I trust that you will break your promises to me."

"Octavian!" She sank onto the bed and sat beside his prone form. "That is very unkind of you to say."

"But it is true, Syd. Do not bother to deny it."

"Is this what you think of me?"

Blast, now she looked ready to cry. But he wanted honesty between them, even if the truth was painful. "You also have many fine qualities, but cooperation is not one of them."

She pursed her lips, for she could not deny this was true. "Is it so terrible that I do what I think is right? My motives are always honorable."

"Honorable? Or hotheaded?" He grunted in exasperation. "And yes, it is terrible because you are not always right. You are sometimes so bent on doing whatever you want to do that you fail to consider the consequences to others or fully consider the consequences to yourself."

"Are you referring to those louts who accosted me and Gory in that tavern near the Royal Society when were trying to help Adela solve the theft of that priceless book from the Huntsford Academy library? The tavern was a respectable place frequented by scholars, and–"

"And you got yourself and Gory hurt because it was not quite as respectable as you believed. You were asking dangerous questions. Did you not consider that the thief would have friends? Because of you, I was left nursing a black eye for a week."

"Which only happened because you interfered."

"Interfered?" He wanted to throttle her for that stupid remark. Instead, he scooted over a little to give her more space to sit beside him on the bed. "I *saved* you. Which is something I had to do because you disobeyed my instructions and went to the tavern instead of going home as you were supposed to do. Syd, you could have been badly hurt had I not followed you there and got the two of you out in time. My black eye was nothing, for it quickly healed. But what bothered me most was that I could not trust you."

"It isn't the same," she insisted. "Yes, I defied you, but I never made you any promises. In fact, Gory and I were adamant about remaining involved in the investigation. You were the one issuing edicts I had no intention of following. But it all worked out in the end, so why are we quarreling about it now?"

"We are not quarreling. We are discussing that old situation as it relates to our current situation. If I tell you that you must do something, it is not because I wish to be an ogre. It is because I know what will happen if you defy me. Syd, at the heart of the matter is that we need to trust each other. I need you to promise that you will not run away from me."

"I won't run away from you. If I decide to leave, then I will tell you. I promise. But you must then allow me to leave if this is what I wish to do. Respect goes both ways."

He rubbed a hand along his jaw and groaned. "We are going to talk in circles. You still intend to do whatever you want to do. It does not give me any confidence. Just because you are going to tell me before you go off on your own doesn't make it right. It leaves me worried that you are going to run into trouble and will not listen to me, no matter how worried I am about you or how dangerous I know the situation to be."

"My valiant protector," she whispered, leaning forward to kiss him primly on the cheek.

Her bosom pressed lightly against his chest, the accidental gesture setting him instantly on fire because this is what Syd seemed able to do to him with her slightest touch.

Gad, why her?

Why could he not have these feelings for some biddable mouse of a girl?

"Give me time, Octavian," she said, her voice shaking with genuine feeling. "If you were raised with a loveable fool of a father and a mother who would rather suffer in silence than ever take a stand or make a decision of her own, you would understand me better."

"Ah, Syd. I do understand you. In fact, sometimes it is scary how well I seem to know your mind."

"You do have an impressive ability to thwart me at every turn," she acknowledged.

"I do not thwart you nearly as often as I wish. In fact, you outwit me constantly. Trying to stay a step ahead of you is usually a losing battle and exhausts me. But we would be quite something if we worked together instead of at cross purposes."

"Where would the fun be in that?" she said playfully, and then drew away when she heard a light knock at their door. "Oh, that will be our refreshments."

She rose and was about to hurry toward the door when he grabbed her gently by the wrist and whispered, "Syd, stop."

She turned to him in confusion. "Why?"

"Exercise a little caution. We don't know who is behind that door."

She frowned lightly and pursed her lips. "Octavian, you are being ridiculous. Who do you think is behind the door?"

CHAPTER 4

SYD WATCHED AS the knob began to turn on its own.

She fell back a step to stand by Octavian's side and quietly berated herself for not thinking about who might be standing on the other side of the door. What if Sir Henry had caught up to them already? Not that she believed it was possible, but Octavian had accused her of being rash and he was right. She had not even considered the danger or expressed any caution before intending to let in whoever stood there.

Octavian had instantly shot to his feet, drawing her behind him, and at the same time reaching for his pistol. He now breathed a sigh of relief and quietly slipped his pistol back in the lip of his boot when the person turned out to be one of the inn's maids rolling in a tea cart.

Completely harmless.

The maid caught sight of Octavian and cast him a beguiling smile. "Do you require anything more, my lord?"

"No, my wife and I have all we need."

The girl eyed him suggestively again, then bobbed a curtsy and sashayed out, quietly closing the door behind her.

Syd regarded him thoughtfully. "Am I mistaken or was she making suggestive overtures to you?"

He grimaced. "You are not mistaken."

"Did she not see me standing right behind you?" Syd was appalled by the brazenness of some women. Who would be so bold as to make such indecent advances to a man while that man's wife was standing right beside him? That she and Octavian were not married was irrelevant since everyone thought they were.

"I don't know. Perhaps you were too well hidden. I'm a big man."

"And what am I? Little and shriveled? I did not think I was all that well hidden," she grumbled and remained staring at him.

He sighed. "What, Syd?"

She blushed. "Are you?"

"Am I what?"

"Going to take her up on her offer?"

"Are you jesting? Blessed saints, no. I have no intention of it. Women approach me all the time."

"Oh, I see." There was no denying he had the good looks to put women in a swoon. No other man had ever made her heart flutter, something he managed to do even when she was irritated with him.

"You seem to be the only one impervious to my charms," he said with a wry arch of his brow. "Syd, we are supposedly married two days now. What sort of knave would I be to cheat on my new wife? But just to be clear, I would never be unfaithful, even to a pretend wife. Not ever. So put it out of your head at once."

"All right. Thank you, Octavian." She went to the cart and began to set out the light fare the brazen maid had brought up. In truth, she wanted to dump it all back out into the hallway, which was something she might have done had Octavian actually been married to her.

But this was her rash and impulsive self getting incensed when she really had no right to be. Octavian was being so wonderfully decent and honorable about their pretend marriage vows. His behavior mattered most, not that of a conniving stranger they would never see again.

Besides, had she not often behaved outrageously herself? Never in any lascivious way, of course. Nor would she ever blatantly proposition any man, much less a happily married one. Having talked herself into calming down, she poured each of them a cup of tea and addressed the comment he had made about her not liking him.

Was it not obvious that she cared for him very much and did not know what to do about it? "I am not impervious to your charms, Octavian. But I was raised to be a lady and taught never to show such feelings."

He laughed. "You may have been raised a lady, but that has not stopped you from expressing your feelings or opinions or doing anything you like. You are a hoyden and a hellion."

She tried not to feel wounded by the remark because it was true and he was stating it as fact without intention of being hurtful. "Is there a difference?"

"Probably not," he said with a shrug, but not a moment later cast her a slow, lazy smile. "Are you suggesting that you find me attractive?"

"Of course, I do. A woman would have to blind not to notice how handsome you are. In fact, you are the handsomest man I have ever set eyes upon. What do you think of that?"

The comment obviously surprised him, but instead of continuing to smile at her, he frowned. "And still, you resent me."

Her eyes widened. "I do not resent you!"

He shook his head. "You do, Syd. But let's drop the discussion for now. I find myself suddenly hungry. What did they bring us?"

"Cold ham, tea cakes, cheese, and apples. I'll set some on a plate for you." She began to fuss with the appetizing fare while he settled into one of the two chairs beside a small table.

He had earlier removed the jacket of his uniform and now looked big and wonderful, his muscles straining against the white lawn of his shirt. How could any woman resist his superb body or those gorgeous, silver-gray eyes?

Still, that maid had no right to blatantly ogle him, even if he was physically perfect in every way. Strong jaw, gorgeous mouth that felt so warm and fine pressed to hers the first and only time he had kissed her. Full head of dark hair trimmed at the sides. The cut of his hair made him look quite rigidly military but also incredibly appealing.

Strength oozed out of his every pore, and the heavenly sinew of his torso had her heart in palpitations.

She wanted to sleep beside this man and feel his arms around her.

Would it be so awful to lose herself in those acres of muscles?

After all, she was ruined whether they slept together or not.

As for their sham marriage, what harm could there be in sharing a bed? It wasn't as though they were going to act upon their proximity. "Octavian," she said, setting the plate of food in front of him, "I have a solution to the problem of who is to sleep on the floor."

"I am not going to flip cards for it."

"We don't even have a deck of cards. That is not my suggestion." She cleared her throat. "The bed is large enough for us to share."

He shook his head and emitted a deep, rich laugh. "No. Absolutely not."

"Why not? We are only going to sleep, so why not allow both of us to be comfortable? It is the only sensible solution. Besides, the staff will think it most odd if only one side of the bed is slept in. They will suspect we are not newlyweds and call in the authorities. Do not be stubborn about this. You know it is the only choice that makes any sense."

He stuffed a bite of cold ham in his mouth in order to avoid responding to her. Why was he so averse to the suggestion? He had told her she was pretty this morning. What had changed? Did she smell of the dirt and heat of the roadway? "Oh, it is me you do not want near you. I...I did not think to take one of Adela's soaps with me. Do you by any chance have some I could use? Perhaps the innkeeper will have–"

"Syd?" He stared at her as though confused, and then amusement shone in his eyes so that they glistened. "Your scent is delightful, as sweet as cherries. Why are you being so dense about this? I am not resisting because of the way you smell."

"Gad, you are such a charmer." She sank into the chair beside his. "How am I being dense?"

He took another bite of his ham and seemed to take forever to swallow it. "You are a woman, quite an attractive one much of the time. You have curves. Very appealing ones."

"And?

"You have a bosom…also very appealing. I do not want any misunderstandings to occur between us while we are asleep."

"So you would rather lay upon a cold, hard floor rather than accidentally brush up against my body?"

"Yes. I do not know what I might do when deep in sleep. I am not a monk and might accidentally shift closer to you, touch you in a way that I should not. You may have a sharp tongue, but–"

"I am not that bad, am I?"

"Do you want me to answer that honestly? My point is, the rest of you is soft and warm. I may not be completely resistant to you."

She placed her elbows on the table and propped her head in her hands while staring at him. This was not quite a declaration of love, but it was still something. "Are you suggesting I entice you? I had no idea I was so sultry and alluring."

"Blessed saints," he said with a groaning chuckle. "Just think about this, Syd. You and I in bed together. It is dark and we are under the covers. You are wearing a thin nightgown and I…well, I had better keep my trousers on, hadn't I?"

"Did you not think to bring a nightshirt?"

"You assume I own one, which I don't because I always sleep naked."

She blushed.

That made him grin. "I am not likely to resist the sweet, womanly scent of your body or the satin feel of your skin. My hands are going to roam all over you…and Lord help us if they land somewhere they should not."

She regarded him thoughtfully for a long moment. "I will wake you if that happens."

"You will slap me if that happens."

"I would never. At worst I would wake you gently." In truth, she would probably let him roam and not say a word because if this make-believe marriage they were about to enter into did not work out, then she wanted to have the memory of sharing a night in bed with him to sustain her upcoming sad and empty years.

No man had ever been as kind to her or as patient with her. If Octavian decided he did not want her, then what chance did she have with anyone else?

If she was going to be a spinster, why not enjoy one wild night with this man who was sinfully handsome? She trusted him to the depths of her soul. He was a dream come true, and she was not going to pass up the chance to experience his lips, hands, and any other bodily organ he wished to use on her.

"I am not finished arguing the matter with you, Octavian. So do not think you have won this point. But I need to get out of my gown and prepare for bed now. You'll have to help me undress," she remarked once they had finished their light repast. There was no lady's maid here to assist and she was *never* going to summon the maid who had brought in the tea cart.

"All right, I'll help you. But I am not discussing the matter of sleeping arrangements with you."

"So that's it? You are going to be a stubborn lout and sleep on the uncomfortable floor where you will catch your death of cold and be of no use to me or the Admiralty, I might point out. Is your mission not important? Besides, I do not wish to travel the rest of the way to Greenock with your dead body moldering in a hired coach."

He grinned. "You'd probably cut me up and examine my body parts under a microscope."

"That is not a bad idea," she teased. "Octavian, there's no hiding from each other. There is no ornamental screen here to shield us while we change out of our clothes or even use a chamber pot. How can we get more intimate than this?"

One eyebrow of his shot up and a gleam sprang into his eyes. "Perhaps I will show you how…one of these days."

Please. Yes.

But she pressed on before she became distracted with thoughts of what he might do. She was eager to learn all she could from him before they parted ways. Even though he had spoken of a possible permanent arrangement, she dared not consider it or give herself hope. She would be crushed when he became disenchanted with her and they returned to leading their separate lives.

"Since we are going to see *all* of each other over these next few weeks, a sensible next step of sharing a bed is not going to be that noteworthy," she said. "If it does not work out, then I will not argue if you choose to move to the floor. Does this not sound fair and sensible? Do we have a deal?"

"No."

Why did he have to be such a stubborn clot?

Well, she could be just as stubborn. "Fine, then you leave me no choice. I shall sleep on the floor, too."

He frowned at her. "You will not."

"You cannot stop me. If you sleep on the floor, then I sleep on the floor. We shall both get sick and die together."

"Bloody blazes, Syd. Why must you be such a nuisance?" He rolled his eyes and then emitted a defeated sigh. "I know I am going to regret this. All right. Deal. We share the bed."

Her hands shook as the import of his agreement rippled through her.

She had just convinced this gorgeous man to sleep with her.

Could she convince him to do more than just sleep with her?

No. No.

What an outrageous thought.

True, they would soon be married.

But they were not married yet.

It was enough of a struggle just getting him to this point.

Perhaps she would raise the matter of *more* in a few days, once he had grown accustomed to having her in bed with him.

Octavian wheeled the tea cart and their dirty dishes into the hall for one of the inn's attendants to pick up while Syd quickly took care of her necessaries and washed up. She wished she could laze in a steaming hot bath, but that luxury would have to wait for another time.

Octavian then had his turn attending to himself while she turned her back to him and began to undress. But she hadn't gotten very far, merely removed her walking boots and stockings, and unpinned her hair before she reached an impasse. "Octavian, will you help me with the hooks and laces?"

Wordlessly, he dried his hands and walked across the chamber to where she was standing.

Syd held her breath as he stepped behind her and then nudged her hair aside before attempting to untie the first lacings. Tingles shot through her as his knuckles grazed her neck and she felt his warm breath upon her skin.

There was a charge between them that felt like bolts of lightning striking the ground.

Sparks lingered in the air.

Her body sizzled with his every touch.

"Silky," he murmured, his fingers sliding through her long tresses as he eased them aside.

"I brushed out the knots," she said for lack of a more clever remark.

"I noticed." He emitted a soft growl watching the curls tumble over her shoulder and come to rest atop her bosom.

She licked her lips. "I usually braid my hair."

"I'm glad you didn't."

So was she, for she never would have experienced this bit of intimacy with Octavian otherwise. There was something quite exciting about him standing behind her, big and masculine. Would he wrap his arms around her if she leaned back ever so slightly to rest against his chest?

"Do you want me to help braid your hair once I am through unlacing your gown?" he asked, his voice deep and resonant.

"Um..." Fashioning a simple braid was something she always did before donning her nightgown and slipping into bed. She did not ever bother with anything intricate, just a loose plait down her back to keep herself from accidentally yanking her hair whenever she turned in her sleep.

But leaving it long and loose, available for him to touch, was so much better. "No, not necessary."

She would never braid her hair again, not while she shared a bedchamber with Octavian.

Once again, she felt his warm breath against her neck as he worked to unfasten the row of hooks along the back of her gown and untie the last of the lacings. "All done," he said finally, his voice unmistakably husky.

"Thank you." She ached to tip back the slightest bit and encourage his embrace, but she could not bring herself to do it.

What if he stepped away instead of drawing her into his arms? The gown was loose and already slipping off her shoulders, so she let it fall further and held her breath in the hope he might do something.

She was scantily clad.

Were men not aroused by this? Several books she had read on the topic indicated this was quite an effective seduction tool.

He muttered something unintelligible and stepped away.

Syd shook off her disappointment, quietly removed the gown, and then carefully set it aside so that it would not wrinkle. But she was not discouraged, for she still needed to remove her corset. Could she tempt him with that? She did not know why it was suddenly so important to wring as much as she could out of this intimate moment.

Perhaps because she did not believe this make-believe marriage would ever work out. Even if they stayed married, would they live together? Share a bedchamber? This was so unlikely. She needed to acquire blissful memories before they parted ways.

They were on good terms at present.

He had just admitted that he was not averse to her.

Why not seize the opportunity before she riled him again?

She turned away from him while removing her corset.

That garment laced up the front so she did not have difficulty removing it. However, she would need assistance tomorrow when doing it up because getting the laces through the eyelets was not nearly as easy to do as pulling them out.

She felt Octavian's scorching gaze on her all the while.

The man had eyes that could burn into her soul.

She sighed as she set the corset over the chair atop her gown. "It is easier if I sleep in my shift, don't you think?"

"Easier for who?" he muttered. "Yes, fine."

He walked to the other side of the bed and removed his boots and shirt while she slipped in between the sheets. When he settled beside her, she realized the bed was not quite as big as she had first imagined. Octavian sank onto the mattress, causing it to dip on his side.

"Oh!" She rolled right into him.

He bolted upright to a sitting position the moment her bosom landed on his chest and firmly pressed against it. "This is why I knew it wouldn't work. I'll sleep on the floor."

She grabbed his arm, requiring both hands to properly wrap them around the rock hard muscle. "Don't you dare. We are smart adults. We shall figure this out. Just lie back and do not utter another word of complaint."

To her surprise, he did no more than growl softly. "Now what?"

They had been given four pillows in all, no doubt because this was the inn's finest and most expensive room. She now propped two of those pillows alongside his body to serve as a barrier between him and her. "See, easily solved."

She lay back down and promptly rolled against the pillows, but she did not see this as a problem since she was not directly against his big body. "Perfect," she mumbled and closed her eyes. Only then did she realize that she should have braided her hair because left unbound, it now spilled over onto his side of the bed.

Well, no matter.

Octavian had just snuffed out the candle and turned away from her. He was not happy with their sleeping arrangements and would do his best to distance himself from her.

Drat.

She was so brave about everything, so why not this? She wanted him to look at her.

She wanted to stare into his silver eyes.

It did not matter that it was too dark to see anything with the candle blown out.

Well, she would just have to content herself with having a giant oak in bed beside her whose skin held the subtly pleasant scent of bergamot and who was taking up most of the mattress.

She liked that he was a big man with big shoulders.

Would he be angry if she told him this was nice?

This was one of her last thoughts before she fell asleep.

Was he thinking of her, too?

CHAPTER 5

THE NIGHT HAD turned cool, but Syd slept comfortably and felt quite cozy come morning. The sky had now lightened from black to bleak gray. She knew it would not be long before one of the inn's staff knocked at their door to deliver their breakfast.

She started to slip out of bed and then suddenly stopped.

Octavian had turned toward her sometime in the night and now had his big, muscled arm around her waist despite the two pillows still between them.

Drat.

Even in sleep, he maintained their barrier.

She placed her hand on the first pillow and ever so slowly tried to ease it out from between them. After all, was it not sensible to remove them before anyone on the inn's staff came in and noticed?

They might grow suspicious and alert the innkeeper something was not right.

Who would ever believe Octavian's wife wanted a barricade between her and that gorgeous ox of a man, especially after she had made such a fuss about theirs being a love match?

But no sooner had she started to move the pillow aside than Octavian emitted a seductive growl. "Don't."

She inhaled lightly. "Ah, you are awake. Why should I not set them aside? We are about to get up anyway. Where is the harm?"

His arm was still wrapped around her waist. Wordlessly, he drew her up against the length of his warm body. "Ooof!

Octavian?"

His eyes were closed, but he now opened one.

Despite its silver glint of menace, she smiled at him. "Good morning."

"It can't be. Still too dark outside."

"Yes, well…it is more gray than inky blackness." She snuggled closer, quite liking the heat of his body. "The first rays of sunlight are just starting to peek through the clouds. May I please remove this barrier between us?"

"No."

"Are you always this grumpy in the morning?"

"Yes. And it is not morning yet."

"I beg to differ." She touched his face because it was such a beautiful, manly face. He had the makings of a beard that scratched against her palm as she rubbed it along his jaw. "Did you sleep well? I did. I think I fell asleep the moment my head hit the pillow."

"I know," he said with a trace of humor in his voice.

"Oh, did I snore? Move too much and accidentally kick you?"

"No, Syd. You didn't snore or kick me. You tossed and turned, then finally curled up in a little ball beside me and purred like a kitten. Were you dreaming of me?" he teased.

She laughed softly. "Since you accused me of purring in my sleep, I was obviously dreaming of cats. In truth, I do not recall dreaming of anything. But is this why you placed your arm around me? To quiet me?"

"You weren't noisy. I did not mind those soft purrs. But I was afraid you were going to fall out of bed since you were shifting around restlessly. Not that I blame you. I was taking up most of the mattress and left you a bit cramped." He yawned as he now shifted onto his back. The sheet drifted lower as he raised his arms over his head and stretched with a soft, animal growl.

Mother in heaven.

She tried not to gawk at the magnificence of his body. But who could overlook the lean, hard length of him, and that broad chest with a dusting of dark hair across its breadth? His skin was bronzed, no doubt due to his years at sea, and his muscles were a masterpiece of sculptured art.

How could she ever be a match for this man?

That he held onto her throughout the night signified nothing. He only held her because he believed she was going to run away from him.

Yes, this was likely the reason.

He did not trust her and meant to keep her restrained.

If only he knew that she would do no such thing.

First of all, her best chance of helping her father was to marry Octavian and have him make whatever bargain necessary with Sir Henry to keep her father safe. Second of all, sometime during the night she had resolved to seduce Octavian.

No matter what happened afterward, she wanted one night of wantonness with him. He would not fully claim her, for he had made the terms of their pretend marriage quite clear. Losing her innocence would seal their fate and make an annulment impossible. But she had read books on the topic of love and knew there were other ways to enjoy each other without need of that final act.

She quickly shook out of the thought before Octavian caught on to what was going through her mind since he knew her so well.

Too well.

It galled her, but also made her feel good that someone understood her as thoroughly as Octavian did.

Perhaps this was an indication they were meant for each other.

So why was she insisting on having them part ways once she came of age and did not need her father's consent to marry? Why would she not think of herself first and encourage Octavian to make theirs a real marriage? Instead, she had made it ever so clear that she wished to maintain a make-believe marriage.

It was her fault that he now carried so many doubts about her. He was not even sure they would exchange vows once they reached Gretna Green.

In failing to agree wholeheartedly to a committed union, she had also given Octavian a way out. What if she wanted to go ahead with their marriage and he decided when standing over the blacksmith's anvil that he would rather not?

The realization that their time together could be over by the end of the week dampened her spirits.

She was going to miss him fiercely.

This left her feeling miserable, but she masked it with a layer of cheerfulness.

Octavian emitted another low, seductive sound, grabbed his shirt from the foot of the bed, and then tossed it on as he rose to peer out the window. "Blast, I think it's going to rain today."

"This is England. It always rains." She climbed out of bed to join him by the window and almost squealed in surprise when he tucked an arm around her shoulders and drew her to him. The gesture felt easy and natural, as though this is how it was meant to be between them.

He grinned when she snuggled against him. "Are you cold, Syd?"

"A little." It was the tiniest fib, for she was in her bare feet and the wooden floor was cool. She wasn't cold yet, but would be if she did not soon don her stockings.

He wrapped both arms around her now. "Better?"

"Yes." Perhaps she would not have to work so hard to gain his agreement about a night of intimacy between them.

Then she noticed the inn's ostler and a few others already moving about the courtyard. Of course, he was not holding her in his arms because he was besotted with her and had to touch her. He was just keeping up the pretense of being a newly married couple on the chance any of them were watching. "I'll need help getting dressed," she reminded him, hoping he did not notice her disappointment.

"All right. Since we're up anyway, let's get you out of those nightclothes." The words came out in a suggestive manner, as though the prospect was arousing to him. But this would mean he was not completely unaffected by her.

Even if he was having intimate thoughts about her, did it signify anything?

She was not the only woman he had ever taken to his bed.

Although he was discreet about it, likely he had taken many, many before her.

Being a kind man by nature, he probably embraced all these young ladies just as he was doing with her now. He must have helped them dress afterward because any young lady would not hesitate to shed her clothing before performing *the act* with Octavian.

Even she wanted to shed her clothing around this man.

This alarmed her, but she also regarded it as a learning opportunity.

Well, none of it mattered.

He was not going to remove his trousers for her and she was a fool for even considering it. Besides, they were in a hurry to get on the road. Was this not far more important? They had almost a full week of illicit bed sharing before they reached Scotland. Plenty of time for them to get better acquainted, and plenty of time for her to work up the courage to seduce him.

Waiting a few days before acting on her plan seemed prudent.

After all, they had both been quite tired after this first day of travel. She was always short-tempered when exhausted and Octavian would likely be the same.

They would settle into a comfortable travel routine within a few days.

It would also give her the chance to get to know him better. Yes, they had been friends for a while now, but had not really seen much of each other since his duties so often took him outside of London.

It was not yet time to do more than sleep together in the same bed.

She watched Octavian move about the room.

Dear heaven, the man was a wonder of nature.

She was going to put her plan into action before they reached Scotland.

There was only the slightest snag.

How was she to get him to cooperate? Especially if he believed she was doing this because she wanted her one night with him and then intended to run off.

Running away was still a possibility.

She would do it for his sake, if it proved necessary.

He wanted to spare her a life of misery with Sir Henry, but she wanted to spare him a life of misery with *her*. In all this time, he had not once mentioned the beautiful debutante everyone in the *ton* was certain he was courting.

She was the one dropping occasional hints to encourage him to talk about Lady Clementine, but he never took her up on it.

Lady Clementine was not merely beautiful, she was considered a matchless beauty.

A true *ton* diamond.

If Octavian was not going to talk about her, then Syd decided that she would not either.

Still, it could not be overlooked that he might have feelings for her.

Nor could Syd ignore that he had reshuffled his plans to run up to Scotland and this may have interfered with his plans to propose to Lady Clementine.

Had he set aside his own happiness in order to rescue her from marriage to Sir Henry?

Syd resolved to have an honest discussion with Octavian about his marital intentions, but not before she had her night of fantasy with him.

In fairness to him, their talk had to take place before they exchanged vows because she would never allow Octavian to bind himself to her in marriage if he loved Lady Clementine.

She inhaled lightly.

When had protecting Octavian become more important to her than her own happiness? Well, she had always felt the need to protect him, whether from a tavern brawl – even if she had started it – or her horrible family.

Warmth curled in her belly as he continued to hold her in his arms.

Could this make-believe situation turn into something wonderful and enduring?

Were the gossips all wrong about his feelings for Lady Clementine?

Getting to the truth was of vital importance, not only for his sake but for hers.

She cared for him.

However, she refused to call this yearning she was feeling love. Love interfered with rational decisions.

Besides, he was never going to fall in love with her. Why fool herself into thinking that he would ever prefer her over Lady Clementine?

CHAPTER 6

OCTAVIAN STUDIED SYD as they sat across from each other in the hired coach. They had made excellent time these past few days on their journey north and would reach Carlisle by this evening. Gretna Green was not far from Carlisle which meant they would soon cross over the border into Scotland and be married by tomorrow afternoon at the latest.

Blessed saints.

By this time tomorrow, he would be Syd's husband.

Of course, this assumed Syd was not going to have a change of heart and run away at the last moment. She had behaved like an angel throughout the journey, showing consideration and in general being charming. Their conversations were intelligent and often witty, but she also knew how to remain silent and lost in her own thoughts.

He could not have asked for a better travel companion.

Or a sweeter bed mate, which was something he had never experienced before. It was not his practice to spend entire nights with any woman. Nor was it his practice to merely sleep when in bed with a woman. Until Syd, having a woman in his bed was purely for the purpose of satisfying his manly urges.

Once done, he and the lady in question would exchange a few pleasantries, and then part ways.

He never brought women to his home, a cardinal rule that he never ignored.

However, he had brought Syd straight to his home without

thinking twice about it on the night she had thrown him off the roof. He could have taken her to the residence of Lady Dayne or Lady Withnall or even to Leo and Marigold's home. Any of them would have protected her quite ably.

But no, he had acted on pure instinct and taken her home with him. He understood the reason for it, although he was not quite ready to accept that he wanted her with him for always.

Syd was a handful.

Headstrong and unpredictable.

And yet, he was ready to risk his heart in the hope of making a love match with her. Syd, who was usually the smartest person in the room, did not seem to grasp the situation.

Would she ever get over her own insecurities to understand he could not bear to be without her?

He did not think so, not yet anyway.

He studied the beautiful swirl and sparkle of her eyes that glistened like pale green crystals, and saw she was troubled once again.

What now?

She was holding something back, a new worry perhaps?

He feared to let down his guard when watching her. One lapse and he risked losing her, especially now that they were so close to their goal. "A few more hours until Carlisle, Syd."

She smiled, but her smile was strained. "And less than twenty-four hours until we are married. How do you feel, Octavian? Any second thoughts?"

"None at all. I feel just fine." He leaned forward and took her hand as they jounced along the uneven roadway in their carriage. "The more important question is, how do you feel about our marriage?"

"I am committed to our make-believe marriage, so you needn't worry that I will run away at the last moment. I can see the doubt in your eyes, but I give you my word of honor that I shall not run. Does this make you feel any better? I know you have been worried about me all along."

"It does ease my mind," he admitted, his tension ebbing now that she had assured him of this fact.

"I know you believe I break promises, but I do not." She glanced out the window. "The more urgent question is whether the impending rain will delay us. Will you look at those dark thunderclouds? They seem to be overtaking us fast."

He followed her gaze and frowned, for those thunderclouds were moving fast and now turning almost black. This meant a serious storm was about to unleash its fury upon them. "We'll be all right, even if we have to stop before reaching Carlisle. We can stay in Penrith tonight, if we must. It is only a few miles away, and we are already within a day's ride of Gretna Green."

In truth, it seemed likely they would have to find themselves a room at one of the nearby inns. There were several good ones up ahead and none would be filled to capacity since the summer hikers had returned to London weeks ago and it was too early for grouse hunting season to begin.

He glanced out the window again, seriously worried the storm was about to swallow them up. "Yes, we had better find shelter right away."

He knocked on the roof and told their driver to stop in Penrith. "Aye, Captain Thorne," the man said with obvious relief.

Syd appeared fretful, but she had to know this was their only choice. Their route traversed the Lake District, a place of majestic beauty and plentiful hills that would be impossible to cross when the ground turned to mud. Also, the roads around here were more isolated than in the south of England. If they broke a wheel on a particularly barren stretch, they might lose days from the time help arrived to the time the carriage was repaired.

Fortunately, their luck held. No more than a few raindrops had fallen by the time they reached the Penrith Inn and drew up in its courtyard. The jovial owner immediately hurried out to greet them. "Good to see you again, Captain Thorne."

"And you, Mr. Burton. May I introduce you to my wife?" He cast Syd a besotted look. "Married almost a week now."

"Newlyweds!" The man clapped his hands and immediately offered them a charming corner room with ample windows overlooking the front yard. Conveniently, it also overlooked the side yard where the inn's staff entered, and the nicely landscaped back garden.

Of course, Mr. Burton was giving them his best guest chamber because he believed they were newly married. But Octavian was pleased with the choice because it gave him a view of whoever came and went from the place, whether from the front entrance or the staff's kitchen entrance.

As the rain began to fall in earnest, he signed the Penrith Inn's guest register as he always did, Captain and Mrs. Thorne.

It amazed him how comfortable and right it felt to sign Syd in as his wife.

After he and Syd settled into their room, he left her there while he sought out the inn's ostler. Perhaps he was being overly concerned, but they had hit a few ruts along the way and he wanted the carriage wheels thoroughly checked.

"The last stretch of road was rough," he told the old man who had a weathered face, calloused hands, and obviously had a wealth of experience with horses and the carriages they drew. "Can you check this hired coach? We need to be on our way at first light tomorrow and I would not like any mishaps."

"At once, Captain Thorne. Never ye worry, this is one of the Carville coaches out of Oxford, isn't it?"

Octavian nodded.

"They're as sturdy as they come." As Octavian looked on, the man took several minutes to poke and prod each wheel and did the same for the carriage frame. "Ye needn't worry, Captain. As I said, she's built sturdy. Nothing wrong with those wheels or anything else."

This came as a great relief to Octavian, for they were so close to Scotland now and he did not want anything to delay their wedding day.

His only regret was that it would not be much of a ceremony for Syd. As for him, he did not care that it would be a five minute affair and then kicked out so another eloping couple could take their vows.

As for his brothers not being present, he knew they would understand. They were practical men and all of a similar mind about wedding ceremonies. These ceremonies were a mere formality. What mattered most were the years of marriage.

But Syd had that traditional side to her and might feel cheated.

He would find a way to make it up to her if it proved important. Of course, this assumed they would stay together.

"It is a nice room, don't you think so, Syd?" he asked, walking back into their chamber and coming to her side when he found her staring out the front window.

"Yes, quite comfortable and cozy." She turned to him and cast him a fragile smile that made his heart lurch.

"But you do not seem comfortable," he remarked. "What is troubling you?"

"Nothing, Octavian. Well, nothing new."

"Still worried that you are imposing on me?" It bothered him that she did not appreciate how lovely she was in every way. She had developed a huge chip on her shoulder due to being raised by an ineffective and often cold mother, and a selfish, wastrel of a father. Whatever doubts she felt about her own worth were only made worse by the snide comments and cruel slights she had endured once out in Society.

Her intelligence was regarded as a mark of insolence.

Her strength of character branded her as difficult and a troublemaker. Well, she certainly was a load of trouble.

But she made him feel more alive than he had ever felt, and he had led a fairly interesting and adventurous life. Syd had not traveled as extensively as he had, nor did she have much experience beyond her book learning.

Still, she held her own against him.

She challenged him constantly, but mostly in a good way.

In truth, she was an inspiration to him because she believed passionately about her causes and would not let the petty thinking of others dissuade her from doing what was right. Her knowledge of medicine was impressive and all of it self-taught because Society and her own family frowned upon her desire for a higher education.

This did not stop Syd from quietly working toward her goal.

Did she realize how much he admired her for overcoming those odds?

Or did she only notice when he rebuked her? He only did so when she was about to run into danger. Ah, well. In time, she might come to accept that he liked her fire and spirit. He had no intention of stifling her, but he was bloody well going to protect her.

He drew aside the curtain so that they could both look out with ease. It was not long before the gentle rain became a gushing torrent, and the courtyard turned into a sea of mud. "Goodness," Syd remarked, "that came on fast."

He grunted in agreement. "I hope it moves out fast, too."

She inhaled lightly. "Octavian, what if it doesn't? Will we ride on to Gretna Green anyway?"

"I don't know. Hopefully, we can. I'd like us to keep moving."

"Because you are worried that Sir Henry and my father will catch up to us? Let's hope they are days behind us still. I know you are eager to get the marriage over and done, but we mustn't act rashly."

Syd being the voice of reason?

That was a rare occurrence.

He arched an eyebrow. "I am not the one who ever acts...never mind. We'll see what tomorrow brings."

She harrumphed. "I know what you were about to say, and it is very mean of you. I do not ever act rashly. Well, only sometimes. Why are ladies thought of as impulsive and men who behave in the same way are deemed decisive and born leaders?"

Octavian avoided the question he preferred not to answer since it would only get him into deeper trouble.

Now, she looked insulted.

He did not blame her. "Are you hungry?" he asked, eager to change the topic of conversation. "Shall I order a meal brought to our room?"

She sighed. "Not yet. I don't have much of an appetite just now."

"Are you feeling all right?"

She looked up at him with big, worried eyes. "I don't know. It is all hitting me at once. I don't know what to think."

He wrapped his arms around her so that her back rested

against his chest as they continued to watch the activity in the courtyard. Carriages were pulling up fast as the rain continued to intensify. His thoughts now turned to Sir Henry, hoping this deluge had slowed him down, too. The man was fierce and determined, especially when it came to claiming Syd as his prize.

Octavian had not been too worried about encountering him at any of the inns where they stayed. His real worry was about tomorrow and whether Sir Henry and Syd's father would be waiting to ambush them at the Gretna Green blacksmith shop. After all, that unsavory pair only needed to catch him and Syd before they married, and everyone knew Gretna Green was the first town across the Scottish border where they could accomplish this task.

Well, nothing to be done about it tonight.

But he would have to scout ahead tomorrow to make certain all was clear before he brought Syd there. They could move on to another village and take their vows further north, if necessary.

Syd's father was a bit of a dolt.

But Sir Henry was wily and dangerous when crossed.

He had to be furious by now.

It would not take Sir Henry longer than a day or two to piece together that she had run off to Scotland with him. He hoped the bounder did not have men already positioned in wait for them at every town along the border.

Octavian believed it unlikely but not altogether impossible.

Syd thought they were well ahead of Sir Henry, but a fast horse could cover more miles in a day than a coach.

Chances were slim that Sir Henry had brought along anyone other than Syd's father. Most of the men around him came from the meanest parts of London. These were ruffians who knew how to prowl the back alleyways and use a blade with skill, but most had never been on a horse.

Riding was a gentleman's sport.

He kept his demeanor casual because he did not wish to worry Syd needlessly.

In truth, she already looked as though something was bothering her. It wasn't the stupid comment he had just made about her rash behavior. No, something more serious was troubling her and had been for several days now.

He studied Syd as she moved to the bed and sat on the plump mattress with yet another sigh. But she wasn't reveling in the comfort of their surroundings. She was pensive and staring down at her hands. "What are you thinking about, Syd?"

A guilty look immediately sprang into her eyes. "Nothing."

Bollocks.

Was she still thinking of returning to her father and allowing herself to be pledged into indentured servitude with that arse, Sir Henry? He thought they had resolved this dispute days ago. And had she not assured him earlier today that she would not run off? He would never allow her to leave his side until he gave her the protection of his name. "Forget it, Syd," he said with a soft growl. "I know what you are thinking and it simply won't work."

Her eyes rounded in surprise. "How can you know what I am thinking?"

"Because your expression reveals everything."

"It does?" Her blush deepened and now spread to the tips of her ears. She moaned and buried her face in her hands when he frowned at her. "How can I ever look at you again? This is so humiliating."

"Why?" he asked, now confused because he did not think describing her decision to return to her father and an odious forced marriage to Sir Henry as humiliating. Well, it was a stupid decision. Upsetting and distasteful, for certain. But she was blushing so furiously, one would think he had accidentally walked in on her while she was naked.

"How can it not be humiliating?" she asked, sticking her head up for a moment before burying it in her hands once again. "Well, I suppose it is quite commonplace for you. But it is not at all for me. Please forget I said anything."

"No, Syd. I won't forget about it. We need to clear the air about this." He did not know what else to say because her response now left him even more confused.

What was commonplace?

She could not be talking about abduction or forced marriage.

She glanced up at him, obviously pained and struggling to maintain her composure. "I will not say another word about my idea. Obviously, I misunderstood your willingness. I thought men were not all that particular about the women they took to bed."

His heart shot into his throat. "To bed? For purposes other than sleeping?"

"Yes. What did you think I was talking about?"

What?

Had he just heard her right? She was asking to leap into bed with him for the purpose of...satisfying their carnal urges?

Syd was completely innocent and had no idea what was involved. However, he breathed a sigh of relief that she was not thinking about running back to London. This is what he'd feared most. But sex? He needed to proceed very carefully before he said or did something unforgivable. "Go on, Syd. Tell me what you have in mind."

"Why? Am I not obvious enough? I did not think you would care that I wanted you to teach me about these intimacies. What is so awful about us doing something more than merely sleeping together?" She groaned softly and continued. "We will be married tomorrow and I do not know what will happen afterward. What if you decide to send me back to London without you?"

Blessed saints.

He tried to form words, but they simply would not come to mind.

His unintentional silence only made things worse.

Syd looked like she wanted to melt into the furniture and never be seen by him again. "Octavian, why won't you say something? How is your refusal, and now your continued silence, anything but humiliating? So, let us forget I asked...well, I did not ask, but you saw the look on my face and knew my intention because you seem to know my mind better than I do."

Ha! That was surely a jest.

How had he gotten it so wrong?

He thought she intended to run away.

Gad, no wonder he was still a bachelor.

Syd looked so hurt, he knew he had to make it right

immediately. He strode to the bed and sat beside her, taking her hands in his so that she could not hide her beautiful face in them. "Syd, look at me."

"No."

"You will make yourself dizzy if you stare down at your feet while we are talking to each other. I do not need you tossing up the remains of your afternoon meal in this confined space."

"But you saw...and you know...and you do not want me even for one night." She shuddered. "I am such an idiot."

"No, I assure you that I am the complete and utter idiot," he said with an ache to his voice, for a soft and vulnerable Syd wreaked havoc on his heart.

He could deal with the firebrand.

But the gentle Syd? She sent his protective instincts into spasms. He wanted to devour her and be with her forever. Having botched this conversation quite badly, he now had to make amends. Of course, he was never going to tell her that he hadn't a clue what she was really thinking. But he knew that he had misunderstood her intentions and inadvertently hurt her feelings.

He had to make it right, but was it wise to have the two of them get too close to each other while things were still so unsettled? What if something went wrong? He did not want to leave her heartsick. "Syd, all I meant is that we are in a delicate situation right now and I do not want to push you into doing anything that you might regret later. What makes you think I am not attracted to you? In fact, I think you are one of the loveliest women I know. The loveliest, actually."

She still would not look up at him, so he pressed on. "Even in sleep, I reached out for you. Is that not telling?"

"You said that you were afraid I was going to fall out of bed because you were taking up too much of it."

"That too, but mostly it was my need to hold onto you."

She gave a little snort. "Because even in sleep, you were afraid I was going to run away."

"No, Syd," he said with a low growl. "I thought I made it clear on our first night together that my reluctance to join you in the bed was because I wanted you more than was wise and might do something untoward while I slept."

"Which is why I thought you would not mind my willingness now. But it is so obviously distasteful to you. If you are worried that I might be in love with you, then let me assure you that my reason has nothing to do with love. I just did not want to spend my life never knowing how things could be between a man and a woman."

"And you think a big ox like me would be the perfect tutor? It is not my practice to despoil virgins, even irritating ones. If you want to know the possibilities, then let me make you my wife in truth."

Her eyes popped wide and she now stared up at him. "How did we go from a mere liaison to husband and wife in a real marriage? I thought we agreed it was only to be make-believe."

"We did, and for now it is. But if I am to bed you – and by bed you, I do not mean merely sleeping in the same bed – if I am to know you intimately, then honor demands that I protect you and keep you as my wife."

"Even if you decide later that you cannot abide me?"

"Yes, because I could never just toss you to the wolves and abandon you."

"But it would not be abandonment if we agreed upon it. And I know you will not leave me destitute. Not that I would be without means if I were permitted to work with Gory in the Huntsford Academy forensic laboratory. Would your brother allow this?"

"Ambrose?"

She nodded. "He is the duke and it is one of his holdings. I know he is generous with his workers and the pay would be sufficient to support me. Perhaps I would no longer be able to move about in the highest social circles, but what do I care about that? Adela, Gory, and I were always considered oddities. Everyone laughed at us."

"My brothers and I never did."

"Because you are decent and honorable men, which is exactly why I would only consider such a thing with you and no one else. Ack!" she cried as he suddenly lifted her onto his lap. "What are you doing?"

He tipped her face up so that she had to meet his gaze. "Stay still, Syd. Do not try to squirm away."

"But–"

"We'll finish this discussion with you in my arms, now that you have conveniently fallen into them."

"Ha! You hauled me onto your lap."

He nodded, but did not relent. "I am not letting go of you. If you want me in your bed, teaching you about love, then we are going to get some rules straight here and now."

"While I sit on your lap? You can spout your rules as I sit on the bed. Need I point out that you have already given me two rules?"

"Those do not count. They were rules of the road. These are to be rules of the bed."

She blushed. "Why must there always be rules with you? Is it your Royal Navy discipline? Or did you have a natural affinity for the navy because you were a little boy who thrived on rules?"

"I have no idea. It isn't relevant. My concern is about your heart. I know you will lose your heart to me once I claim you. And do not accuse me of being full of myself. I know that the act of love cannot be merely a learning experience for you. Syd, you think you are independent and forward thinking. But there is a gentler side to you and it is very traditional. When you give your body to me, it will also come with your heart."

She frowned at him. "I can control my heart."

He laughed. "Not even I, as stone cold as I can sometimes be, am able to control my own heart. Think about it, Syd. If I cannot do it – and I like to control everything – how are you, with your inexperience, to manage it? I assure you, my heart makes its own decisions. Yours will, too. I worry that it will cause you hurt."

"You needn't worry about me. I can take care of myself." She tried to get off his lap, but he was not finished with her yet and had no intention of letting her up. "Octavian, is this not the very reason we will constantly be fighting in our marriage? We are both too stubborn and controlling. This is why I am not trying to alter the agreement about our make-believe marriage. Our deal stands."

"But we now allow for exploration of each other's bodies? No expectation of commitment?" He shook his head and frowned. "I know you love studying your cadavers, but a living person is quite another matter. Shall I give you an example?"

"What sort of example?"

"Just a kiss. It is the safest thing I can think of at the moment."

"A safe, harmless kiss?" she muttered. "Well, that's all right then. Yes, please kiss me and allow me to prove you wrong."

He was going to kiss the slippers off this girl.

He was going to kiss her until her body turned to fire.

He was going to kiss her into forever.

Syd's curiosity was taking over her common sense. But this was Syd, her scientific mind eager to test everything. This had nothing to do with loving him to the point of desperation...not yet, anyway. But he was going to give it his best because he wanted this lovely girl to lose her heart to him by the time he was through with his kissing lesson.

"Stay on my lap, but turn your body slightly toward mine." He drew her up against him so that her breasts now pressed against his chest. He did this purposely because he wanted her to be aware of his body and her physical response to it.

Next, his arms came around her. But he made certain to hold her gently, using just enough strength to keep her from squirming out of his grasp. "If you change your mind, all you have to do is tell me to stop. I will not be angry or irritated."

She looked up at him with a stubborn tilt to her chin. "I am not going to change my mind, so stop treating me like a delicate flower."

He groaned. "You are entirely missing the point of this kiss. Of course I am going to treat you delicately and with loving respect. But I am also going to put heat and passion into the kiss, to have you so hot that you'll want to take your clothes off for me."

She gasped. "That is ridiculous."

"I'll have you so hot, you'll be ripping them off because you cannot work the ties and hooks fast enough." Yet throughout, he would remain watchful and know immediately if she had changed her mind and wanted him to release her. The point was to show her how good a true marriage with all its intimacy could be for them.

She was staring at his lips as he spoke, looking doubtful but not at all scared.

Good, for this meant she trusted him. "Close your eyes, Syd."

She let out a kittenish purr as she closed them.

This immediately raised the temperature within his own body, but he tried not to think of that. The kiss was for her sake, not for his. "Put your arms around my neck."

She made another little purring sound that might have been a soft grumble, but she did as he asked. "You are spouting rules again, Octavian."

"They are merely instructions to allow for a more fulfilling experience. I am not giving you rules about this kiss. In fact, there are no rules. Do as you please, respond as you please. Encourage me as you please."

"That sounds rather daring."

He smiled. "But that is you, Syd. A risk taker. A firebrand. An independent thinker. Shall we forget it? Do you want me to let you go?"

Her eyes popped wide so that all he saw were two big, beautifully green pools. "No."

"I thought not. Close your eyes and let me take the lead in this until you feel ready to take over."

It amazed him that every curve of hers felt so right pressed against him. Up close, her features appeared quite delicate. Softest pink lips and big, lively eyes that had so much going on behind them. Her skin was as smooth as porcelain and a slight blush stained her cheeks, reminding him that she was still innocent and he needed to take it slow with her.

But she was ready for more of a kiss than that first one he had given her on the night she tossed him off the roof. He angled his head so that his mouth could cover hers completely because he did not want her to talk or ask questions while he was seducing her.

He approached it as he would a naval battle, but he was not going in for the kill. He merely wanted her to surrender to him.

No halfway measures either.

Full surrender because it suddenly felt vitally important that Syd remain with him always. Yes, he might regret it by tomorrow.

He would worry about it then.

In truth, he knew there would be no regrets.

Syd was who he wanted as his wife.

He dipped his head and brought his lips down on the plump softness of hers with a determination that turned into something raw and possessive the moment she opened to allow him entrance.

He took her with his mouth in every way possible.

He would teach her tonight what other things he could do with his mouth and tongue.

Cad that he was, he wanted Syd howling with pleasure if she still wanted him to teach her about the act of love. But what he truly wanted was to teach her about actual love, about giving her heart to him and trusting that he would never break it.

His tongue now probed and tangled with hers, teasing and promising.

Syd responded with innocent vigor, not in the least hesitant to give back as good as she got. He should have known the impudent hoyden was never one to back down from a challenge. She clutched his shoulders and pushed her body more firmly against his, squirming against him as though she wanted to get inside of him...or allow him inside of her.

Blessed saints.

Was this not a good thing? She was never going to worry about anything naughty they did together because she trusted him with her heart.

He wished he could trust her as fully as she trusted him.

Syd, for all her good intentions, would ignore his opinions if she thought she was protecting him. Having relied only on herself for so long, she did not know how to work together with him as a team. Nothing and no one would stop her if she believed she was in the right.

The girl was stubborn, for certain. But what troubled him most was that she had a martyr streak and would not hesitate to sacrifice herself to keep *him* safe.

Would she ever accept that it was his duty to protect her, and not the other way around?

He deepened the kiss, wrapping her fully in his embrace so that he could feel the pillowy softness of her breasts against his chest and knew the moment she went beyond mere pleasure to arousal.

Perhaps it was not fair that he knew how to tease her and stroke her near those intimate spots on her body that would arouse her, but he was not yet going to actually touch her anywhere sensitive.

She strained and purred like a kitten, urging him to do more as his hands slid just below her breasts but never actually touched them. He then ran a hand along her leg, sliding his fingers upward to her thigh and stroking the inside of her thigh but going no further.

He felt her frustration, one that he had every intention of easing tonight.

But not here and now.

He wanted her to think about this kiss, to let it wreak havoc on her senses.

He wanted her to love him and make their time together a promise of forever.

"Syd, your turn," he said, his voice deep and raspy as he ended the kiss. "Take possession of me and do whatever you like."

Her eyes were gleaming.

Her lips were deliciously pink and slightly puffed because of the pressure of his lips on hers. "Will you remove your jacket for me?"

"No, clothes do not come off."

"Never?"

He grinned. "Oh, they will tonight. But not before we have our supper."

"All right, then I will wait until tonight to have my turn."

"As you please. Care to enlighten me as to what you are going to do?"

There was an impish gleam in her eyes as she said, "No, I

prefer to keep it a surprise."

Oh, Lord.

He hated surprises.

Especially when they had to do with Syd.

She was a lot to handle even when he knew what she was doing.

Just how wild was she going to get?

CHAPTER 7

"WE OUGHT TO set a few more rules," Octavian said after supper was over and the inn's staff had cleared the trays from their room. The rain was still coming down in torrents, but he and Syd were comfortably ensconced in their chamber. He wanted to take control of this evening's activity…if one could call something just short of coupling a mere activity. Knowing how he felt about Syd, could he maintain his control?

He would do his best because Syd needed to be a virgin when she repeated her marriage vows. Perhaps he was a great fool for insisting on this, but it was important to him. He never wanted Syd to feel trapped by him.

Her family's traps were bad enough.

Sir Henry's trap was even worse.

For this reason, Syd's vow had to be given willingly, and it would not be if she was worried about the consequences of their night together, namely a child conceived from their wanton night of bliss.

He had assured Syd that she would be in charge and was now curious as to what she intended to do.

He wanted her to be bold, but he was also worried she would lose her heart to him as she gave him her body.

On the one hand, he wanted her to love him.

He knew that he would make her a good husband, for no one else understood her and would support her as well as he could. But understanding Syd was also a curse, for he knew she would love him completely once she fell in love with him. This also meant she would sacrifice everything to protect him.

If she got it into her head *not* to marry him because she wanted him to be happy and did not think she could ever satisfy him, then she would run off before the ceremony.

He did not want this to happen.

"Syd, remember this is just trial and exploration. A night of fun."

She nodded. "No hearts involved."

"Right." But he knew both their hearts were already too much involved. "What do you want me to do?"

She crossed to the door and secured the latch, then went to the window and drew the drapes closed so tightly that not a single ray of light got through.

A tallow candle burned on the small table where they had earlier taken their supper and it now served as the only illumination in the room. Syd was cast in a soft, amber glow so that she looked like a fairy princess with silken hair the color of burnished gold. "Take off your clothes, Octavian."

He arched an eyebrow. "All of them?"

She cleared her throat and blushed. "Yes."

He was not the bashful one, and would be her husband by tomorrow anyway. But he slowly removed each item of clothing, taking his time because he did not want any of tonight to be rushed.

When he had nothing left on but his trousers, he began to undo the top button of his falls. "Are you sure, Syd?"

She nodded, but blushed profusely.

He felt it was probably a mistake to take them off, but he could always put them back on if matters began to spin out of control. Of course, it would be agonizing for him to break the flow and don his trousers.

Well, he would not worry about it now.

He took off the last garment.

Her eyes grew big again when she saw his arousal.

"I can put them back on, Syd," he said gently.

She shook her head. "No, I have seen naked male bodies

before."

He stifled the urge to laugh. "But they were dead. You were dissecting cadavers."

"For a noble, scientific purpose," she said defensively as she gave her back to him. "Will you please help me out of my clothes?"

"With pleasure."

Although she tried to hide it from him, he felt her body shaking and knew she was not as calm as she tried to appear. Syd would never admit to being scared, so he was not going to confront her about it since she was safe with him and always would be.

She remained turned away from him once all her clothes were off, perhaps rethinking what she was doing. "Would you like to put your shift back on, Syd?"

"No."

"Do you plan to turn around ever?"

She nodded. "Yes, just working up the courage."

He wanted to take her in his arms, but thought it better not to touch her until she faced him and he knew she was ready to proceed with whatever she had in mind. "This is the thing about intimacy, Syd. It is very…intimate. No one exists in this moment but you and me. I will understand if you are not ready for this. I warned you that feelings are potent. But this thing we are about to do is meant to give you pleasure. On the chance you needed the reminder, you can trust me with your life, with your happiness, and with your heart."

The time stretched before them.

Octavian was about to put an end to this folly when Syd finally turned to face him.

Her eyes glistened with tears that were threatening to spill. "Promise you will not hurt me."

He did not know whether she meant physically because of the size of him, which was irrelevant because he was not going to claim her virginity, or whether she was talking about breaking her heart. "I will never hurt you, Syd. You have my solemn vow."

He held out his arms to her.

She walked into them and tossed her own arms around his neck, holding onto him with unexpected desperation, as though she would drown if she ever let go of him. She was feeling something quite strongly, and it had little to with his arousal or the fact it was poking against her stomach. "Syd?"

"Just for tonight, could you pretend I am Lady Clementine?"

What?

Why was she mentioning that peahen? "Why her?"

"Because she is the one you really want."

"Blessed saints, whatever gave you that ridiculous idea?" he muttered, shaking his head in disbelief. "Let us get something clear before we take this seduction any further. Sharing a dance with a young lady does not mean I wish to marry her."

Syd squeezed her eyes shut. "You danced several dances with her and everyone said you were going to propose to her."

"Everyone? Who cares what *everyone* thinks? I never said any such thing."

"Do you love her, Octavian? Am I ruining your chance for happiness because you are marrying me? Oh, I know it is to be a pretend marriage that will be annulled within the year, but what if she will not wait for you to be free of me?"

He stifled a groan. "Blast it, Syd. There is nothing between me and Lady Clementine. I can assure you that if I loved her, I would never have run off with you."

"Are you certain?"

"Yes. Is this what has been bothering you all this time? Why did you wait so long to mention it to me?"

"I was waiting for you to raise the matter."

"So you had us both get naked to discuss it?" He emitted a laughing groan, for this was such a Syd thing to do. In one way, it made perfect sense. He could not run away from their conversation since he hadn't a stitch of clothing on. "If I cared for Lady Clementine, then I would have found another solution to protect you. Is this all that has been troubling you?"

She nodded.

"Are you certain there is nothing more? Because I want no misunderstandings between us. Dear heaven, Syd. You thought I was interested in Lady Clementine? For this, you were about to destroy your own happiness and freedom? You were eating your guts for days."

"I did not know how to bring up the subject."

More likely, she was afraid to bring it up and have it confirmed out of his own mouth that he was in love with another woman, Octavian realized.

"So you waited until we were standing together naked to mention it? Were you equating baring our bodies to baring our souls? If I were a different sort of scoundrel, I would be tossing you onto the bed and pumping myself into you. Talking to you would be the last thing on my mind. You are not going to take this approach with anyone else, are you?"

"Stop mocking me. You know I would never do this with anyone but you. It made sense to me at the time."

"That baring our arses would act as some kind of a truth serum?" He stifled the urge to laugh. Lord, this girl got the most infuriating ideas in her head.

And yet, she delighted him because this is who she was and there was no one else like her.

"Baring our *hearts* is the truth serum," she insisted, still hugging him just as he still held her in his arms.

"That would only require our going shirtless," he pointed out, feeling the rampant beat of her heart against his chest, not to mention the soft ampleness of her breasts. The sheer pleasure of it left him almost mindless.

"Octavian, do not give me a hard time about this."

He was already hard, how could she not notice?

But he gave her cheek a caress. "All right, no more teasing. Just the naked truth."

"Octavian!"

"Sorry, I couldn't resist the pun." He sighed and shook his head. "There is no one else for me, Syd. You are the only one I ever cared about. You are not interfering with my marital plans because I haven't any, and certainly will never have any regarding Lady Clementine."

"But she is beautiful."

"So are you."

"She is prettier."

"Not to me, so stop trying to diminish yourself in my eyes. You are every bit as worthy as she is, if not more so. My protecting you is not a sacrifice. In fact, quite the opposite is true. It is the only thing my heart will allow me to do. I'm going to put my clothes back on if we need to discuss this further."

"No, don't. It isn't necessary."

"Then you are ready to take your turn kissing me?" And doing whatever else she had in mind to do with him in that bed.

"Yes. And are you certain you do not mind?"

He kissed her lightly on the cheek. "I do not mind, Syd."

"Thank you. I'm so glad we got that straightened out. It pained me to think that by helping me, you were ruining your own chance at happiness." She hugged him tightly once more and made no move to release him.

He debated whether to lift her in his arms and carry her to bed, but quickly realized Syd needed this moment to experience something she had never felt in her entire life.

This was not about a wanton night of sex.

Or a steamy kiss.

This was about her feeling safe and protected. Perhaps this was also about her feeling wanted, yet another thing Octavian did not think she had ever experienced. Her two inept parents must have shown their love to her ineptly as well. What had they said to Syd? Was she made to feel responsible for their financial burdens?

Did they blame her for everything wrong in their lives?

His heart ached for her. "Syd, let me take care of you."

"Isn't this what you are already doing?" she asked, looking up at him with big, hopeful eyes. "Who else would have been foolish enough to offer me marriage as a solution to my problems? Not that you are foolish. You are too good to be true."

"And this scares you?"

She nodded. "More than anything else. Even more than marriage to the odious Sir Henry."

"What if I also considered you to be too good to be true?"

She laughed. "That is not possible."

"Why not? Syd, you are beautiful. Smart. Compassionate. Quick-witted. What makes you think you are not a dream woman for me?"

"How can I be? I am not even sure my own parents love me. I don't think they know how. I convinced myself they did because a child needs this security in their home life. But there was so much heedless disregard going on around me. How can a four-year-old child understand responsibility better than her own parents?"

Yes, that was a good way to describe her parents.

They were irresponsible.

Selfish, too.

"Let's talk about this, Syd. I want you to tell me all about yourself. But can we do this while lying in bed? I'll still hold you, but you'll be warmer under the blankets."

"All right."

She gave a little cry of surprise when he lifted her in his arms and carried her to the bed. Perhaps the gesture was a little grandiose, but he felt it was necessary. Syd was baring her heart to him, allowing her protective shell to come down as she nestled in his arms.

She was about to share her hopes, dreams, and fears with him.

For the first time in her life, she was trusting someone other than herself to know her inner thoughts, to care for her and protect her.

He felt the softness of her cheek against his shoulder as he set her down on the bed and then settled beside her.

She sniffled, but was fiercely determined to hold back her tears. Well, this was Syd. Always reluctant to show weakness, and tears were the most obvious form of weakness.

It did not matter to him whether she fought them off or not. He understood what she needed from him. He was willing to give her everything.

He kissed the top of her head and ran his fingers lightly through her curls, afraid to say anything to put an end to this moment.

Syd was in charge and would tell him what she wanted.

If a talk and a hug was all she needed tonight, then so be it.

He wasn't going to question why they both had to be stark naked for a conversation or a mere hug to take place.

Was she now going to forget about kissing him?

"Am I dreaming you up, Octavian?" she whispered, snuggling against him as they lay in bed.

"No, Syd. I'm real and not leaving your side."

"What if I want you to go?"

His heart skipped several beats. Why was she asking him this? No, how could she be? Not now, not after what they had just shared.

Bloody blazes.

He wasn't leaving her.

More important, he was not letting her go, even if she now thought to leave him.

"Are you bidding me farewell? Is this what our naked hug was all about?" He tried not to sound angry. "Are you showing me your breasts and your body as a consolation gift because you are going to run off?"

Her eyes rounded in obvious surprise. "No, it is just a hypothetical question."

"Syd, do not ask me that again. We are in this together. Stop thinking of yourself as alone against the world."

She frowned. "Stop telling me what to do. The truth is, I am alone against the world. I have always been alone. Oh, now you are frowning back at me."

"I am not frowning at you. I am merely angry at everyone who ought to have protected you and never did. All I am trying to say is that you have me now, and I wish you would learn to rely on me."

"I will. Is this not what our race to Scotland is about?"

"For how long, Syd?"

"What? Rely on you? I don't know…for as long as you can abide me. You are going to get angry with me at some point during our marriage because this is what I seem to do best, infuriate and anger my loved ones. Then you will leave me. So let us not pretend it will be otherwise." She shifted out of his arms and turned away from him.

Gad, would she always doubt her ability to hold his love? "Short of setting fire to the bed while I am in it," he said, drawing her back into his arms, "I doubt there is anything you can do to make me want to walk away from you."

"Oh, now you sound irritated."

"I am not irritated."

"And now we are fighting."

He groaned. "We are in bed together, naked and hugging each other. This is not a fight. This is you trying to learn about trust. I know you trust me because you would not have undone so much as a button if you did not. In fact, you trust me more than you have ever trusted anyone in your entire life including yourself because...need I point out again that we are...naked?"

"No, you do not. I am quite aware."

"Syd, your problem is not me or anyone else. Your problem is that you do not trust yourself. Nor do you trust this feeling of safety because no one in your entire life has ever made you feel safe."

"I know. I'm sorry."

"You needn't apologize to me. I am not chiding you for it. In fact, I admire you even more for accomplishing all you have done while so heavily burdened." He caressed her cheek as she finally eased and nestled against his chest. "You have done nothing wrong."

She emitted a ragged sigh. "Thank you, Octavian. I cherish your opinion of me. Do you mind if I look at your body now?"

He laughed. "Go ahead. Enjoy your fill. I am big and solid and quite real."

He wanted to add that he was also hers forever, but this would only make her skittish again because it was painfully obvious she did not think of herself as loveable.

Unshed tears still glistened in her eyes, poised at the threshold and just waiting to spill. Rather than have her struggle to hold them back, he reached out and gently wiped away the few stray ones that had fallen onto her cheeks. All it took was a light running of his thumb along her cheekbones.

Safe enough.

Nothing too alarming.

"May I kiss you, Octavian?"

"Yes, Syd." Dear heaven, he wanted that kiss. He did not care whether it was prim and meek or hot and heavy.

He would accept whatever she had it in her soul to give him.

She shifted over him for a better angle to his lips, even though he had bent his head toward hers to accommodate her. The kiss was soft, sweet.

Achingly sweet.

Happy and gentle.

Still, his entire body was in a roil because she was once again pressed against him and there was not a blasted stitch between them. They were skin to skin, hers soft as silk and his hot as blazes.

He felt the fullness of her breasts and ached to explore them.

What would they taste like on his tongue? Peaches and cream, no doubt.

"Octavian, may we get dressed now? Well, not all the way dressed because we are going to sleep soon anyway."

"Yes, Syd." He tamped down his disappointment and retrieved her shift.

There would be ample opportunity to explore every inch of her after they were married. After helping her don the shift, he reached for his trousers and put them back on.

She cast him a shy look. "I suppose I am not as hoydenish as you thought. All I did in the end was give you a prim kiss."

He laughed. "Only you would look at it that way. We were naked together. Bodies in unobstructed contact. By definition that kiss was not prim. And you are every bit as hoydenish as I knew you would be. Also every bit as delightful, I might add."

He took a moment to stride to the window, drawing the curtains aside in order to peer out.

The rain was still coming down in torrents. "Still bad out there."

"Oh, dear. Does this mean we are stuck here for another day because the roads will be impassable come morning?"

"Possibly. No reason to fret about it, Syd. If those roads are treacherous for us, they will be just as treacherous for your father and Sir Henry if they happen to be chasing us."

"Octavian, what if this is an omen?"

He rolled his eyes. "This is a storm and nothing more. For pity's sake, Syd. Don't you dare consider reneging on our marriage plan."

"Our make-believe marriage," she reminded him.

"Right, make-believe. After what passed between us just now, is this still all I am to you? A temporary convenience. You bared your body and soul to me," he said, knowing the words sounded like more of an accusation than a mere statement.

Why was she talking about bad omens and not even thinking of their marriage as something permanent? "Did you have me remove my clothes just for a lark? Mere curiosity? Were you bored? Curious?"

"You know it isn't true." She curled her hands into fists. "Why are you being so churlish?"

Because he wanted her to stop lying to herself about their arrangement. Their marriage was never going to be make-believe for him. "Why are you refusing to admit the obvious, Syd? We like each other…as surprising as that may be."

Her fists were still clenched as she regarded him from the bed. "There is nothing obvious to admit."

"Fine, be stubborn about it. I'll ignore our naked moment and pretend it never happened. Or would you like us to dine nakedly tomorrow night? Is this something you plan to have us do on a regular basis? I would just like to understand *your* rules regarding our fake marriage."

"Stop it, Octavian. I am going to beat you about the head if you do not shut up this very instant."

"You are getting scared and defensive again."

"I am not defensive, and I am certainly not scared of you. Why are you making so much of our baring our bodies? You've seen plenty of naked women, I'm sure."

"That is beside the point," he grumbled. "They were not *you*. And you had not seen a *living* man without his clothes until me just now. I make you feel safe and I make you feel happy, and this troubles you to no end. Just don't let it scare you into doing something foolish. You promised me you would not run away."

"And I have every intention of keeping my promise."

"Good, because I intend to hold you to it."

She came up to him and placed her hand on his chest over his heart. "I did not mean to overset you, Octavian. It was just a casual remark."

"About it being a bad omen? Nothing is ever casual with you, Syd. Your mind is always whirling with ideas. I thought we had moved beyond this question of do you marry me or do you not? We took a giant leap forward a few minutes ago and now you are trying to leap backward the entire distance plus some."

She tipped her chin up in defiance. "I am not. You are reading too much into everything I say and do. Are you angry because I had us undress and then did nothing about it?"

He emitted a groaning laugh. "No, I'm not angry about that."

But perhaps he was frustrated and this was skewing his judgment about her intentions. Her claiming the torrential storm was a bad omen was said in jest in all likelihood. But he had leaped on the innocent remark as though it was a wild beast on the loose and about to pounce on him and eat him up. "Sorry, Syd. I think I will be on edge until we are married and I have the legal standing to protect you. Let's be optimistic, shall we? Let's count on the rain being done by morning and the sun out in full force to dry the roads. Let's go to bed. We'll be up at the crack of dawn again tomorrow."

"All right, but no pillows between us tonight. I think I am going to have bad dreams and will need you to hold onto me very tightly."

"Of course. Whatever you wish."

Suited him just fine.

He fully intended to hold onto her. In truth, he would have tied her to the bed if he could have done so without coming across as depraved. Despite the horrendous storm outside, Syd would run off if she set her mind to backing out of their fake marriage plans.

This is why he had been eager to hear her speak of her

childhood. He wanted to learn more about her to better understand what might set her off and make her run from him. He was just as set on preventing her from carrying out any ill-conceived plan that did not include marriage to him.

Anything might pop into her head at the last moment.

Was he being an ogre about it?

Yes, but for her own good.

Did she not understand yet the depth of his feelings for her? She would ruin his life as well as hers if she married someone else.

How could he ever be happy without her?

Gad, why did she force him to think about this?

CHAPTER 8

OCTAVIAN BREATHED A sigh of relief the moment he drew aside the curtain and was hit in the face by brightest sunlight. Syd was still fast asleep, for this ordeal and their impending wedding had left her exhausted.

He turned back to her, his heart warming as he studied her vibrant form while she slept.

With the curtain drawn aside, the sun's rays spilled into the room and shone across their bed. The light seemed to wrap around her, illuminating her mass of golden-red curls so that the gloriously flowing tumble shimmered like sunlight upon a golden meadow.

She had the sweetest body, too.

He saw much of it since she had tossed off the covers as the room began to warm and now slept atop them. Her slender legs were exposed to his view as her shift tangled about her thighs. He liked that he knew her body so well, even though he had yet to touch her intimately. But he had seen plenty because of her stubborn determination to keep nothing between them, whether allegorically, metaphorically, or actually.

A knock sounded at their door.

Syd made not the slightest stir.

Octavian knew it was likely a maid bringing in their breakfast tray, but he grabbed his pistol and went to the door. "Who is it?"

"Yer breakfast, m'lord," a youngish sounding voice replied.

He kept his pistol hidden as he unlatched the door and

cautiously opened it.

"Good morning, m'lord," the maid, who could not have been more than nineteen, said as she entered the chamber and set the tray on the table. She had an ample figure that she displayed to greatest advantage and a less than innocent look in her eyes. "Oh, yer wife's still sleepin'."

"Yes." He remained at the door to encourage the girl to take her leave. "Our travels have tired her out."

She regarded him with a surprisingly sexual frankness, slowly raking her gaze over his chest since he had hastily tossed on his shirt but not bothered to button it up. "I doubt it is the travel that is tiring her out," the girl remarked, her gaze drifting lower as she eyed him quite avidly. "I'm available if she's too done in to accommodate ye."

He dismissed her.

Was he the only fool who took wedding vows seriously? He was glad Syd had not been awake to hear the exchange because she was already worried about his remaining faithful to her over the next nine months. They had stopped at reputable inns along the way, but even in these establishments there were maids who were not shy about propositioning him.

He had given little thought to these sort of offers during his bachelor days, sometimes acting on them and sometimes not. But he no longer considered himself free to do as he pleased. They were not married yet, but he intended to remain faithful to Syd throughout his life.

It would not be a hardship for him since Syd was everything he needed in a wife.

But one had to take small steps with her and slowly get her used to the idea that their marriage would not be temporary. After latching the door, he crossed to the table and peeked under the salvers that covered their food.

Steam poured out as he lifted the lids, and the aroma wafting toward him made his mouth water. Kippers, eggs, and baked scones still hot from the oven were all to be washed down with a freshly brewed pot of tea.

He approached Syd and woke her with a kiss to her brow.

"Time to get up, love."

She yawned and stretched, then sat up with a light grumble. "I could sleep the entire day away. What time is it?"

"Already past seven, I'll wager. You'll have plenty of time to rest once we are in the carriage."

She smiled at him when he sat on the bed beside her and gave her cheek a light caress. "Octavian, you woke me with a kiss."

He nodded. "It felt right."

"And you called me by an endearment."

"You are to be my wife. Should I not?"

"My parents never woke me with endearments. In truth, I don't recall them ever entering my bedroom for any reason. I was put to bed and awakened by a nanny when I was younger, and later by my governess. When I outgrew my need for a governess, it was maids who attended me. My mother never opened her eyes before noon. My father often did not come home until well after I was up and attending to my lessons."

"I'm sorry they were so neglectful of you, Syd. Do you mind that I kissed you?"

"Not at all." She smiled at him again. "Can we add this to one of your rules? I know how you adore them."

He laughed. "Yes, we shall make a new list for our marriage. Top rule shall be to kiss you every morning."

She threw her arms around his neck. "That is perfect. Shall I do the same for you?"

"Kiss me awake? No, Syd."

"Oh." She dropped her arms and cast him a disappointed look. "I see."

"No, you do not see at all. I am trained for battle. My instincts are to lash out and strike whoever sneaks up on me, so do not stick your face in mine until I am awake. Then you may kiss me to your heart's content."

"And you won't complain?"

"No, Syd. I am not ever going to complain about your kissing me." He took her hand in his. "Come on, let's eat. I'm famished."

She inhaled. "That does smell good."

They ate their breakfast, then took turns washing and dressing.

Octavian liked helping Syd each morning with the hooks, tapes, and lace ties of her gowns. Once they were back in London, she would have ample assistance from the maids on the Huntsford staff who would likely do a better job of helping her put herself together. Still, this time spent alone with her was something he would always remember and cherish.

He watched Syd pin her hair in a simply styled chignon. As soon as she was done, he gathered their few belongings and carried them to their waiting carriage. Their driver, a reliable man of about forty years by the name of Felix Henshaw cast him an amiable smile. "Mighty kind of yer lordship to pay for my room at the inn. I could have taken a bed above the stables."

"We pushed hard yesterday, Mr. Henshaw. I appreciated your effort."

"Thank ye, m'lord."

Syd, who was only a few steps behind him, now greeted their driver with cheer. "Good morning, Mr. Henshaw," she said, handing him up a small basket.

The man took it from her with a questioning look. "Mornin', m'lady. What's this?"

"We'll be moving quickly again today, so I had the inn's cook make up a picnic basket for you. I had them make up one for Captain Thorne and myself, as well," she said, now handing Octavian the other small basket to place in the carriage. "It is nothing extravagant, some fruit, cheese, and a loaf of bread to hold us until we stop again. The food was particularly good here, don't you think, Mr. Henshaw?"

"Aye, m'lady. It was."

"Good idea, Syd," Octavian muttered, knowing that having provisions would be useful if they ran into trouble and had to hide out. Today was the day when they would either be married or have their plans thwarted because Sir Henry had caught up to them.

He placed his hands around Syd's waist to help her into the carriage, his body immediately responding to her softness. There was nothing to be done about his feelings for her other than go along with them. He would have time in the carriage to contemplate why his heart had chosen her.

He thought Syd would close her eyes once they were on the road again, but she remained awake and began to fret instead. "Octavian…"

He stifled a groan. "What is on your mind, Syd?"

She regarded him as the carriage jounced along the hills and dales. "I'm glad it is you that I am marrying."

He arched an eyebrow and smiled in relief. Is this all that concerned her? "So am I."

"No regrets?"

He shook his head. "Not a one."

"Do you think my father and Sir Henry are waiting for us in Gretna Green?"

He did not wish to lie to her. "It is a possibility. This is why we are going to pull off the road a short distance outside of town and I will scout the area first."

She nodded. "Yes, that is prudent. I'll go with you."

He sighed. "No, Syd. It is safer if I scout on my own and then come back for you once I am certain all is clear."

Obviously, she did not care for the idea since she was now frowning at him. "You would leave me alone?"

"I would leave you in the capable care of Mr. Henshaw, both of you well hidden. It would only be for a short time, just long enough for me to search the area and make certain Sir Henry and your father are not lying in wait for us."

She nibbled her lip. "I don't think I like that plan at all."

He sighed in resignation. "Would you care to tell me why it is a bad plan?"

Was she going to turn helpless and simpering, afraid to be without him even for fifteen minutes? Syd was a force of nature. If he were Sir Henry, he would sooner face a Royal Navy captain the size of a big ox than an angry Syd.

Why was she fretting? It was a good plan.

"If I am with you," she said, her lips once again pursed, "then we can simply march straight to the blacksmith's shop and marry right away. You would not have to waste time doubling back to find me. What if you forgot where you hid me?"

"I am not going to forget where I hid you," he grumbled. "I scout alone. You will only be a hindrance. What if they are there and you are seen? You cannot run in that gown. Also, they might attempt to shoot me. I cannot risk them hitting you."

"They won't dare shoot you if there is a chance of striking me. Sir Henry wants to marry me. In truth, I think he purposely encouraged my father to run up his debts just so he could possess me. He always had an unnatural way of looking at me. The man is vile and manipulative. Ugh, I shiver just thinking of his odious touch. So you see, you are safer if I am with you."

Oh, lord.

She had that stubborn look in her eye.

He emitted a soft growl to mark his displeasure. "I am not taking you with me, Syd. If it is just me, I can fight back however I wish. Or run, if I wish. Everything changes if I have to worry about you, too. Why make it easy for them to grab you? For the love of heaven, will you not humor me, just this once?"

He could see the request pained her.

She had already decided to stay close to him.

If he left her behind, she would follow.

He was frustrated more than angry, for this was Syd. This is the girl he had chosen to love. Well, his heart had selected her knowing full well she was fiercely independent and willful. It wasn't her fault that he loved her.

"Let's see what happens once we reach Gretna Green," she suggested, no doubt hoping he would see the error of his ways after a few hours of stewing over their difference of opinion.

Rather than fight this losing battle, Octavian decided to spend the time figuring out how to best protect her while keeping her by his side.

In truth, she was agile and resourceful.

And what she had said made sense, for once he determined the village was safe to enter, he would not need to double back and fetch her since she would already be with him.

It was not the worst idea he had ever heard. Indeed, it was not terrible at all. But to his mind, it wasn't the best one available to them.

However, he had to admit there was a risk to leaving her behind.

A travel coach and team of horses was no easy thing to hide. There was also a chance that if Syd – not that it would ever happen – actually obeyed him and remained wherever he put her, she might be found and captured while he was off scouting.

Mr. Henshaw, although amiable and diligent, was in no shape to fight off assailants. Nor did Octavian want their driver to risk his life protecting her. Protecting Syd was his responsibility and he was not going to delegate it to anyone else.

Perhaps she was right to insist on going with him.

"All right," he said with another resigned sigh. "I'll take you with me when I scout."

She cast him a dazzling smile. "Thank you, Octavian. You won't regret the decision."

He shook his head and laughed. "Oh, I'm fairly certain I will."

As the miles rolled by and the road turned smoother, Syd fell asleep.

Octavian watched her, marveling how angelic she looked.

But he did not dwell on her kissable lips or long, sooty eyelashes because he needed to remain alert. There were other conveyances on the road now. They passed several carriages and riders on horseback heading south, and were joined by others heading north.

A few riders galloped ahead of their carriage but Octavian saw nothing suspicious about these men. They appeared to be nothing more than lone riders on their way to Scotland and did not take any particular interest in their hired carriage.

"Syd, we are approaching the next coaching inn. When we arrive, I want you to remain in the carriage while I enter the common room and look around. I'll obtain a private dining room for us since it is best we are not seen by all who come and go. The place will be busy since it is midday and plenty of travelers will be stopping to dine as well as rest their horses."

"So I am to wait for you until you return to fetch me?"

"Yes, same as I plan to do once we reach Gretna Green. We do not enter that village until I am certain Sir Henry has not set a trap for us."

"That again. I've told you that I am going with you."

"And here? Now? So help me, don't you dare poke your head out of this carriage before I know we are safe at this coaching inn."

She rolled her eyes. "It is an empty threat. I know you will never hurt me. Besides, I have every intention of obeying you. It is a fine idea. I only give you trouble when I think your ideas are second best."

"Second best? *Second best.*" Was his heart still aching for this girl? He wanted to throttle her just now. He had years of battle experience and she had none, yet she had the gall to tell him that his plan was weak? "I am one of the finest ship commanders in the Royal Navy. I stayed alive and kept my crew alive because of my tactical prowess. I know how to keep alert to an enemy attack. In fact, I've been in more battles than you have had dances during your come-out Season."

She snorted. "That isn't saying much since no one but you ever asked me to dance."

"Others would have asked if you hadn't frightened the wits out of every man who approached you with talk of cadavers and the science of blood splatters. How could they not worry you planned to experiment on them next?"

"I would never hurt a living soul!"

"That remains to be seen," he muttered, climbing down from the carriage. "Never mind, just stay put."

A quick search revealing nothing worrisome, which meant either they were far ahead of Sir Henry and Syd's father or they would hit trouble at Gretna Green because those two were already there and waiting to ambush them.

Sir Henry did not like to be crossed.

Being that he was so taken with Syd, it was not outside the realm of possibility that he would race across England to prevent her from marrying someone else. In truth, it was not much of a stretch at all. The man was greedy and malevolent. If he saw something he wanted, he would never relent until he'd grabbed it.

Octavian returned to the carriage and held out his hand to assist Syd down. "All safe. Come along, but keep your head down."

She gave him a big-eyed stare. "I know what to do, Octavian. What do you think of this bonnet? Very clever of me to put it on, don't you think?"

The hideous hat completely hid her lush hair, but it could not hide the breathtaking charm of her face. Her big eyes were ensorcelling and her lips were soft as rose petals.

"Is that one of Adela's bonnets?"

She nodded. "She never wears it, so I took it with me. It hides my face rather well, don't you think?"

"Not all that well. You still look beautiful and people will notice." Lord, what was wrong with him? This was no time to be tossing her compliments like a besotted schoolboy. "Keep your head down as much as possible."

She cast him a soft, vulnerable smile. "You think I am beautiful?"

"Sometimes," he muttered, giving her nose a playful tweak. "Mostly, you are aggravating. Being pretty does not excuse your irritating behavior."

She grinned when he ended by giving her cheek a light caress. "You are not always a prize yourself, you know."

Octavian chuckled. "I know. Come along, *wife*. Let's eat and get back on the road."

He helped her down, his heartbeat quickening as it always did whenever he touched her. "The hat is growing on me. You look adorable in it."

He could see why Sir Henry was infatuated with her. Yes, any man with half a brain would fight for this gem of a girl. That old goat was reprehensible in many ways, but no one would ever accuse him of having bad taste in women.

Octavian did not know whether Sir Henry's wives had died in childbirth, which was a common enough occurrence, sadly. Or had he treated them roughly? Rumors circulated about him regarding his efficiency in enforcing his debts. Was he that *efficient* with his wives? He could not allow Syd anywhere near that man.

They attracted little notice while being led to one of the private dining rooms, ate quickly, and were off again as soon as the horses had been adequately tended.

A light mist began to fall as they crossed into Scotland. Syd scooted over to sit by his side as soon as they crossed the border. "Octavian, how far now?"

"Only a few more miles. We'll reach Gretna Green within the next hour for certain, even if the road turns to mud. But let us hope it stays nothing more than a drizzling mist." It was the middle of the afternoon and there was still plenty of daylight remaining, but any pleasured anticipation fled when he heard a rumble of hooves behind them. "Syd, I'm sure there is nothing to be alarmed about…however, just as a precaution." He reached over to the seat bench she had just vacated opposite his and raised the seat. "Spare compartment. All these Carville coaches have them. Climb in and get down. Sorry, but you have to get flat on the floor and curl up in a tight ball. We're about to be stopped."

She inhaled sharply. "Sir Henry and his men?"

He stopped her when she attempted to poke her head out the window to get a better look. "Syd! I don't want them to see you."

"Sorry." She nodded and climbed into the spare compartment. "There must be at least thirty of them, if the thunderous sound of those horses is any indication."

"Yes, no less than twenty men for certain. But it isn't Sir Henry, I'll wager. That old goat would not have chased us with so many men. It is likely Scottish reivers. I'm going to throw this blanket over you, too. Stay hidden. Do not move a muscle and do not talk."

"All right, but give me a weapon."

He hesitated a moment, then handed over the pistol he always kept hidden in the lip of his boot. "You are not to use it unless they fire first and actually shoot me."

She gasped. "That is ridiculous. The entire point is to prevent your getting shot."

"No, the point is to keep *you* alive. They will shoot us both if you fire at them."

He carried another pistol in a sheath within his uniform jacket, not to mention the knife he also carried in his other boot, but he had no intention of drawing either weapon.

His Royal Navy uniform was his best protection.

If these were common reivers, he hoped to talk his way out of any trouble. He was in a uniform familiar to these men. Many of the Highland clans had fought alongside the British during the Napoleonic Wars. Napoleon had long ago been defeated. Octavian had been but a boy at the time and too young to be sent off to fight.

However, he had engaged in many battles during his time as captain of a first-rate naval vessel. He was still in active service in the Royal Navy, for once a naval officer always a naval officer. He had made his fortune capturing enemy vessels and pirate ships, but was now assigned by the Admiralty to supervise the building of the next generation of battle ships for the royal fleet.

He was familiar with the Scots and their sometimes odd ways since a large number of his crew happened to be from Scotland. In fact, several of his officers went by the name of Armstrong, Rutherford, and Kerr.

He would toss out their names and hope someone among the reivers acknowledged a connection. All he needed was for Syd to keep her composure and not go at them like a raging banshee. "Get down now, Syd. I'm closing you in."

"If I were a man, you would have me fighting beside you," she muttered while obeying him.

"But you are not a man. Need I warn you what these oafs might do to you if they are of a mind to be craven? Death would be the easy way out. For the love of heaven, just keep quiet no matter what you hear."

It was the firebrand Syd who glared back at him as he tossed the hideous bonnet in with her, placed the blanket over her head, and then put the seat bench back in place.

Lord, just shut her up and keep her safe.

He commanded Henshaw to stop the carriage and not draw a weapon. "M'lord, they'll shoot us down like dogs if we don't fight back."

"We cannot take down all of them. Just stay calm, Mr. Henshaw. These are reivers, just looking to rob us. Give over whatever they ask. I'll reimburse you for any loss."

"What of Lady Thorne?"

"My wife is hidden. You and I are traveling alone, assuming they bother to ask. Let's hope they did not see us at the coaching inn where we last dined."

Octavian tamped down his frustration as he waited for their leader to approach him. For good measure, he sat atop the bench where Syd was now hiding because he did not want her lifting that lid for any reason.

These border reivers now surrounded his carriage and two of them took hold of the reins so that Mr. Henshaw would not be tempted to drive off. They ordered the frightened driver down from his perch. "Do as they ask, Mr. Henshaw. It is all right."

A big, red-haired man swaggered toward Octavian. "I'll be askin' ye to get out, too."

"As you wish," Octavian said and promptly complied. "Just be aware you are interfering with Royal Navy business. I am on my way to Greenock to meet with your shipbuilders."

The leader took another moment to inspect him. "Ye're a calm one, ain't ye?" he muttered after walking around him.

"Let's hope I have reason to be," Octavian said with an arch of his brow. "All I have with me are documents."

"What sort of documents?" the leader asked.

"Plans for a new battleship. Touch those and that is treason. You'll be betraying your own countrymen as well as the English."

"I have no interest in documents. Do ye have any gold on ye?"

Octavian held his arms out wide. "No, just weapons that I hope you will allow me to keep. I have no intention of using them on you. I have some medals, but I will kill you if you take those. They were hard fought for and earned in battle."

"Ye're not to tell us what we can and canno' take," a young man growled as he dismounted and approached. By his resemblance to their leader, Octavian judged the man was his son or other close male relative, a younger brother perhaps.

The leader stopped the lad with a stern warning. "Angus, we do no' take his medals. Ye'd understand if ye'd ever fought in a war, ye young whelp." He turned back to Octavian. "I was in the Scots Greys."

Octavian nodded. "A fine regiment."

"The finest," the man said with a look of pride. "What's yer name, Captain?"

"Octavian Thorne."

"Thorne? Captain of the Dover Mist?" a man called out from amid the group. "Aw, me eyesight is wretched. Forgive me, Captain. I dinna recognize ye."

"Jamie Armstrong, is that you?" Octavian was never happier to see one of his petty officers, the very one he had insisted on promoting over the pampered son of a powerful English lord. In the end, both men had received their promotions because not even the Admiralty wanted to tangle with the Earl of Oxbridge, a royal favorite. His useless son was given a senior rank he did not deserve and Octavian thought up ways to keep him out of contact with the crew who despised the young lord for his vindictive and heartless ways.

Not that Octavian was soft by any means.

In truth, he was quite demanding of his men.

But he had never raised a fist to them or ever ordered any of them lashed for petty offenses. His father had never raised a hand to any of his sons, and this was how Octavian treated his crew. They obeyed him out of respect, not because he threatened to beat them.

"Aye, Captain. I'm honored ye remembered me," Jamie called back, his voice obviously filled with pride.

"I wouldn't ever forget one of my ablest officers. How are you faring on dry land?"

"Not all that well, Captain," he said with a laugh as he dismounted and limped toward him. "As ye see, we've had to turn to reiving to make it through this season's failed crops. Our sheep got sick and many of them had to be put down, so we dinna have much wool to sell. We're hoping next season will be better."

"Sorry to hear it."

The young man their leader had called Angus now emitted a scornful laugh. "Are ye truly sorry, Captain? I doubt ye give a fig about us, even though ye have our Jamie believing yer lies."

The leader frowned at Angus again. "Shut up, lad. Ye know

not what ye are talking about. All right, Captain. We'll let ye pass. But would ye have any coins to spare for us?"

"I'm traveling to Greenock with just enough to get me there and back to London. I cannot stop you if you are of a mind to take it. But I hope you will accept this proposal...since I already have banking arrangements set up from my prior visits to Greenock, upon my arrival there I will purchase twenty prime wool sheep for you. Is that enough to replenish your stock?"

The leader held out his hand to Octavian. "Fair enough, Captain. You have a deal. Never let it be said Samuel Armstrong is not a man of his word."

Angus cursed. "Are ye daft, Father? He's going to ride off and never think about us again. He'll have a good laugh with his friends, recounting what fools we were to believe him."

Jamie gave the lad a cuff to his head. "Captain Thorne gave us his word. I'd trust him sooner than I'd trust you, ye insolent pup. Good to see ye again, Captain."

Octavian shook Jamie's grimy hand. "I'll be at the Greenock shipyards for several weeks. Would you be willing to work there if I found you a job?"

"Around ships? Aye, Captain. I would. My family needs the money and I would be grateful for it."

Octavian nodded. "Where can I reach you if I have obtained employment for you?"

Angus growled. "Ye're going to give away our location now?"

Jamie cuffed him again. "He has to be told in order to deliver the sheep to us. Aye, I'll be telling him where we live. The man is honorable. He'll no' betray us to the authorities."

"He is the authority!" Angus cried in disgust.

Well, that was true in that Octavian was serving in the Royal Navy. But he was not going to turn these men in for trying to feed their starving families. Most travelers could afford to lose a few coins.

Angus was a hothead but his father was a cool character and had not raised a fist to him or Henshaw. "I give you my oath that I will not give you away to the authorities so long as you do not kill or maim your victims. I'll turn a blind eye to robbery, but not cruelty."

"Fair enough," Samuel Armstrong said, offering his hand. "Safe travels, Captain Thorne."

Octavian climbed back into the carriage and did not release a breath until Henshaw had flicked the reins and gotten the team under way. In truth, he was amazed they had gotten out of the confrontation without incident.

He remained seated atop Syd's hiding spot until they were out of sight of the reivers, then lifted the lid and raised the blanket off her now that it was safe to do so. "Syd, are you all right?"

Beads of perspiration had settled across her brow and her cheeks were a bright pink. "Air," she said, taking a deep breath and then another. "It was hot in there."

"I know. I'm sorry. I did not see any other way out of that encounter but to hide you." He took the pistol from her hand and placed it back in the lip of his boot before helping her out of the secret compartment.

She sat beside him, settling on the seat bench with a grunt. "That Angus fellow was a hothead. I did not like him at all."

"Hopefully, we will never encounter him again. I think he might have liked you all too well and wanted to keep you."

She laughed. "Why? Because I am hotheaded, too? No, even these fiery, thoughtless hounds are looking for biddable wives. No one wants a wife like me."

"Except for me."

Her smile faded.

"For the moment," she said in response.

He did not bother to correct her.

Syd was so drained after being stuffed in that hidden compartment, she would not believe he might want her forever. Besides, they had more trouble in the offing. Those reivers had not gone back into hiding but were following them at a leisurely pace into Gretna Green.

"Bollocks," he muttered, fearing there would be another confrontation once these reivers realized he had hidden Syd from them.

There was no way to hide her now.

Their best chance was to head straight for the blacksmith shop and get the wedding ceremony over and done before the reivers caught up to them and realized he had tricked them.

Bloody blazes.

Now he had not only Sir Henry to worry about, but these Scottish thieves, as well.

He would have to think of something to distract and deter both parties. If Sir Henry and Syd's father were lying in wait for them, perhaps he could talk Jamie and the other Armstrongs into helping him out. After all, what Scot did not love a good brawl?

But it was no sure thing they would join in his fight to marry Syd.

After all, he had lied to them by hiding her and this counted as a lie of omission. Could he rely on Jamie Armstrong or the Armstrong laird understanding why he had to do it?

What if they chose to turn on him and helped Syd's father steal her back?

He glanced at Syd.

Most women would be fluttering and crying by now.

But not Syd.

She was spoiling for a fight.

What would Syd do if they tried to set a hand on her?

CHAPTER 9

OCTAVIAN SAW WHERE this situation was going and knew there was going to be trouble.

"Syd," he muttered as they now stood in front of the Gretna Green blacksmith shop surrounded by a dozen angry Armstrong men who were debating what to do with the two of them. They referred to her as the harpy with blazing green eyes after she punched hotheaded Angus in the nose when he strutted toward her and made the mistake of calling her a scrawny Sassenach.

"Scrawny, am I?" she had retorted and smashed her fist in his face.

Angus was now holding a handkerchief to his nose as blood poured from his nostrils.

Octavian had immediately drawn her behind him, fearing others were going to charge at them now. He had also drawn his pistol and now had it aimed straight at their laird's heart. "I do not wish to hurt anyone, but no one touches my wife and lives. Have your men stand down. Please."

The laird motioned for his men to remain where they were. "No one will draw a weapon on ye, Captain Thorne. Ye may put yers away."

Thank heaven for rational men, Octavian decided and placed his pistol back in the lip of his boot. As he did so, he heard Syd grumble something behind him. "Blessed saints, Syd. All you have to do is keep your mouth shut and let me talk us out of this mess."

She pinched his arse. "As you did not half an hour ago while I was stuffed and suffocating inside the carriage bench? Was I supposed to smile meekly and allow that oaf Angus to call me a common...I cannot even say the awful word!"

"He merely called you a Sassenach, a disdainful term to describe any Englishman. What did you think that word meant?"

"It sounded crude. I will knock out his front teeth if he dares insult me again."

"Dear heaven, will you just let me handle this?" Octavian kept eyes on the enraged men surrounding them and spared only the merest glance at her when she attempted to come out from behind him. But it was enough to notice the soft waves of her hair as the sun slanted across it and turned the lush strands a stunning ginger-gold. "First of all, that big oaf happens to be the son of the laird and you have just humiliated him in front of his men."

"He insulted me!"

"And I would have defended you had you given me the chance, something I could have reasonably done with no punches thrown." He nudged her behind him once more when she tried to step forward again. "You've protected your honor, Syd. Now allow me to save both our lives."

What did she expect would happen when these men realized he had a woman traveling with him? But all would have been corrected after a few words of explanation and an invitation for all of them to serve as witnesses to their wedding.

A second man now dared approach Syd.

Octavian did not like the insolent look in his eyes or the fact he was disobeying his own laird's command. He grabbed the pistol out of that fool's belt and trained it at his head, something he was loathe to do since he wanted to calm the situation, not heighten the confrontation. "My apologies, Laird Armstrong," he said while keeping the pistol trained on this second man. "But we need to talk, and I cannot allow your men to harm the woman I love."

Gad!

Had he just said that?

How had the words flowed so easily from his lips?

The laird motioned for the rest of his men to stand back. "I'll kill the first one of ye who moves," he said in a growled warning. "Have ye grown so base as to not even respect yer own laird's orders?"

Jamie, bless him, also stood firm and repeated the Armstrong leader's warning. "The captain's an honorable man. Can ye blame him for wanting to protect the lovely lass? What would ye have done if strangers surrounded yer carriage and threatened yer wives and sisters? Ye would no' have been so polite or kept yer wits about ye, I'll wager."

The men grumbled but obeyed their laird and held back.

Octavian knew he had to speak fast, for he would not be able to hold them off very long.

These Scots were angry.

Octavian was either going to end up dead or married to Syd, and he wasn't sure which of those outcomes was worse. He quickly explained their situation and why he dared not delay in marrying Syd.

"Captain Thorne," Jamie whispered, "are ye really going to marry the fiery lass? And did ye mean it when ye said ye were going to try to get a job for me?"

"Yes, to both. You know I am a man of my word." He now turned to the laird and spoke to him with all the calm he could muster. "I would be honored if you and your men served as witnesses to our marriage."

"But not your arrogant whelp of a son," Syd blurted, tossing Angus another scowl. "He does not deserve to be present at this sacred rite."

Octavian groaned.

He wanted to throttle Syd. How *bloody* sacred could this ceremony be? They were only going to stand in a blacksmith shop, an anvil as a makeshift altar, as they took less than a minute to repeat their vows.

"The blacksmith shop is quite small," one of the Armstrong men remarked.

Octavian nodded. "We may not all be able to fit, that's true. How about Laird Armstrong and Jamie serve as our witnesses?"

Syd popped her head out from around him. "Yes, I would be

honored to have you both by our side."

Thank The Graces.

Finally, words of compromise from her lips.

They might not die, after all.

Octavian held out a hand in friendship to the laird. "Will you grant us safe passage out of here once we are wed? I did not lie to you about anything, merely neglected to mention that my betrothed was with me. I apologize for that omission, but I did not know how else to protect her without needlessly shedding blood. Can you understand this?"

The laird said nothing, so Octavian continued talking. "I am on my way to Greenock on an Admiralty assignment, as I've told you. And I will purchase those sheep for you." He glanced at Jamie. "I will also use my best efforts to secure employment for you. You have my oath on it."

Jamie nodded. "That's good enough for me, Captain." He now turned to his laird. "He loves the lass. Let him get married."

"Verra well." The laird nodded and took his hand to shake it. "I'll witness yer wedding and grant ye safe passage. But I dinna think ye and the lass ought to pass through here again. Especially the lass. She's insulted my son and there's bad blood between them. Ye should have kept quiet and let yer betrothed handle it, lass."

"Well, I never," Syd mumbled.

Octavian nudged her behind him once again and, as a sign of his good faith, handed back the weapon he had taken from the second oaf who had dared approach Syd.

The laird cast him a wry smile. "Are ye sure about her, Captain Thorne? She's just as likely to smash a tankard of ale over yer head as to kiss ye."

"I am well aware," Octavian said with a chuckle. "She's already thrown me off a roof."

"Octavian!" Syd cried from behind him. "You know it was an accident! I would never purposely hurt you."

"I know, love." He intentionally used the endearment, although he was steaming mad at her right now. Blood was still spurting from Angus's nose and that lad was something worse than angry. He was humiliated, having been defeated by a slip of a girl in front of his friends and family. For this reason, Octavian wanted to get married, then tear out of here before Angus recovered and took his revenge on them.

"She tried to crack my head open," Angus griped, storming to his father's side. "We canno' let her just walk away."

"The lady was frightened and you offended her," Jamie retorted. "Take responsibility for yer actions, Angus. Ye brought this on yerself. Serves ye right. Ye preyed on her because ye thought she was a meek, English rose. Well, she proved ye wrong. I'm telling ye, Angus. Keep yer distance. Anyone can see she is far more trouble than she's worth."

The laird quirked a bushy eyebrow. "Why are ye bothering with her, Captain?"

Octavian took a deep breath. "I have no choice. I love her."

Had that really come out of him again?

The 'love' word?

"The next man who insults me will join Angus with a bloody nose," Syd declared, obviously not willing to take any amount of jesting from these men. Octavian was not saying their behavior was right, but it was how men relieved a tense situation.

He shot her a warning glance.

By all that's holy, keep your mouth shut, Syd.

Of course, Syd could not shut that kissable mouth of hers. "And if any of you dare to harm my husband-to-be," she warned, staring directly at Angus, "rest assured that I will maim as many of you as I can manage before you kill me."

The laird regarded him incredulously. "And ye still want her as yer wife?"

"Yes." Octavian took hold of her hand and gave it a warning squeeze. "She is the only woman I will ever have, and I *really* need to marry her."

The men rolled their eyes, regarded him as though he were mad, and then suddenly began to nod in understanding.

What had he just said?

Oh, bloody hell.

That emphasis on *really* had them believing Syd was carrying his child.

Well, let them think whatever they wished.

He needed to marry her.

Once they exchanged vows, no one would care whether or not they'd had relations outside of marriage.

More important, they would not harm Syd if they believed she was with child.

Two other couples stood ahead of them, for no one had been frightened away by their scene in front of the shop. Eloping couples were desperate and nothing was going to stop them from getting married, not even a horde of angry Scots or a little harpy determined to take them all on.

Octavian took Syd's hand and kept hold of it as they entered the blacksmith's shop. They had yet to exchange vows when he heard the sound of hoofbeats and then shouts to stop the wedding. It could have been anyone else's father or jilted groom bellowing threats, but Octavian recognized Sir Henry's voice, and knew he and Syd had less than thirty seconds to exchange vows.

Octavian pushed them to the front of the queue, smacked double the fee on the table, and confronted the blacksmith. "Captain Octavian Thorne. Lady Sydney Harcourt. Do it now."

The man shrugged. "Do you, Captain Octavian Thorne, take Lady Sydney Harcourt as your lawfully wedded wife?"

"I do."

He now turned to Syd. "Do you, Lady Sydney Harcourt, take Captain Octavian Thorne as your lawfully wedded husband?"

Syd stared up at him.

Sir Henry and her father were angrily pushing their way through the crowd of Armstrongs standing just outside. "Bloody hell, Syd. Do not falter now. You promised me."

"But look at what I am doing to you."

The laird frowned. "Think of the wee bairn."

"What wee bairn?" she asked just as her father and Sir Henry stormed in. Sir Henry had a pistol in hand and now trained it squarely on Octavian's chest.

Syd must have quickly calculated the odds and realized Sir Henry was more likely to shoot him if they were *not* married and could be prevented from taking that final step than if they were married and his efforts were too late. After all, Sir Henry had no incentive to shoot him once Syd was his wife and had the protection of the Thorne name. "I do!"

The blacksmith ever so calmly pronounced them husband and wife.

Syd threw her arms around Octavian, protecting his chest. "You big ox," she muttered, sounding desperately heartbroken. "What have I done to you?"

"Married me," he said, relief washing over him. "No one will ever hurt you now, Syd. You are mine to love and protect."

She looked up at him, her expression one of joy mingled with dismay. "Am I truly your wife?"

"Yes," the blacksmith said with a calm bordering on utter boredom. No doubt, this was an every day occurrence for him. Escaping bride and groom. Father on the chase, sometimes successful in stopping the wedding and sometimes not. "Follow my wife to sign the certificate. It is a mere formality for recording purposes. You are married whether you sign it or not."

The danger had not yet passed, Octavian knew. There was nothing to stop Sir Henry from shooting him out of sheer vengeance. But the old goat must have thought twice about taking on a Thorne since there was no profit in it for him. Syd was his wife and that immediately put her out of Sir Henry's reach even if he made her a widow.

Besides, his brothers would go after Sir Henry and not stop until they saw his businesses destroyed and him drawn, quartered, and then hanged.

Sir Henry lowered his weapon and emitted a string of curses. "This isn't over, Thorne."

"Yes, it is," Octavian intoned. "I'll be back in London in a month's time. Come see me about Lord Harcourt's debt. I will repay it."

"Excellent!" Harcourt cried, obviously pleased he was now to be saved.

Octavian was disgusted, for there was not a hint of remorse in his expression. He had put Syd through hell and had not even a soothing word for her as he called her over. "Come give your father a hug, Sydney. I knew it would all work out. Did I not tell you so?"

Octavian drew her back instead, for he would not allow her go near the loathsome man who had been willing to sell her into servitude to save his worthless hide. "You little weasel," he said, unable to hide his rage, "you put your daughter in danger for your own irresponsible pleasures. How could you do this to her?"

Her father held out his arms to her again. "It's all been a silly misunderstanding. Come to me, daughter."

Octavian refused to let her go. "No, she's mine now. I'll honor your debt to Sir Henry, but not a farthing more after this. Get out of my sight. You don't deserve this gem of a girl."

All eyes remained on Sir Henry and the Earl of Harcourt while they strode out of the place. Octavian would not release Syd when she tried to bid her father farewell. "Octavian, he's my father!"

"He put you through this ordeal. Have you forgiven him already, Syd?" He continued to hold her until the pair left Gretna Green.

Could she not see that it was for her own good?

He was fully prepared to take a punch in the nose from her if she remained truly angry with him. But after seeing the pain this man had put her through, how could she be so quick to forgive and forget?

"He never meant to hurt me," she said, sounding so wounded that it tugged at his heart. But he was not going to allow her to delude herself about her father's love. The man placed his indulgent wants and needs above regard for his own daughter, and Octavian was not going to allow Syd ever to be trod on like that again.

"Stop lying to yourself," Octavian growled back, wondering if she would ever be this loyal to him. Perhaps in time, she might. "The only person your father cares about is himself."

Octavian and the Armstrong clan watched Sir Henry and Syd's father ride out of town, none of them speaking until the pair disappeared from view.

All the bravado Syd had shown when confronted by the

Armstrongs and then her father and Sir Henry now deserted her.

She broke down and emitted a sob.

"Oh, Syd. You are my wife now. You are safe, love." Octavian wrapped her firmly in his arms, for her entire body was shaking.

"I am not crying," she said when he withdrew his handkerchief to dry her tears.

Octavian did not believe her since tiny trails of water were sliding down her cheeks, but he was not about to make an issue of it. They were married and she was safely under his protection now.

Nothing else mattered.

He kept an arm around her shoulders as they walked to their carriage.

The Armstrongs followed them.

Mr. Henshaw was waiting beside the conveyance and must have taken in the entire spectacle. "I thought you were already married," he muttered with a shake of his head, obviously uncertain whether to approve or disapprove their sharing a room at the various inns along the way.

Octavian cast him a warning glance.

Syd was already overset and did not need more guilt piled on her.

"Well, there was no mistaking you were lovebirds. You did what you had to do, considering you got her in that delicate condition."

"What?" Syd's entire body went stiff. "I am not–"

"Syd, leave it alone," Octavian said, for everyone was listening in. "What does it matter? We are married now."

The Armstrong laird and his men surrounded them.

Bollocks.

What now?

The laird stepped forward. "M'lady, no one is condemning ye," he tried to assure Syd, who may have appeared tearful, but she was quietly seething and getting angrier by the moment. "He's a handsome lad and ye could not have resisted giving him yer body as well as yer heart."

Jamie now stepped forward. "But it all worked out in the end.

The captain did the honorable thing."

"Let me be clear," Octavian said before Syd exploded and hurled another insult. Or worse, revealed that she was not with child, which would anger these Armstrongs into thinking he had deceived them again. "It was love at first sight for me. I knew I wanted to marry Lady Sydney from the moment we met. I did not *have* to marry her. I *wanted* to marry her. Never a doubt in my mind. I love her. I have always loved her. And I will always love her."

Syd stiffened and glanced up at him.

The laird nodded and then turned to Syd. "Yer father is a foolish man, lass. He should have consented to yer marriage to Captain Thorne and spared ye the difficulty of traveling all the way to Scotland. How far are ye along?"

Fortunately, the shock of his words and the laird's question kept Syd quiet for the moment.

"Too early to tell," Octavian hastily interjected. "What matters is that she is a lady and now my wife. You will treat her with respect."

The laird assured him they would do so. "But the father's actions still make no sense to me. Why would he choose that old goat over you?"

The curious Scots were not going to allow them to leave until their questions were answered, so Octavian obliged. "Lady Sydney's father got heavily into debt with Sir Henry. The only way he could repay it was to bend to Sir Henry's demand to give Syd over to him. Her father did not hesitate to sacrifice her in order to save his own hide. She is not yet of age and needed her father's consent to marry me. He was never going to give it while under threat to Sir Henry."

The laird nodded. "I see. But surely Sir Henry would have backed off once he knew she carried your child."

Oh, hell.

Syd curled her hands into fists. "What makes you think–"

"Right! What makes you think that old, vindictive beast would release her? He was obsessed with her. She's quite beautiful, as you all can see. What better way to make us suffer than to claim the child as his? Or harm it because it was not his?"

Kindhearted Jamie gasped. "That is pure evil. Surely, her father could not condone it."

Octavian nodded. "He should not have done any of what he did. But he was in fear for his own life, and willing to sacrifice his daughter rather than himself. Neither of them knew of her condition." He glanced at Syd who once again looked angry. "The worst is over, and I thank you for your assistance. You must excuse us now and let us be on our way. Defying her father has taken quite a bit out of my wife. She is overset and there is no telling what she might say or do."

Jamie cast her a sympathetic smile. "Ye are safe now, lass. Captain Thorne loves ye deeply. Do ye think he would have taken them on the chase if ye hadn't claimed his heart? And now ye and the bairn are safe."

Her eyes narrowed in frustration. "I am not–"

"Quite yourself just now," Octavian interrupted her again. "I'm sure you are confused and exhausted, but thrilled at the prospect of giving me a son." He lifted her into the carriage and firmly set her in it. "Shut up, Syd," he whispered.

She was bent on defending her honor while he was desperate to get them out of here without further trouble. "Good to see you again, Jamie. Laird Armstrong, an honor. Thank you for your hospitality."

Octavian did not release a breath until they were north of Gretna Green and he was certain they had not been followed.

Syd was glowering at him.

Octavian stifled a groan. "What?"

"They think I gave myself to you," she said, sounding more hurt than angry. He could manage her anger, but her shame devastated his heart. "Oh, I know you wanted to shut me up, and I understand your reasons why. But they did not question for a moment that you had bedded me. This is what I found galling."

Syd was fiery and independent in so many ways, and yet remarkably traditional when it came to love and marriage.

"Their willingness to believe me is what saved us," he said gently. "I'm sorry I encouraged their mistake. It curled my stomach to pile on those lies. In truth, I uttered more lies in this past hour than I have done in all my life. I never even lied as a child when I did something stupid. I always told my father the truth and took the punishment. But this was about protecting you. How else was I to keep you safe? They were not going to harm a woman with child, and that's all I cared about…that they would not harm you. Syd, I could not come up with a better idea on the spur of the moment. Could you?"

She let out a breath, but said nothing.

"You are my wife now. Even if you weren't, the Scots would not think any less of you for taking me into your bed. They have a hand-fasting tradition. Do you know what that is?"

She continued to look at him with pain in her eyes.

He sighed and continued. "The couple declare their intention to marry in front of witnesses and then go live together. If they are still together after a year, they are considered married. If the woman carries his child, they are considered married. It is nothing formal, just tradition. Nothing like our English ceremonial rites. They do not think less of you for giving yourself to me."

"But this is entirely the point! I did *not* give myself to you."

"You were willing last night," he dared to point out. "Why deny it? I was the one who insisted on waiting until we were married." He ran a hand through his hair, concerned he was digging himself into a deeper pit every time he opened his mouth. But they had to speak about this or else Syd's resentment would fester. "We've traveled together for over a week, slept in the same bed, and seen each other without a stitch of clothing on. We did all that, so do not make too much of the fact you are still a virgin. I assure you, no one cares whether we did the deed or not. You were thoroughly ruined the night you tossed me off the roof and I took you to my home. Our marriage will save you from any scandal. More important, our marriage has saved you from Sir Henry."

"Still, it hurts me, Octavian. Can you not see that?"

"Yes, I do. I see it more clearly than you think. But I am not turning back to explain to the Scots that you are *not* carrying my child. Nor am I sorry they misinterpreted my haste to marry you.

Their misunderstanding saved us. Correcting them, and then explaining your father intended to sell you to Sir Henry, would not have been as effective."

"It might have been."

"Syd, you know that is not true. Many fathers believe their daughters are their possession to do with as they wish. Your father is not the only scoundrel who thinks this way. These Scots might have sided with him and felt he had the right to choose your husband, even as poor a choice as Sir Henry. They might have prevented our wedding ceremony. But to keep a man from making an honest woman of the lass who is carrying his child? *His child.* No man was going to stop the ceremony and interfere with my act of honor."

She stared down at her hands. "Still, it stings."

"I know." He spoke gently, for he understood how embarrassed she felt. Her father had not only gambled away his assets but stolen her funds as well as her inheritance from her grandmother and her dowry. He had probably pawned anything of value she had ever owned. This prideful girl had come into the marriage with nothing left but her maidenhood. To have that stripped away because the Armstrongs misunderstood his need for haste and thought he had bedded her was a final humiliation. "We'll have a proper wedding reception once we are back in London. How does that sound to you?"

She continued to stare down at her clasped hands. "I don't know."

"All right, fair enough. Just know that I am going to treat you with respect as my wife. I cannot repair what has already been done, but I can promise you that I will honor our marriage vows."

"Our make-believe marriage vows."

He raked a hand through his hair again. "Can you not bring that up for the rest of the day?"

She looked up now. "Why, Octavian?"

"I just don't want to talk about a sham marriage. All right?"

"If you insist." She gave a careless shrug. "You seem to have no trouble lying about my honor. So why get irate when pretending this marriage is something other than fake?"

"Because it does not have to be fake." He took her hands in his, surprised by how cold they were, for the weather was relatively mild. However, he knew the Scottish climate was not to blame. She was bereft and feeling cold inside, their hasty ceremony having left much to be desired. She'd spent more time this morning deciding on whether to drink tea or cocoa than in repeating wedding vows.

His morning piss had taken longer than the entire ceremony.

He rubbed her hands lightly to warm them. "Syd, we could make this work. We could turn this into something real and lasting. Will you give us the chance?"

CHAPTER 10

SYD WANTED THEIR marriage to be real, but how could it be when she had come to Octavian with nothing? She might have gotten over her pride and agreed to try and make it work, if not for her own horrible family. How long before her father brought more shame upon them all?

Did Octavian not understand what a future with her would bring him?

Even if he could overlook the failures of her parents, he still had to deal with her own faults. Was she not too independent? Too stubborn and irreverent? In short, she was no prize. It was only a matter of time before he realized she was not what he had bargained for and wanted out of the marriage.

Why would he want to stay married to an unbiddable, opinionated *ton* misfit?

As for her, she longed for a happy family life with Octavian. How likely was it to happen? To make matters worse, she was already falling in love with him. Was this not a dangerous thing? How was she to maintain a happy marriage when she did not even know how to be a good wife? If her mother was to be believed, she had never even been a good daughter.

What had she done to bring her mother such disappointment? It was a mystery to Syd. She had tried so hard to gain her approval, but nothing ever worked. As for her hopes and dreams, both parents dismissed those as frivolous and irrelevant. "No man wants a wife more educated than him," her father had remarked, thinking to give her a kindly warning.

Yes, he was always kind to her, even as he wasted the Harcourt assets and made all sorts of idiotic decisions.

"Syd, you are fretting again," Octavian said when they stopped at a charming inn known as the Abbott's Cross located somewhere north of the town of Moffat.

She nodded. "I was thinking of you and what you said about making this real."

His hands stilled on her waist as he helped her descend from the carriage. "Have you come to a decision?"

"I haven't made up my mind yet, Octavian."

He sighed and helped her down. "All right. But try not to look so miserable on our wedding day. Can you pretend to be a happy newlywed until we are settled in our chamber?"

"I am happy," she insisted. "You are the best thing that has ever happened to me. But how can I ever be more than a curse to you?"

"Ah, Syd. It is shameful what your parents have done to you. They did not appreciate the gem they had in you, and now they have broken you."

"And you think you can fix me?" She tried not to sound hopeful because this was such a difficult task.

"I'm willing to spend a lifetime trying," he said in earnest.

This is why she was doomed to love him desperately and devotedly for the rest of her days. She gave him a playful poke in the ribs. "Then you may start trying after we eat. I'm starved."

He laughed and escorted her inside.

Syd watched as Octavian signed them in as Captain and Mrs. Thorne, surprised by the warmth that curled in her belly as the truth struck her. She was his wife, and Octavian wanted to make it a permanent arrangement.

She ought to be leaping for joy.

Well, she was.

But she was also scared to death his good intentions would fail.

This was ironic because Octavian believed she was fearless.

Quite the opposite was true when it came to matters of love.

She quaked inside, her fear was that great she might lose him.

But she smiled at him when he set down the quill pen after inking their names in the register.

"You mentioned you are hungry, Syd. Shall I order supper sent to our room?"

"Would you mind if we ate in the inn's dining room this evening?" She was now his wife by law and wanted everyone to know she was proud of this fact.

"Dining room it is." Octavian now turned to the innkeeper. "Is it possible to have a tub brought up to our room straight away? We've been on the road since London and are in desperate need of cleaning up." To make his point, he gave his jacket a light pat. A cloud of dust wafted up from the fabric into the air.

"I'll have one of my maids freshen yer travel clothes while ye bathe. Aye, Captain Thorne. Won't be a problem."

"That was considerate of you, Octavian," Syd remarked once they were settled in their guest chamber and awaited the tub to be rolled in. It was a cozy room situated above the common room, but the noise did not carry upward from downstairs. The inn was sturdily built and had obviously been around for centuries. However, their quarters were well-appointed but small. Octavian could not turn around without bumping into something because of his size.

"Bollocks," he muttered, hitting his head on one of the low ceiling beams. The roof had a sharp slope to it, making it impossible for him to stand fully upright other than in the center of the room.

Syd had no problem because she was a full head and shoulders shorter than him. But this did not stop her from taking command. "Sit on the bed and let me have a look at your forehead, Octavian."

"It isn't necessary."

"Sit," she repeated, nudging him lightly onto the bed. It was not very large, which meant they would have to sleep curled against each other. Her heart fluttered, for she looked forward to sleeping beside him as his wife. "Is it the same spot bruised when you fell off Sir Henry's roof?"

"No, a new spot." He winced as she gently examined the area.

"That other one is fully healed. Do not start fretting again, Syd."

"Should I not worry about my husband? Especially when I have some medical knowledge and can help ease your pain?" She grabbed a clean cloth beside a basin and ewer filled with fresh water atop their bureau. "Stay seated, Octavian.

She moistened the cloth, then returned to his side to press it gently against his forehead. "Octavian!" She had yet to place it on his brow before he pulled her onto his lap, a big grin on his face. "What are you doing, you big ox?"

"You'll be more comfortable working on me while seated on my lap."

She laughed softly, relieved the bump was not all that severe. He would have been moaning and not at all playful if it hurt like blazes. "Fine, but stop grinning at me. What do you find so funny?"

"You called me your husband." He cast her a devastatingly appealing smile. "I liked it very much."

"Should I not call you that? This is what you are to me, no matter what happens in the coming year." He might even be hers forever, if she did not anger him to the point he gave up on her and wanted out of the marriage.

Losing him once she got used to falling asleep every night in his arms would be so hard for her.

Devastating, actually.

He made her feel safe.

He understood her better than anyone ever had, even better than her dearest friends, Adela, Gory, and Marigold, the youngest of them who had recently been added to their trusted circle. They were the sisters she had always wished to have. They shared similar academic interests, and refused to abide by Society's strict rules on appropriate feminine behavior.

Their friendship meant everything to her, and she intended to seek their advice on how to build a successful marriage when she returned to London. Adela and Marigold had husbands who understood their hopes and dreams, and encouraged them with their full support.

She never thought Octavian would be such a man because he

liked to be in command and also had very strong protective instincts. For this reason, she assumed he would want to keep her under his thumb. She had been so wrong about that. Yes, he was demanding, but he was also very thoughtful and often gave into her ideas. He was protective, but how could she fault that trait when he had saved her from a horrific marriage to Sir Henry?

He was fierce, and yet always gentle with her. This was important because he could otherwise be quite intimidating.

Not that she would ever buckle to intimidation.

For a strong man, he was remarkably averse to using his fists. She'd noticed how often he managed to talk his way out of a situation rather than fight, even when he had the better odds on his side.

Was it shameful that she had gotten into more tavern brawls than he had?

This said something about her, did it not?

He cast her a soft look as she tended to the lump on his brow. His lips were so close to hers, she wanted to lean in the littlest bit and kiss him. Did she not have the right to kiss him now that she was his wife?

"Syd, are you fretting again? You do that a lot, you know."

"I do?" She nodded, realizing she had been nibbling her lip while tending to him, thinking about him, and debating whether or not to kiss him. "Yes, I do. You seem to bring it out in me. Not on purpose, mind you. The blame is on me. I don't know what to do about you."

He had been surprisingly agreeable for much of this trip, but would it always be this way between them?

"Don't think too hard, Syd. Open up your heart and allow your feelings to flow. The rest will take care of itself."

She groaned. "That requires letting down my guard, and I'm not sure how to do that. I've spent my life worrying about what calamity might happen next. I've built this protective shell around me ever since I was a child. My parents could never be described as doting. I think I often disappointed them."

"They were in the wrong, Syd. It wasn't you."

She wanted to believe him, but did it matter now? The damage had been done to her and the past could not be changed. "Because of my father's profligate ways, I was raised to always been on alert and ready to run at a moment's notice when creditors bore down on us. Did you know they often come around at night?"

"No, I did not. My family has little experience with debt collectors because we always pay our debts."

"Your family is wonderful. So are you." She cast him a worried smile. "Octavian, what's going to happen tonight?"

He arched an eyebrow. "In the marital bed?"

She nodded.

"Oh, Syd. We are husband and wife, not debtor and creditor. Whatever happens tonight shall be whatever you wish to happen."

She released a breath, but was not truly relieved. Their marriage ought to be a partnership, and yet he was conceding everything to her on their wedding night. "What about your wishes? They ought to matter, too."

He cast her a remarkably affectionate smile. "You surprise me. That is quite a wifely thing to say."

She looked up at him.

He appeared so pleased by her simple remark. "Is it? I should think it was common courtesy. Oh, and I am so rarely courteous. Is that what you mean?"

She tried to scramble off his lap, but he would not release her. "That is not what I said or ever meant. Why are you twisting my words?"

"How am I twisting them?"

"First of all, you are courteous and know how to comport yourself like a lady. However, there are times you get a bug up your arse and–"

"Octavian!"

"You know this what you do, Syd. You are quick to toss courtesy aside whenever someone says or does something that is not to your liking. I am not faulting you for standing up for yourself or others."

"Sometimes you do."

"Only when you disregard obvious dangers. Otherwise, I like

this trait in you. There are many things I like about you in addition to your being beautiful."

She blushed.

He really thought she was beautiful? More than merely pretty? He had once told her she was prettier than Lady Clementine. Had he truly meant it?

"You are intelligent, resourceful, honest, and you are not afraid to stand up to me. I admire this so much."

Her eyes widened. "You do?"

He nodded. "As for your *wifely* comment, I have already told you that you are a traditional girl at heart. You would make any man a good wife, if only you were not so prickly all the time. All I meant by my remark is that I did not expect you to let down your guard and be kind and nurturing so soon. I thought breaking down your defenses would take longer."

"Well, obviously I have not broken them down since I was ready to poke you in the nose for your remark. Sorry, Octavian." She removed the cloth from his brow and rose to dampen it again. "This is why I fear our marriage will not work out. The fault lies with me, not you."

He stretched out on the bed and regarded her while she wet the cloth and returned to his side. "You are a work in progress, Syd. Don't give up on us before we've ever gotten started."

They said nothing more as there was a knock on the door.

"That's our tub." Octavian rose to answer the door.

"Look out for those low beams or you'll bump your head again," Syd warned.

He smiled. "Another wifely comment. See, it comes naturally to you."

She snorted in dismissal.

He gave her cheek a light caress. "Only a few hours married and you are already invaluable to me."

She gave him a playful shove. "Answer the door, you big ox."

But she was smiling.

Two men rolled in a hip tub and then carried in buckets of hot water. When they left, Octavian secured the door latch and then returned to her side. "I can leave, if you prefer privacy. I'll grab an ale and return in half an hour. How does that sound to you?"

"A good plan." She turned her back to him. "Would you help me out of my gown first?"

"With pleasure. I've quite enjoyed undressing you."

"Octavian!" But she tingled as he moved closer and placed his hands on her body to loosen her ties.

"What? Am I not permitted to enjoy my wife? Seems a shame to get dressed again to dine in the common room," he muttered. "Are you sure you want to bother, Syd?"

"Yes, but it isn't to avoid being alone with you. I want to enjoy being lawfully married to you, having us step out together as husband and wife without it being a lie." She glanced at him, wincing as she met his gaze. "And yet, I am giving you an awful time about our marital situation. I don't know what you must be thinking when I am as inconstant as the shifting winds."

He gave her a light kiss on the neck as he undid the last hook and helped her slip out of her gown. "I'm a patient man. In truth, I am not giving our situation any thought right now. Nor should you. We have nothing to prove to anyone here in Scotland. Nor do we need to fool anyone here. So, enjoy these next few weeks. That's what I plan to do."

"You are right. I'll try my best to enjoy our time together and not worry about everything that could go wrong." She sighed. "But I am sure I will do something to get you angry. It seems to be what I do best."

"You are kicking yourself again," he remarked, pulling something out of the travel pouch he had brought in for himself. "Soap," he said, in response to the questioning arch of her eyebrow. "For us to share."

She took a sniff when he handed it to her. "Is it sandalwood?"

He nodded. "There was nothing else available at the coaching inn where we stopped at midday. We'll shop for something more suitable for you when we reach Greenock, although they won't have the variety of choices that are available to us in London. You'll also need a few more gowns, especially warmer fabrics as the weather turns cold."

She listened to him plan out their next few weeks.

As he spoke, the one thing that struck her was how dependent she was going to be on him. Not his fault, of course. "You'll need pin money," he said. "And I'll arrange credit with the local shops as soon as we arrive in Greenock."

She pursed her lips, feeling quite awful that her father had left her with nothing. Octavian was not blaming her or looking down on her in any way, but this only made her feel worse.

"Syd, what have I said now? You are fretting again."

She shook her head vehemently. "No, I was just giving thought to what I would need while in Scotland. Will we have to find private lodgings? The Admiralty must have expected you to stay in the local military barracks. Do they have separate lodgings for the officers?"

He nodded. "Yes, they do. But these are not meant to house their wives, too. I'll settle you comfortably at one of the local inns and then we can figure out what to do next."

"Will you leave me to myself at the inn?"

"And spend my nights on a mangy cot with a regiment of snoring Scots? No, I'd rather sleep next to your sweet body." He kissed her on the nose before crossing to the door. "Latch it after me. I'll knock twice sharply when I return. All right, Syd? Two quick knocks, then a pause, then two more quick knocks."

Syd stared a moment at the door after latching it, her thoughts on Octavian and what he had just said about wanting to sleep with her.

That was nice.

She liked the idea of curling up next to his body, too.

However, she did not dwell on the thought, instead concentrating on washing the road dust off her skin and out of her hair. Since Octavian would bathe in the same water after her, she decided to use the ewer and basin to wash her hair first. She then lightly rinsed off her body using a wash cloth. Only afterward did she step into the bath. She hoped it would remain fairly clean for Octavian's use.

Well, this was just her being fussy.

She doubted Octavian would think twice about sinking into the same water she had used since he was accustomed to far greater battlefield hardships.

She eased into the water with a sigh of relief, allowing the warmth to soak into her bones.

Oh, it felt so good.

But after a few minute of luxuriating, she realized that she was taking too long and hurried out of the tub to dry herself off. She had just donned her shift and was combing out her hair when she heard a sharp knock at the door. Three sharp raps. Hadn't he said that he would knock twice?

What did it matter?

He must have forgotten.

"Just a moment." She hastened to unlatch the door. "Come in, Octavian. I was–"

The breath rushed out of her.

Sir Henry pushed his way in and slammed the door shut behind him. "Did you think your farce of a wedding ceremony would be the end of it, my little dove? Your husband shall return to find you a *soiled* dove."

Syd backed away from this man with wild, gleaming eyes, hoping to reach the fire irons beside the hearth before he realized what she intended and stopped her. "Where's my father?" she asked, glancing over his shoulder. "He would never allow you to harm me."

"Your father is a fool. We parted ways outside of Gretna Green," he said, advancing on her as a predator would advance on his prey.

She continued to back up as he stalked closer, trying not to exhibit fear. But her heart was in her throat and she was trembling. "Parted ways? How?"

By the menacing emphasis he'd placed on the words *parted ways*, she feared Sir Henry had injured her father. He must have been livid when seeing her wed to Octavian and had then taken his fury out on her father.

She would never forgive herself if that evil man injured him...or worse, killed him. "What have you done to my father?"

Sir Henry sneered. "Oh, he'll make his way back to London one way or another...eventually. As for you, I've saved the best of my anger for you."

He turned to fasten the door latch.

Syd took advantage of his momentary distraction to grab one of the fire irons. At the same time, she began to shout for help.

Would anyone hear her?

Were any of the adjoining rooms occupied? Would those occupants respond or merely ignore her?

She knew her voice would never carry into the common room. *Octavian, where are you? Come upstairs.*

Sir Henry reached into the lip of his boot and withdrew a pistol.

At the same moment, Syd lunged forward and struck him with the fire iron. The blow grazed his head, but it was enough to bring him to his knees and momentarily stun him.

Since he still blocked the door, she dared not run past him.

Nor could she bring herself to hit him again and crack his skull open.

Instead, she threw open the window, tossed down the fire iron, and then climbed down a conveniently placed rose trestle beside her chamber. Thorns dug into her hands and feet, but she ignored the pain. It was nothing compared to what Sir Henry meant to do to her.

She picked up the fire iron the moment her feet touched the cold ground, and quickly looked around for any rogues Sir Henry might have brought along with him.

But there was no one else around.

She started to run back into the inn and immediately stepped into a puddle of mud.

So much for bathing.

Her hands and feet were dirty again…and she was wearing nothing but a thin shift that hid little from view.

Well, there was nothing to do but brazen it out.

She entered the now crowded common room and desperately searched for Octavian. The place quieted as everyone turned to stare at her.

She must have looked like a demented harpy.

Feet covered in mud, half-combed wet hair, dressed

shamelessly and too much of her body revealed. She was gripping that fire iron with hands torn up by those thorns.

Perhaps she ought to have taken a moment to find the proprietor or even a cloak room where she might grab something to cover herself. But she hadn't thought of it, and now there was no time to spare. Sir Henry was hobbling down the stairs, pistol in hand, and mad enough to breathe fire.

"Octavian!" Syd cried. "Where are you?"

Octavian had just finished his ale and was tossing a coin to the serving maid when she had rushed in. "Syd! What the…?"

He immediately removed his jacket and wrapped it around her, pushed her behind him, and in the same motion retrieved his own pistol just as Sir Henry stepped through the door. The patrons all scrambled as far away from her and Octavian as possible.

"Put your weapon down, Sir Henry," Octavian said with a remarkably calming voice of authority. But Syd knew Sir Henry was too enraged to listen to reason.

"She's mine! You stole her from me!" He snarled like a vicious dog and aimed his weapon at Octavian's chest.

Syd tried to step around Octavian to stand in front of him, but he kept pushing her behind him. "Don't be a fool, Sir Henry. She was never yours and never will be. Put down your pistol. Don't make me have to kill you."

This seemed to be Octavian's way, always preferring to come to terms without need of resorting to violence. Syd adored him for it, but was worried. Sir Henry was a snake and had no code of honor.

"Get down, Syd," Octavian whispered urgently.

She crouched behind a sturdy wooden chair and closed her eyes just as two shots were fired.

She screamed.

Before she could move, Octavian's arms came around her. "Syd, are you all right?"

She let out a sob. "Are you?"

"Yes, love."

Not ready to believe him, she ran her hands up and down his

body. His arms, his chest, his legs. His face. She felt no blood. Maybe she had missed something. "Did he hit you, Octavian? Please, tell me the truth. I need to tend to you right away if he did."

"Love, I'm fine. The same cannot be said of Sir Henry."

She peered over Octavian's shoulder and caught a glimpse of the evil man lying motionless on the floor. "Is he dead? He looks dead."

The inn's patrons were now starting to gather around the body, obscuring her view.

"Yes, he is," Octavian said. "But I didn't shoot him."

"You didn't? Then who did?"

The proprietor, who had been standing over Sir Henry's body along with his fellow countrymen, now came toward them. "The man attacked one of my sons and left him for dead in the stable. My ten-year-old was doing nothing but tending the horses, his nightly chore before retiring to bed, and that beast bludgeoned him."

Syd emitted a soft cry.

"My eldest found him and his ma's tending him now. Are ye all right, Mrs. Thorne? Did he harm ye? Och, yer hands are all cut up. Did he take a knife to ye?"

"No, Mr. Douglas. I struck him with this," she said, glancing at the fire iron Octavian had just taken out of her hands, "and escaped by climbing out the window."

"Then that beast followed ye down here? And pointed his pistol at ye, Mrs. Thorne? Well, he'll never do that in my place again, will he?"

"Mr. Douglas, I'm so sorry," Syd said with unmistakable anguish. "This is all my fault."

"Syd," Octavian said with a wrenching ache, wrapping his arms around her. "He was mad and determined to hurt you. None of this is your fault."

She was not convinced, but Mr. Douglas seemed to side with Octavian and not blame her. Still, she felt the need to apologize to him. "I am truly sorry. I never thought he would follow us here. Will you let me look at your son? I have some medical knowledge."

He shook his head. "My wife is a healer. She'll look after him. Besides, ye're a bit of a mess yerself, if ye pardon my saying."

Syd laughed. "I was shaken, but I will be all right."

Octavian gave her a heartfelt hug. "Love, one of the maids will take you back to our room. I'll have her stay with you until this ugly business is finished down here. The authorities must be called in and told what happened."

"All right, but I'll get dressed and come back down to join you."

"Syd, you're trembling and overset. Can you not let me handle it?"

"No, he came after *me*. He tried to attack *me*. And what of Mr. Douglas's poor boy? I need to see him, too."

Octavian sighed. "All right. I'm so sorry, Syd. I should have realized he was not going to give up even after we were married. I should have stayed upstairs with you and protected you."

"Don't you dare blame yourself for Sir Henry's evildoing." She placed a hand on his cheek to stroke it lightly, but Octavian caught her hand in his and then held up the other, too. "These cuts and scratches on your hands, did he do this to you?"

"No, those happened while I escaped. They're from climbing down the rose trestle, that's all. You know how good I am with scampering up and down roofs and such."

"A veritable little squirrel," he remarked affectionately and hugged her again.

"The cuts aren't serious. A little bit of good Scottish whiskey will cleanse them adequately."

"I'll fetch a bottle at once. My wife can tend to–"

"No, she's busy with your son. I'll see to these myself. My medical training, you know."

Octavian let out a breath. "I'll take you upstairs and make sure there's no one lurking nearby. He might have an accomplice."

"I doubt he did. He would have had the man hold me down while...never mind." She emitted a ragged breath and gave silent thanks that he did have no one with him or else she would not have escaped the fate he had intended for her. "But he was on his own."

"I'll search anyway." He swept her up in his arms.

"Octavian! What are you doing?" Had they not attracted enough attention? "Put me down! I am not helpless. I can walk."

"You are barefoot and probably have cuts on your feet, as well." He ignored her and told one of the maids to grab the unopened bottle of whiskey the innkeeper had set on the table beside them. He then ordered her to follow him up to their chamber. "Make certain my wife tends to her wounds before she returns down here."

"They are tiny scratches," Syd muttered.

"They are *cuts* that drew blood and need to be properly cleaned out," he said with a low growl to mark his frustration over the situation. He turned once more to the maid. "My wife is stubborn. Keep a sharp eye on her and make certain she takes care of herself properly."

"Yes, Captain Thorne," the girl said, bobbing a curtsy.

Syd knew she looked a fright.

The proprietor was not going to let her near his son.

So she did not make a fuss.

Once in her chamber, she set to work cleaning her hands and feet quite thoroughly, placing the whiskey on each scratch and cut, and repeating the process again before she donned her gown and slippers.

The maid assisted her with the fastenings of her gown and then helped her pin her hair in a simple bun at the nape of her neck. "It ain't anything fancy, m'lady."

"Moira, it is perfect. Thank you. Let's join the men."

The shy girl nodded and followed her out. "You were very brave, m'lady."

Syd shook her head. "I was scared out of my wits. But I did my best to hold myself together and find a way to escape. I should have been more careful. I thought it was my husband knocking at the door, so I did not think twice before I let him in."

"Ye weren't to know it was that devil."

Syd nodded. "Mr. Douglas's boy is most important now, that is my greatest concern."

"Och, aye. We are all worried about him. He looked lifeless as his brother carried him in."

Syd gasped. "Then I must go to them at once."

She hurried to the innkeeper's private quarters, eager to look upon the injured lad and do anything she could to help. "Mrs. Douglas, how is he?"

The innkeeper's wife cast her a kindly smile. "He'll recover. He has a small lump on his head and will no doubt have a headache for the next few days, but I have him resting comfortably now. Come, look for yourself."

Syd did, but she cast one look at him and frowned. "He also has marks around his neck. Dear heaven! Did Sir Henry attempt to strangle him?"

The woman nodded, hastily wiping a tear from her eye. "But my eldest boy must have interrupted them when he walked into the stable and called out for him. Thank the Good Lord. As he spotted his brother and knelt to take care of him, the villain must have run off to go after you next. My eldest did not realize something foul was afoot at the time. He thought his brother had fallen and bumped his head. My husband realized what must have happened when you came into the common room in hysterics."

Syd nodded, although she did not think she had been in the least hysterical. Yes, she looked like a mad woman living in a swamp, but…well, it did not matter now. "Any nosebleed? Bleeding from the ears?"

"No, Mrs. Thorne."

"Good. May I check his eyes?" At the woman's nod she raised a finger and asked the boy, who was thankfully conscious now, to follow her finger as she moved it around. He seemed to do it without much difficulty. "You're a very brave fellow," she said kindly. "What's your name?"

"Matthew," the boy replied with a promptness that eased her mind. One of the ways to determine the severity of a blow to the head was to test someone's acuity. The lad's eyes were clear, he knew his name, and now engaged her in conversation without a hint of slurred speech or confusion. "Matthew, you'll need to rest for several days."

The boy grinned and glanced at his mother. "I can do that. Right?"

His mother chuckled. "Yes, my love. We'll take good care of you."

When Syd was ready to join the men in the common room, Mrs. Douglas walked her out. "I'll sit up with him tonight and tomorrow as well," she assured Syd. "It is plain to see ye've done a bit of healing, as well."

Syd nodded. "Although it is not appreciated in London as it seems to be here. I am more often ridiculed than welcomed."

"Our menfolk are about as stubborn as they come, but they are also very practical. Anyone with a useful talent is accepted and appreciated."

She took the woman's hands in hers and emitted a shaky breath. "I am so relieved your boy will be all right, Mrs. Douglas. Please do not hesitate to wake me if he takes an unexpected turn for the worse. My husband and I are at your service."

"Oh, ye dear thing. I shall, if it is needed. That boy is our heart. We'll do everything we can to protect him. Ye just let yer husband take care of yerself now. Matthew will be fine. Ye saw that his eyes were sharp and in focus, and his words weren't slurred or thoughts jumbled. These are very good signs."

"Yes, they are. I can only repeat how sorry I am for what happened tonight."

"Tush! Go back to yer husband who must be worried about ye."

Syd nodded and hurried into the common room. Octavian rose to escort her to a chair, relief washing over his face when she entered.

Sir Henry's body was still on the floor where he had been shot, so she kept clear of it. However, the sight of him stirred up a well of ugly feelings. Anger, frustration, rage, and resentment. "Is it wicked of me to want to kick him?" she muttered.

Octavian grunted as he wrapped an arm around her shoulders. "Not at all. I wish he was still alive so I could kill him with my bare hands. Love, the constable has some questions for you."

She liked that he was using the endearment, but they were both shaken and Octavian's protective instincts had to be on fire at the moment. She could see that he was blaming himself for what happened tonight, thinking he had let her down.

How could he ever believe he had failed her when all he had done and continued to do was aimed at keeping her safe?

Octavian gave her hand a light squeeze to regain her attention since her thoughts were obviously wandering. He introduced her to another man with the surname of Douglas who turned out to be the local constable, and no doubt related to the innkeeper. When the constable drew up a chair beside her, Octavian did the same for himself. He took a seat beside her and kept hold of her hand while the man asked his questions.

Syd tried to keep calm as she detailed everything that happened. "He knocked three times. I should have paid more attention."

She turned to Octavian with a look of apology. "I wasn't thinking and just let him in believing it was you."

Octavian gave her hand another light squeeze. "It's all right, love. You couldn't have known. I should have kept closer watch on who was coming in and out of the inn. It is more my fault than yours."

"It is Sir Henry's fault," the constable replied. "Neither of ye should cast blame on yerselves. He must have been following ye, Mrs. Thorne. Were ye aware?"

"Not that he had followed us into Scotland beyond Gretna Green," Octavian said. "This surprised us. You see, he and the Earl of Harcourt, who is my wife's father–"

"Yer father's an earl, m'lady?"

She nodded.

The man now looked worried.

"But Sir Henry is merely a knight. Somehow rewarded with a knighthood for his shady dealings," she muttered.

Octavian cleared his throat. "The pair chased us to Gretna Green from London. But they caught up to us too late to prevent our marriage. We thought they had returned home. We watched them leave and believed that would be the end of it."

"But I think Sir Henry may have harmed my father, too."

Octavian frowned. "What makes you think he did? What reason would he have to hurt him when he knew I was going to pay off his debt?"

Syd felt her heart twist as she turned to the constable and related what Sir Henry had growled at her. "It was in the way he said they had parted ways. It made my skin crawl. My husband and I will have to go back and search the area just south of Gretna Green."

"What? No, Syd. I cannot go back," Octavian said with a groan. "I have to report to Greenock no later than Friday morning."

"That gives us two days to return and search." She did not understand why this would be a problem.

Octavian's expression turned stubborn. "It will take us a full day to return, and then it will be too dark to search by the time we arrive. We'll have to wait until the following morning. By then, we'll have no more than two or three hours at best to look for him before we have to head north again."

The constable left their side a moment, no doubt eager to keep out of this marital dispute.

Octavian drew her into the opposite corner of the room to be sure they were out of everyone's hearing, and then continued to argue the matter. "Syd, not only will we have little chance of finding your father in that limited time, but we will also be heading straight back into Armstrong territory. Who knows what they will do to us if they see me again without their promised sheep?" He motioned to his uniform, his jacket now back on so that he looked every inch the dashing Royal Navy captain. "I am on assignment. This is not a holiday for me."

Syd did not want to hear his excuses.

This was her father.

He could be injured and lying helpless.

Every moment lost in saving him was precious. "The Admiralty would not penalize you if your carriage broke down or a torrential storm slowed you down, would they? How could they punish you if you stopped to save an injured man?"

"I will have word sent to the Gretna Green constable to

conduct a thorough search of the area. If a broader search is necessary, I'll see if a scouting force can be spared from the Greenock barracks to be sent down there."

"*If* necessary? *If* they can be spared? What are they doing other than whiling their time away doing marching exercises? No one is attacking Greenock." Syd tried to remain calm, but did a dismal job of it. "How can you be so casual about this? Time is precious."

"So is my career. I am not going to jeopardize it for your arse of a father. He's cost me enough, as it is. Not to mention, he almost cost you your life tonight."

She gasped. "He is not...all right, he is not the best father, I will grant you. But he is *my* father and I love him despite his numerous faults. Why will you not do this for me? I am begging you."

His eyes turned as cold as ice. "If you were the object of my search, I would move heaven and earth to find you. But your father is not you. He is a selfish, inconsiderate excuse for a man, completely useless and worthless. I will do all I can for him, but not at the peril of my Royal Navy obligations. Enough, Syd. You are not going to change my mind."

"You think he is worthless."

He gave her another cold, hard look. "I will not deny it."

"Do you think I am worthless, too?"

CHAPTER 11

OCTAVIAN SPENT MOST of the evening giving the local constable information about Sir Henry and his obsessive desire for Syd. He also relented for the sake of Syd and arranged for the constable to send out a search party for her father. He supposed it made sense to send this constable and his men down immediately rather than merely sending word to the Gretna Green authorities. This constable had seen the damage caused by Sir Henry and might search more diligently because of it.

He still felt this was a big concession to Syd. However, she was so worried her father was sill alive but too injured to seek help for himself, that he could not find it in his heart to deny her.

As they were about to return to their bedchamber, Syd implored the constable not to give up the search until his men had found her father.

"Aye, m'lady. I assume there's to be a reward for the safe recovery of the earl?" the man asked.

"Yes," Octavian said in resignation, knowing it would be coming out of his pocket. He had already agreed to pay the entire cost of the search, so what was a little more tossed in as a reward?

He tried not to show his irritation, but Syd was no fool and understood what the heavy air of his silence meant. They had been married only a few hours and he was already piling up expense on top of expense to save the undeserving man. Octavian had already agreed to pay her father's debts to Sir Henry. Now it was costing him the cost of a search party *and* a reward.

Syd had asked nothing for herself.

Could she not see her father was a worthless leech who sucked the life and coin out of everyone he touched? In truth, Octavian would not be surprised if he was not hurt at all and merrily cheating his way back to London. The man was a master at avoiding harm to himself while piling it on others.

Unfortunately, Syd did not see it the same way. "I do not see why we cannot return to Gretna Green and search along with the others. We are the only ones who know what he looks like."

"We've given the constable a good description, and any of the Armstrongs will be able to identify him, assuming they are still in the area. That is enough."

"It isn't nearly enough," Syd muttered, allowing herself to stew and worry with renewed fervor now that they were back in their guest chamber. The tub had been rolled out sometime while the chaos and interrogations had taken place downstairs, so Octavian did not even have the chance to bathe.

The tub itself, or lack thereof, was not the point.

He resorted to obtaining fresh water to refill the ewer and scrubbed himself clean with a damp cloth. Using the last of the fresh water, he washed his hair. Since Syd had taken their one comb to brush out her long tresses, he merely used his fingers to rake through the wet strands of his own and brush them off his face.

As if this was not bad enough, Octavian watched with mounting irritation as she set out a pallet for herself beside the hearth in their already cramped quarters.

Well, it could have been worse.

She could have demanded separate rooms.

"Great," Octavian muttered. "You're still angry because I am refusing to return to Gretna Green even though I am now paying through the nose to find your father?"

Syd said nothing, merely continued to set out her pallet.

What a way to spend their wedding night.

Her father had once again managed to interfere with his daughter's happiness and his own, Octavian thought with some resentment. Even if he and Syd were in a make-believe marriage, were they not entitled to a wedding night? This would have been their chance to warm up to each other. Of course, he was not going to claim her without her willingness. But there were so many other ways they could have enjoyed each other and experienced intimacy.

"Syd, don't do this. Come to bed, please." He had removed his boots and clothing, leaving only his trousers on. She had allowed him to untie the hooks and laces of her gown, and now wore only her shift.

He was glad she had disrobed instead of piling clothes on herself and buttoning them to her throat.

Was this not a hopeful sign?

"The proprietor shot Sir Henry," Syd replied, sounding pained. "He did not give us the chance to ask what he had done with my father."

"Sir Henry, when attacking *you*, told you that your father would eventually make his way back to London. Were these not his exact words?"

She nodded. "How is that helpful? What did he mean? Did he kill my father? Is he dead? Is he injured and unable to move? Will he make his way home in a coffin? Is this what he meant by *eventually*?"

"I think Sir Henry would have told you outright if he had killed him, Syd. This is how his sordid mind worked, taking pleasure in another's pain. He would not have spared you the anguish. In fact, it would have heightened his pleasure even as he…it makes me ill just thinking of what he might have done to you."

He groaned and continued. "A search party is being put together as we speak, including hunting dogs. They'll find your precious father if he is anywhere in the vicinity of Gretna Green. I've arranged payment for a full search and spared no expense. Your presence or mine will not make a difference. In fact, it will complicate it."

"Because of the risk of encountering the Armstrongs? So you've mentioned several times already."

"I only mention it because you stubbornly refuse to

acknowledge its importance."

She shook out her blanket. "Well, that is me. Isn't it? Stubborn. Unyielding. Infuriating."

He sighed. "Good night, Syd. Join me in bed if you change your mind."

Not that she would.

The blasted girl was too stubborn by half.

Octavian was still awake an hour later, grinding his teeth and debating whether to put Syd in the bed and move himself onto the pallet, when he heard a stirring and suddenly felt her slip into bed beside him. "Syd?"

She sniffled.

He held out his arms to her.

She nestled in them without hesitation. "Do not make too much of this. There are mice scurrying on the floor."

"All right." He knew there were no mice. This establishment was meticulously clean. "Sweet dreams, love."

She let out long, ragged breath. "Thank you, Octavian. I'm so sorry I got angry with you. I know you aren't to blame for any of this. You've been far more generous than I or my father deserve. I just feel so frustrated and helpless. The strain has worn me down. But I could not fall asleep knowing I had been so terribly unfair to you. I'm glad you are awake because I need to apologize to you." She told him again how sorry she was. "Will you let me stay in your arms?"

"Always, Syd."

"I'm so tired," she whispered. "And cold."

"I know, love. I'll keep you warm." It was surprising how rapidly he fell asleep now that she was in his arms.

Never mind the possibility of sex.

That was not happening tonight short of a bolt of lightning from the heavens delivering a miracle.

But having Syd curled up beside him was enough to satisfy Octavian.

That she had come to him of her own accord meant everything, even if she blamed it on non-existent mice.

The inn was shrouded in mist by the time dawn broke, but

Octavian knew the sun would come out soon and burn away the haze of gray. Syd was sleeping peacefully, her body wrapped around his so that it took him a while to ease out of her grasp and cross the small room to peer out the window.

He bumped his head as he stood by the window and emitted a muffled curse.

Syd stirred and opened her eyes.

He returned to her side and sat on the bed. "I didn't mean to wake you."

She cast him a smile as sweet as heaven. "I heard the *thunk* as your head struck the wooden beam. Does it hurt? Shall I have a look at it?"

"No, it's fine. Go back to sleep, if you like. It's early yet. Mr. Henshaw won't bring the carriage around for another two hours."

Syd shook her head and sat up beside him, trying to stifle her yawn. "Should we not get an early start?"

"After last night's ordeal? No, I did not want to rush you." He let out a groaning breath suddenly. "Syd, I did not even think to ask Mr. Douglas to give us a different room. How thoughtless of me. Why did you not say something?"

"It wasn't necessary. Nothing happened in here other than my hitting Sir Henry over the head with a fire iron. A change of rooms would not have mattered since I was most upset about my father, not myself."

He gave her rosy cheek a light caress. "You need to think more about yourself and less about others...except me, of course," he added with a grin. "Feel free to worship and adore me to your heart's content."

She laughed. "Do I have a choice? You are not an easy man to ignore."

He wanted to give her a light kiss on the brow, but decided to let her make the first moves. If she wanted affection, she had only to say so and he was willing to reciprocate. But he did not dwell on it long because he heard voices in the courtyard and was curious to know who was up and about.

He rose and walked over to the window once again to peer out of it. "Young Matthew Douglas and his brothers. Now Matthew is walking to the stable. Syd, should he be walking around this soon?"

She scrambled out of bed and joined him by the window. "Yes, he can so long as he does not undertake any physically strenuous duties. I don't think his mother would have allowed him to step out of his room if she did not think he was fit enough. It is a good sign that he is too restless to remain in bed.

"Something I would like to do," Octavian muttered, and then sighed. "I'll give you a moment alone to tend to your necessaries. Shall I send a maid up to assist you to dress?"

"All right, although you do a commendable job of putting me together. I would rather have your touch, but will understand if you have had enough of me."

What he would rather do was a commendable job of getting her *out* of her clothes and showing her the sins of pleasure.

Perhaps tonight, assuming Syd was willing.

He ached to put his hands and lips on her sweet body.

But she was now bustling around the room and organizing their belongings. She appeared eager to get on the road, so there was not going to be anything amorous happening now. Not that he wanted to take her in this room, not after Sir Henry had come after her in here.

New place, new memory.

Or he could wait until they arrived in Greenock and settled in.

Since Octavian already had his trousers on, he tossed on the rest of his uniform and donned his boots. "Shall I order breakfast delivered up here for us, Syd? Ouch!" He winced as he bumped his head against another of those infernal, low ceiling beams.

"I don't think it is safe for you in here." She stifled a laugh but could not hold back another of her beautiful smiles. "Let's eat downstairs."

They had a filling meal, although Octavian noted that Syd merely picked at her food. He left it alone because urging her *not* to worry about her father would only serve to make her worry all the more.

After finishing his meal, he left Syd in the company of Mrs. Douglas, the two ladies sharing a pot of tea, while he went with their eldest son to seek out the constable and make certain his search party was assembled and ready to ride south. The constable had only three men and two dogs with him. "Can't bring more men," the constable explained. "Our clan feuds are long over, but the Armstrongs will be alarmed if I ride into their territory with a small army."

Octavian nodded. "I understand."

"Will yer wife?" he asked, arching a bushy eyebrow.

Octavian groaned lightly. "Probably not, but she's mine to worry about. I appreciate all you are doing for us. She does, too."

Syd had their bags packed and in their carriage by the time Octavian returned. He saw her walking out of the stable just as he reached the inn's courtyard. "I wanted to see Matthew one last time and remind him not to overdo it," she explained.

"How is he?"

She smiled. "Good as new, but I dare not tell him so because he will overdo it and strain himself by returning to his full duties far too soon."

They were on the road by midmorning and traveled north for the next two days, arriving in Greenock on the second evening in a light rain. Since Octavian had been to this Scottish town several times before, he knew of a good inn where they could settle for the night. If Syd liked the place, he would have them stay for the next few days, and possibly for the remainder of their stay. He did not expect this visit to last longer than two or three weeks before they headed to the Glasgow shipyards and then eventually home to London.

It did not take them long to reach the Seafarer's Inn.

Octavian made certain Syd was comfortably settled, and then left her behind to unpack their meager belongings while he reported to the commanding officer. The town had originally been nothing but a row of houses along the harbor, only recently becoming a center of activity for the sugar trade and shipbuilding industry. His assignment was to assess the potential for building navy battle-ready vessels here as well as in the port city of Glasgow, which had an established shipbuilding industry and would likely be awarded the lion's share of the work.

If Syd was willing, he would take her along with him on his expeditions around the area. First on his list was to learn all he could about the depth of the waters in and around the Greenock harbor. He knew it was deep enough for most vessels, but the naval fleet required battleships much larger than a standard merchant schooner. The keel had to clear all shoals and other obstructions as the ship sailed in and out of port.

If the harbor wasn't deep enough, he would have to assess the cost of enlarging it and determine whether the time, men, and materials necessary to make it work was worth the effort. Finding able workers was not the problem. Too many Scots were unemployed and desperate to find a means to make a living wage. Labor, in more than adequate supply, could be had at a reasonable cost. Whether the proper materials could be found close by was another matter.

Since it was already well past suppertime, Octavian knew his meeting with the fort commander would be a short one tonight, merely to advise him of his and Syd's arrival. Tomorrow was Friday, so he had only to officially report to duty in the morning. Right on time, and just as planned.

The commander, an older gentleman with a shock of white hair and a jovial disposition, greeted him warmly. "Captain Thorne, good to see you again. Come in out of the rain. Come in!"

"How are you, Commodore Wainright?"

"I could do with a warmer, drier climate. But no complaints, otherwise." Wainright gave him a friendly pat on the shoulder. "Are you settled in at the fort? Have you had your supper, lad?"

Octavian shook his head. "I've settled at the Seafarer's Inn and will return there for a bite to eat shortly. I'm here with my wife, so we'll either remain at the inn for the few weeks necessary to complete my duties, or we'll find a suitable short-term accommodation."

"Your wife?" Wainright's eyes widened and he smiled in obvious delight. "When did this happen? I had no idea you were courting a young lady. In fact, to hear you talk when you were last here a few months ago, one would think you weren't going to marry for another five years."

Octavian cast the man a sheepish look. "You must have thought I was a fool."

"Not at all, lad. Not at all." Abner Wainright had been happily married for decades until his wife passed away last year. Octavian had met the woman several years earlier and enjoyed watching the pair together. He would best describe them as old lovebirds, for they fussed and cooed on each other with a charming ease. Their affection for each other was sincere but never cloying. Watching them was a revelation, for it seemed as though they were each a natural extension of the other.

He ached for this same ease with Syd.

Yes, he wanted passion, too.

But he also wanted the comfortable familiarity that came with complete trust in each other and an unbreakable bond of love.

Lord, he and Syd had a long way to go to achieve this.

They spoke for a short while, exchanging pleasantries before Octavian politely excused himself. "I've left my wife at the inn. She's awaiting me for supper."

Wainright rose along with him. "Dine with me tomorrow night, you and Mrs. Thorne. I'm eager to meet this paragon who has stolen your heart. You cannot make mention of her without smiling, so do not think to deny it is a love match."

Octavian smiled. "Yes, she certainly has my heart."

Usually, she had his heart twisted in knots because she was often too fearless.

But he was not about to discuss all the ways Syd overset him.

Still, he loved her for those very strengths that also tended to rile him.

Could it count as a love match if he was the only one in love? Well, Syd might feel the same, but she was not ready to admit it to him or to herself yet. Perhaps in time. He was hopeful of it, but it was no sure thing. "Until tomorrow," he said and stepped out into a heightening wind and a pattering rain.

He hurried back to the inn which was not very far from the commodore's residence. Nothing was far in this small town. Syd was just coming down the stairs when he strode in. She hurried toward him as he shook off the dampness like a dog might do after a swim.

She giggled and skittered back a few steps. "You might have warned me!"

"Sorry, Syd. It's damn wet out there." He shook off the last of the rain as he asked about her. "You must be hungry. Did I keep you waiting too long?"

"No, not at all. But I will admit that I am glad you are back. Oh, but your uniform is still soaked. Take off your jacket and I'll hang it up to dry in our room. Did all go smoothly?"

"Yes, most pleasant." He grinned as she fussed over him, and allowed her to unbutton his jacket for him before he shrugged out of it. But he merely set it near the warming fire in the common room for now. Several men were at the bar, and others were seated at tables eating and enjoying an ale or a stronger libation. "The commodore has invited us to supper tomorrow evening."

"Oh, that is lovely. Tell me about your visit with him as we eat. You look hungry, and I think you shall expire if you have to wait another moment for a meal. Me, too. I'm famished. I spoke to Mr. MacLean earlier," she said, making mention of the innkeeper. "Lamb stew is on offer for tonight. Doesn't it smell heavenly?"

"Yes, it's making my mouth water." They settled at a quiet corner table and gave the innkeeper their order. Octavian then ordered an ale for himself while Syd ordered a cup of tea. "Are you cold, Syd?"

She shrugged. "Just a little. I thought I could get away with Adela's borrowed gowns, but the fabrics are too light for this climate. It is quite cool up north, even if only early autumn. I'll need a woolen shawl to get me through the days and nights."

"Not just a shawl," he said with a frown. "There's a seamstress in town. I'll walk you over to her shop before I start my official duties in the morning. I think you'll need two sturdy gowns at a minimum, in addition to your shawl. Wool stockings, too. Might not be a bad idea to purchase a wool blanket for us while you are shopping."

"How long do you think we will be in Greenock? I dare not go on a spending binge. I think I've been too much of a burden for you already." Her face paled a little. "It is now sinking in just how much my father is costing you, and I am appalled. His debt to Sir Henry alone was bad enough, but to add a reward and the costs of a search party…I'm so sorry. I'll make it up to you somehow."

Octavian placed a hand over hers as it rested on the table. "You are my wife now. I am not looking to you for money. Nor should you ever feel the need to scrimp or deprive yourself of whatever you require."

"My father has wasted everything I ever had. I never want to do this to you. It galls me that I came to you with nothing. It shames me that there is nothing for you to take even if you did want something from me. Oh, and as for the added cost to you…I forgot to mention the sheep to be purchased for the Armstrong clan. It is yet another expense incurred by you because we had to race up to Scotland to marry."

He wanted to tell her that it was nothing compared to the contentment he felt being married to her. But he kept silent because Syd would not believe him. Even if she did, the admission would only upset her because of those large chips of shame and blame she carried on her slight shoulders.

How was he to convince her that she was not at fault for any of it? Or that she was more than worthy to be his wife?

"Octavian…"

"Yes, Syd."

Whatever she was about to tell him was interrupted as the innkeeper brought out their drinks and generous portions of lamb stew.

"Here you go," Mr. MacLean said, setting two large plates piled high in front of them. He then remained to chat with them for a few minutes, thinking to be amiable.

Octavian wanted to tell him to go away, but Syd was going on about a simple cure for a boil she had noticed on the man's neck. It was a rather nasty red, swollen lump on his skin and resembled a blister. "Soak a clean cloth in warm water and apply it to the boil for about ten minutes several times a day, Mr. MacLean," Syd prescribed. "It may take a few days to finally burst, but once it does, you must continue to do the same, but add salt to the water before putting it to your neck. I can burst it for you if in pains you too much to wait for the healing to happen naturally."

"Could I trouble you for your assistance, Mrs. Thorne? My sister is afraid to touch it, and it does pain me something awful."

Syd nodded. "Of course, I'll tend to it right after my husband and I finish our supper."

The innkeeper walked off, all the happier, while Octavian now stared into his plate of stew and tried not to think of popping boils. "Syd, you could have waited until after supper to talk about medical treatments."

She laughed softly. "Oh, dear. I did not think about it dampening your appetite. It is hardly a medical treatment, just a matter of applying warm water. He's probably been poking and scratching around that irritation, which only makes it worse."

"Syd, no talk of boils!" he said with a groaning chuckle.

She sighed and watched him dig into his meal. "I knew the talk would not dissuade you for long. The lamb is good, isn't it?"

"Yes," he admitted, shoveling another spoonful into his mouth. The meat was tender and fell off the bone with a mere touch of his spoon. He piled on more and added a chunk of potato to go with it.

Syd continued to chatter while he ate, but she was also devouring the delicious stew, pausing to eat a bite and then prattle on. He liked listening to her, for there was a melodic liveliness to her voice that he found quite pleasant. "His sister is the cook here. She came down from the Highlands to help him run the inn after his wife died. The poor dear succumbed to the influenza. I spoke to his sister briefly while you were visiting Commodore Wainright."

Octavian took a sip of his ale. "Briefly? Sounds like you got some fairly personal information out of her in a short time."

"I am a misfit among the *ton*, but people in general find me approachable and like to confide in me."

"Because you have a reassuring quality about you," he mumbled, taking another spoonful of stew into his mouth and quickly swallowing it. "What else did you talk about?"

"Sheep," she said with a triumphant smile.

He arched an eyebrow. "Sheep? Because of the lamb stew?"

"Well, the aroma of the stew is what lured me into the kitchen. But then we got to speaking about the local farmers and which of them were interested in selling their sheep. Not just any sheep, mind you. Apparently, one of these farmers used to be a sailor and smuggled a cargo of merino sheep out of Spain several decades ago. Isn't this exciting?"

Her eyes were sparkling.

He grinned. "Yes, Syd. I am agog. Tell me more about these merino sheep."

"You beast," she said with a light laugh, "you are just humoring me. But there is a point to this story. The herd has grown and thrived here. I thought they might be perfect for the Armstrong clan, assuming they don't waste their precious value and eat them. Do you think they would be so foolish as to eat these sheep, Octavian?"

"Probably, although their leader appeared to have a good dose of sense. His son was a fool, however. What do you have in mind?"

"I'm thinking the Armstrongs can develop an active woolen trade with them. There's no finer quality wool around and people will pay a higher price for these goods. Few farmers in England or Scotland are likely to have these sheep since Spain is very protective of its merino breed and will hang anyone caught trying to transport them out of the country. The only way they can be acquired is to be smuggled out. They are not quite as rare as the silkworms in China that spun the purest silk. That secret was guarded successfully for centuries before European traders figured it out."

She took a sip of her tea and continued. "As for these merino sheep, their sheared wool can be spun into spools and sold to any of the weavers in Moffat. These weavers can turn them into shawls, gowns, stockings, waistcoats, and the like, and sell their goods at a considerable profit in which the Armstrongs might share. But I think purchasing just ten merino sheep ought to do it. Of course, one of them must be a virile ram for obvious reasons."

Octavian chuckled. "Syd, you are blushing."

"I'm sure I am not," she muttered as her blush deepened,

staining her cheeks an inescapably bright pink. "I am speaking of farm animals of the male persuasion, not discussing you. I'm sure you are virile, but you are not a ram."

"No, I am a big ox."

She sighed. "I only call you that when you irritate me, as you are doing now. I suppose that is not very nice of me. I'm sorry. I won't do that again. You've been wonderful to me. If anything, I am the big ox."

He placed his hand over hers. "Syd, you will never be mistaken for that. A swan, perhaps. Or a golden dove. Do not worry about hurting me. I always want you to tell me what is on your mind and how you are feeling. My hide is quite thick, and I do not care what you call me. Tell me more about your thoughts on the Armstrong sheep."

She set down her fork and sighed. "I thought to acquire ten of another local Highland breed for eating, if they are that hard pressed to survive. But I think all these sheep should be kept alive and bred for their wool. While you are off working, I can visit the farmer and ask what price for his sheep. Do you have any farms, Octavian?"

"As part of my holdings?" He found himself grinning once more as he watched the ideas spin in Syd's head. "No, but Ambrose does. As Duke of Huntsford, he owns farms, country manors, a townhouse in London, and a dozen other land holdings, all of them as part of his entailment. Are you thinking to acquire sheep for us? I would not mind purchasing a dozen for Ambrose. He's done a lot for me and Julius as we were growing up and even now. We are all grown men but still live under his roof. True, Julius and I are rarely there, but we've always considered Ambrose's townhouse our home as well. He has always made us feel welcomed, even now that he is married."

"I wish I had been raised in a family like yours," she muttered, but did not dwell on her past. Instead, she continued to chatter about the possibility of his turning to farming and raising sheep.

"Me? Become a gentleman farmer?" He laughed and shook his head. "Oh, Syd. I don't know. This would require my purchasing a farm, something I would only do if I had a wife in truth and we were preparing to set down roots and raise a family," he said gently, not wishing to start on that sensitive topic.

The light faded from her eyes. "Oh, I see your point. Why bother to build up something that will come tumbling down because it is a sham? Isn't that right?"

"All I am saying is, things can change between us. For the better, I hope. But I was speaking about the practicality of transporting sheep to London. Won't Ambrose and Adela be surprised to find a dozen bleating creatures tearing up their townhouse garden? As it is, we'll have to make arrangements to get the first flock to the Armstrongs."

Syd laughed. "I think we can drop the second flock, should we purchase any for Ambrose and Adela, off at one of Ambrose's farms before we return to London."

"We'll still have to arrange for them to be transported. Our carriage, as spacious as it is, will not fit us and a single sheep, must less an entire flock. But get all the information you can from the farmer tomorrow, negotiate terms you think are fair, and let me know what he says."

The idea seemed to please her. "You would trust me to do the negotiation?"

He nodded. "Syd, you are one of the smartest, most resourceful people I know."

She blushed. "Thank you, Octavian. I'll see what terms he proposes and then report back to you. I've never shopped for sheep before and don't want to make a misstep and overpay. It is your funds I would be spending, so you should have the final say. Seems I've already followed in my father's footsteps and been quick to spare no expense at *your* cost."

He placed a hand over hers again. "You are not your father, Syd. I will remind you of this as often as you need to hear it."

"But–"

"You are not your father," he repeated yet again. "He would never have considered keeping a promise to the Armstrongs or thought about acquiring sheep for himself."

"And yet, you have agreed to help him."

"For you, Syd. You are my wife now. I would do anything for

you. If he is lying injured on an isolated stretch of road, which I sincerely doubt…but if he is, then I would not forgive myself for doing nothing and allowing him to die. I know sending others to search in place of us is not what you had in mind, but they know the terrain better and will be more effective. I suppose I have not handled it perfectly, but–"

"Don't say that, Octavian. You have done so much."

"While we are married, I hope you know that you can come to me for anything you need. This is what it means to be husband and wife. Trust, support, sharing."

"Octavian, stop," she said in a ragged whisper. "You are overwhelming me. This is so different from my life growing up. There was no trust in my family. My parents did not support each other or me. No one shared. They just took."

"And you are deathly afraid to be like them in our marriage." He said it as a fact, not asking it in the form of a question. He knew the answer already. Syd was fearless about many things, but one fear she had yet to overcome was that of becoming as vain and vapid as her parents.

She looked down at her plate and nodded. "I dread it."

"Syd, you won't be like them. You care too much about people and always go out of your way to support your friends. Your outlook on life is completely different from that of your father or your mother. When have you ever indulged yourself at the cost of others? I'll answer that question for you…never."

"But I've done exactly this throughout our rushed trip to Scotland."

"You've been running for your life. That is not indulgent."

"Perhaps you are right, but people can change. What if I do?" She gazed up at him with big, hopeful eyes, so obviously desperate for answers about herself. If only she could see herself for who she truly was, but it would take time for her to understand and appreciate her strengths.

"People, at their core, do not change," Octavian insisted. "A sneaky, petty child is going to turn into a sneaky, petty adult. A kind, compassionate child is going to turn into a kind, compassionate adult."

"Unless they are so badly hurt, they become embittered."

He still had hold of her hand and gave it another light squeeze. "But they also have the capacity to become unembittered when their fortunes turn."

"Or they become cynical and never trust again."

"Is that you, Syd? Too cynical to ever trust me?"

She frowned. "No…that is…I do trust you. In fact, I trust you more than I trust myself." Her frown now faded into a smile. "It is a nice feeling, Octavian. But that does not stop me from being stubborn and irritating to you."

He laughed. "I'll accept that, so long as you trust me. That is good enough for me."

"You have no idea how much I do," she said, surprising even herself by the revelation. "To the depths of my soul. This is how deeply I trust you, Octavian."

"I know. That much was clear the night you bared *everything* to me."

She blushed again. "I did do that, didn't I?"

"Sweet heaven, yes." He cast her a rakish smile. "Care to do that again?"

Her blush deepened to the brightest shade of pink and she began to fidget in her chair. "What would you do if I said yes?"

CHAPTER 12

SYD STIFLED HER laughter at the look of surprise on Octavian's face.

In the next moment, he rose, almost knocking over his chair in his haste. "Are you done, Syd?"

"Yes." She set aside her table linen and rose along with him. "Did I just shock you?"

"You delighted me. Care to go upstairs?"

She nodded and placed her arm in the crook of his elbow. "I'm ready."

In truth, she was ready in so many ways.

Ready to retire upstairs to their guest chamber.

Ready to shed her clothes.

Ready to be intimate with Octavian.

She was still scared beyond belief because he was too good to be true. How could he accept her with all her faults? He had none, that was for certain. In truth, it was terrifying because he was so perfect and she was so imperfect.

"Love, you are fretting again," he said, sparing her a glance as they walked to their room.

Love.

The endearment warmed her soul.

How did one go about making this feeling last and grow deeper over time? "Yes, I am not very good yet at handling happiness. It worries me."

He gave her cheek a light caress. "Trust me to show you the

way."

Her heart was in palpitations as they entered their room.

Octavian closed the door and secured the latch.

However, Syd did not feel trapped with him. Despite his brawn and often stern demeanor, he was soft as pudding on the inside when it came to her. She did not understand why he was so kind and caring, or accepting of her prickly disposition when she so often riled him.

"Will you trust me, Syd?" he asked again, coming to her side to assist in unlacing the ties of her gown.

She raised her arm to give him easier access. "Yes, not a doubt."

He gave her a light, lingering kiss on the neck that completely shattered her resistance. Not that she had any intention of resisting. But with one kiss, he had turned her body liquid. When he planted another lingering kiss on her neck and wrapped her in his arms, her body turned to fire. "Octavian, I...oh, dear heaven. Do all the ladies respond like this?"

"Syd, it is just you and me. No one else matters."

"But I've never done anything like this before. You are the only man who has ever kissed me. For all my book learning, I am at a loss when it comes to real life experience. I suppose I spent too much time with cadavers instead of living, breathing men, just as you have often accused."

"No talk of dead people just now, all right?" he muttered with a chuckle.

She nodded. "Yes, I see your point. Forgive me. As you can see, I am quite the fluttering peahen just now. Especially since you have removed my gown and are starting to unpin my hair."

"Do you want me to stop?"

"No!" She sighed. "Just ignore my rambling. I am very eager to do this, but you mustn't take that *last* step, Octavian. Not yet."

His hands stilled as they were gently sliding through her tumble of curls. "Exploration but no claiming the treasure?"

"For your sake, not mine. I have no doubts or concerns for myself."

He turned her to face him and tipped her chin up to meet his gaze. "Your concerns are for me? Syd, I do not want this to be a pretend marriage. I do not want you to leave me when you turn one and twenty. I want to be with you until you are one *hundred* and twenty. Why are you resisting?"

She tried not to tremble, for he would feel it in the cup of his hand as he held her delicately by the chin. "You mustn't be so quick to accept me," she tried to explain. Why was he being so thick about this? She was a Harcourt, which meant something was going to happen to disappoint him and have him running from their marriage. "Please, Octavian. Can we not take this slowly?"

He emitted a groaning laugh and gave her chin a light tweak before releasing her. "Of course, Syd. We'll go at your pace. I want to devour you. But, very well. I am not going to rush you."

"Oh, I've squashed your ardor, haven't I?" She cast him a worried glance.

His smile in response was affectionate. "If you are asking whether I still want to undress you and carry you to bed, the answer to that is…yes, I do. I'll just have to work a little harder to keep myself in control."

"And by demanding this, I am spoiling your pleasure." She silently kicked herself for saying anything to this wonderful man. But this was what she did best, ruin things. Isn't this what her mother had always said about her?

He took a moment to hang up his jacket on a peg by the hearth. "It's almost dry," he commented while feeling along the fabric. Next, he removed his shirt and came back toward her with his glorious muscles on full display. "The only way you would disappoint me is not to join me in that bed. With or without clothes. It is entirely your choice."

She cast him a determined look. "Without."

"And so it shall be." He sank onto their bed, smiling and chuckling as he began to remove his boots.

She watched him. "Will you help me out of my corset and shift?"

He nodded and came to her side. He had gotten as far as undoing one of the buttons of his falls before she had asked the question. There was something quite arousing about the way that one side of the fabric dipped down to *almost* reveal him.

His grin meant he knew the effect he was having on her.

By the time he stripped her out of her corset and shift, she was awash in intimate sensations, most of them hot enough to make a courtesan blush. He settled her on the bed and pressed on, now naked himself while positioning himself atop her on the soft mattress. His weight rested on his arms so as not to crush her, but she adored the feel of his body atop hers.

And deeply regretted insisting he keep to her wishes and not claim her maidenhead. But she soon found out there were other ways to claim her and Octavian appeared to have mastered them all.

He savored her breasts, licking and teasing the hardened buds. Then he moved between her legs and put his mouth *there*, suckling her and swirling his tongue until...oh, heavens. Powerful sensations washed over her, catching her up in a tidal wave of feelings. Unstoppable heat and pressure that kept building inside her until the pressure released and she was carried off to an unknown place.

She cried out Octavian's name.

Goodness, she loved his name.

It suited him so perfectly.

She cried out for him, repeating his name with ache and wonder.

"I have you, love," he whispered, stroking her body with exquisite gentleness as she soared and then soared even higher.

She held onto him when he wrapped his arms around her to hold her in his protective embrace. She held on as she tumbled over the edge of reason into the deep waters of indescribably passionate sensations.

All the while, Octavian soothed her and told her she was beautiful. "You are, Syd. So beautiful," he said and kissed her with searing heat and tender possession.

He made her feel cherished while he soothed her and held her until this storm of new sensations passed and she calmed.

She was still breathing heavily when he rolled onto his back and brought her along with him so that she was comfortably settled atop him.

"Syd," he said softly, "how do you feel?"

She wanted to cry because she felt so happy, but did not want to end this moment with tears, even if they were good tears. Instead, she smiled back at him and gazed into his gorgeous, gray eyes that still held the heat of smoldering embers. "I feel wonderful," she admitted. "And scared by these feelings you stirred in me. They are so potent, Octavian. Does this happen with all the women you take into your bed?"

"Do not compare yourself to anyone. Nor could I tell you truly how anyone else felt, for they never meant anything to me and I meant little to them. I know it sounds harsh, but it was reciprocal apathy. Those women were using me as much as I was using them. They could have been faking, for all I know."

"With you? No." She shook her head emphatically. "I do not think any woman could resist you."

He kissed her gently on the cheek. "That is because you genuinely like me. Indeed, you like me more than you are willing to admit. But these others ladies? I have no idea. Nor do I particularly care. Perhaps that does not speak well of me. I never sought out women of sterling character to satisfy my urges. The ones I bedded would lie to me through their teeth if they thought there was advantage to be had. Not you, though. You would always be honest with me."

"Even if I lied, you would see through me." Indeed, he would see straight into her heart because he understood her so well, her every gesture, her every nuance. Even if she were stone-faced, he could still tell what she was thinking.

"Syd, you do not have it in you to ever lie to me. Defy me, yes. Irritate me, constantly."

"Octavian!" She had remained atop him, warmed in the circle of his arms and the heat of his skin. But she laughed because this is what she was – defiant and stubborn – and there was no denying it. "You are a beast to say such things to me."

He gave a low growl and kissed her. "And you are also beautiful, smart, passionate, and my heart fills with elation whenever I am around you."

"I feel the same around you…and yet, I am still so scared it will all come undone. The Harcourt curse. I don't want to end up miserable like my parents."

"You won't, sweetheart. You are nothing like your parents. We are not going to repeat their mistakes."

She nodded against his chest. "I hope you are right. But I cannot shake this awful feeling that something will arise to put a rift between us."

He ran his fingers lightly through her hair. "You will be of age in less than nine months, Syd. If no disasters strike, will you make our marriage permanent? Do this for us, won't you? Give us a chance."

"Octavian, by the time I come of age, you will be eager to get rid of me."

He frowned. "I am not getting rid of you. Put it out of your mind and stop wishing for it to happen."

"Wishing for it?" She shook her head and let out a mirthless laugh. "I am desperately hoping it does not happen. Please, no more speaking of this tonight. Let us enjoy the moment. I'd rather fall asleep with a smile on my face."

"Fine," he said, obviously wondering how to deal with her dread. It was going to hang over her head like the sword of Damocles unless she learned to simply accept they could be happy together.

She was trying, but it was still so hard for her to do. "Can we try this again, Octavian? Soon?"

"*This* being my hands and lips all over you?"

She nodded. "I like the way you touch me."

"Yes, Syd. As often as you desire."

She nibbled her lip, suddenly finding another reason to fret.

Did he now think her too forward? She was setting rules, refusing to consider their arrangement permanent, and yet wanting this intimacy often. How often was too often? What was not often enough?

Since her head was still resting on his chest, she felt his rumble of laughter. "Octavian, why are you laughing?"

"Because you are fretting over nothing. Only you would be

worried about the terms of our intimacy. I'm a man, Syd. If you want to get naked and give me your body, I am not going to refuse you. If you want me to get naked and allow you to explore my body, have at it."

"You would allow this? Even with my rules?"

"Even with your rules. There is no right or wrong number of times we engage in…giving each other pleasure or how we choose to do it," he said with that uncanny ability to read her mind. "How far we go is up to you. If you want limits, then there shall be limits. That's all there is to it."

"What if one of us wants to do more and the other one doesn't?"

"I am not going to force you to do anything you are not ready to do, Syd. We will figure it out at that time."

"You make it sound so easy," she grumbled, because if it really was as simple as he made it out to be, then why were her parents so horrible to each other?

"It is easy because we are sensible people who care about each other and have the wisdom to deal with their differences intelligently."

"You think I am sensible?"

His chest shook as another rumble of laughter escaped him. "Yes, Syd. I think you will come to the right decision…although it won't be without giving me a headache or two along the way, because that is you. In turn, I'm sure I will give you a headache or two because that is me. We are both obstinate when we want to be. But our marriage will be unbreakable as long as we are understanding and forgiving of each other."

"I would add another caveat, that it shall not be one of us always doing the taking and forcing the other to do all the forgiving."

"It won't happen, Syd. Stop fretting about it. I would not call either of us *takers*."

"But I took everything tonight and gave you nothing in return."

He arched an eyebrow. "Are you referring to my neglected male parts? We'll address that next time or the time after.

Whenever you are ready. Seeing you respond to my touch was pleasure enough for me tonight. You gave me that, and it is no small thing on your part."

"Because I trust you."

"I know."

Syd listened to the rain pelt their window.

She fell asleep to the pitter-patter against the panes and the steady rise and fall of Octavian's chest against her cheek. Her last memory before she dozed off was of the gentle stroke of his hand as he ran his fingers through her hair to caress her.

Let this be our life.

Please.

Please.

Don't take this away from me.

The sun was shining by the time Syd awoke the following morning. She sat up, noticed Octavian's side of the bed was empty, and hastily gathered the sheet around her body. Neither of them had bothered to put on nightclothes before falling asleep, and she was not used to sleeping naked. It helped to have Octavian's big, warm body beside her during the chill of the rainy night.

But their lack of clothing was still embarrassing.

She could have tossed on a shift or nightgown afterward.

She wiped the sleep from her eyes and then realized she must have slept quite soundly because Octavian was already washed, shaved, and dressed in his uniform.

He smiled at her. "Good morning."

She smiled back. "Good morning. You look rather marvelous this morning."

"So do you. That sheet is quite becoming on you. The height of fashion."

She playfully tossed the pillow at him.

He came to her side and gave her a scorching kiss on the lips. "I know I said I would walk you to the seamstress shop, but I did not have the heart to wake you. You were curled up like a kitten beside me and did not respond when I kissed you earlier. I thought it best to let you sleep, especially after last night's exertions."

Heat shot into her cheeks. "I did not exert myself."

He arched an eyebrow.

"I was merely engaged and curious. Mostly, I lay there and responded to your touch."

He laughed. "Is that all?"

"You were very manly," she said with a sigh, recalling last night's pleasure. "I was transported."

"Go on." He kissed her lightly on the nose.

She could not contain her smile. "It was most satisfying, as you well know. Just look at the smug grin on your face. But the fact remains, you did the lion's share of the work."

Oh, he did look so proud of himself.

"It was all pleasure on my part," he said. "Not a bit of work. And you were *very* responsive. I think you howled."

"Octavian! The very idea!"

He gave her cheek an affectionate caress. "The seamstress shop is just down the street. The innkeeper or anyone one on his staff can direct you. I'll be gone most of the day, but will return to collect you at six. Don't forget, we have that early supper with Commodore Wainright. Have the innkeeper send word to me if you need me to return sooner."

She shook her head. "I'll be all right on my own. I'm used to it. Don't worry about me. I won't bother you."

"You are never a bother," he said, casting her a hot, hungry look. "Gad, you're pretty."

She rolled her eyes and smiled at him. "I am sure I look a mess."

"No, you are perfect." He kissed her again, claiming her mouth with a ravenous urgency. "I'll send up one of the maids to help you with your gown."

As soon as he left, Syd grabbed her shift and tossed it on. She then set about readying herself for the day. First stop would be the seamstress because she needed warmer garments. The light muslins she had taken from Adela's armoire were never going to protect her from this harsher, northern climate where the air cooled precipitously once the sun went down.

She decided that her first purchase ought to be a woolen shawl that she could use immediately since she intended to hike to the Campbell farm next to inspect the merino sheep for the Armstrongs.

Miss Granger was the local seamstress, a charming woman who appeared to be about forty years old, and had a crisp, efficient manner about her. "Och, Mrs. Thorne. Good morning," she said, bustling to the front of the shop to greet Syd. "Yer husband said to expect ye. I should have known ye were lovely by the sparkle in his eyes when he spoke of ye."

Syd smiled. "A pleasure to meet you, Miss Granger. What else did my husband say?"

The seamstress waved her hand lightly in the air. "Ah, men. He gave me explicit instructions you were to have the best of everything. No less than five gowns with all the trimmings and accessories."

"Five!" Syd shook her head in resignation. "I only thought to acquire two. We're only here for a fortnight."

"Well, it gets rather cool at night and often in the daytime as well. Ye'll freeze if ye go around wearing those thin clothes. Let's choose the fabrics and colors, and then I'll make up three gowns for everyday wear and something a little nicer for evening entertainments. Captain Thorne is soon to be promoted to admiral, and him already in the highest social circles means you and he will be invited to dine with all the best families in the area. Ye'll catch yer death if ye go out in that thin material, even if it is elegant. I have girls in town that I'll call in to help me get these new gowns sewn fast."

Syd spent more time than she intended in the shop, but she had fun chatting with Miss Granger as they selected the color and style for each gown. She also acquired stockings, shawls, and gloves, making certain at least one of the gowns and its accompanying shawl featured the Earl of Greenock's clan colors. Just as important, she relied on Miss Granger to alert her to the colors not to be chosen because they belonged to an enemy clan.

The bitter violence between these families had long since ended, but some lingering rivalries remained. Most were lighthearted disagreements and some were more serious, but she was not looking to inadvertently give insult no matter the reason.

Being measured and pinned took longer than Syd realized.

It was already past noon by the time she returned to the inn. The kindly innkeeper hustled toward her when she spotted him in the common room. "How long do you think it will take me to walk to Mr. Campbell's farm and back?"

"Och, no, Mrs. Thorne. Let me have one of my boys drive ye in our rig. Ye'll never make it there and back in time for supper with Commodore Wainright."

Did everybody know of their plans?

Well, it was a small town and Octavian was probably the most exciting outsider to visit this place in ages.

Goodness, he had looked so handsome in his uniform this morning. Dark hair, striking gray eyes as sharp as those of a jungle cat, broad shoulders, and trim, muscled torso. How could any woman ever resist him?

Well, she could have done so if he'd turned out to be a complete ass.

But he wasn't.

He was intelligent and kind.

His perfection still scared her to death.

The innkeeper's sister packed a lunch for her and had it ready when her nephew drove the rig around. "I'll be escorting ye, Mrs. Thorne. Let me help ye up," the young man called Ewan said. He hopped down and then held out a hand to give her a boost into the seat beside his. "My wife is one of the seamstresses who'll be helping Miss Granger with yer gowns."

"Oh, that is lovely."

"The town is abuzz over ye and the captain. He's a good man. Been here several times already."

"Yes, he's told me how much he loves the area."

"We're hoping he finds Greenock meets the navy's needs. Canno' lie to ye. We need the work."

Syd nodded soberly. "It is his wish, too."

The horse jogged along country roads and beautiful scenery for almost an hour before Ewan turned the rig inland down a small lane. A gray stone farmhouse with smoke wafting from its chimney came into view. The farmhouse looked to be small, perhaps containing only a common room and a small bedroom, but the barn was much larger and appeared to be very well maintained. Mr. Campbell obviously valued the comfort of his sheep more than his own.

A tall, lean man leaning heavily on a cane ambled toward them followed by four big dogs. By the look of them, Syd surmised two were border collies designed to herd sheep and the other two were just big and scary looking, designed to keep strangers such as the Armstrong reivers from stealing said sheep.

However, she doubted these lowland reivers ever ventured this far north to steal from their countrymen. It was quite all right to steal from the English, however. "Ewan, lad. What brings ye out here?" the old man asked the innkeeper's son, but stared directly at Syd.

"This here is Mrs. Thorne, wife of Captain Octavian Thorne. Do ye remember him, Mr. Campbell?"

"Och, aye. Big fellow."

Syd smiled. "Yes, that's him."

"Mrs. Thorne would like to purchase a few of yer sheep," Ewan said.

The smile on his sun-leathered face faded as his old eyes regarded her thoughtfully. "Ye've made the trip for nothing, Mrs. Thorne. My sheep are not for sale."

"Not at any price?"

He arched an eyebrow. "Looking to toss money at me?"

"Within reason," she said with a nod. "You see, my husband and I encountered a clan on our journey north a few days ago, fellow Scotsmen of yours who have fallen upon hard times. They need an industry to support their clan, so when I heard of your fine sheep, I–"

"Ye thought I'd sell some to ye for those lowland reivers?" He huffed in disgust. "So they sent a woman, a Sassenach, at that, to do their bidding?"

Syd tried not to bridle at the term commonly used to describe the English. *Sassenach.* Octavian had told her what it meant when

Angus Armstrong had used the word to describe her. It was usually spoken in a dismissive tone that revealed it was not a compliment. Indeed, there was a long history of hatred for the English among the Scots, and perhaps she ought to have considered this fact before undertaking the journey to the Campbell farm.

However, she maintained her friendly smile rather than resort to usual form and toss back a cutting remark. The crotchety, old man was looking for any reason to kick her off his farm and she was not about to give him one.

Octavian would have been proud of her poise.

She was showing remarkable restraint. "They did not send me, Mr. Campbell," she patiently explained. "I expect they would be highly insulted if they knew what I was doing."

"Then why are ye doing it?"

"That is a fair question," she replied with a nod. "You Scots are too proud to accept help from anyone. In fact, you'd rather cut off your nose to spite your face."

Ewan chuckled. "Och, aye."

"But there are women and children to think about, not to mention injured soldiers whose wounds will never heal sufficiently to allow them back into military service. The sick and the elderly. What is to happen to them if we do not extend a hand to help? My husband and I are not offering charity, but only hoping to provide the means for them to survive. These are your countrymen. All I am asking for is ten sheep to get them started."

"And compete with my woolen prices?"

"You are a three day journey from the English border. Any wool produced by them would be sold no further north than Moffat. In all likelihood, they would go south to sell their wool in the English cities of Carlisle and Chester where they can command higher prices. They would not be competing with you at all. I understand you sell your wool in Glasgow and Aberdeen."

"Who told ye that?"

She shrugged. "One hears things."

He scowled. "Ye've been poking yer pert, little nose in my business and I dinna like it."

She cleared her throat. "And I would require another ten sheep for me."

Mr. Campbell emitted a bark of laughter. "For ye, lass? What use would ye have for my sheep?"

"I intend them as a gift to the Thorne family, in gratitude for all they have done for me."

He arched a thick, gray eyebrow. "And what is it they've done for ye, Mrs. Thorne?"

"Saved my life," she said with a wealth of feeling, surprising even herself when tears suddenly formed in her eyes. "Oh, dear."

She quickly wiped them away.

Ewan cast her a worried glance. "Yer driver, Mr. Henshaw, told my aunt what happened to ye. Ye were indeed brave, Mrs. Thorne."

"Her? Brave?" Mr. Campbell sighed. "Come in, lass. You too, Ewan. I'll put on some water for tea and ye'll tell me what happened to ye."

She understood that honesty was the only way to be with him, so she related a shortened account of Sir Henry's obsession with her, omitting mention of Mr. Douglas having shot the villain because it was sufficient to relate that he'd met a just end after his attempt to harm her. She also mentioned her worries about her missing father. However, she made no mention of her marriage to Octavian being a sham.

That was no one's business but hers and Octavian's.

In truth, she and Octavian cared for each other deeply. If not for this looming fear she had that something dreadful was going to happen to destroy their chance at happiness, she would have grabbed onto him with both hands and continued to hold onto him with all her heart and all her might until her dying breath.

"Others have suffered far worse than me," she said, bringing an end to the abbreviated tale. "But I do understand fear and despair. This is why my husband and I hope to provide help wherever we can. I am doing it with the purchase of sheep and my husband is doing it with the hope of bringing the navy shipbuilding contracts to Greenock."

Ewan grinned at the old man. "What do ye have to say to

that?"

"Mind yer business, Ewan," he barked back. "I'll think about it, Mrs. Thorne. But dinna get yer hopes up. Those sheep are my livelihood. I canno' afford to give them away at any price."

Syd tried not to look disappointed as she thanked him for his time. "It was a pleasure to meet you, Mr. Campbell."

"And ye, Mrs. Thorne. Ye're all right for a *Sassenach*."

Ewan turned to her once they were back on the road to Greenock. "Ye gave it yer best try. He hasn't parted with a single one of his flock since he stole them out of Spain decades ago."

Syd nodded and wrapped her newly purchased shawl tighter about her shoulders as the wind picked up and now had a decided chill to it. "Well, I got a cup of tea and shortbread out of the visit. Thank you for taking the time to escort me to his farm. Brrr, the weather turned nasty rather quickly." She glanced up at the darkening clouds in the sky. "Will we make it back to the inn before it rains?"

"Aye, just about make it." Ewan flicked the reins to get their horse moving at a trot.

The first raindrops fell just as Syd darted into the inn. "That was close!" she said with a laugh, greeting the innkeeper with a breathless smile.

"Och, aye. Yer husband was worried for ye."

Her eyes widened. "He's here?"

"Aye, Mrs. Thorne. Came back almost an hour ago and has been fretting over yer safe return ever since. I sent him into the common room for an ale because he was pacing back and forth in front of the door with a fearsome scowl on his face and chasing my customers away," he joked.

She hurried into the common room that was quite crowded, which proved even Octavian's fearsome scowl was not enough to scare a determined Scot away from his pint of ale. "Octavian!" she called to him from the doorway, but he had already seen her and was coming toward her with relief etched on his handsome features.

"You're back. I was so worried about you." He picked her up and gave her a quick twirl before kissing her and then setting her back on her feet with a quick hug. "Tell me all about your day."

Everyone had been watching them and grinning as Octavian behaved most improperly by kissing her in public.

Their smirks were good-natured, and she certainly did not mind Octavian kissing her. Even his briefest kisses were packed with steam and turned her insides liquid.

He led her back to his table and held out a chair for her. "We're to have supper in two hours with Commodore Wainright, but are you hungry now? Shall we order a little something to hold you over?"

She cast him an impish grin. "I always knew you were a mother hen at heart."

He laughed. "No, just a worried husband."

"A doting husband," she said warmly. "You're back early. Is everything all right?"

He nodded. "I accomplished all I could today. It took less time than I expected, so I returned here."

"Oh, I'm sorry I kept you waiting."

"You couldn't have known. It's all right, although it felt like an eternity. I'm glad you had one of the MacLean boys as escort and did not walk all the way to the Campbell farm on your own."

"The fitting for my new gowns took much longer than expected since *someone* insisted that I acquire no less than *five* gowns," she teased. "I had a lovely time chatting with the seamstress."

He placed a hand over both of hers as they rested on the table. "I would have ordered an entire new wardrobe for you, but that would have made you angry."

"Not angry," she hastened to assure him. "Your generosity is much appreciated, but not necessary. Perhaps it will be needed when we return to London. My father will be angry and might not allow me to get my clothes out of the house, that is assuming he is still alive."

"I'm sure he is alive," Octavian said with a nod of certainty. "As for your wardrobe, don't think twice about it. We shall deal with the situation when the time comes. I'll have every modiste in town attend to you, if necessary. How did your sheep-purchasing jaunt go?"

She sighed. "It didn't. Mr. Campbell is a lovely fellow, but he is not going to part with any of his flock."

"Sorry, Syd. I know you had your heart set on those merino sheep. We'll come up with another plan."

"Seems we have no choice but to acquire local breeds. They won't turn as much of a profit for the Armstrongs, but it is better than their having no wool at all."

"You gave it your best. That counts for something."

"I don't know. He has over a hundred in his herd now. I wish he had agreed to sell me a few. He would not even negotiate."

"We'll be here for at least another week. Perhaps you'll wear him down."

She laughed. "Yes, irritating people is my specialty. Isn't it?"

He brought her hand to his lips and kissed it softly. "Syd, after last night," he said with a delicious huskiness to his voice, "you can do no wrong in my eyes. I have no complaints about you."

She blushed.

Yes, last night.

She couldn't wait to leap into bed with Octavian again tonight.

His conquering grin revealed that he had read her thoughts.

"You have to stop doing that," she muttered.

He leaned back and held his hands out while casting her an innocent, but unmistakably smug, look. "Doing what?"

The man did not have an innocent bone in his body.

He was gorgeous and he knew it.

He also knew how to pleasure women.

The big ox knew he had left her well pleased.

"Reading my mind." Worst of all, he knew she had absolutely no resistence to his charms and would melt, moan, writhe, and do other embarrassing things the moment he got her back in bed. "You are a rogue and a scoundrel. You do know this, don't you?"

"I beg to differ. I am neither a rogue nor a scoundrel."

"Then what are you?"

He leaned closer and took her hands in his once again. "A husband who wants this marriage to be real. Who wants to wake up to find you beside him every morning of his life."

Did he not understand she was desperate for this, too?

"Octavian..." She struggled to breathe, for his words were a painful ache to her heart. What if she allowed him in and then lost him? She would never recover from that.

"Bollocks." He shook his head and sighed. "Never mind. Forget I said that. It was not my intention to pressure you into making a decision. Are you hungry, Syd? Want something to tide you over until supper? Mr. MacLean's come to take your order."

Yes, she was famished.

It wasn't for food but for the happiness Octavian offered her.

Why was her heart so filled with dread?

Why was she so certain their marriage would not work out?

CHAPTER 13

THEIR TWO WEEKS in Greenock had flown by, Syd realized as she spent the last few days visiting the new friends she had made here. It was said that no Scot would ever consider anyone a true friend until they had known that person for over a dozen years. But Syd felt truly welcomed into the Greenock community. She understood it was sensible to be wary of strangers, and that the span of time would bring out the good and bad in anyone, revealing their true nature. But these rules seemed to fall aside because she was so quickly accepted as one of their own.

This was something new for her.

Other than her friendship with Adela, Gory, and Marigold, she had never felt accepted by London society, and especially never her parents. For this reason, she was loathe to leave Scotland, even though she missed her three friends and her work at the Huntsford Academy.

She and Octavian now maintained a surprisingly busy social life in this quiet port town. She had grown quite friendly with several of the villagers from Miss Granger, the seamstress, to Lady Lennox, who was the *grande-dame* of Greenock society and had taken a liking to Syd, claiming that Syd reminded her of herself in her younger days.

Syd was also warmed by how easily the locals accepted her love of medicine and desire to learn. Unlike those in England who imposed stiff rules and moral regulations designed to keep a woman in her place, these Scots admired anyone who yearned for higher learning.

While Octavian busied himself with plans for the harbor and expanding the shipbuilding operations, she had gone to local lectures hosted by Lady Lennox, taken hikes along coastal paths with the Greenock bird-watching society, and even followed the local doctor and midwife on their round of calls. She was accepted by everyone without so much as the blink of an eye, most surprisingly receiving the praises and warm regard of the doctor and midwife. She learned so much about the natural healing arts from each of them.

But her greatest pride was in being able to teach the villagers, especially these local healers, a few things she had discovered during her forensic studies at the Huntsford Academy. The academy was the museum and center for scholastic studies that Octavian's brother, Ambrose, Duke of Huntsford, had established to honor their father.

The Huntsford Academy was situated across from the British Museum and was just as renowned, for visitors came from all over the world to view the ancient creatures her friends, Adela and Marigold had discovered buried in Adela's Devonshire caves. Their Dragons of the Ancient World exhibits were all the rage in London.

She shook out of her wandering thoughts upon spotting Octavian walking up the street toward her as she was returning from assisting the local midwife in a birth. Her eyes must have been alight and her cheeks glowing because Octavian's smile was particularly affectionate when he saw her. "You look happy, Syd."

She nodded, for she was content in so many ways, not the least of which was their sham marriage that had felt blissfully real ever since arriving in Greenock. Sharing Octavian's bed every night, enjoying his touch, and waking in his arms was beyond perfection. She dreaded its idyllic end, for that feeling of doom had not left her despite how happy she was.

Something terrible was going to happen upon their return to London and she had no idea what it was or how to prevent it from occurring. "I assisted in a birth," she said proudly. "It was amazing, Octavian."

His smile turned tender and indulgent. "Nicer than working on cadavers?"

"Much nicer," she admitted, letting out a lengthy breath of laughter that formed a vapor as she exhaled because the day was surprisingly cold for this time of year. However, she was prepared for the weather now that she had five new gowns, several of them of softest merino wool from the sheep Mr. Campbell still would not sell to her. "Were you looking for me?"

He nodded and took her arm to lead her back to the inn.

They had kept matters simple and chosen to remain at the Seafarer's Inn since they were quite comfortable there and did not need more than a bedchamber for themselves. "I've just heard news about your father," he said as they neared the inn.

She paled and gripped his arm. "And?"

"It is all good, Syd," he assured, stopping along the bustling street to place a comforting hand over hers. "He wasn't hurt. Sir Henry did not harm him. They merely parted ways and your father set off by himself, imposing upon friends and acquaintances while he made his way home."

"Are you certain?"

He nodded. "I expect he's made it safely back to London by now, at no cost to himself."

She shook her head and gave a mirthless laugh. "So typical of my father. He never pays his own way. But I am relieved he is safe. However, you do not look pleased. What else was said in the report?"

"You mistake my expression. I am pleased he wasn't hurt, but he hasn't changed his ways, Syd. I expect he will disrupt our lives again soon."

She groaned while nodding in agreement. "What happened?"

"The Armstrong clan assisted in the search when the Moffat constable and his men arrived in Gretna Green. Several of Laird Armstrong's men rode south into England and caught up with your father at one of the local inns just across the border. He was playing cards and probably cheating the other players since they reported he was on a remarkable winning streak."

Syd sighed. "Typical."

"But he is safe, and this is what matters. As for the Armstrong men, perhaps I misjudged them. They did us a good turn."

"And now I feel worse for not obtaining Mr. Campbell's sheep for them. That man is such a stubborn clot. He is quite galling. And those sheep aren't even legitimately his. He *stole* them out of Spain."

Octavian grinned. "The Armstrongs will survive the disappointment since it will be softened with my news. The Greenock harbor meets our requirements, so we are going to build two navy battleships here to start. Probably more will be ordered in the years to come. That means we'll need men to build them. Locals will be hired, of course. But I'm also going to offer jobs to more of the Armstrong men. At least ten, to start. Perhaps more, depending on the local shortage."

"Octavian, that's wonderful," she said with genuine cheer.

"I'll put Jamie in charge because of his experience and knowledge of seamanship. He's a good man and can be trusted. I just hope the laird's son isn't among those choosing to work here. That one's trouble."

Syd nodded. "Let's hope his father decides to keep him close to home since he is next in line to be laird of their clan."

"It is not a given," Octavian said when they resumed walking to the inn. "A clan can vote for someone else to take over the role if they find the son lacking. Their hierarchy does not work the same as our order of ranks and titles that are pretty much carved in stone. A Scottish duke or earl is secure in his title which is granted through Letters Patent by the monarch. Those usually contain terms requiring passage of the title and entailed estate by primogeniture to the eldest son. But a clan laird does not receive any such grant of title. He has no guarantees that his eldest son will be next to succeed him."

Syd was fairly well versed in such matters and had done quite a bit of reading about Scotland, especially in the field of medicine, long before their mad dash to elope. She already knew this about Scottish traditions, but did not interrupt Octavian because she enjoyed listening to him speak. There was much she still did not know, so she made it a daily practice to read up on as much history as she could while here.

She planned to do the same upon their return to England because she expected Octavian would be dashing back and forth between London and Greenock, and she hoped to join him on each trip. The inn had a small library and she often spent time in there reading everything she could find. She had even developed an interest in novels and poetry written by Scottish authors and poets.

In truth, she was developing a love for the area and its people, finding a tolerance in them and a freedom for herself that she had never experienced in London.

When they reached their bedchamber, Octavian showed her the correspondence he had received from the Armstrong laird and another from the constable. "Thank you for this, Octavian. It is a great weight off my heart."

He stared at her a moment and grunted. "But you are still troubled. Why, Syd? Sir Henry is dead…" He paused another moment to clear his throat. "By the way, the official report states he was shot by persons unknown in an apparent robbery attempt. This is what was sent to the London magistrate by the constable in the hope of closing the investigation."

"And that is as it shall remain," Syd assured him. "I will never say or do anything to bring harm to the Douglas family. That beast would have killed young Matthew had he not been interrupted by the older brother. It is best to point the finger at no one."

Octavian nodded. "Yet, you are still fretting. What is wrong, Syd? I thought the news would please you."

"It does." She took a moment to wash her hands properly since she hadn't had the chance to do more than rinse them lightly after assisting in the birth. "It pleases me immensely. But we will be returning to London the day after tomorrow and…"

He arched an eyebrow. "Is it the sheep?"

She laughed lightly. "No, although it does irk me that Mr. Campbell will not sell me a single one. That man is stubborn."

"And you're not?" Octavian grinned and gave her a light kiss on the lips. "He's just protecting his business, even though it is a business built on stolen goods. No competitors means higher prices for him. Basic economic theory. What really irks *you* is that you could not sway him. Rest assured, not even Methuselah haranguing him for a thousand years would have accomplished it. The Armstrongs will get their sheep, albeit not the prize merinos."

"It isn't that, Octavian." She dried her hands, then sank onto the bed and sighed.

He settled beside her, his closeness quite comforting to her. "Then what? Tell me, love."

She stared into the silvery embers of his eyes and saw the depth of his concern reflected in them. "*Love,*" she said in a soft voice. "This is what you affectionately call me. It is my greatest joy and also my greatest worry. We've gotten along remarkably well these past few weeks, haven't we?"

He nodded. "It's been wonderful for me, Syd. That's the honest truth."

"For me, too. Here we are in a bedchamber that is so small we cannot turn around without bumping into each other, in a town that is hardly a speck on a map, and I feel freer than I ever have felt in my life. I was sure our marriage would be nothing but constant bickering, but we've hardly had any disagreements." She let out a breathy sigh. "Knowing you are beside me is nourishment to my soul, Octavian. I had no idea how starved I was for it until you came along."

He regarded her with obvious surprise, saying nothing for a long moment. This was her fault. She so rarely reciprocated the loving gestures. But he must have seen into her heart because a slow smile crept across his face. "How is my making you happy a bad thing?"

"It isn't. But this dark cloud of dread will not leave me." She searched his expression, hoping he might know the answer to this worry that plagued her. But how could he when she could not explain it herself? "I hope it is just me being afraid to accept this affection growing between us. It is such a wonderful feeling."

"But?"

"This sense of doom will not leave me. It is like a sword hovering over my head and just waiting to drop on me. I wish we could stay here and never return to London. Is it horrible of me to admit I would not care if I ever saw my parents again?"

"They leave a lot to be desired, but I thought you loved them? You were so worried that Sir Henry had harmed your father. Does this sense of doom you feel concern them? Shall we talk about it, Syd?"

"That's just it. I don't know to begin to explain it. What I *feel* does concern my parents, but only in the sense they will play a part in my undoing. Hasn't my father already wreaked havoc on our lives?"

Octavian nodded. "I don't think I can ever forgive him for trying to sell you to Sir Henry."

She felt the anger seethe inside of him at the reminder of what had brought them to this point. She was also angry, but much of it was tempered by her love for her father. Yet, she also felt so much resentment. Perhaps this is why she was overset, this mix of feelings so at odds with each other. "What worries me most is that something terrible is going to happen to split you and me apart once we are back in London. I am usually so logical, but I cannot make sense of this foreboding."

He cleared his throat. "Syd, do not get angry with me...but you are not always as sensible or logical as you think you are. There's a depth of feeling in you that often controls your actions and compels you to do things that are not always wise or safe."

"Which you refer to as rash and foolhardy," she said with some dismay. "But it is not so. I am logical. However, it is merely a logic different from yours."

He gave her hand a gentle squeeze. "You took risks for your friends and charged into places where you should not have gone."

"I had to help Adela, and would do so again if the need arose. Same for helping Marigold. Gory never needed my help, but I would have done whatever I could for her if ever it was necessary."

"Then let's hope it is never necessary," Octavian grumbled. "I do not ever wish to see you hurt."

"I know. You have always been my protector, although I never understood why you ever bothered with me when you had women aplenty fawning over you. Not to mention, the gossip rags were all reporting that you and Lady Clementine were an item."

"We were never an item," he insisted.

Syd regarded him dubiously. "Perhaps not in your mind, but everyone else thought you were going to offer for her. However, my point is that Adela, Gory, Marigold and I are a sisterhood, and each of us would not hesitate to run to the aid of whichever of us was in trouble. Oh, and that isn't the point I was trying to make, either."

He nodded. "You are trying to make sense of your feeling of doom."

"Yes, and it is this inability to understand why I feel the way I do that troubles me. My skin prickles. I shiver at the thought of returning to England. I want to cling to these days of bliss so fiercely because I know they will disappear once we are back in London. Is it just me being foolish? Or am I sensing something real?"

"It is real in that you are dealing with a new experience and struggling to accept it."

"New experience?"

"That of a normal family life. The life you deserved but was always denied to you. Throughout your childhood, all you remember is having happiness snatched from you."

She nodded. "Yes, it was always this way."

"The impact on you was profound, Syd. Every time you felt safe or content, that feeling was soon upended by something your parents said or did. But I am here by your side now, aching to protect you and keep you safe. I'll be here forever if you want me to be."

Octavian had such a soothing way about him, providing a comfort and assurance she had never felt before. His kindness made her want to cry, for this was the push and pull inside of her. She wanted to reach for that happiness, but was so afraid it would be snatched from her grasp as soon as she let down her defenses.

For this reason, she was so afraid to open her heart.

But she was so ready to do so.

Octavian was her dream man, and she wanted theirs to be a

true and loving marriage.

"Syd, do you want this, too?"

"Do I want us to be together forever?" She nodded. "I want this probably more than you. I am just so awful at showing it."

"Because you have always been disappointed when giving anyone – meaning your parents – your love. Now, you are struggling with giving your heart to me and having it crushed. Your fear will fade with time. It will fade," he insisted. "All you have to do is make our marriage real. Commit to me, Syd."

She dared not.

It still felt as though she was jumping into dark waters.

Dangerous waters where she might drown.

To give him her love, to accept this happiness, and then have it all cruelly taken from her…she would never recover from losing Octavian.

Octavian sighed and drew her into his arms when she buried her face in her hands to avoid his gaze. "I need more time, Octavian."

"All right, love."

But how much longer would he wait?

Did he mean it when he said forever?

Adela and Marigold had made happy marriages. They were in love with their husbands and completely committed to them, yet still maintained their own desires, hopes, and dreams. Neither of them, as far as she knew, ever walked around in fear of their marriage suddenly falling apart. They trusted their husbands and adored them.

She certainly felt the same way about Octavian.

Had she not always said she trusted him more than she trusted herself? No man was ever more worthy of her adoration. "Thank you for being so understanding, Octavian."

"I have no choice, Syd."

She lifted her head and turned to him. "What do you mean? Our marriage can still be annulled. You know I will not fight you if you decide to walk away."

"My heart will never allow me to walk away from you. How many times must I say it before you will believe me? I do not want to spend my life without you. So, you see. It is not about your taking the choice from me. I have already taken it away from myself."

"And you are waiting for me to do the same for myself."

He nodded. "You are the bravest girl I have ever met, Syd. Find the courage to make our marriage permanent and unbreakable."

She said nothing, now eager to see her friends when she returned to London and confide in them. They would help her find the courage to do what she already knew was the right step for her.

Octavian was convinced it was the right step for him, too.

She hated these doubts that were holding her back.

Octavian regarded her thoughtfully.

"Never mind," she said. "Let's prepare for Lady Lennox's dinner party. Which gown should I wear?" She left his side and crossed the small room to open the armoire and draw out her two evening gowns. She held them up against herself for his perusal. "The lilac or the rose?"

"The rose. It picks up the color in your cheeks."

"So, you don't like the lilac?"

He chuckled. "I like them both. But the lilac shows a little too much of your bosom, and I would rather not share your *assets* with others."

"It is modest by London standards of fashion. And I always wear it with a fichu, anyway."

"Then wear the lilac, but I prefer the rose."

"The rose, it is." She set about preparing for the evening.

He stretched out on the bed and watched her, his grin rakish and admiring as she slipped out of her day gown and began to wash up.

"Your *assets* are glorious, by the way."

She blushed. "Shouldn't you start getting ready?"

"No, it'll take me five minutes and we still have almost an hour before we have to be on our way. I'm enjoying the show."

"I'm going to hit you with this wet cloth if you don't behave. But I'm glad you like my body."

"That is an understatement. I cannot keep my hands off you whenever we are in bed together. Which brings up something that has been on my mind. What sleeping arrangements do you want for us when we return to London? We'll be staying with Ambrose and Adela for the moment, but we can search for a place of our own to let, if you prefer."

"I think it makes more sense to stay with Ambrose and Adela until your Admiralty assignment is better settled."

"Separate bedrooms?"

Her heart tugged. "If that is your wish."

He rose to come to her side, his magnificence hard to overlook while he stood so close. "You know it isn't. My preference is one bedchamber and one bed to share. You seem comfortable with this arrangement here, but London will be quite different for you, especially if we are not going to make our marriage real."

"I know." She set aside her wash cloth and turned to face him. "It is on my mind constantly, but can we please leave it unanswered for now? This feeling of dread that plagues me does not come from any doubts I have about you. The fear is of an outside force destroying our happiness."

"And you think that outside force will show itself once we are in London?"

She nodded.

He caressed her cheek. "All right, I'll leave it alone for now. You'll make the decisions once we are in London. Just keep in mind that we are stronger together than apart."

She melted into his arms when he put them around her. "It would be so much simpler if we hated each other."

"Syd, never say that."

"All right, I'm sorry. Let's hope for the best."

He kissed her on the brow and then eased away. "Come on, Cheerful. We'll be late if we don't get moving."

She laughed and flicked a few droplets of water at him. "You are the one who is moving slow as a turtle, you fiend."

Lady Lennox's dinner party was bittersweet and Syd felt more sentimental than usual. But she made it through the evening without bursting into tears or begging Octavian to leave her behind while he returned to London. Avoiding London would ease her feeling of doom, but it would also mean being without Octavian, and this felt even worse.

That night, she held onto him tightly.

Her dreams were full of gathering storms and howling winds roiling an angry sea. She was lost amid the vast sea, calling out for Octavian to save her from drowning, but he could not hear her as she drifted away from him. The harder she tried to swim back to him, the fiercer the current and tumultuous waves pulled them apart.

Then, she could no longer see him.

She began to shiver.

She would not stop shivering.

"Syd. Syd, love." She heard Octavian talking to her and realized he was trying to shake her awake. "Open your eyes, love. You're having a bad dream."

It took her a moment to shake out of her dream and regain her senses. "What?" She groaned. "What time is it?"

"Still early, sweetheart."

She noticed the grayness of the night and realized it was approaching dawn, but still too early even for the cock's crow.

"Rough night, Syd? Want to tell me about it?"

She snuggled against him and nodded. "Horrible night," she admitted. "I kept trying to swim to you but kept getting pulled away. It was awful. I kept losing you."

"I'm sorry, love. That's why you were crying out in your sleep."

"Yes. I'm so sorry."

"Don't be. That's what I'm here for."

He was her wonderful protector, and now he had her cradled in his arms. "Octavian, I've come to a decision."

"You have? What decision might that be?" Although he sounded calm and revealed nothing in his expression, she felt his body tense and understood he was worried about what she was about to tell him.

"No separate bedchambers for us in London. We stay together, for you are my husband and I am your wife. Whatever our fate, we must face it together. You said last night that you cannot be apart from me. It is the same for me concerning you. This is what my horrible dream was about, the agony of not being with you."

"Blessed saints, Syd. Dare I ask? Are you ready to make this make-believe marriage real?"

CHAPTER 14

OCTAVIAN REALIZED THEY would be married slightly over a month by the time he and Syd returned to London. Their trip home necessitated several detours, the first being a three-day stopover in Glasgow to confirm the navy ships awarded under previous contracts were properly underway and no unauthorized changes had been made to their designs.

Glasgow was a dingy, rainy city, but one would think it was clear skies and sunshine the way Syd chirped about the city and its *enlightened* residents. "You will never believe what I did today, Octavian," she told him while they dined in the privacy of their guestroom later that evening in Glasgow's fanciest hotel, The Harley. It was quite a change from the simple Seafarer's Inn, for it was far grander in size, had marble floors and crystal chandeliers, and larger beds. But Syd still managed to paste herself to his side during the night, something Octavian did not mind at all.

"What did you do?" he replied between bites, eager to hear what had Syd's eyes alight and a beaming smile on her pretty lips.

"Well, first I went…"

The simple question turned into a twenty minute recitation, but he leaned back, sipping his wine and devouring a most delicious roast duck in plum sauce while he listened in good cheer. Syd was happier than he had ever seen her, chattering like a magpie between bites of her salmon and potatoes. "Can you believe it, Octavian?"

While he spent his time at the navy shipyard, Syd frequented the Glagow museums and medical school where she was permitted to observe the medical students in their studies. "Did you really observe the students dissecting cadavers?"

"Yes, and the professor let me lead the class when he learned I was involved in research projects at the Huntsford Academy forensic laboratory. He begged me to give an impromptu lecture."

Octavian chuckled. "Of course. Why am I not surprised?"

"It is not surprising at all," she insisted, taking a sip of her wine.

He motioned for the wine steward to pour him another glass, then turned to respond to her. "That's what I said, Syd."

"Thank you, Octavian. If I were a man, I would be renowned in the field of forensics by now," she insisted. "London society believes I am quite the ghoul. But everyone here accepts me as quite the scholar."

"I know that. I am glad they have realized it." He leaned over and kissed her on the hand while she was in the middle of expounding on her achievements.

"Stop giving me those steamy looks or you will make me forget what I was saying." She sighed and cast him a loving look, a sign she did not really mind his warm regard. "Afterward, the dean of the medical school gave me a private tour of their classrooms and laboratories, and asked if I had any suggestions for their improvement. Can you believe it?"

"Yes, I can. I keep telling you that you are a treasure. See, others believe it, too. Did you give him any suggestions?"

She rolled her eyes. "Have you ever known me to keep my mouth shut?"

He laughed.

"I gave him at least a dozen. He thought they were very good and promised to implement them."

"That's my girl."

"Are you truly proud of what I did?"

The question surprised him. "Syd, do you still not know me at all? I am tremendously proud of you. If I had wanted a goose-brain for a wife, I would have settled on Lady Clementine. Who, by the way, is a vicious goose-brain, so I probably would not have chosen her under any circumstances. Tell me about the museums you visited. Did you stop running around at all today?"

"I will admit to being exhausted now. But we have so little time here and there is so much to see and do. The museum director afforded me the same courtesy as the medical school dean had done." She cleared her throat. "I might have let slip that I was the sister-in-law of the Duke of Huntsford and could put in a good word with him about their museum."

Octavian arched an eyebrow as he took a sip of his ale. "Indeed, having connections has its privileges."

She winced. "I know I overstepped and took advantage, but there is so much still to see. As I just said, there is so little time in which to do it."

"I'll be traveling between London, Glasgow, and Greenock regularly. Come with me whenever you wish. Just slow down on this visit, will you? You'll have time to do whatever you find of interest over the coming months."

"You would take me with you?"

He groaned. "Yes, I have no desire to be without you."

She set down her fork and cast him a dazzling smile. "Octavian, that is a lovely thing to say."

"It's the truth, Syd. You know it is. I haven't kept my feelings to myself."

"I know. You are wonderful."

He grunted. "So are you. Who else but you would have accomplished all this in a day? You haven't once complained about being left on your own. Nor did you tear through the shops and buy trinkets you did not need, or bemoan the lack of decent modistes or the miserable Scottish weather." He glanced out the window, noting the rain pounding against the panes with a rapid *pik-pok*. "I like being married to you."

"Feeling is mutual, you big ox." She blushed and shifted uncomfortably in her chair because any mention of permanence in their marital relation was still upsetting to her.

He ought to have kept quiet about it, for her fear of their marriage crumbling once they reached London was deeply embedded within her and not a jest to be treated lightly. He reached for her hand. "Tell me about the rest of your day."

She placed her small hand in his. "Was this not enough for one day? I start again bright and early tomorrow. How was yours? Can you talk about any of it?"

"No, it is all top secret. A few minor issues but nothing serious."

They finished their meal and retired to bed.

Syd had truly worn herself out and was asleep before her head hit the pillow. Octavian drew her up against him because Syd slept better while pressed to his warm body. Perhaps he was the one who slept better knowing she was beside him.

He had grown used to her shapely softness and the lovely scent of her skin that reminded him of wild roses kissed by the morning dew.

Ah, well.

Who could explain why they felt so comfortable with each other and craved each other's touch? The sense of rightness was primal in him, arising from somewhere deep within his soul. It had nothing to do with reason or logic.

He read quietly in bed for a few hours, and then set aside his book and fell asleep himself. But before he did, he made certain to draw her into his arms.

Octavian was in good spirits, for Syd's expeditions over the following days pleased her to no end, and that in turn pleased him. However, he was not all that delighted when she began returning to their hotel after nightfall. She did this for two days in a row, and would have driven him mad with worry had he not arranged for a carriage and driver to remain with her all the while. Syd was adventurous, and he wanted someone armed with a weapon and knowledgeable about the city to escort her wherever she wished to go.

He was relieved when they left Glasgow, although Syd did not really give him serious cause to worry. She spent almost all her time either at the medical school or at the museum. But she often lost all sense of time and only left when they politely kicked her out.

The rest of their week was spent in travel, his assignment

taking him next to Edinburgh for a brief visit, and then finally to making their way south to London. As the sun began to set, they passed by the Eildon Hills and then turned slightly north to come upon the ancient wonder of Melrose Abbey, a magnificent structure built by the Cistercian monks.

Octavian noticed a fair going on in the nearby town of Melrose. "Care to stay over and stroll through the fair tomorrow, Syd?"

At her nod, he had their driver stop at one of the local inns on the chance they might have a room available for the night. This slight change in plans would not take them out of the way since they would have had to stop within an hour's time as darkness fell.

"I see sheep!" Syd poked her head out of the carriage window for a better view of the fairgrounds.

So did he.

There were tents of all sizes flying their pennants of brilliant colors. Reds, golds, greens. The tents were mostly plain, but some were emblazoned with a clan insignia. Many bore designs of dragons, thistles, and claymores.

"Sheep! Sheep!" Syd cried out excitedly as they drew closer.

Octavian loved this vitality about her.

He laughed. "Ah, then we are compelled to stop here and explore."

If the weather held, they could spend tomorrow at leisure, browsing the stalls and enjoying the food and entertainment provided. This was no small affair, he realized while taking note of the sizeable crowd.

It was obvious that visitors had converged on this spot from all over the country.

He worried about finding a place to spend the night, but the task was accomplished with surprising ease. They found a charming inn on an elegant Melrose square across the field from the fairgrounds, and were settled into their cozy quarters just before dusk.

Syd was delighted and continually cast him breathtaking smiles as they dined in the crowded common room. She had more smiles for him when they retired to bed. "Are you going to dream of me or sheep?" he teased, taking her into his arms, as had become his habit, when she climbed in beside him.

"If I bleat in my sleep, then you'll know that you have lost out."

He laughed and kissed her. "Sweet dreams, love."

"Sweet dreams, Octavian," she purred and kissed him back.

He knew Syd was happy because she fell asleep right away, her head resting against his chest and her body curled up against his own.

He followed soon after, for there were sheep to be purchased come morning and Syd viewed it as serious business. An entire flock to be purchased, to be precise, and his first chore tomorrow morning would be to acquire them for the Armstrong clan.

Since Melrose was within a day's ride of Gretna Green, he and Syd were not all that surprised to encounter Laird Armstrong and his men wandering the fairgrounds the following afternoon.

Syd dragged Octavian along as she rushed forward to greet them. "Laird Armstrong! What a fortunate coincidence." She cast the laird an enchanting smile that did not fail to charm him. "My husband and I were just deciding how best to deliver the sheep to you, and here you are. It is most convenient. Would you be able to take delivery of them right here and now?"

The laird glanced at Octavian, obviously surprised. "Ye bought sheep for us?"

He nodded. "We promised you, did we not?"

"Och, aye. But I seriously did not think an Englishman would keep to his word."

"I always do."

Syd nodded. "He always does. He is the most honest man you will ever encounter."

Octavian grinned, not minding at all that Syd sang his praises. He was no longer surprised by her compliments because there was a traditional side to her that did love and honor him. It was the obeying part she had yet to get right, and he fully expected her to run amok at some point during the fair. There was too much going on and too many people around for something *not* to happen.

Perhaps he was turning into a mother hen and worrying too much.

Jamie Armstrong had accompanied his laird, another fortunate circumstance because Octavian could discuss hiring workers for the Greenock shipyard contracts now, as well. "Jamie, the manager position is yours if you want it." He then turned to the laird. "Armstrong, I have a place for nine more workers. Let me be clear, Jamie will be in charge. He will assign each man to his daily task and oversee what they are doing. Any of your men interested?"

The old lord's eyes widened and then began to sparkle with amusement. "Blessed saints, Thorne. Seems attempting to rob ye was the best thing we could have done. Ye're keeping to that promise, as well? In truth, I would not have blamed ye if ye could no' have delivered on those jobs."

"What say you? Would your men be willing? I need good workers. No idlers."

Syd, who had been standing by Octavian's side all the while, now cleared her throat. "Not your son, however."

Octavian groaned. "Syd, hush."

She tipped her chin up in defiance. "He was rude, hotheaded, and meant to cause trouble. My lord, I believe your son is best kept with you if you ever hope to mold him into a proper leader. Don't you agree?"

Octavian put an arm around her waist and drew her up against his side, the gesture instinctively protective because – true to herself – Syd had formed an ill opinion of the laird's son, was determined not to let him anywhere near those ships being built, and had now insulted the father by telling him that his son was a fool and a lout.

She viewed it as her moral duty to be honest.

At this moment, Octavian thought tact, not honesty, was the better virtue.

That they were not *her* ships nor was it her decision to make, did not stop her from spouting her opinion. This was Syd at her righteous best. "For pity's sake, Syd."

While the laird might have accepted the insult quietly, the

laird's son had come up behind her and heard every word.

"A hotheaded lout, am I?" he shouted.

Octavian gave Syd a light squeeze in the hope of keeping her quiet while he took care of the man and calmed the situation, but she had other ideas. "I was speaking to your father, not to you. However, since you overheard, I am not taking it back until you apologize to me for your boorish behavior toward me when we first met."

"Blessed saints, Syd," Octavian muttered.

She gasped. "I–"

And then clamped her mouth shut upon finally noticing the laird's son had withdrawn a knife. "Oh."

"Does yer wife always lead ye about by the nose, Thorne? A proper beating will cure her of her outspoken ways."

Octavian growled low in his throat. "My wife leads me about by the *heart*. Let me be clear, I will never raise a hand to her nor will I ever allow anyone else to do so."

The laird's son sneered.

The laird marched over and cuffed his offspring. "Grow up, lad. How do ye think to lead our clan when all ye know how to do is bully and insult? Put yer dirk away or I shall take it away from ye. Is yer behavior not proving Mrs. Thorne's exact point?"

His son stormed off, no doubt to the closest tavern to drown his sorrows in ale. Octavian doubted the young man would ever reform his ways, for there were such people who could not see beyond their noses. They blamed everyone but themselves for anything that went wrong, and always looked upon others for what they could do for *him* rather than what *he* could do for them.

He hoped he was wrong, for the father was a man Octavian respected.

Had the son inherited any of the older man's qualities?

Octavian and the laird exchanged apologies, then agreed to meet by the sheep pens an hour from now to finalize the ownership papers for the flock.

Once Jamie and the laird had left them, Octavian turned to Syd.

She gazed at him with defiance in her eyes. "Do not say it. That man is trouble and his father knows it. Jamie could not have handled him if he were part of the Armstrong crew sent up to Greenock. The arrogant oaf would have undercut Jamie's authority at every turn and possibly sabotaged the ships being built out of spite."

Octavian raked a hand through his hair. "We all know he has some growing up to do, Syd. Even his father cannot deny it. But you should not have said it aloud. As for sabotage, that is a hanging offense. Not even he, as petulant and shortsighted as he is, would ever do anything so foolish. That would be a betrayal of his country."

"The ships may be built in Scotland, but they are English ships. He would view it as betraying the English and think of himself as a hero. I know you did not want him in Greenock. Was it not better that I take the blame in forbidding him rather than you? Everyone in England already thinks of me as unreasonable. Let the Scots think so, too."

He wanted to remain angry with her, but it seemed he was incapable of holding anything but love for her. Lord, he was in trouble if this is how their exchanges would always end. "Syd, blast it. You are my wife. I want people to think of you as a princess, not an impertinent, outspoken pest."

"A princess?" She shook her head and laughed. "There is no one in the world who would think this of me."

"I do," he said in all seriousness.

She stared at him in stunned silence.

Was she waiting for him to declare it a jest? She would have to wait forever because he was not taking back his words. Yes, she was irritating. Yes, she was outspoken.

And yes, he loved her.

After a moment, she released a ragged breath. "Octavian, you cannot say such things to me."

"Why not?" In truth, it hurt his heart to see the damage her parents had done to make her feel so undeserving. This was the very reason she was struggling to accept the permanence of their marriage. The happier she was, the more anxious she became. "Why will you not accept that you have good qualities?"

"Because it isn't true. I am no one's princess. Never have been."

"As told to you by an inept mother and a worthless father." He struggled to subdue his anger at everyone who had ever cast her down. "Who are you going to believe? Them or me? Moments ago, you declared to Laird Armstrong that I was the most honest man you knew. Were you lying to him?"

"No!"

"Then why will you not believe me?" He did not mean to growl at her, but this discussion seemed to come up every day. Instead of accepting the truth, she always retreated to this familiar position of denigrating herself.

Dismissing affection was how she protected herself.

He would not allow her to do this with him any longer. "Are you telling me that I have made a poor choice in a wife? Or that the brightest minds in Glasgow, Greenock, and London are wrong to think you are clever?"

Syd glanced around the crowded fair, obviously unhappy to be having this discussion amid sheep, goats, and other cattle, or amid the crushing crowd. Many of the fair goers were already in their cups, if the shouts and jeers from the nearby ale tent were any indication. "How about you be honest with yourself for a change and admit Lady Clementine would have been a better fit for you. A proper, biddable wife."

"Where did that come from?" he asked, making a strangled sound of disbelief. "Surely, you are jesting. Lady Clementine would have made me miserable. Marriage to her would have been the true farce."

She fixed her stubborn stare on him. "Men were tripping over each other to gain her attention and win her hand."

"I wasn't."

She snorted. "You were first in line, Octavian. Do you forget already? It must be so convenient to have a selective memory."

"I will not deny that I once considered her, but I just as quickly dismissed her. She was not *you*."

Syd snorted again. "Oh, yes. I am such a prize."

"To me you are. Stop doing that, Syd. You come up with all

sorts of ridiculous reasons to push me away whenever you fear we are getting too close. You are terrified you will inevitably disappoint me, and I am telling you that it will never happen."

She turned away and started to walk off, but he took her hand and kept her close for fear of losing her in the crowd.

Perhaps one day she would agree with him when he told her that she was worthy.

Obviously, it would not be today.

It irked him how contradictory Syd could be. "Be angry with me, if you must. But stop tossing Lady Clementine's name in my face. All right? You know there was never anything between us. She's just a convenient cannonball you hurl at me to deflect the truth."

She folded her arms across her chest and frowned at him. "And what is that truth?"

"That our marriage has never been make-believe. We are burned into each other's heart. Just accept it."

He felt awful when she practically crumbled before him. He was frustrated, but she was scared and he should have taken it easy on her today. She worked so hard to achieve all she had done despite the obstacles Society tossed in her way.

No medical school would accept her, so she had learned anatomy and the healing arts all on her own. She had mastered them to the point he would trust her before he trusted most doctors in London. Her forensic knowledge was above anyone else in the field, which was why his brother, the Duke of Huntsford, had given her unlimited access to the Huntsford Academy's forensic laboratory.

She was beautiful, honest, and compassionate, and yet, she saw herself as lacking.

The blame lay squarely with her parents.

To bloody hell with them.

"Are you thirsty, Syd? I think we've both gotten a little hot under the collar."

She nodded. "Yes, I'd like that. I'm sorry I am being so difficult."

"I'm no prize," he said with a grunt. "I just want you to be happy."

"I want the same for you," she said softly, placing her arm in his.

"I know." He knew she was in love with him.

Deeply and forever in love with him.

Did this not add to his frustration?

That he had not claimed her as a husband ought to claim his wife was his greatest worry. He had shown her how to satisfy him in other ways. It was not about the sexual pleasure, but about the commitment.

The sex was great.

Syd would have kicked him in the bollocks had she not desired him or wanted his touch. What she felt for him was not a mere, wanton desire but a deep and abiding love. The little hellion had a lot of passion in her, and it was all for him.

All she had to do was accept they were meant for each other.

Octavian kept her close as they made their way through the crowd, but as they neared the one of the refreshment stands, Octavian realized the line was impossibly long. "We'll be standing her into the night. Anyway, I'm not just thirsty but hungry, too. Shall we grab a meal at the inn before I meet with Laird Armstrong?"

"All right. Yes, let's get out of this crush."

The day was not particularly warm, but no one felt the light chill in the air because there were too many bodies in close proximity producing sweat and heat. Nor could he and Syd avoid the odors carried on the breeze since they were standing downwind of the ale tent and the animal pens.

He now led her back to the inn where they were staying for tonight, as well. It was too close to the fairgrounds for his liking, but there was not a spare room to be had elsewhere in Melrose or within twenty miles of the town. They were fortunate that a sudden departure had opened the room for them.

Bribes were not uncommon when rooms were this scarce, but the innkeeper appeared to be an honest man and did not charge them extra. As Syd was quick to point out upon their arrival, no one would dare cheat him since he was the brother of the Duke of

Huntsford. "Yer brother is known in these parts, Captain Thorne. He's an excellent man. Excellent. Ye just call upon me for anything ye or yer wife need. Aye, His Grace is an excellent man."

Octavian grumbled a bit as the man had gushed about Ambrose. Yes, he was a good brother and marvelous man. But he and Julius had worked hard to stand on their own and make something of themselves. However, in instances such as this, he knew better than to allow his pride to stand in the way. There was nothing wrong with occasionally taking advantage of the privileges afforded because of one's connections.

The inn, being in such close proximity to the fairgrounds and having an excellent common room, was packed to the rafters. "Blast, let me see if there is a private dining room to be had. Wait here, Syd. I'll be right back."

Although she had mighty opinions, she herself was not all that big and could not possibly make her way through a throng as tightly packed as this one was.

She surveyed the room and nodded. "All right. Hurry back."

"I will, love." He left her standing at the entrance and brusquely shouldered his way through the mob of diners, many of whom were already unruly and drunk. The wooden floorboards were slippery in some places and sticky in others from all the ale sloshed onto them.

Octavian marveled at the ability of the inn's maids to avoid the outstretched hands and crude advances of several louts who tried to pinch their bottoms or draw them onto their laps as the maids sailed past them. These ladies managed to smoothly dart and dodge between these men while carrying large trays piled high with food for their hungry guests.

This was how he hoped these newly designed navy warships would maneuver at sea, swiftly able to change course, shifting left or right with ease, and agile enough to sail between enemy ships and blast them with their cannons.

He laughed at the idea of comparing these able maids to first rate battleships. The designs for those ships had been in the works for years. They were now drawn and ready to be realized. He was to spend the next few years traveling from shipyard to shipyard to oversee their construction.

He shook out of the thought.

The immediate problem was getting food for him and Syd, and obtaining a quiet place for them to dine.

The harried innkeeper had little time for him just now, but a few coins placed in his gnarled fingers quickly did the trick. There was only one dish served to the crowd, a hearty stew with bits of whatever meat and vegetables remained in the inn's larder. "We've been so busy because of the fair," the innkeeper explained, "that our kitchen ran out of our usual fare hours ago."

"Bring us whatever you have," he said, shouting to be heard above the noise. "And drinks, too. Ale for me and cider for my wife."

He then tossed the man another coin before shoving his way through the crowd to return to Syd. His heart shot into his throat when he reached the entrance to the common room and could not find her. "Syd! Syd!"

Calling her name was useless since noisy crowds were everywhere inside and out in front of the inn. He walked down the street in search of her. People chattered, musicians played, couples were dancing. He asked a few older ladies seated on a bench if they had seen Syd walk by.

"No, captain."

He returned to the inn, his path interrupted by drunks who were roaring with laughter, and a few others who were fighting among themselves. Fortunately, they were too wasted to actually land any solid blows against each other, and one of them passed out at his feet.

Things would only get worse as night fell.

Where was Syd?

He tore up to their room, but she wasn't there.

He ran back downstairs and finally saw her in the small yard behind the inn, surrounded by a group of angry Scots. "Botheration, what did you do now, Syd?" he muttered and hastened outside. The group surrounding her were all men, and some of them had drawn their dirks. "Lord, give me strength," he prayed under his breath and walked out.

That giant chip Syd carried on her shoulder was going to get her into serious trouble one of these days.

He hoped today was not the day.

Blessed saints.

What had she said to get these Scots so riled?

CHAPTER 15

OCTAVIAN DID NOT recognize any of these men who were standing around Syd and scowling at her. Syd was scowling just as fiercely back at them. Had he thought her clever? Sometimes, the girl did not have a lick of sense and would get them both killed if she opened her mouth again. "There you are, love," he said, striding into the fray and placing a protective arm around her. "Our table is ready."

He tried to walk her out of the circle, but several men barred his way. "Is she yers?" one of them asked.

He nodded. "Yes, unfortunately. I would love for you to take her off my hands, but I made a vow to protect her when we married and I aim to keep it. Captain Octavian Thorne, at your service."

"A *Sassenach*," another man said and spat on the ground in a purposeful attempt to insult him.

"I will not deny it," he replied, unwilling to take the bait. "Nor am I looking for trouble. I merely want to escort my wife to the inn for our supper."

The man who appeared to be their leader peered at Syd for what felt like a very long while. "And ye say he is yer husband?"

"That big ox?" She turned her scowl on Octavian. "*Unfortunately?* You said *unfortunately*, I was your wife?"

"Syd! This is no time for games. And can you blame me? I leave you alone for two minutes and you've gotten yourself into a fight." Octavian had spent years in the Royal Navy in command of one of the finest fleet ships battling pirates, foreign privateers, and enemy frigates throughout the world. He was not used to losing battles, and he was not about to lose this one, either. He did not want to hurt any of these men, but he would if they dared set a hand on her.

But Syd was on the warpath and not about to back down. "What is it with you arrogant Scots? Do you think women really want to be ogled and pawed by drunken strangers? And you dare to draw a knife on me for interfering with your debauched advances? I'll have you know, my husband is the finest warrior ever in existence and he'll take all of you on if you do not apologize to me immediately. Would you ever allow anyone to behave in this abominable fashion with your wives, sisters, or daughters? Or treat your mother in this fashion? Of course not! So who will be the first one of you man enough to apologize to me?"

"Bloody, little fool," Octavian muttered, staring down at her when she edged back to his side, "do you wish to see blood shed? Specifically mine?"

Fortunately, no one heard her answer as a mail coach thundered up to their inn, which happened to be a popular coaching inn, and rolled to a stop beside them at just that moment.

Syd eyed it, no doubt hoping to escape onto it before it took off again.

Octavian wanted to slap manacles on her, one on her wrist and the other on his because this brash bluestocking wife of his was not going anywhere but back to London with him.

He still did not know what had happened to cause this confrontation or who these men were. Obviously, they were not from the Armstrong clan.

He could do with a few Armstrong men to back him up right now.

Syd seemed determined to have him die in a blaze of glory because she was still berating these louts who looked as confused as he had ever seen any men look.

Well, Syd had a knack for evoking this response from every male she came across.

Why was he bothering with her?

How had he fallen so deeply in love with her?

And why was he stifling a rumble of laughter as she drew another breath and continued to excoriate these stunned Scots.

But there was never a doubt in his mind that he needed to be with Syd forever, even if forever was another few minutes before they were both carved to little pieces by these dirk-wielding men. He still did not question his sanity or the rightness of his decision to marry her.

He would marry her a thousand times over, even if it meant racing north to Gretna Green each time.

The brash bluestocking got under his skin.

He hadn't had a decent night's sleep since meeting her.

She was his wife. *His wife.* And he had yet to properly bed her.

He did not want to die without staking that claim on her.

"Does the lass never shut up?" the one who appeared to be their leader asked him.

Octavian shrugged. "Not when she is this angry. What did you do to rile her?"

"We did no' touch her," another in their group retorted.

But Octavian knew they had done something sinful.

The fun was over.

It was time for him to defend Syd's honor.

He simply was not sure how to manage it and stay alive. Twelve to one odds did not look promising. "Syd, is this true? Did any of them touch you in an inappropriate way?"

She glowered at a big, redheaded lad who was holding his hands protectively over his male parts. "That oaf tried, but I set him straight."

Gad, she must have kicked him in the bollocks and doubled him over. That man was not going to be standing *straight* any time soon.

But why quibble?

She turned to another man who had a bleeding lip. "He tried, too. Shameful! Where is your mother? I am going to tell her what you did."

"Me ma's dead," the man retorted.

Syd's expression turned sympathetic. "Oh, I am truly sorry."

She then walked over and kicked him in the shin. "All the more shameful of you! She must be weeping for your soul in heaven."

Octavian turned upon hearing a burst of laughter from behind him, and recognized Laird Armstrong's son, Angus, and his loutish friends as they now approached the other Scots. "What's the problem, MacGregor?"

"This Sassenach witch insulted my men."

Angus inspected the two injured men. "Looks like she did more than insult them. What did they attempt to do to her?"

"They did not set a hand on her," MacGregor replied.

Syd gasped. "But they tried! Do not pass them off as innocent. They ought to be praising the saints that I fended them off because my husband would be tearing them limb from limb right now if they had succeeded in setting a finger on me." She cast the Armstrong lad a look of reproof and curled her hands into fists. "Are you going to defend them?"

He raised his hands in mock surrender. "No, I'm here to defend you."

Her eyes widened. "You are?"

She glanced at Octavian, obviously surprised and seeking his assurance before returning her attention to the laird's son. "Truly, Angus?"

He nodded. "Yes, ye little troublemaker. Ye may be a Sassenach witch, but ye're *our* Sassenach witch, and my father will no' let anyone harm ye in our territory."

The MacGregor laird scoffed. "Ye're well outside of yer territory here in Melrose."

"It is close enough, and I say ye are not to harm her or her husband. Ye ought to be grateful I've stopped ye before ye attacked him. That man is Captain Octavian Thorne, brother of the Duke of Huntsford."

"*That* Captain Thorne of the Royal Navy?" asked the man with the bleeding lip. "My brother sailed under yer command. Ye should have told us who ye were."

"I did." Obviously, the man had been too busy nursing his cuts and bruises to pay attention when he introduced himself.

"Is this really yer wife, Captain Thorne?"

Syd gasped again. "Of course, I am! Did you think I made it up? Or that my husband would go along with the ruse if he wasn't really my husband? Of all the inconceivable gall!"

Laird Armstrong's son burst out laughing again. "Ye know, Thorne, it is not difficult to divorce her. Are ye certain ye wish to stay married to the little harpy?"

Octavian grinned, realizing the situation was no longer dire. The arrival of the Armstrong men, and the fact that a MacGregor's brother had served under him, had cooled their bloodlust. Still, he wanted to get Syd back inside the inn as soon as possible. He also meant to let them all know this was a love match and he would kill any man who harmed his wife. "I'm certain. I would marry her a thousand times over."

The MacGregor lord eyed him dubiously. "Well then, I'm thinking ye need to marry the lass once more. Here and now. Any objections?"

Syd was getting angry again. "Are you doubting my word? Or my husband's? Are you calling us liars? Are you calling the Armstrongs liars? Their laird witnessed our ceremony. Just ask any of these men and they will answer truthfully," she said, pointing to the laird's son and his friends.

"Well, lass," the laird's son said with a rather smug look on his face. "I saw ye and Captain Thorne in Gretna Green. I saw ye enter the blacksmith's shop. But I did not actually see the ceremony."

"What ceremony?" Syd said in a huff. "It was nothing more than an exchange of names and a paper to sign. Your father was a witness. You know he was. Why are you being so difficult? If you wished for revenge, well now you've had it. If you are not going to tell the MacGregors the truth, then just go away."

Octavian groaned, for Syd had reached her breaking point and was going to get them back in serious trouble if she did not walk away now. But now the MacGregors and the Armstrongs blocked their way when he attempted to escort her back inside the inn.

He really did not want to start throwing punches, for the odds were now even more against him. Since these Scots would not allow them to leave, Octavian saw no other alternative to mitigate the situation. "Syd, will you marry me again?"

"What?"

He took both of her hands in his. "MacGregor did not have a bad idea. Our ceremony was nothing you had ever dreamed of or deserve. So, marry me again."

"A second ceremony? But that will not change anything."

"I've told you before, I would marry you a thousand times over. I mean to prove it."

She sank against his chest and burst into tears.

That sobered all the men fast.

Apparently, he was not the only one left helpless by a woman's tears.

He wrapped his arms tightly around her. "Oh, Syd. I'm sorry I left you even for a moment."

"It wasn't your fault. But I didn't know what else to do when I saw them grabbing that young girl and she cried out for help, but no one else stopped to help her. I could not just leave her to their mercy."

"Hush, love." When he turned again, he realized the crowd had doubled. There were now a dozen women gathered around them. "She's the one who saved me," an equally tearful, young woman said, pointing to Syd. "I'm sorry it took me so long to come back to ye, but the oafs drinking at the inn would no' listen to me or lift a finger to come to yer rescue when I turned to them for help."

"Shameful," an older woman beside her said.

"And then I tried to find my grandmother." She motioned to the woman beside her. "Did they harm ye, missus? We'll see them hanged if they did."

None of the men were laughing now.

An older gentleman pushed his way through the crowd. Octavian realized this was the MacGregor laird. *The* MacGregor, for there was no denying his commanding air of authority. He turned in anger toward the two men Syd had managed to injure. "What is going on here? Was this more than having a little sport with a Sassenach lass? Did ye assault the Campbell girl?"

The two men cast their eyes down.

MacGregor began to pace in front of his men. "Of all the stupid, reckless, idiotic…I have no' the words to sufficiently describe how disappointing and reprehensible yer behavior…dear heaven, a *Campbell* lass? Have I raised two idiot sons? A plague on both of ye!" He looked up at the sky. "Take me now! Strike me down with a lightning bolt so I need no longer endure this shame!"

Of course, the skies were clear and no bolt was going to come down out of the blue and roast him. After a moment, the MacGregor laird sighed in dismay and turned to the elegant woman who had to be the Campbell girl's grandmother. In truth, she appeared to be the respected matriarch of the entire Campbell clan. "I shall make this right, Lady Campbell. What will ye ask of us?"

The matriarch came over to Syd and lovingly stroked her hair. "Tell me what happened to ye after ye saved my granddaughter."

Syd wiped her tears and turned to the woman. "I hit them, and was berating them when the other MacGregors arrived. Then a moment later my husband arrived to save me. Then the Armstrongs arrived to save *him* because they saw he was outnumbered."

"So, these MacGregor lads did not manage to lay a hand on you?"

"No, ma'am, but it wasn't from want of trying."

The old woman sighed, and then turned to the MacGregor laird. "Yer sons are fortunate the girl was able to fight back. But for this egregious misdeed, I'll take ten of yer merino sheep."

Syd's eyes widened. "You have—"

Octavian tightened his arms around her. "Hush, Syd. Let's see how this plays out."

He felt her excitement as he held her against his chest, the quickening beat of her heart because of those blasted sheep. Never mind that two oafs attempted to accost her and might have hurt her when she ran to the rescue of the Campbell girl.

MacGregor let out a howl. "Och, no! Not my blessed sheep! Ask anything else of me. Ye have enough of yer own merino sheep. Ye dinna need mine."

"Will ye already go back on yer word?" the old woman remarked. "I see now where yer sons learned their reprehensible–"

"Och, dinna start on me. Ye'll get them, Lady Campbell. Ye know I am a man of my word." The concession obviously pained MacGregor. It was obvious to Octavian that the laird would have preferred to give up a limb rather than those precious animals. It seemed the crusty, old farmer in Greenock was not the only Scot who had stolen them out of Spain.

Come to think of it, he was a Campbell, too.

Obviously, the MacGregors and the Campbells had sailed to Spain and stolen those sheep. Whether they had done so together or each clan on their own, Octavian had no idea.

Laird Armstrong's son now stepped forward to address Lady Campbell. "I'll buy those sheep from ye."

She arched a silver eyebrow. "And why would I ever sell them to ye, Angus?"

"Because they are not for me or those in the Armstrong clan. They are for Mrs. Thorne."

Syd gasped. "For me?"

He nodded. "Aye, by way of apology for my behavior toward you. Despite my rudeness, ye still found it in yer heart to help us. Ye could have demanded yer husband not help us, but ye went out of yer way to support our clan. Yer husband told my father of yer attempts to acquire those merino sheep for us."

"But I didn't succeed," she said with notable disappointment.

"Ye tried with all yer heart."

She nodded. "I did, and you know how persistent I can be."

The laird's son laughed. "Och, aye. Painfully aware."

Lady Campbell cleared her throat. "I will not give ye the sheep, Angus. However, I will give them to Mrs. Thorne as reward for protecting my granddaughter." She turned to Syd. "They are yers to do with as ye wish."

Octavian could not suppress his smile.

Syd had gotten her merino sheep.

Of course, she had.

Was there ever a doubt that she would somehow work this miracle? Which now meant the Armstrongs would get their woolen industry underway because she was going to turn them over to Laird Armstrong.

Which she did when the laird arrived a few moments later and was told all that had transpired. "Ye mean my son was not the instigator?"

"Father! How can ye think that of me? No, I saw Mrs. Thorne and her husband were in trouble and rushed over to help them."

"Is that true?" he asked Syd instead of Octavian, but Octavian was not insulted. He knew the man wanted an honest answer, not a tactful one which he would have given.

"Yes, it is true," Syd said, then turned to his son. "Although you could have assured the MacGregors that Captain Thorne and I were married. Even if it was a nothing of a ceremony, it was still legal under Scottish law."

The laird's son raked a hand through his mass of unruly curls. "Aye, Mrs. Thorne. Ye are right. Perhaps I did make light of yer wedding. But ye must admit, it is an amusing thing to watch ye English in a mad race over the Scottish border to marry in haste."

"It is not what I would have chosen," she answered softly, her pain evident to Octavian because he understood how traditional Syd was in such things. "But I could not allow my father to give me away to anyone else."

"Och, I dinna blame ye. He's proven to be a fine man," the laird's son admitted. "And ye've proven to be a fine lass. I apologize for callin' ye an Armstrong witch. In truth, ye've proved to be our angel."

His father beamed with pride. "That's the truth, son."

Octavian nodded in agreement. Perhaps there was hope for Angus to become a good laird when his father passed on. Of course, it was too soon to tell. That he recognized his fault was promising, but a hot temper was not an easy thing to overcome and would require more work on his part.

But this was a matter for the Armstrong clan to sort out.

There was one thing Octavian needed to do before they left the town of Melrose.

As the Armstrongs, MacGregors, and Campbells were about to leave, Octavian asked them all to remain a moment longer. He bent on one knee in front of Syd. "Will you marry me again? Properly, this time. With words of love exchanged in front of an alter instead of an anvil?"

"Are you serious?" She sank onto her knees in front of him and searched his expression.

"Lass, he's awaiting yer answer," Lady Campbell called out.

Syd began to nibble her lip.

Octavian groaned. "Syd, please. Do not give me a hard time about this."

"Two weddings?"

He nodded.

She leaned close, pretending to hug him and whispered, "Does this mean we must divorce twice?"

"No, only one divorce...but it will never happen," he growled back softly.

She threw her arms around him and kissed him brazenly on the lips. "Of course, I will marry you. In the sight of all these people, I will declare how much I–"

A cheer arose among the crowd.

Everyone thought she had finished the thought and declared how much she loved him. In truth, she had stopped herself before uttering the word 'love'. Octavian swallowed that kernel of disappointment. In truth, it did not matter. He knew she loved him. She did not have to declare it because it was evident in so many important ways.

Still, it would have been nice to hear it from her lips.

The fair would go on for one more day.

Fair goers would start leaving by midday tomorrow as the hawkers, musicians, and farmers began to break down their tents and animal pens.

Octavian invited everyone to join them in front of Melrose Abbey at ten o'clock the following morning.

For this, he had brought Syd all the way to Scotland.

He'd loved her from the moment he'd set eyes on her and vowed to himself to protect her always. She was his and there would be no undoing of either the first ceremony taking less than a minute in the blacksmith shop, or this one in full sight of three of the major lowlands clans.

The usually sleepy town of Melrose was known for little other than its once magnificent Melrose Abbey that now lay in ruins. Well, the area was beautiful, and he and Syd might have enjoyed riding over its hills and dales and across its glistening streams if they weren't in such a rush for time.

A light breeze swept across the hills and nearby meadows.

The sun shone brightly down on them once again as they stood before the ruins of the abbey on the following day.

The Armstrong laird himself officiated the ceremony.

Octavian had no idea whether or not he had actual authority, but it did not matter. He was already lawfully married to Syd. Even if he were not, this ceremony would have been considered a hand-fasting, which was as good as a marriage ceremony under Scottish law.

The laird recited several prayers, a Scottish poem, then gave a sermon on the importance of faithfulness and trust. At last, he brought the ceremony to an end with some all-important final words. "Captain Thorne, in the eyes of God and all these good people, do ye take Lady Sydney Harcourt to be yer lawful wife?"

"I do."

"Will ye honor her and protect her for all the days of yer life?"

"I will."

He then turned to Syd who looked like an angel in her gown of rose merino wool, a gown she had donned with pride this morning, especially now that she was the proud owner of ten merino sheep. Those would officially be turned over to Laird Armstrong after this ceremony.

Syd had let her hair down, the lovely, tumbling mane gleaming a rich, golden-red as the sun illuminated every silken strand. Her hair was adorned with nothing more than a circlet of flowers. "Lady Sydney Harcourt do ye take Captain Octavian Thorne as yer lawful wedded husband?"

Her eyes sparkled as she studied him, looking him up and down, and obviously deciding he looked splendid in his navy dress uniform. He did not usually wear his medals, but always carried them with him, and had pinned them onto his jacket in honor of his wedding. "I do," Syd said, her smile achingly beautiful.

"Will ye honor him and...och, lass, we all know how contrary ye can be. Will ye promise to obey him sometimes?"

The crowd laughed.

"Yes," she said with another beaming smile. "For better or for worse. In sickness and in health. I shall always honor him and be faithful to him, for he shall always have my heart even if he does not always have my agreement."

The crowd laughed again.

"I now pronounce ye husband and wife!" the laird declared mirthfully. "Ye may kiss yer bride, Captain Thorne. But be quick about it. We're all thirsty and in sore need of a drink."

Octavian kissed Syd with every ounce of love he had in his heart for her.

She kissed him back with equal fervor.

Octavian then bought several rounds of drinks for everyone when they headed to the inn's common room. As the noon hour approached, he ordered meals for everyone to sober them up. The last thing any of them needed was a repeat of yesterday's friction.

But he need not have worried. Their wedding put everyone in good humor on this last day of the fair.

There was dancing.

Armstrongs, Campbells, and MacGregors all put on displays of sword dancing that fascinated Syd. The Campbell granddaughter gave her a lesson in Scottish dancing. Syd took to it with the fervor of a bee taking to honey and was soon leaping and twirling along with the other Scottish women as though she had been born to it.

There were Scottish games that Octavian was goaded to participate in, such as a log toss, shot put, and an arm wrestle that he won. He doubted even he had the strength to defeat the Scottish champion, but Syd was hopping up and down and cheering him on in the sincerely heartwarming belief he was winning fair and square.

Of course, he wasn't.

The Scottish champion had been given the word to allow this bridegroom to win.

His shirt was off and sweat was gleaming on his skin by the time the games ended.

Syd did not care.

She hurled herself into his arms and rained kisses all over his face.

"Are you happy, love?" he asked her, for there was no denying it was a very good day for them.

"Yes," she said with heartfelt sincerity. "I got my sheep. I got my proper wedding. Most of all, I got you."

He wrapped his arms around her. "That last one was easy. You've always had me."

She hugged him fiercely. "I hope so."

He muffled his disappointment.

After all this, why was Syd still scared?

CHAPTER 16

A LITTLE OVER a week had passed since her second wedding in front of Melrose Abbey. The memories of Scotland were fading away as though in a dream, Syd realized while waiting for her friends to arrive at the elegant Huntsford townhouse for tea. The townhouse, situated in one of London's most elegant squares, was far more magnificent than the one she had grown up in with her parents.

Their home had always been a shambles because of her father's spendthrift ways. Whatever funds came into the family coffers were quickly spent on gambling, speculation, and frivolities, leaving nothing to spare for repairs or basic necessities. Her mother also grabbed whatever she could, and Syd had no idea where those funds were squirreled away, for her mother never used them to improve the household. It was a wonder their home had not yet collapsed, for it was held together with little more than spit and her father's high hopes.

Syd's heart soared when her friends began to arrive. "Gory! Marigold! Come in. Oh, do come in. I have so much to tell you!"

She gave each a heartfelt hug, and then led them into the elegant drawing room where their tea service had already been set up.

Her favorite dowagers, Lady Withnall and Lady Dayne, arrived next, along with Marigold's aunt, Sophie Farthingale. The two dowagers had generously offered to sponsor a Season for her and Gory, while Sophie had been one of their stalwart supporters, encouraging their love of education in addition to the traditional accomplishments expected of a debutante.

This was not all that surprising since Sophie's daughter, Lily, was a highly respected scientist and renowned for her intelligence. While Sophie and her husband held no titles, their daughters and nieces, including Marigold who was a marchioness, had married well, so that she was now considered one of the most powerful matriarchs in London society.

The dowagers had started their matchmaking efforts with Adela first, gaining a reputation for success when Syd's shy friend had married a duke. That duke was London's most sought-after bachelor, Octavian's brother, Ambrose.

Syd had grown quite friendly with these powerful matriarchs, but she no longer required their assistance since she was now married to Octavian. However, she would need their help when their marriage ended.

If it ended.

Oh, it would end.

Was this not her nightmare about to come alive now that she and Octavian were back in London?

It was only a matter of time before disaster struck and he wanted out of their marriage.

Syd kept up a casual conversation with her friends while waiting for the Huntsford butler to serve them and then leave. As soon as the drawing room doors closed, she had yet to set down her teacup when the ever sharp Lady Withnall leaned forward and said, "Now, Syd. You must tell us everything that happened, and why you still look so unhappy."

"Are you unhappy with Octavian?" Gory asked with some surprise.

The others were now curious and stared at her.

"It is complicated. This is why I invited you here." She glanced at her buttered bread, wishing she could stuff it in her mouth and not speak. But this was important. Her stomach had been in knots all morning, and everything she ate had felt dry in her mouth. "I'm just sorry Adela could not be with us, but unearthing that trove of ancient bones is far more important than listening to my troubles."

Lady Dayne frowned. "You are newly married to a man who cares deeply for you, Syd. A smart, handsome, and accomplished man who has encouraged your forensic work at the Huntsford Academy. Why are you troubled?"

"This is what I have been asking myself." She let out a ragged breath. "I have no answer for you."

"Has he been unkind to you?" Sophie asked.

"No, he's been wonderful." She and Octavian had been back in London for almost a week now. They had fallen back into their daily routines which kept them busy. This was the excuse she gave herself for not seeing these friends until now or calling upon her parents.

Ah, yes.

Her parents.

She had to face them eventually and dreaded it.

With Sir Henry dead, her father had gained a reprieve from repaying his debts. Octavian had agreed to help him pay off those debts, but no one had yet taken charge of Sir Henry's affairs or come around to collect what had been due him.

Octavian was keeping close watch on the situation.

Meanwhile, true to form, her father had reverted to his scoundrel ways and was reportedly running up new debts.

How could her mother endure this?

A good daughter would have run to her side to offer solace and assistance, but she had not done this yet. She would in time, she supposed. However, she felt no urgency to lend aid to a mother had not lifted a finger to prevent her father's scheme to marry her off to the odious Sir Henry. In truth, Syd had the uneasy suspicion her mother had encouraged Sir Henry.

It was a dreadful thing to think ill of one's mother.

But her mother had never been loving or supportive, Syd was coming to realize. In truth, Marigold's aunt, Sophie, had shown more concern for her than her own mother ever had.

Perhaps she had not gone to see her parents because she was still too angry with them for using her to pay off her father's debts.

She shook off the thought and returned to the conversation because she needed to seek guidance from her friends.

"Will you be living here with Adela and Ambrose?" Lady Dayne asked.

"For now," Syd said with a nod. "Octavian's assignment may require us to settle in Scotland for a few years, so we are in no hurry to acquire a London residence for ourselves when it might remain empty for months at a time."

Marigold voiced her agreement. "There's certainly no urgency since Adela and Ambrose spend most of their time in Devon digging up fossils, and Julius is often in Oxford or York attending to the Huntsford holdings. Using the Huntsford townhouse as a home base for all of you makes eminent sense for now."

"Exactly," Syd said. Besides, what point was there in building up memories with Octavian when it might all come undone at any moment?

Gory finally asked her the question they were all eager to have answered. "What happened?"

Marigold scooted forward in her chair and nodded. "Yes! We have all been dying to know since receiving your cryptic messages. All you revealed was that you were safe and on the run with Octavian. That he married you to protect your honor is so romantic."

Syd smiled at the comment.

Marigold was the sweetest of them all and firmly believed in the power of love to overcome all woes.

"Tell us everything," Gory insisted.

All of the ladies listened attentively as she related what happened on the night she tried to steal into Sir Henry's townhouse. The dowagers must have seen and heard a lot in their day, for they were not overly impressed by her attempt to destroy proof of her father's debt to Sir Henry.

"That was quite foolish of you," Lady Dayne said, her reproof mild because the lady was too kind to ever condescend or berate her. "You might have fallen off that slippery roof and hurt yourself, not to mention Octavian might have been seriously hurt when he fell off."

She nodded. "I know. But I was desperate. I loathed having to bow to my father's wishes and marry the odious Sir Henry. But I could not leave my father in danger, either. I thought destroying those vouchers would give him some bargaining power."

Lady Withnall shook her head. "Sir Henry was a villain through and through. Realizing those vouchers had been stolen would only have enraged him. Did you not consider that he would take his rage out on your father?"

"That's what Octavian said." Heat crept up her cheeks, for she was ashamed to admit that she had given this possibility little consideration. Her father was a little weasel who always managed to slip out of his problems, as Octavian often remarked.

"I'm sure you only meant to provide your father more time until you came up with a better plan," Marigold said, and gave her a comforting pat on the hand.

Syd nodded. "Yes, that was my hope."

Gory pursed her lips. "I wish you had come to me. We could have killed the old goat and buried his body somewhere he would never be found."

Syd's mouth gaped open. "Gory!"

The others responded with equal shock, especially Marigold who was too gentle to even hurt a mouse.

Gory rolled her eyes. "For pity's sake. I'm jesting! Do you honestly believe I am capable of killing anyone? Believe me, if ever I went on a murderous spree, it would be my uncle I'd go after first. But I would not be obvious about it. An obscure poison is what I would use in order to make his death appear natural. Is this not the cleverest way to murder someone? A murder no one suspects ever occurred?"

Sophie grunted in disapproval. "We all know your uncle is a toad. But dreaming up ways to dispatch him? That is not at all the thing, Gory."

Gory sighed. "I would never actually do it. But what is so wrong with hoping he gets back a little of what he deserves? He is not a good man. In fact, he's gotten involved in some very shady dealings lately. The class of gentlemen coming around to our house these past few weeks is enough to chill your blood. I only call them gentlemen out of politeness."

Lady Dayne frowned. "This sounds serious, Gory. Have these men frightened you? Or approached you inappropriately? Do you need our help? Come stay with me if you are worried for your safety."

"Thank you for the offer, but I am capable of taking care of myself."

"Still," Lady Withnall said with a shake of her head, "it sounds like a bad business. Do not hesitate to come to me or Lady Dayne if ever you feel at risk. We have big, empty houses now that our children are grown and have their own homes. We would enjoy having your companionship."

"Thank you. That is very kind of you, and I will take you up on the offer should the need arise." Gory then purposely changed the course of the conversation. "Oh, yum. Ginger cake. My favorite. I'll have a slice, Syd. Now, tell us more about your adventures with Octavian."

Lady Dayne wagged a finger at Gory. "Your ploy to distract us will not work. In fact, it has made me even more determined. With Syd now married, there is no reason to put off our sponsoring you this Season."

"My thoughts exactly," Lady Withnall said. "It is time we spoke to your uncle about our taking you under our wing. Is this not sensible? Your home life sounds deplorable and possibly dangerous, so move in with me or Lady Dayne without delay. You'll need a new wardrobe, of course. And there's to be no more talk of cadavers or digging up graves while dancing with any young men. You purposely do this to scare them away. That ghoulish talk must end. Is that clear?"

Gory smiled as she nodded. "Quite clear."

"And you are to wear soft colors when going about in Society," Lady Dayne added. "No more walking around looking like the harbinger of death."

"I like dark colors," Gory grumbled. "Besides, is it not proper for me to be in mourning for my parents?"

"It has been well over a year now," Lady Withnall shot back, but gave Gory's hand a gentle pat. "I know you miss them. But they would not be happy to see you behaving as you are."

After a little more discussion about Gory's future, something of which they all held opinions, the topic returned to Syd and her dash to Scotland with Octavian. "I knew he was in love with you," Lady Dayne insisted.

Lady Withnall nodded. "I knew it, too. So ridiculously obvious. Dozens of women flitting about him like butterflies, some brazenly propositioning him, and he had no interest in any of them from the moment he set eyes on you, Syd."

Syd had just taken a sip of her tea, and now coughed as it went down the wrong way. "I know he cares for me," she said, quickly recovering.

"As you do for him," Lady Withnall stated. "You must not hide your feelings from him any longer Syd. He must be told what is in your heart, or..."

"Or what?" Syd asked.

Lady Withnall frowned. "Lady Clementine is still smarting over Octavian's slighting her. She is furious that he chose you over her, and I fear she will do something about it."

"Would this not make her look more of a fool?" Syd asked. "I thought they were not an item. Octavian assured me they were not together."

"Well, seems he forgot to mention it to Lady Clementine," Lady Dayne remarked.

"Perhaps he thought by no longer coming around to see her, she would understand he had lost interest in her," Marigold said. "Or, she might have refused to listen to him when he broke it off. Is this not something she would do if she still wanted him?"

Lady Withnall took a sip of her tea. "Yes, that is a possibility. And an apt description. She is not a nice girl. Being the daughter of a duke, she is used to getting her way in all things. Whatever the pampered princess wants, she gets. Her papa sees to it."

Marigold frowned. "But Syd and Octavian are married now. Not even a duke can break up a lawful marriage, especially when it is a love match."

Lady Withnall cast Marigold a wry glance. "Never underestimate the power of evil."

Syd was worried, not for herself but for Octavian. "You think she is evil?"

The dowager shrugged her slight shoulders. "Malicious, to be sure. Spoiled. Inconsiderate. I would not ever describe her as kind or affectionate. Possessive and demanding, that's what she is."

"What does it matter?" Gory placed another slice of ginger cake on her plate. "Syd is married to Octavian now, and there is no undoing it. Is there? Especially if Syd is with child. I cannot imagine that he has been a monk with you, Syd. Surely, you have...um..." She paused to clear her throat. "My point is, your marriage is secure."

Syd blushed and turned away.

Lady Withnall gasped.

That woman had the eyes of an eagle and the instinctive scent of a bloodhound. This feared matriarch of the *ton*, missed nothing.

It did not help that Syd was terrible at hiding her thoughts and feelings.

And now Octavian would be shamed once they all understood what Lady Withnall had picked up on immediately...that she and Octavian had never consummated the marriage.

How was this fair to him?

He had done nothing but be kind to her and protective.

Lady Withnall was a tiny thing. No one knew quite how old she was, but she knew everyone's family secrets dating back generations, to their parents, grandparents, and even great-grandparents.

"It isn't his fault. The blame is all on me," Syd said, her hands now shaking. "He is the best man who ever existed."

Lady Withnall sighed. "Syd, what is going on? You cannot be thinking of undoing this marriage. It would ruin Octavian's career."

Marigold now stared at her in dismay. "Why would you ever want to divorce him? Are you suggesting your marriage is make-believe? How can it be? He obviously loves you. Just as important, you obviously love him."

Gory nodded as she also gaped at Syd. "Does he still have the ability to annul your marriage. Have you been pushing him away?"

"Why, Syd?" Marigold asked, sincerely distressed because she was such a believer in true love.

Gory was now frowning at her, too. "Syd, of all the stupid notions you've ever gotten into your head, this one takes the cake. She would do it for love, Marigold. She would leave him if she thought he was better off without her."

Marigold leaped to her feet. "You mustn't ever leave him! You would break his heart. He does not deserve such an end after all he has done for you. Nor can you make such a decision on your own. He is your husband and deserves to have a say in what happens. If he wants to build a lifetime of dreams with you, then you cannot take that away from him."

Syd did not know whether to be angry or simply fall apart and cry. "Do you think I ever want to leave him? I never understood the meaning of happiness until I met him. He is my very own miracle. But what if something terrible happens and he can no longer stand to be with me?"

"Such as what, Syd?" Lady Dayne asked, setting aside her cup of tea as their discussion intensified. "Were you already married? And now you are hiding a first husband?"

"No! How can you suggest such a thing, Lady Dayne? There's never been anyone else. I had never even been kissed until Octavian kissed me. There are no secret marriages. No tawdry affairs. I was a virgin when we married."

And still am.

Marigold sank back into her chair and sighed. "You had me scared for a moment. Why are you so on edge if there are no dark secrets in your past?"

Syd buried her face in her hands. "I don't know. Octavian thinks I have never experienced true happiness before and this is what brings on my distress. He says I am at a loss and don't know how to deal with it."

"Is he wrong?" Lady Dayne said.

"He is being sensible and reasonable, trying to make logical sense of something that is illogical. He is not wrong, but there is more to it. I am happy with him and dearly want to stay in this marriage. But I cannot shake off this sense of doom. Something terrible is going to happen to destroy us. I just know it."

The two dowagers exchanged worried looks.

Lady Withnall spoke up. "My dear, if you keep looking for this to happen, then it will happen. You will cause it."

"Pushing Octavian away is the wrong thing to do," Lady Dayne added. "Every marriage has problems along the way. I do not care how perfect a couple may appear to others. Nothing is ever ideal. What matters is how the two of you approach these problems. If you love him and he loves you, then fight for each other. Solve whatever troubles come your way by working together."

Marigold agreed. "Octavian's greatest pain will be in losing you. Keeping him at arm's length, abandoning him because *you* believe it is best for him, will only cause him greater hurt. Will ending your marriage make you feel any better? No, it would not. Your own heart would never forgive you for betraying his love."

Syd knew they all meant well, but none of them understood. "So you are saying I must stay with him even though I would bring shame and disgrace upon him and his family?"

Lady Withnall frowned at her. "Syd, you must tell us the truth. Do you know something we do not? What are you not telling us?"

"Nothing. Upon my word. Whatever it is, has not happened yet."

"Or may never happen," Sophie added. "Will you throw away everything for this?"

Lady Withnall grunted as she eased back in her chair. "The solution is easy."

Syd stared at her. "It is?"

"Yes, my dear. Whatever this terrible thing is that you are convinced will happen can only be overcome by love. If it brings shame on you and Octavian, then will it not bring shame whether you are together or apart? He is already tainted because you are married to each other. Spurning you later will not help him remove the taint."

"Yes," Gory said, latching onto the idea. "It is like indelible ink. Once spilled, the stain will never come out."

"So, how better to fight whatever problem arises than together?" Lady Withnall asked. "Octavian is never going to turn around and run anyway. His every instinct will be, and has always been, to protect you."

"And my every instinct has always been to protect him. If my leaving can save his career, does it not make sense for me to go?"

"Are you not listening to anything we've said?" Marigold frowned at her and huffed.

"Precisely, Marigold," Lady Withnall remarked, and then once again turned to Syd. "Anything bad enough to destroy his career will destroy it whether you stay or go because he has already committed to you and all of London knows it. And what makes you think Octavian would care more for his career than for you? Who are you to make that choice for him? Is it not something that ought to be decided upon together?"

Marigold, who truly was softhearted, took out her handkerchief as her tears began to flow.

Syd groaned. "Marigold, why are you crying?"

"For you. Is it not obvious? You cannot give up on true love, Syd. Look at what Leo and I had to endure, but did I ever consider leaving him? No. Not once. Not for a moment." She paused and groaned. "But he considered leaving me. That is true. He thought to protect me. But how was losing him ever the better choice? My heart would have shattered in a thousand pieces and never mended. I told him so."

"Did he listen?" Syd asked, knowing the answer, for Leo could be stubborn when he wanted to be. Nothing Marigold said was going to change his mind.

"No, he was too thickheaded and refused. But he eventually realized I was right because love always find a way, Syd. Love *always* finds a way. I found the mate of my soul in Leo. I do not think I am mistaken in saying Octavian is yours. So why are you giving up on this precious gift?"

Gory agreed. "I know you better than anyone else does, Syd. You would never have married Octavian, no matter how dire your circumstances, if you had a single doubt about your feelings for him. And you married him twice. Who marries *twice*? You never even believed you would marry once. Does this not tell you something?"

Lady Dayne decided to add her opinion. "Oh, my goodness. I could see the sparks fly between you and Octavian every time you two met. You riled him at every turn. He constantly wanted to throttle you. But mostly, he wanted to kiss you. The poor man ached for it."

Sophie laughed lightly. "It was such fun to watch him struggle with these feelings that bemused him and probably terrified him, for his life had been quite trouble-free until you came along. But he knew the moment he set eyes on you that his rakish lifestyle had come to an end. Whether he was ready or not, his heart had chosen you. Well, Syd? Have we resolved your situation? You may not know what is going to happen, but the solution will not be found by running away from Octavian."

In truth, they were very helpful.

Perhaps they were right.

Octavian had never come out and said he loved her, but he was clear about wanting their marriage to last, and often called her *love* or *my love* as an endearment.

Nor had she ever told him that she loved him.

Yet, keeping silent did not change the fact that she did love him.

Had she been wrong to deny him the privileges of their marriage bed?

She clasped her hands together as they began to shake.

Was it time to take that leap?

CHAPTER 17

OCTAVIAN SENSED SOMETHING was amiss when he returned to the Huntsford townhouse that evening and saw Syd pacing in the entry hall while awaiting his arrival. "Love, what's wrong?"

She surprised him by rushing into his arms. "Nothing is wrong. I missed you."

He emitted a rumble of laughter as he gathered her in his embrace. "Now I am certain something is wrong."

She smiled as she looked up at him. "Actually, something is very right. I saw my friends today."

He gave her cheek a light caress. "You did? I'm glad. How are they? Do you wish to throw a dinner party and have them all join us? I should have mentioned it sooner, but we each got involved in catching up on the work waiting for us here in London. You with your forensic research and me with my navy assignment. It took me days of just writing reports. I've only now started to make a dent in the other work piled on my desk."

She reached up and kissed him on the lips. "A dinner party would be lovely. Will this coming Saturday do? I know it is short notice, but I would not invite many people. I'll show you my list before I send out invitations."

"Not necessary. I trust your judgement."

She burst out laughing. "Dear heaven, I never thought to hear those words spill from your lips. You must be more exhausted than I realized."

He joined her in a chuckle. "You can be obstinate, at times. But mostly you are perfect and wonderful."

"Oh, I am not. Octavian, I have been so unfair to you." She dragged him upstairs because she did not wish the Huntsford servants to overhear their conversation. She was about to seduce Octavian and did not care for anyone to listen in. Not that she really needed to say anything other than *take me now.*

He would drop everything and carry her to bed.

"Syd?" He arched an eyebrow in question once she got him in their bedchamber and locked the door.

A smile tugged at his lips when she tossed him what she hoped was a sultry smile. "What are you doing, Syd?"

She considered slinking toward him, but how exactly did one slink and still look alluring? "Am I not permitted a private moment with my husband?"

"Private, as in talking to me in private? Or private as in…?" He glanced toward their bed.

She pointed to the bed and emitted a shaky breath.

His expression gentled the moment he realized what she was doing. "Oh, Syd. Come here, love."

She ran into his arms when he held them out to her. "I've been so stupid, Octavian."

"No, love. You've been in pain." It was disconcerting how well he understood her.

But it also proved how strongly they were connected. "Would you mind if we had supper in our bedchamber tonight?"

He cupped her face in his hands and kissed her with aching tenderness. "An excellent idea. May I ask what has put you in this amorous mood?" But he now turned serious. "Are you truly ready to take this next step in our marriage?"

She nodded.

He said nothing for the longest moment, and then released a breath in obvious relief. "Dare I ask, what changed your mind?"

"The way I spoke about you to my friends." Not to mention, her friends beating sense into her. Marigold had burst into tears while chattering about the endurance of love. She was right. Love mattered. Love could not be denied.

Love *should* not be denied.

"I told them how smart, insanely gorgeous, gentle and kind you were to me," she said. "I told them how happy I was with you."

"What else did you tell them?" he asked, groaning as he realized she may have confided their most intimate moments to her friends.

She winced. "I told them everything."

"Blessed saints, Syd. You told them our marriage was make-believe?" He looked hurt more than angry.

This only made Syd feel worse. "Quite the opposite. They now know our marriage is real...or will be as soon as we have our clothes off. If I understood the first thing about seduction, I would be using every feminine wile on you right now instead of talking. But I am not wily, apparently."

He was still staring at her and not making a move to undo a single one of her laces or any of his buttons. "Must I say it, Octavian?"

"Say what?"

She let out a breath. "Do not be difficult about this. Can you not see? I want you to take me, for I am yours and wish to be yours...forever."

He stared at her in silence for a long moment before the hint of a smile crossed his lips. "Yes, there is a very important thing we must say to each other before we go at it like a pair of wild monkeys."

"Octavian!" But she laughed. "I am trying to make this a tender moment and bare my soul to you."

He caressed her cheek. "You know how I feel about you. Do you feel the same way?"

He loved her.

His every action spoke of his affection.

He hadn't said the words because she had refused to hear them until now. Idiotically refused, as though not hearing them or saying them back to him would make this pain she still felt ripping through her more endurable.

She had it all backwards.

His love was the cure for her pain.

It was time she told him how she felt.

To her surprise, tears formed in her eyes.

Why was she turning into a blubbering peahen at this critical moment? She was almost as bad as Marigold who was sentimental about everything.

"Syd, shall I say it first?"

"No, I want to say it to you. It is important, Octavian. I have to say it first."

He took her hands and held them in those big, rough hands of his that never failed to stir her to passion with a mere touch. "I'm listening, love."

"Octavian…Octavian…"

He gave them a light squeeze. "You needn't force it, Syd. You'll say it when the time feels right."

"But it has always been right. That's just it. There has never been a moment when I have not loved you." She gasped. "I just said it, didn't I? I just said that I loved you."

His grin was ear to ear. "Indeed, you did. Care to say it again?"

She nodded. "I love you, Octavian."

"There's my girl." His voice was achingly soft.

"I'm so sorry I waited this long to tell you. But you knew I felt it." She was going to cry again because this admission had her heart in spasms and she had no idea how to control it.

"I love you, too," he said in a husky murmur.

He released her hands and began to unbutton the jacket of his uniform.

She smiled as she watched him shrug out of it.

He winked at her. "This is quite the momentous moment, isn't it?"

She laughed. "Yes, it is."

"Are you ready for this, Syd? You need to be sure because there is no undoing it once it is done."

She was shamefully eager, truth be told. "Octavian, you need to consider this next step, too. It is just as irrevocable for you. Once you claim me, there is no getting out of our marriage. The make-believe is gone."

"Hallelujah," he said without hesitation. "I never wanted our marriage to be a sham. I want to spend the rest of my life with you. What is your preference? Slow and romantic? Or wild and passionate?"

She laughed again. "It does not matter. I have a feeling we are going to do this every which way tonight. By the gleam in your eyes, I do not think it shall be one and done."

"But it will be," he said with affection, "if you are too sore. Syd, you need to be honest with me as we do this. I think you will like it, but I am big and you…well, you are going to be tight because you are untried."

She smiled at him. "That is most considerate of you, but I doubt there will be a problem since I melt whenever you touch me. As you well know, since you are always so smug about it afterward."

He grinned as he removed his shirt next.

Syd never tired of watching the beautiful flex and tension of his muscled torso. "Um, in truth, I think you know my body so well, that you will sense precisely what I need and at what moment."

He removed the clips from her stylish curls and set them aside on the bureau. "It is not difficult to do. You are quite vocal when expressing your pleasure."

"Octavian! I am not loud when…*you know*."

"Love, they can hear you all the way to the Thames."

She playfully swatted his shoulder. "Stop gloating! You are supposed to be complimenting me, not teasing me."

"And you were never supposed to steal my heart. Gad, it happened so quickly. I lost it to you before I drew a second breath." He turned her to face away from him in order to get at the laces of her gown. "You drive me wild, you little minx."

"Minx?" She gave a soft, purring laugh when he nuzzled her neck.

"Yes." He ran his hands all over her body, arousing her with remarkable efficiency.

Her skin tingled wherever he touched.

She sighed.

"Minx," he whispered, nibbling her earlobe. "You'll find the word defined in Samuel Johnson's dictionary…an exceptionally attractive and playful woman who often causes trouble. Sound familiar? Particularly the trouble part."

"That is completely unfair. Have I not been on my best behavior since marrying you?"

"Yes, if one overlooks poking Laird Armstrong's son in the nose and drawing blood. Not to mention the clan war you almost started when taking on the MacGregors by yourself."

"How could I ignore the poor Campbell girl in need of help? And how was this a bad thing when I got those merino sheep for the Armstrongs as reward?"

Once they were both fully undressed, he lifted her in his arms and carried her to bed. "Only you would still be obsessed with those blasted sheep."

"They make the finest wool. Have you ever run your hands over anything softer?"

"Your sweet body, for one." He eyed her with heat as he shifted over her, his body pressing lightly on hers as he dipped his head and covered her mouth in a kiss that left her breathless and aching for more of him. "I love you, Syd."

What a stupid goose she had been to delay this moment for so long. "I love you, too."

No more words were necessary.

The exquisite sensation of his touch and her eager response said it all.

Dear heaven.

Why had she ever resisted this man?

His kisses were scorching and exquisite.

His hands were calloused but his touch always gentle.

He played her body with the agile expertise of a master musician. She thrummed and hummed as he kissed her, suckled her breasts, and flicked his tongue over their straining buds until they were hard points. "Octavian," she moaned, clutching his hair and tugging on it to hold him closer.

"I'm here, love," he crooned, stroking his finger along the sensitive nub between her legs and evoking fires within her.

"I love you, Syd," he repeated. "I love you so much."

He nudged her legs apart and positioned himself between them as he prepared to claim her. *Dear heaven.* Had he not already claimed every other ounce of her? How could she resist? His every word and deed during the weeks of their marriage, and even before they had ever exchanged vows, proved how much he loved and cherished her.

She felt a momentary pinch of pain when he broke through her maiden's barrier, but he had prepared her and there was only pleasure after that first, fleeting moment. She wrapped her arms around his neck as his big, muscled body filled her and he embedded himself inside her. He cast her a conquering, yet still affectionate smile, and kept her in the cradle of his arms to guide her through this rhythm of love. They were two dancers moving in perfect harmony to their music. Although she was not quite perfect, sometimes rushing her movements because she wanted so much of him, and craved all of him *now.*

Her big, protective ox.

That guardian-protector part of him was so ingrained in his soul.

Little fires burned everywhere within her body.

His skin was hot to the touch, too.

He made her burn with an intensity, the like of which she had never experienced before, not even all the prior times he'd guided her to pleasure. But this…*this*…was different, for this was truly their shared pleasure.

Yes, sharing.

Was not this the entire point of marriage?

He watched her with his silver eyes that resembled smoldering embers and kindled her passion.

She writhed beneath him, impatiently rubbing against his body as a familiar pressure built within her. She knew this hot, liquid feeling, for she had experienced it before under his touch. But this was different. He hadn't been inside her before. He hadn't shared in her pleasure until now. "Octavian!"

"Let yourself go, love. I'm right here to catch you."

She kissed him and set free all of her inhibitions, all of her worries, and allowed the sensation of *him* to flood her senses. She felt his strength, inhaled his scent of bergamot, savored the warmth of his mouth and heat of his tongue.

Her eyes had been closed to better absorb these sensations, but she now opened them to find him once again smiling at her. "My tender beast," she whispered. "My one and only true love."

There was wonder in the way he looked at her.

She felt a soul-deep contentment, a joy she had never experienced before.

She loved him so much and told him so.

"I love you, too," he whispered.

Fire tore through her and consumed her, so that there was nothing left of her but wisps of ash floating and soaring through the air.

Octavian continued to watch her.

He hugged her to his broad chest as she cried out in pleasure, and held her safe as she tumbled back to earth. Then with a low growl, he thrust twice and followed her, spilling his seed in her and claiming her as forever his.

"*Oh, Lord.* That was good," he said, carefully easing out of her with a groaning laugh and collapsed atop her. All sweat. All heat. All glorious muscles.

She loved the sensation of his weight upon her, but he quickly moved off to avoid crushing her and fell back against the mattress with a grunt of satisfaction. He then drew her into his arms and grunted again. "That was really, really good, Syd. How do you feel?"

"Really, really good," she replied, mimicking his grunts as she planted kisses on his chest. Her lips were still tingling from his kisses as she tasted the light sheen of sweat on his skin. "I love you, you big ox. I am yours forever and there is no getting rid of me now."

"I never wanted our marriage to end. You and me, minx. Into our dotage."

They never bothered to order supper brought up since they were too busy feasting on each other. Octavian claimed her twice more over the course of the night, but would not take her again come morning, even though they were both still naked and he was obviously aroused. "You're going to be sore, Syd. I am big and we did not hold back."

She meant to assure him that she could handle it, but the words escaped her when he leaned over and cupped her breast, smiling when the mound filled the palm of his hand. She gasped as he ran his thumb lightly across its pink bud, and was completely undone, lost to him when he closed his mouth over the bud and began to suckle and tease it.

Apparently, this is all it took to turn her wanton.

She was not even fully awake yet, but her body responded immediately and she reached her ecstasy before he had hardly started. Had even a minute passed? He had not even touched her anywhere else.

He regarded her with a smug, conquering grin. "Good morning."

She snuggled against him. "You are a wicked lout."

"Why? Because I know your body so well?" He kissed her on the brow. "I had such dreams about that glorious body of yours. Every night from the moment I met you. Agonizing nights because my heart was yours and there could never be anyone else for me. Because of you, I became celibate as a monk."

This surprised her. "Not even to relieve your urges? We were more enemies than friends at the time. You owed me nothing."

He groaned. "It made no difference to my heart. We Thornes tend to be one-woman men. There it was…I loved you and did not want to be with anyone else."

"I had no idea I was such an enchantress," she teased.

She had assumed he was continuing his rakehell ways because he had not shown any inclination to court her. In truth, she had died a little inside when rumor began to spread about his courting Lady Clementine.

Was she really as horrible as Octavian insisted?

How could Clementine be worse than her? She had behaved abominably toward Octavian. Riling him. Disobeying him. Defying him. And all along, he loved her.

She sighed, feeling ashamed of herself.

In her own defense, she had only been difficult because she

loved him.

"Syd, why are you frowning?"

"There is something I need to tell you."

He moaned. "Is this something you should have told me *before* we had sex?"

"No." She sat up and wrapped the sheet around her, as much as she could grab of it without leaving him naked. Not that he would care. He wasn't a bashful man. "Lady Withnall mentioned that Clementine was not happy to learn of our marriage. Clementine believed you were courting her, and now she is angry."

"But I wasn't ever courting her. I shared a dance or two with her, escorted her and her father to the theater once."

"And escorted them to a ball or two," Syd added.

"At her father's request, not my idea. I hadn't even seen her for months before that night you tossed me off Sir Henry's roof. Speaking of which, there is something I need to tell *you*."

"Oh?"

"Gad, you look pretty, Syd. Your hair's in a tumble and you look adorably sleepy."

She arched an eyebrow. "Sleepy? Not after that morning wake-up surprise you gave me."

He laughed. "I couldn't help myself. I am besotted."

"What is it you had to tell me? Only that I am pretty and you love me?"

He sighed. "Sir Henry's family has asked the London magistrate to make inquiries into his death. I meant to tell you last night but was distracted by our...er, going at it like a pair of wild monkeys."

"Octavian! Stop describing us as that." She rolled her eyes. "You are such a big ox."

He grinned. "And you are a kitten."

She rolled her eyes again. "I thought I was a minx? Stop being naughty and just tell me."

"The magistrate intends to question your father."

Syd thought on it a moment. "But he doesn't know anything about the night Sir Henry died. He was already on his way to

London. Does the magistrate believe my father might have done it? He certainly had enough motive. But you and I know he is innocent. He can provide witnesses to attest to his whereabouts. The Armstrongs and those gamblers he swindled along the way. Thank goodness he was nowhere near the Abbott's Cross Inn at the time."

"Indeed," Octavian muttered. "Otherwise, your father would be thinking up ways to blackmail poor Mr. Douglas."

"No! My father would never...well, perhaps you are right. He is wretched, isn't he?"

Octavian nodded. "The magistrate is sure to come around to us next. I am not concerned about proving your father's innocence. As you said, we all know he was in England and not in Scotland at the time. It is Mr. Douglas I am most worried about. The magistrate must be kept in the dark about what really happened. For this, we have to keep our story consistent, Syd."

"I understand."

"We must tell him that we were at the inn, but none of us heard anything. We assume he was set upon and robbed while following us to the inn. He must have resisted and fought back, so this assailant, or unknown assailants, killed him."

She nibbled her lip as she began to fret. "The magistrate will question why he was following us. I'm sure my father will tell him about Sir Henry's desire to marry me."

"His filthy obsession," Octavian said in disgust. "There's no reason to lie about any of it."

"What about the Armstrongs? What do you think they might tell him? And the Gretna Green blacksmith? What will he tell the magistrate? He is not going to lie for us."

"They can all swear to the truth about our wedding ceremony, and so should we. Why should they lie about your father and Sir Henry attempting to stop our marriage? It happened. Everyone saw them try to stop us."

"But this will give us a motive for killing him."

"Syd, it doesn't matter. We did not kill him and can attest to it because it is the truth. There is only one fact that needs omitting...that we know who did it."

Syd acknowledged his concern with a nod.

"If asked, all we need to say is Sir Henry must have followed us. But we were unaware because he never made it to the inn. There's no need to deny Sir Henry was angry or wanted revenge. We did not even consider the possibility of his following us because we saw him and your father ride out of Gretna Green on their way back to London. Everyone saw them ride south and assumed their chase was over."

"Octavian, you know I am not a good liar. What if the magistrate senses I am holding something back?"

He pursed his lips. "I'll request that he question only me."

"Will he agree?"

"Yes. I will let him know that Sir Henry was a brute who was obsessed with you and scared the wits out of you. Just speaking about him oversets you because you are such a delicate, fluttery thing."

She poked him in the ribs. "Don't you dare call me delicate or fluttery."

"Would you rather I describe you as a harpy? A tavern brawler? But there really is no reason to involve you since we were together the entire time, and whatever you saw, I saw. Or more to the point, it was our wedding night and we were in bed, doing something *other* than thinking of Sir Henry."

"Octavian! You cannot say that."

"Why not? The magistrate is not going to ask more questions after that statement."

"It is not right to discuss our wedding night."

"I am not going to describe how you and I were naked together and–"

"Beast!"

"Ouch," he said with a chuckle, releasing her as she wriggled out of his arms. "No more teasing you, I promise."

She gathered the sheet around her body once again. "You had better behave. How can you treat the matter so lightly?"

"Believe me, I am not." He rested his hands behind his head as he leaned back against their pillows and admired her. "I will feel much better when the inquiry is over. It will amount to no more than a few questions and done. His family detested him. Their request is more for show than any true concern. Behind closed doors, they are probably toasting his demise. Nor will his business acquaintances grieve for him. There's probably a battle going on behind the scenes as to who will take control of his illicit operations."

"I'll hold my breath until it is all over." She tugged the sheet back when he tried to draw it off her. "I am not going to fall naked into your arms, you wicked man. Besides, I am not done talking to you."

"What else is there to discuss, love?"

His smile was making her melt and lose the trail of her thoughts. "My father. My parents, actually. I thought I would visit them today. But I dare not go now or risk encountering the magistrate. Perhaps I had better wait until the matter of Sir Henry is completely put to rest."

"You could invite your parents here."

"No!" She sighed. "My father will probably steal the silverware."

"Syd, you cannot put off seeing your parents. Shall I go with you? Even though Sir Henry is gone, your father's debt vouchers remain. Someone is going to come around to their home soon asking for repayment. I need to square this with your father."

She nodded. "If it were up to me, I would never see them again."

He frowned as he studied her. "Syd, what is going on? Why are you suddenly so loathe to see your parents?"

CHAPTER 18

SYD ALLOWED ANOTHER week to go by without contacting either her mother or her father. She made every excuse possible not to see them, until she had run out of reasons and could no longer delay the inevitable. Even London's popular gossip rag, The Tattler, was hinting of a rift within the family, a circumstance she found most odd because her family had never been known for their close ties. So what made it suddenly of interest to anyone?

Octavian, always sensible to the point of irritation, had not been pleased to learn the Harcourts had been in the news. He had just returned home after a long day at the Admiralty, and now set the most recent edition down on the writing table where Syd was seated. "Octavian, what is that?" she asked, putting down her quill pen as she rose to greet him.

"More gossip about you and your parents," he muttered.

"This is most curious." She shot him a questioning gaze. "Why would anyone care or notice that I had not seen them since returning to London? Someone is planting this information to stir mischief."

"No doubt, but this changes nothing. Love, you cannot avoid seeing them. My concern is not for us, but for the Douglas family. I've dealt with the London magistrate. He has accepted my statement and closed the investigation. But if gossip continues about this split among the Harcourt family, some eager reporter might dig a little deeper and uncover something that is better left buried."

She knew he was right. "I'm sorry. I'll write to my parents as soon as I finish this note to Lady Withnall accepting her invitation to tea. I'll arrange to call upon them early next week. Is that all right?"

"Yes, of course." He took her into his arms and kissed her with a wealth of tenderness, and then kept her in his arms when he sensed she needed to be held a little longer. "I know this is hard for you. But your fear in facing them will–"

"It is fear of the unknown," she insisted. "I am not afraid of my mother or father."

"Fine, but whatever this unknown fear is, it is obviously rooted in your unsettled feelings for them. Otherwise, you would not hesitate to visit them."

She squirmed in his arms.

He held her gently, but would not let her go just yet. "You would not even stop by there to pack up your belongings. I had to ask the Harcourt housekeeper to ensure it was done. You cannot let this dread fester, Syd. It will grow worse over time. Isn't it better we address it now?" he pointed out.

She rested her head against his broad chest, taking comfort in his nearness. "Everything you are saying is right, Octavian."

"I've offered to go with you. You know I will always stand by you."

"To catch me if I fall," she said with a mirthless lilt of laughter. "I can do this on my own."

"Are you certain, Syd?"

She nodded. "As I said, I am not afraid of them."

While Octavian went upstairs to their bedchamber to wash up and change out of his uniform, she finished her note to Lady Withnall, and then jotted another to her mother. By the time she joined him in their chamber, he was comfortably ensconced in one of the large, tufted chairs beside the hearth, glass of wine in hand while staring into the fire and lost in his thoughts.

He smiled when she came over to sit on his lap.

He had taken off all but his trousers and shirt that was now unbuttoned down the front to expose much of his chest. She settled cozily against him, resting a hand atop the light spray of hair across his chest.

The silver of his eyes captured the golden glow of firelight so that he looked devilishly handsome as he welcomed her into his embrace. "The note is done and will be delivered to my mother in the morning. We'll see if she responds."

"I'm proud of you, love."

She sighed. "I would reserve judgement, if I were you. Your *Sassenach* witch of a wife might still make a mess of the reconciliation."

He gave a deep, rumbling chuckle. "First of all, my wife is a gem and not a witch. She is also exceptionally clever. She can do anything she puts her mind to doing."

"I am sure you are referring to a wife you may have had in a prior lifetime," she said with a light laugh. "You cannot possibly be referring to me." But she paused a moment to kiss him, loving the warmth of his lips as they covered hers. She tasted the wine he had been drinking, just a hint of its full-bodied, fruitiness. "Thank you, Octavian. You always have a kind word for me."

"Because you are that special, Syd."

"I'm not sure my mother will agree. I don't think she will be all that thrilled to see me. She never is. But one can only hope her opinion of me will improve now that I am married to you and you have a lot of money."

He kissed her on the nose. "Aha," he teased, "I knew you only married me for my wealth. The truth finally comes out. You went about it very cleverly, too. Never asking me for so much as a shilling. Never complaining about our accommodations as we traveled throughout Scotland. Berating me for insisting on acquiring *five* gowns for you when you only wanted two."

"Dare I point out that you spent a fortune on my father."

"But I got you in the bargain, and it is the best bargain I have ever made. I love you, Syd."

A pang tore through her.

She loved him, too.

She loved him so much, she ached with it. But the feeling of dread once again seized her and would not let go of her now. Something was going to happen when she saw her parents, something awful that would have her losing this man she loved with all her being.

This fear sent prickling sensations up her spine.

Was this real? Or was she simply going mad?

Three days later, she walked up the steps of the Harcourt townhouse, her legs feeling as heavy as blocks of granite. Her father's reception would be warm because Octavian had since taken care of the vowels owed to Sir Henry. He had paid them over to that villain's brother who turned out not to be a villain at all and agreed to cancel the debt upon repayment of a mere thirty percent of it. "Henry had no moral scruples," the brother had told Octavian. "I do not know who was cheated and who was not, but I suspect not all of these vowels were honestly acquired. I have no way of knowing which were and which were not. I expect he cheated most, for this is the manipulative, evil man he was. I would forgive every last debt if I could. But there is a cost to cleaning up his affairs and putting the Maxwell businesses back in legitimate order. So, I must ask for a thirty percent settlement. I think this is fair."

Octavian had agreed and settled the account.

Syd knew he intended to set aside the remaining seventy percent and use it to assist her parents when her father ran up more debts, which he inevitably would. The only question was how soon and how much?

Her mother ought to have been pleased by the outcome, but Syd knew that she would not be. It was not in her nature ever to be satisfied. She would find a reason to ignore the fact they had been saved from ruin by Octavian's generosity.

"Good afternoon, Stanford," she said with a smile when the Harcourt butler opened the door of her former residence to find her standing on the other side of it.

"Lady Sydney!" His stoic expression melted away as he cast her a beaming smile in return. "What a joy it is to see you again."

That he appeared genuinely surprised only meant her parents had neglected to inform the staff of her visit. "Typical," she muttered under her breath, for there was nothing prepared to receive a guest, even though the arrangements had been made several days ago. Her mother was aware of the date and time agreed upon for her visit.

Had she bothered to tell her father?

Syd began to doubt herself, and now wondered whether she ought to have sent a note off to him, too.

She should have done so, she realized.

Those two moved about the household like two wraiths passing in the night. They rarely spoke to each other. Rarely acknowledged the other was there. Mostly, it was her mother who ignored them all. Her father often tried to be affable.

This meeting would be their first after she had married, but her mother would not care, nor would she rejoice in her daughter's happiness. Her mother had never viewed her role as one of bringing the family together.

Syd chided herself again.

How foolish of her not to send separate notes. But was her mother not mostly to blame? Even though her parents led fairly separate lives, they did live under the same roof and spoke on occasion. Would a recently married daughter's visit not be something worth mentioning to him? Or the staff?

Apparently not.

She stifled her hurt.

Why did she think her mother would ever change?

She followed the Harcourt butler into the parlor. "How are my parents, Stanford?"

His smile faltered. "Same as always."

"I'm sorry for that."

"May I congratulate you on your marriage? Captain Thorne came by several days ago to meet with your father. He seems an excellent man."

Syd nodded. "He is, Stanford. The very best of men."

"I am happy for you, Lady Sydney. Well, you are Lady Thorne now. You deserve the best. I shall advise your parents that you have arrived. Will you be staying long? Shall I bring in tea and cakes?"

"No, that won't be necessary. Please convey my best regards to the rest of the staff."

"I will." He left her on her own while he went in search of her parents.

It felt odd to be sitting in the visitor's parlor while awaiting them, to be sitting here as though she were a stranger calling upon an earl and countess she hardly knew when this had always been her home. In truth, none of the servants would stop her if she waltzed up to her bedchamber and had a look around.

One of the things Octavian had done when arranging to meet with her father was to order her clothes packed up and sent to the Huntsford residence. Her father had agreed without rancor and advised their housekeeper to attend to it, for he was always most amiable, especially when swindling someone. The clothes had arrived in a jumbled mess, no doubt her mother's doing. A sign of her resentment? Why did the woman wish her any ill? Should a mother not rejoice in her own daughter's happiness? But this had never been her mother's way. She was as vain as her father, except lacking his charm.

As the minutes passed, Syd felt the walls begin to close in around her. She took several deep breaths.

The parlor felt like a mausoleum.

Dark drapes.

Dark furnishings that were in obvious need of replacing since most were chipped or frayed.

As she was about to conduct her own search of the house for her parents, her mother walked in.

Syd smiled and rose to greet her. "Mama, how are you?"

"How do you expect me to feel?" Her mother stiffened as Syd kissed her on the cheek. "I have a husband who has burned through his inheritance and mine."

"Not to mention mine," Syd muttered. "But Papa's debts are cleared now. With a little effort, the entailed properties will once more provide enough of an income to get you back on your feet."

"Do not be absurd, girl! Effort? When has your father ever lifted a finger? The only thing he has ever been diligent about is gambling. He will toss the entirety of his earnings away before a single coin ever reaches his hands. That is your miserable father for you. He has never had a care for me, nor did he ever care for you."

Syd tamped down the urge to turn around and walk out.

She had a home with Octavian now and did not need to endure this constant criticism. Yes, most of it was aimed at her father and most of it was true.

Still, why could she not ease up on him just this once? "I know he is quite flawed, Mama. But he never beat us or mistreated us. I agree, at times we could have lived better. But we went about in the best circles, had a roof over our heads, and food on the table. We did on occasion have to run from creditors, but it wasn't all that often. Father always found a way to land on his feet. And we did have some happy times together, did we not?"

Her mother took a seat on the settee and motioned for Syd to take the chair across from hers. "Happy times? Are you deluded, girl? It was all fakery. Make-believe. Just as our marriage has always been."

Syd cringed, for was this not exactly how she had insisted her marriage to Octavian needed to be? Sham. Fake. Make-believe.

Dear heaven.

Would she resemble this angry, sour woman in twenty years?

No. No.

She would never be like this. Her flaw was that she had too much compassion. She was the opposite of this woman in every way. In truth, she had never resembled her mother either physically or in temperament.

She did not have much in common with her father, either. Perhaps the color of their hair was similar, although his was much lighter, more of a cornsilk blond in his younger days. His hair was shot through with strands of white now. His eyes were green, but a much darker shade than hers. More of a forest green.

But they did often laugh together.

The mere sight of her always cheered her father whenever he felt particularly defeated. He always had a smile for her, and would make her smile if she appeared to be overset. Despite his many flaws, she still loved him. In time, she might forgive him for agreeing to sell her off to Sir Henry.

What did it matter?

She had escaped that evil man's clutches and was happily married to Octavian now. Best of all, theirs was a love match.

She placed a hand over her stomach as it began to churn with this perpetual dread she could not seem to shake off.

Why did it plague her?

Octavian was nothing like her father, and would never repeat any of his mistakes, for he was fine and brave.

Abandoning her was out of the question.

He would never gamble away his fortune.

They were truly husband and wife in every possible way now, and he would always put her and any children they were blessed to have first in his heart.

"Oh, he smiles and struts about like a fine gentleman," her mother grumbled, regaining Syd's attention as she bemoaned her father. "He pats you on the head and tells you what a pretty thing you are, but he lies through his teeth. You are *nothing* to him. You, my girl, with your smug smile and new husband who will soon deceive and disappoint you, were never anything more than a useful tool for him to access an inheritance."

"What do you mean?"

Her mother said nothing, merely responded with another smug look.

"Mama, why do you stay under the same roof with my father if you are so miserable with him?" Syd asked.

"And where else would I stay?"

"You have family who would help establish you elsewhere."

Her mother huffed. "Are you suggesting I retire to Bath? Move about in that lesser Society? Entertain graceless rustics and creaky-kneed gentry who have settled there for the healing waters?"

"It is second only to London in our social circles and more popular than London in the summers," she replied, wondering why her mother appeared more agitated than usual.

"You are just like your father. Always hoping to get rid of me. But I am a countess and will not be demeaned. I will not give up the privileges of my rank."

Syd reached over to take her mother's hand in comfort, but her mother drew it away and cast her an icy look. "I only married him because he was an earl. What good has it done me? I should be living in style instead of always scrounging for pin money. And you certainly gave us a worry."

Warmth spread through Syd. "You were worried about me? I'm sorry I ran away, but you and Papa left me with no choice. I did not want to marry Sir Henry."

Now, she felt badly about not telling her parents about her elopement plans. But how could she let on when the information would have quickly fallen into Sir Henry's hands and he would have stopped them? Nor could her father simply agree to let her marry Octavian, for Sir Henry had a stranglehold on him because of his gambling debts. The villain would have killed her father had he given his consent to a union between her and anyone other than himself. "Truly, Mama. I am so sorry I gave you cause to worry for my safety."

She laughed bitterly. "It wasn't about you, Syd. It has never been about you. Are you so blind to what you are to us?"

What was her mother going on about? Syd hated these cryptic comments designed to be vague and cruel. Why could she not simply get to the point? "What do you mean?"

She stared at her mother, noting the age lines across her brow and at the corners of her eyes. Her mouth had a downward dip to it, so that she never looked happy even when her face was relaxed. Her dark brown hair was threaded with gray, and she sat with a slight stoop, as though bowed by the weight of her age. She was only in her mid-forties, but the dark orbs staring back at Syd looked aged beyond their years.

"Have you not guessed the truth by now, stupid girl?"

Another knot formed in Syd's belly. She no longer saw her mother's face but waves of darkness swirling around her. "You've had your cruel fun. Just tell me what this is about."

"Harcourt and I are not–"

"Lady Harcourt, shut up!" her father commanded, striding in at just that moment and looking angrier than she had ever seen him.

Syd had been too caught up studying her mother to realize he had been standing in the doorway. Had he been there all the while? How much had he overheard? She and her mother had said nothing outrageous. Although her mother's words were not complimentary to him, this was nothing new.

When had her mother ever had a kind word for him?

Never.

Nor had she ever expressed a kindness for her.

But this hatred she had always harbored for her father was in full blossom now. In truth, her father was no less critical of his wife. This is why they always addressed each other as though strangers. He was always Harcourt to her. She was always Lady Harcourt to him.

The complaints had always been the same.

She hated his gambling.

He disliked her constantly berating him.

Syd rose and hesitantly smiled at her father. "Good to see you, Papa."

She was uncertain whether his present anger extended to her as well. But why should it? He had come out of his scrape with Sir Henry smelling like a rose. His debt was paid. Sir Henry was dead and could never threaten him again. And his daughter was happily married to Octavian, the very man who had paid that debt.

"Good afternoon, Syd." He had a glorious smile for her that felt genuine, but one could never be certain with her father. He was awfully smooth. "You are a sight for sore eyes, child. Why did you not tell us you were stopping by? I'll have Stanford bring in refreshments."

Her mother shot to her feet. "What are you doing home at this hour, Harcourt? What happened? Are the odds-makers refusing to accept your bets?"

Dear heaven.

Syd did not miss this constant bickering.

She was going to hug Octavian and kiss every inch of his face when she saw him next. "Papa, did you not know I was coming over?" She glanced at her mother, curious as to why she would hide the news from him. It wasn't as though they were going to have a loving mother-daughter exchange.

Had her mother said a single kind word yet?

She had never been a loving mother.

If not for Syd's genuinely compassionate nanny and later her equally caring governess, she would never have known a gentle, female touch. Her mother had never tucked her into bed or nursed her when she was ill. Nor had she ever cheered any of her accomplishments.

Was this not odd?

Syd had never given it much thought until seeing the mothering instincts come out in her married friends, Adela and Marigold.

Only then did she realize how wholly devoid of feeling this woman standing before her was.

Her father made up for some of the lack, for he had a genial nature. He was always joking, and always had a pretty compliment for her. But he was never as protective or responsible as Octavian. In truth, he never rolled up his sleeves and worked hard at anything. It galled her to admit that her mother had been right about that.

But for a child starved for affection, his smiles and pats on the head were everything. Despite his inept ways, Syd had always felt he loved her. "Mama, why did you not tell him?"

"I'll answer that," her father said. "She means to spread her poison. Have you not noticed how we are suddenly the topic of interest in the gossip rags?"

Syd nodded. "Yes, what is that about?"

Her mother laughed with unmasked bitterness.

Her father frowned. "Do not believe anything she tells you, Syd. She only means to hurt you."

Syd's stomach now ached so badly, she could feel the pain radiating throughout her body. "How can she hurt me? I already know she does not love me. Nor does she love you. Mama, is it just us? Or do you hate everyone?"

She gave another bitter laugh. "Oh, it is just you and your father. I've kept quiet all these years, but no more."

Her father looked upon his wife, still enraged. "There is no reason for your cruelty, Lady Harcourt. Why can you not let any of the past go? Captain Thorne has saved us from ruin. Your status is secure. Is this not all you care about? Is this not all you have ever cared about? You certainly never gave me a thought."

Her mother made a snide sound of dismissal.

Her father pressed on. "You and I shall never be reconciled. It is far too late for us now. But is this how you are to show your gratitude to our daughter? By filling her good heart with your poison?"

Her mother's expression turned chilling. "Our daughter? *Our* daughter? Oh, that is amusing. But you were always a great jester. How easily you charm everyone and make them laugh."

"Dear heaven." Her father now turned to her. "Go home, Syd. Go home to your husband, my precious girl," he said in all seriousness.

"Papa?" Syd wanted to run, but before she could move, her mother grabbed her by the wrist and held on so tight that Syd yelped. "Mama, let me go!"

"Know this before you run away like a scared, little rabbit. This man is hardly worthy to claim himself as your father. Who knows if he really is your father? He's always told me that he is not. Is that not a wonderfully dirty, little secret? But who can tell if it is true or not when he never tells the truth? More important, I was *never* your mother. Do you hear me? You are not my daughter. You are *nothing* to us. We've used you all these years. To us, you are just a foolish nobody."

Her father hurriedly shut the door and turned to her mother…this woman…this unrecognizable, mad person holding onto her wrist with enough force that Syd feared she might actually snap a bone. "You have gone too far," her father growled, turning on her mother. "Do not utter another word or I shall have you locked away forever. Did I not assure you that I would take care of you? Have I not kept to my word all these years? There is no question of divorce, as you well know. Your status is secure. Why are you causing trouble now?"

"My status secure? Ha! You have taken every last shred of dignity from me. It was the only thing I had left because you stripped away everything else. And now you think to bring a mistress into this house? My home? I will not have it!"

Syd gasped. "Papa? Is this true?"

"No, sweetheart. But I do intend to move out and get some joy in my life now that I know you are happily settled and safely away from this woman."

Her mother's laughter was more of a witch's cackle. "See how he continues to lie? How sweetly he does it, too. Joy in his life? He's found himself a rich widow and she is to be his next victim. He'll abandon her as soon as he's lost all her money, too."

"Syd, please. Do not believe her." Her father looked pained as he turned pleading eyes on her. "Yes, I am a gambler. I readily admit I am a lowly hound. I know I have not been the best father to you, but I have given you whatever I could. Everything possible within my means."

Her mother gasped. "You've stolen whatever you could! This is what you do best. Steal. Lie. Take. Take. *Take.* You never give." She squeezed Syd's wrist hard again. "Who are you going to believe? Him or me?"

She had no wish to take sides. "I love both of you."

This turned out to be the wrong thing to say to her mother, apparently an incendiary statement that put her in a rage. She finally released Syd, but only did so in order to raise a hand to slap her.

Syd had been fearless when fending off those Armstrong reivers and drunken MacGregors. But she watched in horror as her mother's bony fingers whipped closer, and she was too stunned to defend herself.

Her father stepped between them in time to prevent the blow from striking her. "Enough, Lady Harcourt! Calm down and apologize to our daughter immediately, or I shall have you declared mad and put away."

"Mad, am I? If so, then you have driven me to it. You and this *thing* you picked up off the streets." She glowered at Syd. "You think you are so high and mighty. You think you are an earl's daughter. Well, you are not. You are *nothing*. Just some lowly by-blow acquired as a useful tool to gain an inheritance."

Her father looked thoroughly stricken. "Do not believe a word she says, Syd. She is only trying to hurt you."

"She'll hear the truth now, you lying scoundrel." This woman she had always considered a mother now turned the force of her anger on Syd. "You were brought here because I could not bear children, and there was all this money just lying untouched in a trust established by my family for any children of mine. Your father was on his way to gambling through his inheritance."

"They were business ventures gone bad. How was I to know?" he argued.

Her mother ignored him. "Then he began to gamble through my dowry. As our resources dwindled, he came up with the bright idea of claiming this children's trust. It is all gone now. Everything lost in a puff of smoke. So, now he intends to leave me because I am no longer of any use to him."

Syd was ready to toss up her accounts.

She felt nauseated.

Her father put an arm around her. "My dear girl, do not believe a word of the bile spewing from her lips. She is angry and trying to hurt us."

But Syd knew it was the truth.

This is exactly who her father was. Jovial. Amiable. But also lazy, selfish, and not above swindling anyone and everyone. Having used up all his resources, he was about to move on to more fertile ground and cheat an unsuspecting widow out of her life savings. He would do this rather than put any effort into restoring the Harcourt properties.

As for herself, had she not felt this iciness in her mother for all of her life? And if this embittered woman believed herself so righteous, then why did she not say a word when he began to dip into the children's trust? She was as much in on his lies and schemes, keeping silent as he used the funds that were not his. She did this in order to maintain her position in Society. She did this to live in stylish fashion. New gowns. Jewelry. A town carriage. The lavish parties they once held because appearance was everything to both of them.

Was it any surprise the money ran out?

He may have swindled. But she spent as much of those ill-gotten gains as he did.

Syd was going to toss up her accounts if she did not get out of here right away. But how could she leave with so many unanswered questions? What was true and what were lies? "Who am I, Papa?"

His pain seemed genuine, but he had gotten so good at weaving his stories, she could no longer tell. Perhaps he was so convincing that he had also convinced himself his lies were true. "You are my daughter."

"And yet, he was ready to sell you to Sir Henry Maxwell," her mother retorted. "Think of that, Syd. Would a true father do this to his daughter?"

No...but some did...but, no.

She hated to agree with her mother...or whoever this woman was to her. What loving father would ever sacrifice his true daughter? "I need to go. Octavian is expecting me. I dare not be late."

"Yes," her mother said with so much venom threaded through that one word. "Go home and tell him that you are not an earl's daughter. Let him know that you are a nobody the Earl of Harcourt picked up off the streets. Won't he be cheered? There's an end to your happy marriage. His family will be tainted and his career in ruins once the scandal breaks. And I assure you, I will see to it. What have I got to lose now?"

Her harsh laughter resounded through the parlor.

Syd blindly raced toward the front door.

She wanted to get away from these miserable people and rush home to Octavian.

Home.

In truth, she had no home to truly call her own.

The Huntsford townhouse belonged to Ambrose, not to her or Octavian. Still, it was somewhere away from her family. It was where should would find Octavian, although who was to say when he would get home this evening? He had been working late all week on his presentation to the Admiralty which he claimed was almost completed.

What would she say to him?

She had to tell him the truth.

But what was true and what were lies? She would repeat the conversation and let him decide what to believe.

Greeves took one look at her as she walked in and his eyes widened. "My lady," he said, noticeably alarmed, "you do not look well. Shall I summon a doctor?"

"No, please do not make a fuss. It is nothing serious. Have Mrs. Quinn bring me up a pot of tea. I'll be in my bedchamber. I need to rest."

"Right away." He cast her another worried look. "I shall send word to Captain Thorne."

"No, you mustn't disturb his important work. Just send him upstairs when he arrives home."

Her legs once again felt like granite blocks as she made her way up the stairs. This was it. This was the dread that had haunted her from the moment she opened her heart and accepted a true and forever marriage.

Why had she done this?

She ought to have waited the full nine months before committing to Octavian. Instead, she had held out less than two months.

If only she had waited.

She knew all along, did she not? She knew that her marriage could never be anything more than make-believe.

Her dreams of forever could never come true, for she had come to Octavian with nothing but her good name.

And now, she did not even have that.

Dread filled her.

She felt more ill than she had ever felt in her life.

Would Octavian demand that she move out this very night?

CHAPTER 19

OCTAVIAN RACED UP to his bedchamber as soon as Greeves told him Syd was not feeling well. He cursed under his breath, knowing the visit to her parents must have badly overset her. He should have gone with her. Why did he not go with her? Those blasted Admiralty reports could have waited an extra day. It made no difference whether he turned them in tomorrow or two days from now.

He felt a heaviness in the air as he strode down the hall toward their chamber. His heart twisted in knots. What had her parents done to her? Greeves said she had returned home looking ashen and pale, and had practically crawled up the stairs.

She was in utter despair, if his butler was to be believed.

Of course, he believed Greeves.

The man was loyal and never lied.

The room was dark when he entered, the curtains drawn tightly closed to hide the late afternoon sunlight. "Syd?"

He saw the littlest lump beneath the covers and knew she was lying there, curled in a tight ball. He crossed to the drapes to draw them wide and allow in all the light because he wanted to see her face while he spoke to her.

She groaned as the fading rays of sunlight streamed in. "Why did you do that?"

He marched to the bed and sat beside her prone form. Her head was barely peeking out from under the covers, so all he could see was the top of her head and a little of her nose. "Syd, sweetheart. Talk to me. Tell me what happened."

An ill feeling overtook him. He knew this dread haunting her for weeks had finally reared its ugly head and become horribly real. It was no longer a wispy specter that hovered on the outer edges of her mind. He waited for her to speak, but all that came out were hitching breaths and soul-deep sobs. "Syd, please. I'm here. We'll deal with the problem together."

"That's just it. We cannot be together," she said between hiccups and more ragged breaths. "I'm so sorry, Octavian. You are completely blameless in all this. I will do whatever I can to spare you. It has all been make-believe. I feared it. Did I not tell you how much I feared it? Not just our marriage, but my entire life. A complete sham. Please believe I never knew. And now I've got you into this scandal and ruined your life, too."

He had never seen Syd this vulnerable and shaken.

The fight had gone out of her.

The impassioned fires had been stomped out.

It tore him up inside.

"You haven't ruined anything for me," he growled. "And what is it that you never knew?"

She tried to speak, but was aching so badly that she couldn't.

Blessed saints.

What had her parents done to her?

He sighed. "Sweetheart, start at the beginning."

Her father was a despicable cheat and a weasel, but his method was to charm and cajole. It was not his fashion to intimidate and destroy. Whatever took place during her visit to her parents was no mere argument.

Syd looked broken.

"No more hiding, love. Come here." Despite her token protest, he slid the coverlet aside and hauled her onto his lap because he wanted to look at her face and hold her in his arms as they spoke. Her eyes were red and her cheeks blotched from all her crying. He withdrew his handkerchief and gave it over to her since hers was thoroughly soaked from her tears. "Tell me, Syd. What has this to do with your parents?"

She took several deep breaths to calm herself. "I knew

something bad was going to happen. Did I not tell you so?"

He nodded. "Yes, love. You did."

And he blamed himself for dismissing her concerns.

Syd was no feather-headed fribble of a girl. Nor was she a mouse who shrank at her own shadow. She was often too brave for her own good. For this reason, he ought to have taken her distress more seriously. That she could not explain exactly what was troubling her was no excuse to absolve him of blame.

He should not have let her go into the Harcourt house alone.

"My skin prickled as I walked through the front door," she said, her words still hitching because she could not calm herself. "I wanted to turn and run. But I made myself enter, even though I could not stop shivering. That sense of doom fell over me as Stanford led me into the parlor. I felt a darkness surrounding me. Our parlor is the ugliest room. Truly, such an ugly room. Austere. Devoid of all cheer. It sucks all the joy out of one's soul."

Octavian caressed her cheek while waiting for her to continue.

He did not want to hear about the Harcourt parlor, but understood that Syd needed to build up the strength to talk about the fight that obviously took place between her and her parents. Did they both attack her? Verbally, that is. Her father, for all his faults, was not a physically brutal man. He could not say the same about her mother, however. Syd appeared to have a small bruise on her wrist.

Had one of them done this to her?

The mere thought of Syd being hurt shot his heart into his throat. Not that she couldn't defend herself. Syd was fearless and had not backed down when any of those Scots had tried to put a hand on her.

But this was her parents.

She would not fight back because she loved them. They were most undeserving, but he had no control over her soft feelings toward them.

In any event, Octavian could not imagine both of them assaulting Syd since the husband and wife never agreed on anything. If one claimed it was day, the other said it was night. If one said the moon was out, the other would claim it was the sun.

If one attempted to hurt Syd, would not the other prevent it? "Sweetheart, what did they say to you?"

"The dread," she said with shattered breath. "The fear. The lies. The schemes. The depravity."

He wrapped her in his embrace. "Blessed saints, Syd. What happened?"

"The end to our marriage. That is what happened. We were happy together, weren't we Octavian?"

"And still are," he said, trying to contain his mounting anger. It was not aimed at Syd, of course. He wanted to protect her to the end of his days. He wanted to shield her from hurt and pain, but he hadn't shielded her from whatever torment this was. "I love you, Syd."

"No." She shook her head vehemently. "You won't after this."

She started crying again.

Syd did shed tears on occasion, but she was hardly a watering pot. However, rivers of water were now flowing out of her. Oceans of it. "I came to you with nothing…and this is what I am. *Nothing*. Not even an earl's daughter. *Less than nothing*. I do not even know who I am."

It took another half hour to get the entire story out of her because she spent so much of the time catching her breath and going on about that awful parlor that he did not give a fig about. But he finally understood what had taken place.

Syd believed she was some illegitimate newborn taken from her dying mother's arms and given over to Harcourt and his wife for the sole purpose of getting their hands on a children's trust set up by Lady Harcourt's family.

Dear heaven.

This sounded like some hatched up scheme out of a cheap novel. A gothic tale of treachery and the innocent orphan girl used for a villain's depraved purpose. Only this girl was Syd and this was real.

Well, he wasn't sure if any of it was true. Syd obviously believed it because of the coldness she had endured from the woman she had always thought of as her mother. Lady Harcourt was a bitter woman who did not know the meaning of love.

Octavian had never seen her crack a smile or ever utter a kind word to Syd. It was not farfetched that she now lied to Syd for the sheer purpose of hurting her.

It likely was more for the sheer pleasure of hurting her husband. Unfortunately, Syd was caught in the middle. Her mother would not care that her words also destroyed her daughter.

"I'll move out," Syd said, letting out another trembling breath. "I'm not sure where I can go yet. I don't even know if my friends will accept me once they learn the truth. I think they will, even though they will be scorned if they dare keep me in their social circle. But you and I must deal with this problem first. Perhaps we ought to return to Scotland and quietly annul the marriage. It is easier done there, don't you think? Can we annul it?"

"No, we cannot," he said with determination, for he'd gained Syd's love and was not about to toss it away.

"Oh, because we've made the marriage real in *that* way. But there must be other legal grounds for an annulment. Lying about my identity should be an acceptable reason. A commoner masquerading as an earl's daughter. They will declare me a liar and a fraud, and grant your freedom. Oh, Octavian. I don't even know my real name!"

He wrapped his fingers gently around her shoulders, holding her so that she could not turn away while he spoke to her. "You are Sydney Thorne now. Lady Thorne because I am the son of a duke and you are my wife. Whether you should have been addressed as a lady in your past is no longer of any relevance. You are a lady now because of your connection to me. The only question is, do you prefer to be addressed as Mrs. Thorne or Lady Thorne? It is up to you, but does not change your right to be Lady Thorne."

"My mother…if she is even that…is going to spread the story of my illegitimacy around London because she is so angry with my father. He tried to reason with her, but it enraged her all the more. He even agreed to end all relations with the other woman he had recently taken up with. A rich widow, my mother claims. He vowed never to see her again and that he would remain under the same roof with my mother, but this was also to no avail."

Octavian doubted her father would ever keep to his word. If he was going after this rich widow to gain access to her wealth, then nothing would deter him. Also, if he truly cared for this new woman, he would not be deterred either.

Even scoundrels fell in love.

"Octavian, my mother never cared a jot for him. Truly, she has always detested the sight of him. So, why does she care that he is now taking up with another woman? It is not uncommon among members of the *ton* to look elsewhere for affection."

"Perhaps she loves him and has always been afraid to admit it because he might spurn her." In truth, he dismissed this as a possibility. The woman was cold as an iceberg. If one peered beneath the surface, one would only find more ice.

"Oh, no. It isn't possible," Syd said, confirming his own thoughts. "Well, who knows what happened between them in the early years? Perhaps she did regard him with affection in the beginning. And as you say, he might have spurned her. Yet, I have never known my father to be unfaithful. For all his faults, this was never one of them."

She sighed and continued. "How could my mother have loved him and to this day never bothered to tell him so? Or ever shown him a scintilla of caring or compassion? In this I cannot condemn my father for finally having had enough. She never smiles. She never has a kind word to say for anyone, least of all him. You've referred to her as icy. But that is just her facade. Inside, she is a bubbling cauldron of dark thoughts and feelings. The irony is that she does not even realize she will be destroying herself along with him. Social standing is everything to her. Perhaps she does realize it and no longer cares. She certainly has never cared for me."

She looked up at Octavian, her beautiful eyes filled with so much pain. "Are there such people, Octavian? Those who cannot abide happiness and seek to destroy it in others? Is this what she is doing? Destroying everything my father holds dear? How can I have been so blind not to see the depth of her resentment? I am such an idiot."

He still had his hands on her slight shoulders and now rubbed them lightly in a gesture meant to comfort her. "You are not an idiot, Syd."

She shook her head in disagreement. "But I am. I walked around thinking I was so clever. A bluestocking know-it-all. Yet, I could not see what was going on under my very nose."

"How could you know, love? Your heart has always been filled with hope and compassion. What a strong, little heart yours must have been as a child to overcome her vindictive bile. This is your heart now, too. Strong, resilient, full of compassion and goodness."

She threw her arms around him and hugged him fiercely. "I love you, Octavian. I love you with all my heart and soul. But I will give you the annulment because I will not have your good name ruined by all this. If an annulment is not possible, then I shall grant you the divorce. We can accomplish this as quietly as possible. I never cared for any of the privileges of rank. I don't want anything from you. I am not afraid to work hard and make my own way. Well, I may need your help in securing employment. I would enjoy working in a museum or other place of knowledge. I understand that any position at the Huntsford Academy would be out of the question now, of course. You would need to cut all ties with me."

He eased out of the hug and took her hands in his. "Are you done with your list of demands?"

"What demands? I have only asked for your help in seeking employment." She stared at him through her misty eyes. "Am I not being reasonable?"

"Not at all. You are assuming I wish to end our marriage, which I do not."

Her eyes widened. "But once the scandal breaks–"

"I do not care. Lord, Syd. How could you think I would?"

"What about your Admiralty work? Your career. Your impending promotion."

He kissed her with raw abandon, wanting her to feel the tingle on her lips long after the kiss ended. Wanting her to feel *him* on her lips and not forget him. "It is all worth nothing if I do not have you beside me. I do not care who you are or where you came from. In truth, I think you are an angel sent from heaven."

She gave a wistful laugh. "I'm not sure you understand the definition of angel, if you think I am that."

"I understand it perfectly. An angel is a good, sweet soul who is beautiful in appearance but occasionally irritating, often impossibly independent, and incredibly opinionated. An angel is also recklessly fearless in her defense of others. Sound familiar? Because you are exactly that. This is why you have *always* been perfect for me. No matter how much of what your parents told you is true, even if all of it is true, I do not care. All that matters is you are mine now. Mine to love and protect."

"Octavian, you cannot mean that."

"Every bloody word. You are my happiness. You are my heart and my future. I have no intention of giving you up."

She place a finger to his lips and slid it lightly back and forth across his mouth to quiet him as she gazed at him in wonder. "I will not hold you to this. You need to sleep on such an important decision that will change the course of your life. Think about it overnight, Octavian. Or take longer. I do not intend to force you into making a rash choice."

"I am not the rash one in this marriage," he reminded her, his manner light and affectionate.

She managed a small smile. "I know, but you are very quick to dismiss the potential damage to your future. You sounded very much like me just now. Hotheaded. Impassioned. Stubbornly certain you were right."

"Because I am right. There is nothing to consider."

"The repercussions of this scandal might take weeks or months to unfold," she needlessly warned because he was fully aware of all that could happen, especially the damage to his chances of promotion to the rank of admiral.

It all paled in comparison to losing her.

"You need to think calmly about this without my interference. I'll ask Mrs. Quinn to prepare one of the guest chambers for me."

He held her fast to him when she attempted to rise. "No, you won't. Syd, so help me...don't you dare turn martyr on me. Sacrificing your happiness is not going to save me from strife. We are married and will stay married, and that's an end to it."

She frowned at him. "Why are you being so difficult?"

"Me?" Octavian shook his head and laughed. "Have I not been clear enough? I do not care who your true parents might be. They could not possibly be any worse than Harcourt and his wife. In truth, I would cheer loudest and longest upon having it confirmed that you are no blood relation to them. Could anyone have in-laws worse than them?"

He tipped her chin up to bring her face closer to his, and then dipped his head and kissed her full on the mouth again. She had the prettiest bow lips, soft and slightly plump. Lips a man could sink into and lose himself in their splendor.

Her body was the same, soft in all the right places, and curved in all the best places. In addition, she loved him truly. There was never any guile or artifice about Syd. He knew exactly where she stood on any subject, especially those she was passionate about, because she gave her opinion whether asked for or not. "I married you for better or for worse, minx."

"Ugh, don't call me that," she muttered, managing a small smile even though she was overset.

He nuzzled her neck, inhaling the soft, sweet scent of her skin while he suckled the pulse now throbbing at the base of her throat. "You started off as a thorn in my side, and shall now always be a Thorne *by* my side," he said with a husky ache to his voice, intending the pun on rose thorns and his family's surname of Thorne.

Syd stared at him, although he doubted she could see much beyond the veil of tears still clouding her eyes. "Why are you being so obstinate when I am trying to save you?"

"I do not wish to be saved from you. How many ways must I tell you that I do not want to be without you, Syd?"

"How can you be so wonderful to me? What did I ever do right to deserve a husband like you?"

"I could ask the same about you. Why did good fortune smile down on me and give me the perfect wife?"

She laughed. "Dear heaven, I am far from perfect."

"Neither am I."

"Oh, you are so wrong about that, Octavian. There is not a man in all England better than you. So, how can you attach yourself to a wife who is not even real?"

"I did not marry a name. I married *you*. We may have questions about your true identity, questions that will be addressed in time. If this requires Homer Barrow and his army of Bow Street runners to dig into your past, then so be it. But one thing I know for certain is that you are not Joan of Arc. So kindly stop tossing yourself onto that burning sacrificial pyre for my sake. I would rather have you in the lovely, pink flesh and not as the ashen remains of a burnt offering."

"Octavian!"

"What? Am I not entitled to my opinion?"

She furrowed her brow and pursed her lips, making him want to kiss her again even though she was frowning at him. But then, he always wanted to kiss her. "You have not given this problem enough thought," she chided.

"I have given it all the thought it merits. Shall I have supper sent up here? We can dine quietly in our chamber tonight. And we shall both sleep in this bed tonight and every night hereafter. End of discussion, Syd."

"You are being most highhanded."

"Sorry, but the thought of losing my wife over something that was not her fault has put me in ill humor. I'll arrange to meet your parents tomorrow and find out what is really going on."

"We'll go together," she said, easing back to look up at him. "I want to do this with you."

He was not thrilled with that idea. "Syd, today's visit devastated you. Are you sure you want to accompany me?"

"Yes." She nodded emphatically. "I can face anything when you are by my side. You wonderful, big ox. How can you not hate me?"

He tweaked her chin. "Your parents caught you by surprise today. Your mother's words were meant to be cruel, her barbs tipped with poisonous bile aimed at your lovely heart where they would cause the most damage. You were alone and unprepared for her attack. But you have me by your side for now and always.

We shall deal with her tomorrow."

She cast him a breathtakingly tender smile.

He ordered their supper brought up.

Syd hardly touched her food, merely pecked at her vegetables like a little bird.

Once all had been cleared away, they readied for bed. Octavian usually stayed awake later than Syd. His routine was to settle in one of the tufted chairs beside the hearth with a book and a glass of wine in hand. But Syd never fell into more than a light sleep until he joined her in bed and took her into his arms. Only then would she let down her guard and drift into a deep and unreserved slumber.

The more he learned about Syd, the more he grew to understand how much she had kept bottled up inside for much of her life. That she had grown to trust him and rely on him was an enormous compliment. It could not have been easy for her to let anyone in. In truth, no one had ever gotten this close to her before.

But she had let him in, trusting him to keep her safe.

This is why she held onto him even while asleep.

It was his touch that allowed her to shed her defenses.

For this reason, he altered his routine this evening. He still read, but did so while in bed. This allowed Syd to burrow against him and be comforted by his body beside hers.

This was a comfort to him, too.

He needed her beside him...whoever she was...wherever she had come from. She was his wife and nothing else mattered to him.

But it mattered to her.

Despite his presence beside her, he saw that her sleep was not as peaceful as it could have been. She tossed and turned, unable to find a comfortable position. "Syd, love. Your fretting won't help anything. Try to rest."

"I'm trying, but it is hard to fall asleep when I don't know who I am."

"You are my wife, that's who you are. No matter your lineage, you are the woman I love and nothing is going to change that." He set aside his book and simply held her, stroking her hair and caressing her until she finally drifted off, her body half sprawled atop him.

Yes, she was his to love and protect.

Would her parents tell them the truth when confronted tomorrow?

CHAPTER 20

OCTAVIAN TUCKED SYD'S arm in his and placed his hand over hers for extra reassurance as they stood in front of the Harcourt townhouse the following morning awaiting the inevitable confrontation. Not that she needed him to hold her hand, really. Her flood of tears last night had not been about her mother's hurtful words, but about her fear of losing him because of those accusations hurled by the woman who had not a trace of maternal feeling in her.

Now that Syd was assured their marriage would endure, she seemed to be back in fighting spirit. However, she was still uncertain that it *should* endure because of the damage she feared to his family and his Admiralty career. For this reason, she continued to behave like a martyr. All morning long, she had insisted on his needing to give their situation more thought. "No thought needed, Syd. My mind is made up," he had told her every time she brought it up. "You are my wife and the only woman I want beside me. That is an end to it."

"You do not know all the facts yet," she would counter.

"Nor do you. Stop trying to save me when I am not in need of rescue."

"Perhaps you need rescuing from yourself."

He did not want martyr Syd.

Martyr Syd was going to sacrifice her happiness to protect his good name when he couldn't give a fig about what others thought of him. Martyr Syd was going to run off and hide somewhere because she did not want to be a burden to him when she was actually the light in his life and eased the weight on his shoulders.

Nor would his brothers care for any supposed stain she might attach to the Thorne family name. How could anyone consider it her fault when she had been an innocent newborn when taken by the Harcourts?

"Good morning, Stanford," she greeted the Harcourt butler when he opened the door, her smile sweet but her chin pointed upward in defiance.

"Good morning, Lady Thorne. Captain Thorne." He tried to maintain a stoic facade even though he was clearly surprised to find them standing in front of him at this early hour. But it was not all that early. Syd knew the schedules each parent kept and had mentioned her father would be up by now. It was shortly after ten o'clock and who really cared whether it was socially acceptable or not to call upon them when dealing with a situation of this importance? "Neither Lord Harcourt nor Lady Harcourt has come down yet."

Syd did not appear in the least put off. "That's too bad, but we shall await them in the parlor. It is a most hideous room, is it not Stanford?"

"Yes, m'lady. Without a doubt."

She cast him another warm smile. "Which is why I hope they will not keep us waiting. Tell them they have ten minutes to get down here or Captain Thorne shall bodily remove them from their beds and haul their miserable personages down the stairs."

Stanford stared at her in dismay.

"Forgive me if I've shocked you, Stanford. But I'm sure you overheard more than you ought yesterday and know what this is about." Syd pointed to the large clock in the corner of the entry hall. "Time is wasting. Do not bother to show us into the parlor. We know the way. But do send in refreshments. Our visit may take a while."

Since she already had her arm wrapped in Octavian's, she now tugged him along. The drapes were drawn and the room was dark even though it was a bright morning. Syd marched to the windows and drew the heavy damask drapes aside to allow in a flood of sunlight. "Much better," she muttered as dust filtered into the air.

She settled on the settee beside him. "But it is still a hideous room."

He readily agreed. "Syd, I am not going to march upstairs and drag your parents down here."

"Then I will do it," she said with a stubborn look on her face. "But you are the big ox, not me. My mother will probably push me down the stairs if I were the one to do it. Is it bloodthirsty of me to want to poke her in the nose? My father deserves a poke in the nose, too. He really does. Do you think they are the most incompetent parents ever to exist? I am going to tell them so."

"I'm sure they'll be delighted to hear it," he said dryly. The situation was serious and he should not be grinning, but Octavian could not hold back. Syd hopped back and forth between behaving like a martyr and behaving like a hellion.

He had gotten to know and love the hellion.

If it were up to him, he would declare the martyr banished.

The wait ended up dragging on for another thirty minutes, but Octavian was in no hurry. As it turned out, neither was Syd. When Stanford wheeled in the tea cart filled with some of Syd's favorite treats, she pounced on the scones that were served along with their tea. This was because she hadn't eaten anything last night or this morning, and was now hungry.

She was also primed for battle.

Her father was the first to walk in.

"Thorne," he muttered as Octavian rose to greet him with an outstretched hand. "I know you think very little of me, and with good reason. But not even I was prepared for what happened yesterday. Shall we start? I do not think Lady Harcourt will be down anytime soon. She never leaves her bedchamber before noon."

Syd jumped to her feet, her hands curled into fists to mark her irritation. "I'll fetch her."

"No," Octavian said. "I'd rather we speak to your father first."

He knew Syd was impatient to learn the truth. However, it was best learned by keeping those two apart and hearing each version of the story. He expected each of them to lie, but somewhere along the way they might drop a few kernels of truth.

Syd sat back down without protest. "All right. You know best, Octavian."

He chuckled.

Was he hearing right? Headstrong Syd deferring to his judgement?

She cast him an impishly loving grin. "You do on occasion make good sense."

Now that she had finished her second scone, he took her hand and held it in his. He intended to keep hold of her for no logical reason. She was no longer fragile or suffering. Nor was she going to run away from this meeting. She had been extremely hurt by her parents and wanted answers.

He was here to protect her.

In truth, Syd had him and his family, along with her circle of excellent friends to make up for any loss of family connection, should it turn out she was not their daughter.

Her so-called mother would surely sever all ties.

However, he did not think Harcourt would. Even if they were not related by blood, there was no mistaking he and Syd cared for each other.

The bounder, for all his lying, cheating ways, appeared to have a place in his heart for her. Not enough to prevent him from selling her off, however. His words of contrition were not enough to absolve him of that selfish act.

Octavian still did not like the man and was in no rush to forgive him his sins.

He liked Syd's mother even less. Syd had tried to be a good daughter to her. For all her efforts, she had been icily rebuffed every time. As far as Octavian was concerned, Syd had fulfilled any duty she owed this woman. Why should Syd ache over her when the cold witch did not care enough to join them in the parlor?

"Papa," Syd said, "it is time to tell me the truth."

"All of it," Octavian added. "Syd deserves to know."

Her father nodded. "I will not come out looking very good in this."

"Papa, how much worse can you look? You are a liar, a very bad gambler, and an even worse businessman. You sold my cousin to your last creditor, and–"

"It was a love match! It all worked out, did it not?"

"Yes," Syd admitted. "But you did not know it would. And do not forget, you tried to fob me off on him first."

Her father shook his head in disagreement. "I knew he was a good man. That's why I hoped to marry you off to him last year. It would have been the perfect solution, but you wouldn't do it. I suppose you loved Thorne even back then. You could have told me. So, your cousin got him instead and is deliriously happy now that she is married to him."

"Lucky for you," Syd muttered.

"No, not lucky for me at all. In truth, I was sorry that I had tried to swindle him. He was sharp and quickly caught me in the act. And now he owns the business entirely and is making a fortune off it. Is this not punishment enough for me?"

"You could have shared in the profits if you had kept your larcenous hands out of the till." Syd frowned at him. "And having learned not a single lesson from it, you quickly got yourself caught up with Sir Henry Maxwell."

Her father frowned. "I'm sure he cheated me."

"He beat you at your own game," Syd insisted. "And you were ready to hand me over to that beast to save your hide. Is it because I am not really your daughter? Was I expendable? Is this all you thought of me? Having drained the assets of the children's trust, you had no more use for me and did not care who took me next?"

"No! It wasn't that way at all!" He raked a hand through his thinning hair. "You are my daughter...my daughter of the heart."

Syd inhaled lightly. "But not of the blood?"

"Whether of the heart or of the blood does not matter. You are mine, Syd. I have loved you from the moment I brought you home. I loved watching you grow up into the splendid young lady you are today. I am so proud of you, although I have a rotten way of showing it."

"Indeed," Syd grumbled.

"I know I pledged you to Sir Henry. It was the last thing I ever wanted to do. But the man was ruthless and obsessed with you. He threatened to kill me if I did not give you over to him." He shrugged. "I did not care and told him to go ahead and do it. When he saw that threat had failed, he then vowed to harm *you* if I did not comply. I could not put him off when he demanded you in exchange for my debt vowels." He cast her a weak smile and continued. "But you are a resourceful girl, Syd. I knew you would think of something to save yourself."

She frowned. "You believed me resourceful enough to handle that brute?"

Her father nodded. "Yes, you would have got the better of him."

"You are deluded if you think so. He would have beaten me down. Physically beaten me until I had no soul or spirit left."

"No. No!" Her father looked stricken. "You would have found a way to best him. And see, this is exactly what you did by marrying Captain Thorne. I have not always been lucky in life, but you have. Syd, you have that golden touch. You've always had it, even as a little girl. I wish I could have taken you into the gambling hells with me back then. I would have won a fortune with you as my charm."

She gave a light, dismissive snort. "And would you have paid off your creditors?"

Her father sighed. "In time. If pressed. Most of them. But the point is, I would have won at cards had you been with me. No debts. No bothersome collectors banging on our door. This is why I was sure something would come up to save you from Sir Henry. I was not surprised in the least to learn you had eloped to Gretna Green with Captain Thorne. See? Lucky."

Syd now frowned at her father. "I'm sorry he married me. As reward, he is burdened with a penniless wife who does not even know her own name, and a looming scandal that will destroy his career and his family's good name."

"No, child." He glanced at Octavian and smiled. "He has married a gem and he knows it. In turn, you have the best husband. He moved heaven and earth to keep you safe. Do you think he cares what anyone thinks of your parentage? One might say, you owe me a debt of gratitude for bringing the two of you together. Admit it, Captain Thorne. Would you have offered for my daughter had circumstances not pushed you together?"

Syd leaped to her feet. "Of all the gall! Only you would be so vain as to congratulate yourself for bringing about our match."

"And why should I not? It is a love match, is it not? Or will you now pretend you do not love him?"

A blush crept up Syd's neck and into her cheeks. "Of course, I love him. I have always loved him, but you could not know this. Do not dare take credit for bringing us together. You had no part in it. We would have come around to it in time."

"How?" her father asked. "Gossip had it that Captain Thorne was courting Lady Clementine Renfield. Would you have said anything to him before you lost him for good? Not you, Syd. You are too proud. You would have hidden your feelings and wept in silence as he married the wrong woman."

Octavian thought they were getting a little off the point. "Lord Harcourt, you said that you brought Syd home as a newborn. From where? Who are her natural parents?"

"Does it matter? They are both long since dead."

Syd gasped.

Octavian wrapped an arm around her. "Harcourt, be careful what you say. Can you not see how painful this is for your…" He let his voice trail away, for he did not know who Syd was to this man.

"Who were my parents? I have a right to know."

Octavian nudged Syd closer to him as tears now stung her eyes.

"Who?" she insisted, her heart laid bare for this man to crush.

Her father pondered the matter for a long moment and then nodded. "All right, child. You may as well hear it from me rather than from the gossip rags. You are the child of my best friend, the Marquess of Sutton and the squire's daughter he loved. They never married, Syd. At least, I do not believe they did. Nor were they ever likely to marry because he was already betrothed to another. In the end, none of it mattered because he caught a lung fever before he ever had the chance to wed either of those ladies, and died before you were born."

"And my mother?" she asked in trembling voice.

"She died shortly after giving birth to you. I was there at the convent for the birth, waiting in the antechamber for news she had delivered you. I was anxiously pacing back and forth as though I were the father. I was there by her side when she passed. You see, I was fulfilling a deathbed promise made to Sutton to ensure his beloved and their child would always be kept safe. Your mother's name was Catriona Langley, and she looked quite a bit like you, Syd. She named you before she died. *Sydney.* You must be called Sydney she insisted, for that was the family surname of the Marquess of Sutton. He was Douglas Sydney."

Tears were streaming down Syd's cheeks as she listened to Harcourt.

Octavian felt his own eyes moisten, but Syd had tears enough and did not need him crying, too. "Harcourt," he said, hesitating to ask the next question because Syd was already so fragile, but it had to be asked, "do the Langleys and the Sydneys know about Syd?"

He nodded. "Yes, for I approached them both. Catriona's family had cut her off and did not want anything to do with her or her child. I paid for her burial, for they would not take care of her even in death. The same for Sutton's father who was the Duke of Parkhurst. Sutton's mother had died years earlier. Perhaps she would have been kinder, but Parkhurst was not. He was enraged that Sutton wanted to break off the arranged betrothal and marry Catriona instead. Sutton's brother ended up marrying the lady originally meant for Sutton. He knew what had transpired but could not take you in, even though he wanted to. To do so meant fighting his own father and forcing you on the very woman his own brother was about to jilt."

"So, you took me in?"

He nodded. "I was not always the depraved hound you believe me to be, Syd. I was a good man once. My first thoughts were of honoring my pledge to my best friend and protecting you. Please believe me. Only a few weeks had passed by the time I had exhausted all efforts and realized neither family would take you in or ever acknowledge you. By this time, I was relieved. I had already fallen in love with you, even though you were Sutton's child. But you were mine to raise now, and I meant to claim you as mine and give you a happy home."

He snorted and shook his head. "Lady Harcourt and I had been wed for several years by then, and I was coming to realize what a cold woman she was and that we would never have children of our own. She could not stand me...and I could not stand to touch her. I brought you home and told her about Sutton. In this, I laid down the law. You were our child and no one was to be told otherwise."

Syd's eyes widened. "But how could you get away with it? Others knew she was not carrying a child."

"Who was to know? Our few retainers were loyal and never uttered a word. We were not in London at the time, so it was easy to get away with the ruse. I had taken her on a tour of my holdings, so we were traveling from one remote farm to another. She was haughty and never befriended any of the local gentry. She kept to herself. Few people other than a maid or two ever saw her up close. She wanted to take up residence in London, flaunt her status as countess, and become a notable among the *ton* elite. I agreed to all of her demands, so long as we passed you off as our daughter."

Syd shook her head. "And she went along with it?"

Harcourt nodded. "However, she was never accepted as the *ton* darling she'd hoped to become. I could have told her she would never be adored. How could she be when she had not an ounce of warmth or compassion? People sensed her coldness and stayed away. But she had made her deal with me and feared the consequences if she were to renege. I would have shipped her off to one of those remote farms and left her there to tend the hogs. I was tempted to do it so many times, but she kept silent about you, and so we kept up the pretense of a marriage while going about in London. Her resentment of me festered and extended to you. She never believed you were Sutton's daughter. She has always thought you were mine."

"This is why she detested me," Syd said brokenly.

"She would have found a reason to detest you even if you had been ours and delivered from her own body. It took me a while to understand how truly empty her heart was." He gave a bitter laugh. "I thought it was just me she disliked. But she hated the world and everything beautiful in it. It is easy to blame her for the man I am today. Oh, she had an important part to play in it, for certain. However, I could have made changes to better my life and never did. I am trying now. That widow…I have no intention of taking her money, although we will be living off her income because the Harcourt properties are in a shambles and bring almost nothing in now. Perhaps the next earl will do better. Syd, it could be your son that inherits. He would be next in line."

Octavian felt her entire body grow tense. In the next moment, she leaped to her feet again and frowned at Harcourt. "You've just told me I am not your daughter. How can any child of mine inherit?"

"I have claimed you as mine and will claim to my dying breath that you are our legitimate offspring. Who is to know? And why should you not inherit? What do I care if some distant relation is cut out because of it?"

"If Lady Harcourt reports this to the gossip rags, as you obviously fear she will, then everyone will know," Octavian pointed out. "More important, Syd now knows the truth and she will not lie about this, whether or not it remains a secret."

"Added to the fact that an experienced medical practitioner will know whether a woman has ever had a child," Syd said. "All it would take is a simple examination of her body."

"She will never let anyone touch her," Harcourt replied, his bitterness once more evident. "And by not allowing a doctor's examination, everyone will conclude she was the liar."

Syd turned to Octavian, her expression one of frustration.

Well, this was her father.

He could not stop scheming, even as he supposedly confessed all. If what he said was true and Syd was not his legitimate daughter, that did not dissuade him in the least from plotting to cheat the rightful heir from assuming the title.

Syd was so embroiled, her heart in a jumble over a thousand conflicting feelings, that Octavian knew it was up to him to sort out the lies. He wanted to hear from Lady Harcourt next, but would the woman condescend to speak to him? He was not above bribing her to keep her mouth shut, if this is what was needed to protect Syd.

The woman finally made her way downstairs as the earl's confession came to an end. She stood in the doorway, seething as she looked upon her husband and Syd. "He lies to you. He cannot stop his lies."

The earl rose to offer her his seat. "No, I have told them the complete truth. They now know everything. You cannot hurt them, and you cannot hurt me any longer. Captain Thorne, you shall find me at my club if you have need of me again." With that, he strode out, leaving them to deal with his wife.

Octavian rose. "Please, Lady Harcourt. Join us."

She shook her head. "Not with *that* woman here."

Blessed saints.

Is this how she referred to Syd?

He reached out to take Syd's hand, but Syd was once more on her feet and staring back at the woman. "The feeling is mutual, I assure you."

She cast him a look that revealed it was all right, that he should speak with Lady Harcourt on his own, and then turned to walk out.

Octavian had no idea where she meant to go. He started after her, but she stopped him with a smile and slight wave of her hand. "You'll find me in the kitchen with Cook. Her scones were delicious. I think I will have a few more. I'm all right, my love."

He breathed a sigh of relief. "I'll come to you when I'm done."

Lady Harcourt took a seat on the settee, as grim looking a piece of furniture as he had ever seen. Dark color. Heavy fabric. Overly carved ebony frame. The lady herself looked quite grim, too. She sat with her hands primly folded on her lap and her back as stiff as a board. "What has my wretched husband told you?"

Octavian took the seat across from hers and then leaned forward. "Does it matter? I am here to listen to what you have to say. Is Syd your daughter or not?"

"Not."

"Care to be more forthcoming? No one is ever going to believe you if this is all you will say."

Octavian now leaned back in his chair and stretched his long legs before him. "You opened up this Pandora's Box by threatening to reveal all to the gossip rags, Lady Harcourt. Your husband has prepared his defenses. It is a very good story, too. He will have the *ton* embracing him and declaring him a hero. Is this what you want?"

"He charms everyone," she said with disdain. "What has he told you? That Syd was the daughter of his friend?" Her bitter laughter resounded through the room. "He is such a lying rat. The squire's daughter was *his* mistress, not Sutton's. Then he has the gall to bring his own by-blow into our home. How could I ever accept her as my own? To look upon her every day and know he was unfaithful to me so early in our marriage."

"How can you be sure he was lying to you?"

"Because this is what he does best. He lies and lies, and then he lies some more. Fool that I was, I agreed to his scheme so that I could be assured of remaining in London and going about in Society. But he had planned ahead and was already scheming to take control of the trust my family had established for any children of mine. Once we had presented *her* as our daughter, there was no going back or else I would lose not only him, but my family. I was trapped, and that little girl had trapped me."

"That little girl was a mere babe at the time and not to blame for anything you or Lord Harcourt did." Octavian tried to stifle his anger, but it was hard to do when both Harcourts were so quick to deny responsibility for their own selfish actions. "Why are you so eager for your version of the truth to come out now? Other families will be hurt by it."

"Why should I care about the mistress's family? They are nothing but common gentry. They had already disowned their daughter for taking up with Harcourt and being so stupid as to get with child. I'm sure he's told you the woman was Sutton's beloved. Ha! Sutton merely played along because he wanted out of his own betrothal and hoped fabricating a scandal might have the desired effect. He hoped that his betrothed's family would be furious and break it off."

"Then Sutton died unexpectedly," Octavian said, prodding her to continue.

"Yes, and then Harcourt's beloved Miss Langley died in childbirth. So he brought the child home to me. Sutton's father knew the harlot was Harcourt's lover and not his son's. The Langley's knew their daughter had taken up with a married man – again, not Sutton who was not yet married. Harcourt could not unload the child, not even with all of his powers of persuasion."

"The child, Syd, was blameless."

"She was Harcourt's and I've hated her from the moment he brought her into this house," she said with enough venom to shock Octavian who was never easily shocked. "I would have beaten her every day, if I could. But Harcourt threatened to beat me if ever I laid a hand on her. If I starved her, then he would starve me. If I sent her away, then he would do the same to me. So I endured. And suffered. And encouraged that vile Sir Henry Maxwell to take her when I noticed his interest in her. I did not care if he married her or not."

"You just wanted to see her hurt," Octavian said, unable to hold down the bile rising in his throat.

He had never wished death on any man, but was relieved beyond measure to know Sir Henry was now dead and unable to get his brutal hands on Syd. As for this woman, she needed to be banished to some devil's island where she would never be seen or heard from again.

She no longer maintained her genteel facade, so carried away was she in her quest to reveal the truth.

Her warped idea of the truth.

Octavian now saw the intensity of her hatred reflected in her eyes. He was glad Syd was not beside him and could be spared this wickedness. Not even he, with all his battle experience, was prepared for the extent of her hatred. Syd never stood a chance with this woman. "He plans to leave me. So I will see him and his bastard daughter destroyed."

Octavian rose, for he had heard enough.

Even if everything she said about her husband and Catriona Langley was true, she had taken her rage beyond any bounds of reason.

He meant to escort Syd to Lady Withnall's residence next. If anyone knew of the gossip circulating back then, she would. He would also hire Homer Barrow, the best Bow Street man in London, to dig deeper and ferret out to the truth. Both Lady Withnall and Mr. Barrow could be counted on for their discretion.

One thing was for certain, Syd was not related in any way to Lady Harcourt. Whether she was Harcourt's child or Sutton's was yet to be determined. Octavian wanted the matter resolved before he and Syd had their own children. He wasn't worried that Syd would become a mother from hell as Lady Harcourt had been. There was too much kindness in Syd for that. She would never blame a child or turn away from it because of circumstances out of that child's control.

Nor was he ever going to be unfaithful to Syd and create such an impossible situation in his own home. If ever it happened – which was as likely as hell freezing over – but if it did ever happen, Syd would be the first to protect that child.

He shook off the unsavory thought of any dalliances, for he could not conceive of a situation where he would be unfaithful to her. He had not considered cheating on her before they had even entered into their make-believe marriage.

Now, their marriage was real.

If their nightly activities were any indication, they were probably already on their way to creating a family. It might take a month or two to be certain, but he would not be surprised if Syd was already with child.

Still too soon to tell, of course.

He struggled to contain his disgust as Lady Harcourt now rose to draw an end to their conversation.

His admiration for Syd only increased. He could not imagination what he would have become had his mother been like this witch standing before him. He was going to kiss Syd every moment he could. He was going to kiss her and tell her that he loved her until she grew fed up with him and smacked him over the head.

Octavian made his way to the Harcourt kitchen, hoping to keep his expression unreadable. He did not want Syd to see how shaken he was by his conversation with Lady Harcourt. He needn't have worried. Her beaming smile the moment she caught sight of him had him grinning in response. "Love, it is time to go."

The cook and kitchen staff cooed upon hearing his endearment for Syd. It was obvious she was their favorite Harcourt. Their smiles were genuine. She rose and kissed the cook. "Mrs. Simmons, I fear I am no longer favored in this house and we shall not have the opportunity to meet again. Thank you for all your wonderful meals. I shall miss you."

"Aw, my lady. Ye have yer husband to think about now." She cast Octavian a look of approval. "Take care of our Lady Syd."

He nodded. "I will."

They walked out, each of them saying nothing until they were in their carriage and on their way to drop in on Lady Withnall. As soon as the carriage rolled away, they each let out a breath of relief. Syd immediately began to toss questions at him. "What did she say? I thought she would speak more openly to you than she would if I were present. Do you mind that I left you and sat in the kitchen? What did she say about my father? Whose child am I?"

"Love, I did not mind that you sat in the kitchen. It was for the best. She did speak openly."

"And?"

"She's a hateful person."

Syd nodded as she cast him a mirthless smile. "I knew she did not like me."

That was an understatement.

The woman not only loathed her, but had been a danger to her for most of her life.

The only reason Lady Harcourt had kept Syd alive was because of the earl's threat to banish her from London and all genteel Society if she ever harmed Syd. That witch had accused the earl of scheming to take hold of the trust funds, but she had done nothing to stop him. In fact, she spent those funds as freely as he had.

Harcourt had not immediately gone through the children's trust, only depleting it once Syd was about to come of age. Octavian now understood why the earl had waited until recently to spend it all down. He feared what his wife might do to Syd if he'd spent it earlier. She would have unleashed her rage once she felt Syd was no longer of use to them.

Syd nudged him gently. "Octavian, what did she say? Who am I?"

He stifled a shudder. "She claims you are Harcourt's daughter, just as Harcourt indicated she would say. She insists he was the one to have the affair with Miss Langley, not his friend Sutton."

"Do you believe her?"

"I truly do not know which of them to believe. This is why we need to speak to Lady Withnall. She might shed some light on the matter. She knows everyone's secrets and will also be discreet in not repeating whatever we confide in her."

Syd sighed. "No matter what we learn, the ugly rumors will still come out because Lady Harcourt will make certain of it."

"We will deal with it when it happens. We are still best armed by knowing the truth." She looked so forlorn, Octavian couldn't bear it. He drew her onto his lap and held her there as their carriage rolled through the busy London streets. "I love you, Syd."

She nestled against him. "Lady Harcourt must have been brutal. She has you rattled."

He groaned. "I marvel that you did not become a twisted, gnarled thing growing up with that woman. You are a beautiful rose she could not spoil no matter how much poison she attempted to inject in you. A delicate, but very hardy rose."

"I survived because my father, for all his faults, was very good to me."

"Yes, you've told me. I begin to see it now. He's such a wretch in so many ways, Syd."

She laughed lightly. "I know. Do you realize that if what he said is true, and that Douglas Sydney, the Marquess of Sutton, is my father, that I could be Lady Sydney Sydney? What a terribly ridiculous name."

Octavian chuckled. "It sprang to my mind when I heard Sutton's name, but I dared not say anything about it. However, all jesting aside. I am beginning to understand how much Harcourt does love you. However, I still will not forgive him for trying to sell you to Sir Henry."

They arrived at Lady Withnall's residence and were quickly shown into her drawing room, a light and airy, elegant room decorated in sky blue silks and florals. The tiny woman bustled in moments later, the quick *thuck, thuck, thuck* of her cane indicating her brisk walk. "I heard you had quite a row with your parents yesterday, Syd," she said, marching in and motioning for them to take a seat. "And now you are here after visiting them again this morning. How can I help you?"

Octavian marveled at this woman's web of contacts. She had more people spying for her than the Home Office or Foreign Office combined. He and Syd quickly related all that had happened.

Lady Withnall was a tiny woman, but she had a towering and commanding presence. Those with secrets feared her. Those who were honorable adored her. Everyone knew she was probably the best connected person in London.

"Lady Withnall, do you know who I am?" Syd asked, her voice so fragile that Octavian ached for her.

He took her hand in his as Lady Withnall began her response. "I had heard rumors, my dear. Long ago hints that you were not Lady Harcourt's child. But the whispers quickly died, for everyone could see how your father doted on you."

Octavian leaned forward. "He is a detestable man in many ways, but it seems he always did care for Syd. Is he Syd's father?"

CHAPTER 21

SYD BEGAN TO tremble as Lady Withnall cast her a pained look. "Syd, I truly do not know the answer. What I do know is that Harcourt raised you as though you were his own flesh and blood. Whether or not you are of his blood, he considers you his daughter. I have always believed he cared deeply for you, although his trying to sell you to Sir Henry was not one of his finer moments."

Syd nodded. "Well, we do know for certain that Lady Harcourt is not my mother. I believe my mother's name was Catriona Langley. The only question is, which man was in love with her? My father or his best friend, Sutton."

"Your father was blond and Sutton had dark red hair," Lady Withnall remarked. "Your father was tall and slender while Sutton was stockier in build. Someone in Miss Langley's family or in service to her family at the time might know which one of them she was secretly meeting."

"I plan to engage Homer Barrow to investigate," Octavian said.

Lady Withnall nodded. "He is a most reliable man. Syd, I see by your stubborn expression that you think to run off and investigate on your own. I strongly recommend against this idea. It will be too hurtful for you, my dear. You do not know how you will be received or what vile things Catriona's embittered family might say against her. Let Mr. Barrow ask his questions and deliver his report to you. Then you and Octavian can consider what is to come next."

Syd glanced at her husband, this man who was proving to be a bedrock foundation for her, and arched an eyebrow in question.

He sighed. "I agree with Lady Withnall, Syd. Let Mr. Barrow do his job and report back to us. I'll get him on the task this very day. Your mother is at a breaking point and will snap soon. Then she will unleash the gossip rags on you and your father."

"And destroy you as well, Octavian. In truth, you will be hurt most by this ugly affair because you have the most to lose," Syd muttered. "I meant what I said about protecting you. I could–"

"No," he said roughly. "I am not ending our marriage or distancing myself from you in any way. Forget it, Syd. And do not bother to ask Lady Withnall for her opinion. I do not care to hear it. My mind is made up. I'm in this with you to the end."

"Big, stubborn ox," she retorted affectionately.

"Minx," he teased her right back and grinned at her with equal affection.

Lady Withnall shook her head. "Your husband is right, Syd. He took a vow on your wedding day to love and protect you, so let him do it."

Syd did not recall their exchanging anything but their names and a quick 'I do' from each of them before they were shoved off to the side and the next couple stepped up. They had said those vows at their second wedding, but she had no idea if that counted as official even under the lax Scottish laws.

"I will also contact some reliable sources of my own and see what I can dig up," the dowager continued. "If you are Harcourt's natural daughter, then you will be looked upon with scorn by some. But it is not all that unusual to have a father claim a child born out of wedlock and give that child the benefit of his status. Of course, that child would not be able to claim his title or entailed properties. But what if you were Sutton's child and he had secretly married Miss Langley?"

Syd stared at her. "Lady Withnall, what are you saying?"

"Any son of yours might not be heir to Harcourt's earldom, but he could be heir to the Duke of Parkhurst. Would that not be ironic? In trying to hurt you, Syd…it may turn out that Lady Harcourt's efforts will elevate your status instead of diminish it."

On that remark, their visit ended.

Lady Withnall hugged her. "Oh, Syd. My dear girl. Whatever will be, will be. You will sail past the malicious gossip, for scandals always blow over. Yours will soon become old news, especially when everyone sees how strong your marriage remains. In all of this jumble, pay attention to all that truly matters. Octavian loves you and you love him. Stand together. Love will always triumph."

Syd felt drained but also elated.

Her elation had nothing to do with the possibility of her eldest son – assuming she and Octavian had children – being in line for the Parkhurst dukedom. Was this possibility not too farfetched? Of course, it would please her to no end to see Lady Harcourt's vile attempts to destroy her blow up in the woman's face. Syd was compassionate by nature, but she was not a saint and that woman was a demon. A little gloating would not be sinful.

Her elation had to do with realizing how precious her marriage was and what a good man she had married. She also realized how much Lord Harcourt, whether he turned out to be her father or not, had done for her. She knew there was a reason why she loved him even though he was such a weasel.

She also gained an appreciation for her friends. Not only Lady Withnall, who had taken on so many roles for her. Friend. Confidante. Grandmother. Benefactor. Same for Lady Dayne. Those two dowagers had been a blessing to Adela and now to her.

She was surprised to find Marigold and Gory waiting for her when she and Octavian returned to the Huntsford residence after making a stop at Mr. Barrow's office to engage his services. She handed over her pelisse, gloves, and reticule to a maid and hurried into the parlor. "Did I forget a meeting? I'm so sorry."

Marigold and Gory assured her that she did not.

"Oh, then why are you here?"

Marigold, who was always so sweet and compassionate, took hold of her hand. "We heard you had a terrible row with your parents yesterday. And now there are ridiculous whispers going around. We were worried about you and wanted to see that you were all right."

Syd hugged them both. "I am now."

Octavian came in a few minutes later. "Syd, since your friends are here…"

She nodded as he came to her side. "You need to report to the Admiralty, I know. Yes, please do. I've distracted you long enough. I will be fine here with my friends." But she followed him out because she wanted to tell him how much she loved him and appreciated him.

Poor Greeves tried not to look or listen as she kissed Octavian, and cooed words of love to him. Yes, she sounded like an infatuated peahen. But how could she not worship and adore Octavian after all he had done for her?

Before Octavian departed for the Admiralty, she reminded him of tonight's plans. "We are to dine at Lady Dayne's this evening. Shall I pick you up at your office? Or will you come home to change?"

He groaned and glanced down at himself. "Pick me up on your way over, will you? Well, it is a bit out of your way."

"No, it's fine," she insisted.

He kissed her on the brow. "Can you bring me a change of clothes? I'll wash up and change into them there. Do you mind?"

She laughed and shook her head. "Not at all. It is no inconvenience. I would go to the ends of the earth for you if you asked it of me."

Greeves made a sound somewhere between a groan and a chuckle.

Syd sighed.

Octavian kissed her. "I love you, Syd."

She floated back to the parlor to join her friends.

Neither Marigold nor Gory stayed long after seeing she was fine because they had all been invited to supper at Lady Dayne's residence on Chipping Way and needed to prepare. "Until later," Marigold said and gave her a hug.

Marigold loved to hug.

Usually, she hugged her husband, Leo, who did not seem to mind her displays of affection at all.

Gory, who preferred dissecting cadavers rather than dealing

with living people, also gave her a sincere embrace. "We'll stand by your side no matter what lies are spread about you. Friends forever."

Marigold agreed. "Friends forever."

Syd smiled. "Yes, forever in friendship."

The day had started with so much trepidation that Syd marveled she was able to begin the evening in such good spirits. Amid the dark clouds of turmoil, she had discovered the light that true love and true friends had brought to her.

So it was with a dancing step that she walked into the Admiralty building and made her way up to Octavian's office in the early evening to pick up Octavian. Most of the staff had gone home by now, so she encountered hardly anyone other than a guard at the entry and another few guards along the empty hallways.

Her footsteps resounded as she walked down the dimly lit hall to his office while carrying his change of clothes. She held the garments carefully so that they would not wrinkle. "Octavian, I–"

Her stomach sank into her toes.

Her world fell apart.

Standing before her, with her octopus arms wrapped around Octavian's neck and her body pasted to his, was Lady Clementine. "Oops," the horrid debutante said with a malicious gleam in her eyes. "Your wife has caught us, Captain Thorne. Why did you not tell me you expected her here?"

If Octavian was a dragon, he would be breathing fire.

Syd wanted to run away, but her legs seemed bolted to the floor.

"Syd, seriously? Lady Clementine must have heard you coming down the hall and this is why she suddenly threw herself at me," he said, trying to extricate himself from her grip. "You cannot believe I would ever...Syd? For pity's sake. I knew you were coming to pick me up. Do you think I would be so stupid as to arrange a tryst with another woman at the same time? In my office, no less?"

Was it cruel of her to make him squirm?

Especially since she knew Lady Clementine had purposely set

him up. She knew it because she could see the malice still gleaming in the odious debutante's eyes. Revenge. This is what Clementine wanted, revenge on the man who had spurned her. She was another just like Lady Harcourt.

Octavian had told her so, but she had dismissed the warning until now.

Syd also noted the honest anguish in Octavian's eyes, and knew this valiant man did not have it in him ever to be unfaithful to her.

But feelings of hurt did ripple through her.

It made no sense, for she truly did not doubt him for a moment. Was this not a wonderful revelation? Octavian was her guardian and protector, proving himself worthy in countless ways.

He wanted to build a life and family with her.

He was the one insisting on continuing their marriage, even knowing she was likely born out of wedlock.

That Lady Clementine was here meant the scandal surrounding her birth was already making its way around the *ton*. Lady Harcourt must have gone to the London gossip rags as soon as she and Octavian had left her this morning.

With rumors no doubt abounding, Lady Clementine, who was ever the predator, had seen her opportunity to add to their wounds and grabbed it. "My father will see that your fake marriage is annulled," she said, eyeing Syd with disdain. "No court will uphold a marriage based on fraud. You are not an earl's daughter. You are a baseborn nobody and the Thornes are well rid of you. Then your husband will be free to marry me."

"That does it," Octavian growled and grabbed hold of Lady Clementine's arm. "No one insults my wife. Out. Get out of here and never come back, or I will order the guards to bodily toss you out." He dragged her into the hall and slammed the door in her face when she attempted to walk back in.

He growled again, ignoring her screeches as he locked the door and turned to Syd, his body taut and shaking with anger. "Syd...you have to believe me. I had no idea...*bloody hell*."

She set down his suit of clothes. "Octavian, I do believe you. I–"

"Because she walked into my office less than a minute before you did. I had no idea what she was doing here, and I had just come around to the front of my desk to escort her out when..." He raked a hand through his hair. "Wait...did you just say that you believed me?"

Syd smiled at him and nodded.

He released a groaning sigh of relief. "Thank heaven for that. The look of hurt when you saw us..."

"She caught me off my guard, that's all. She still wants you."

He laughed and shook his head. "No, love. She just wanted to hurt me. She was hoping to ruin whatever feelings you and I have for each other, undermine the trust we have in each other. Even if she does want me, you know that I never wanted her. Syd, you have to know this. Have I not always told you so? Now can you understand why I wanted nothing to do with her? She is another one who only knows to spit poison. I–"

She reached up on tiptoes and kissed him. "You wonderful, big ox. I believe you. I *trust* you. I could have found you naked in here with her and still trusted you...just don't put that one to the test, however."

He chuckled. "No, love. My clothes stay on except for you."

"All right, then. Speaking of clothes, let's start by removing yours," she said with an impish grin, carefully shifting aside some papers he must have been working on, in order to sit atop his desk. "We are going to be late if you do not start scrambling, Captain Thorne."

He unbuttoned the jacket of his uniform. "Are you all right, Syd?"

She nodded. "A little rattled, but only because I did not expect her to behave so brazenly. She did not waste a moment in coming after you, did she?"

"Blessed saints, she's a shark. She smelled blood in the water and attacked." He tossed his jacket aside and removed his shirt, his muscles flexing in graceful motion and making her wish they did not have plans tonight.

A sharp, constricting pang shot through Syd's heart.

Octavian immediately noticed her pained expression and came

to her side. "Love, are you sure that you are all right?"

She nodded.

He kissed her on the brow and then stepped back as he began to unbutton the falls of his trousers. "As if I would ever consider exchanging you for her," he muttered in disgust. "I don't know how she got through the guards in the first place. They don't let just anyone up here."

"She is a duke's daughter."

"That still should not have given her access. We're supposed to have tight security in this building." He cursed under his breath. "I did not invite her up here, Syd. I never would."

"I know." She put her arms around him when he came back to her side, loving the strength of his own and the warmth of his skin that covered his exceptionally fine body. "Your every thought and every action from the moment we met has been to protect me. You've taken a punch in the face for me. Fallen off a roof for me. Even married me twice. And now I think you are more rattled about Lady Clementine's attempt to split us up than I am."

"You are calm about this?"

"No, I am still angry and quite a bit shaken. But I trust you. I also know you are irresistible to women. That is your lot in life, to be so handsome that every woman wants you."

He relaxed and emitted a playfully laughing sigh. "Indeed, it is a curse."

She gave him a light swat to his arm, but turned serious a moment later. "You are irresistible. I cannot blame others for desiring you. I'm still not sure what you find so perfect about me. I feel as though I have put you through the labors of Hercules."

"No, love." He donned his elegant dinner trousers and crossed to a ewer and basin on a sideboard in order to wash up. "They were labors of love."

She came to his side and watched as he scrubbed his hands and face.

His was such a handsome face.

Firm jaw and masculine angles.

His hands were big and his palms calloused. She loved the feel of them when he touched her body. "They were labors of endurance, Octavian."

He dried himself off. "I would go through the fires of hell for you, Syd."

"You are going to make me cry if you continue to say such nice things to me."

Octavian took her into his arms. "I will always be nice to you. We still have a few minutes before we must leave. I could show you how just nice I can be to you," he said, his voice now husky and seductive.

She could be seductive, too.

But heavens, she hoped he would not laugh at her attempt to be sultry. "Forget about nice," she purred. "I would rather you were naughty with me."

He lifted her in his arms and set her back atop his desk. "How naughty?"

"Octavian, don't you dare grin at me so wickedly," she teased, laughing because she knew exactly what he meant to do, and now that she had goaded him, she had no intention of stopping him. "Oh! Um...is this is something new?" she asked as he moved between her legs and now trailed his fingers up her thighs.

"Close your eyes, love. You're going to like this."

They arrived late to Lady Dayne's party.

The dear dowager might have believed their sincere apologies had Octavian not been grinning from ear to ear. As for her, she was blushing furiously.

Honestly, where did this man learn these tricks of seduction?

She was going to embarrass herself if she did not stop thinking of what he had just done to her.

"Oh, dear heaven. Spare me, you two," Lady Dayne admonished them, and then had her ancient butler, Watling, ring the dinner bell to summon them all into the dining room.

The dinner party was a quiet affair among friends.

They made passing mention of the breaking scandal, but only for the purpose of assuring Syd of their support. Mostly, they spoke of the latest Huntsford Academy finds, the excellent wine and dessert courses served, upcoming horse auctions, and the abysmal weather.

Syd knew tomorrow's ball at Lord Winstone's was not going to be anywhere near as pleasant. However, she could endure the snide cuts and malicious whispers if Octavian stood beside her. Nor was she without her supporters, for Marigold and her Aunt Sophie were Farthingales, which meant she would have a host of their family members coming to her aid if the insults got out of hand.

This was most appreciated since most of the Thorne family was out of town and not able to come to her rescue.

Octavian carried her up the stairs when they got home.

It still amazed her how fiercely Octavian believed in them as a couple. But she was growing to understand these Thornes were family men, and none were more ready to settle into that staid, everyday life than Octavian.

His eagerness to be a good husband and father surprised Syd, for she thought he was the handsomest of all, and never had a problem luring women into his bed. Yet, he had not given a second thought to abandoning his rakehell ways and committing to their marriage. Not even a glimmer of regret.

Dear heaven.

Even she would have jumped into bed with him had he attempted to seduce her instead of marry her, although she would have made him work harder to accomplish his seduction than others might have done.

Perhaps this is what made them a good fit.

He did not want a woman who would give him his way in everything. He liked a challenge.

She was certainly proving to be that.

Had she not given him enough challenges in a month of marriage to last a lifetime?

His hand brushed lightly over her bare shoulder as he helped her to undress now that they were back in their shared quarters. "You look beautiful, Syd. That rose color is nice on you. I should have mentioned it earlier, but I was too steamed."

She sighed. "Octavian…"

"Do not ask me again if I am sure of my choice, Syd. Every moment, every incident, only confirms I have made the right decision."

She turned to face him. "We are going to have some serious battles coming up. I'm glad to have a big fellow like you to watch my back. But are you certain?"

"Never a doubt. Always at your service, ma'am."

Later that night, after settling in bed together, Octavian grew pensive. "We need a place of our own, Syd," he said, taking her into his arms. "Time to establish some roots."

She nodded. "I agree."

"We should start looking tomorrow."

She nodded again. "Yes, that is a fine idea."

"A big house with a large nursery to accommodate our children."

"Perfect. I already have decorating ideas in mind."

"I would like our home to be close to this house. Ambrose and I have always been close. Julius, too. I like the idea of their being able to pop in whenever they wish."

"Absolutely."

He chuckled. "You are being quite agreeable. What have you done to my Syd?"

"She is right here beside you, where she always wishes to be. I love you, Octavian."

He kissed her on the brow. "Back at you, minx."

Syd fell asleep contentedly in her husband's arms, but she wondered what tomorrow would bring. She did not think either Lady Harcourt or the horrible Clementine were done with them yet.

What would they try next?

CHAPTER 22

THE SCANDAL HIT the front pages of every gossip rag in Town the following day.

There was no way to escape the embarrassment, especially now that they were about to enter Lord Winstone's elegant townhouse on the night of his ball. The Winstones had spared no expense to make this the affair of the year. Scented wax candles shone amid crystal chandeliers in a grand display of light as they walked in and advanced in queue.

Everything glittered and sparkled.

Champagne was plentiful.

One had only to glance around to see that no expense was spared.

Syd kept on the lookout for her mother or Lady Clementine. If there was to be a battle tonight, she wished to get a sense of where her opponents were positioned on this dazzling battlefield.

In truth, Syd did not want to engage in any battles.

However, she was never one to shrink from a fight.

She also had an army of friends to guard her back.

Not that she would ever impose on them.

She could fight her own battles and was ready to give the odious Lady Clementine a poke in the nose if the girl dared insult her beyond merely giving her the cut direct. Syd did not care about that insignificant slight. That was to be expected since the wicked *ton* diamond routinely snubbed all those who fell out of her favor, and there were many hapless souls who had fallen victim to her wrath.

One might even consider it a badge of honor to be cut by her.

It meant one was worthy of her notice, in the first place.

But Syd would not allow her to get away with anything more.

As for her mother...Lady Harcourt...Syd had no idea what to do about her. The woman was going to spew her poison.

Well, Syd could only wait and see what happened next.

Octavian was going to stand beside her and be the voice of reason should there be an altercation.

He was the most sensible, thoughtful man she had ever met.

She might even surprise him by following his advice to remain dignified in the face of hurled insults.

She glanced at him and her heart began to flutter.

He looked quite magnificent in his black tie and tails. He had always looked wonderful in his uniform, but now stole her breath away while dressed in his evening clothes that accentuated his broad shoulders and masculine physique.

He arched an eyebrow. "Syd, why are you smiling at me?"

"Can a wife not be happy to be standing beside her handsome husband?"

"Perhaps, but you are no ordinary wife. Are you going to behave yourself tonight?"

She gasped. "Me? What about–"

"It matters not what Clementine or your mother do. It is up to you to show the world that you are the better lady."

"I hate it when you are being reasonable," she muttered, but tossed him an endearing smile.

They did not have long to wait before trouble started.

Clementine purposely walked by them with her group of snide friends, all of whom sauntered past her and sneered as they gave her the cut.

No big surprise there.

Was she supposed to beat her chest in despair and weep?

Their feeble attempt to insult her was completely neutralized when Marigold and her Farthingale cousins, some of whom she did not know, rushed toward her and greeted her effusively. To all who were watching – and everyone was, since this erupting scandal was quite juicy – she and the Farthingales could have been lifelong friends.

How was she ever to repay this family's kindness?

Marigold was a marchioness, and the list of titles among her cousins included duchess, baroness, viscountess, and there were several countesses. Indeed, Daffodil Farthingale was the Duchess of Edgeware and Syd did not think there was a more powerful duke in the realm.

Take that, Lady Clementine.

When the two dowagers walked in, Lady Dayne and Lady Withnall, the first thing they also did was greet Syd warmly.

This was another victory shot across the bow, for no one was more respected among the *ton* than these two ladies.

First skirmish won.

Clementine defeated.

Not only defeated, but rendered insignificant.

Syd tried not to gloat, but this first win over the wretched girl felt awfully good.

Of greater concern was Lady Harcourt.

Syd felt her venom from across the ballroom.

Lord Winstone and his wife had opened the ball with a waltz, to the surprise of the elders in the crowd who looked upon this with disapproval. But many of the younger couples were delighted and eagerly stepped onto the dance floor to join in the first dance.

Octavian took her hand. "Come on, Syd. Try to look up at me adoringly as we waltz."

She laughed. "It shall be quite a struggle, but I will do my best."

If anyone questioned whether theirs was a love match, this waltz removed all doubt. Syd could not hold back. Everyone saw the love in her eyes the moment Octavian took her in his arms and began to twirl her around the dance floor.

No one could overlook the happiness gleaming in his eyes, either.

When Lady Harcourt approached them at the end of the dance, hatred oozing from her every pore, the guests were already inclined to dismiss the scandal as the nonsensical ranting of a troubled woman.

Octavian placed a protective arm around Syd's waist.

Perhaps some of his good sense flowed into her, because she suddenly had no desire to destroy this pathetic woman. How better to disarm her than to show sympathy instead of rage? "Lady Harcourt, you need not do this," she said, reaching out to offer her hand. "You are only hurting yourself."

"Me? Hurt? I am beyond hurt." She laughed loudly, her laughter bordering on the maniacal. "Your very presence is a blight that will never be removed until you die. I wish you both dead, you and Harcourt!"

That earned several gasps from those who were listening in.

Syd was also shocked and deeply wounded by the remark. She dropped her hand to her side, feeling quite sad rather than angry. This was the woman she had always believed was her mother. Yes, a flawed and icy mother, but still the woman she had always thought would nurture and protect her, if ever the need arose.

Children were like this, needing no more than a speck of affection to soothe their young hearts. Syd was no longer that hopeful child. But even now, despite knowing the truth, she never wanted to hurt this woman. "Please, let us not do this here."

"Who are you to tell me what to do? You are soiled and baseborn. You are a nobody and do not belong here!"

"Enough!" Lord Winstone roared as he approached, the look on his face seething.

Syd was not certain to whom he was directing this anger...well, it had to be Lady Harcourt or else he would have quietly rescinded the invitation to her and Octavian upon the scandal breaking if he did not want them here. Behind him strode two men. One was her father...well, she would always think of Lord Harcourt as her father. But she did not know who the other man was.

Others apparently did, for she quickly heard a murmur rolling through the crowd like a gentle wave upon the water. "Parkhurst," was the name on everyone's lips.

"His Grace," some guests whispered, pressing closer to see

what would next unfold.

"Reclusive duke," others whispered. "Just come out of mourning."

Syd realized this man whose name was Parkhurst had to be the brother who had now succeeded to the title of duke upon the passing of his father. If what Syd's father had told her was true, this brother was the one who had married the Marquess of Sutton's betrothed after his death.

Syd's heart broke as she looked upon him. Was the Marquess of Sutton truly her father? Did the present duke standing before her now resemble him in any way? Was she in the presence of her uncle?

Octavian drew her closer to his side, his protective instincts on fire. This man who did not flinch in the face of battle, who had calmly stood his ground when surrounded by reivers and Scottish warriors, this man who was the very definition of poise under fire, looked ready to throw punches if another insult was hurled at her.

She was now the one to take his hand and give it a light squeeze to assure him that she was all right.

She felt his tension, and knew he was riled and had reached his tipping point. She would never allow him to throw a punch.

No, she was going to throw the punches if any were warranted.

Octavian must have sensed her thoughts, for his tension suddenly eased and he grinned at her. "Behave yourself, minx," he whispered.

"You too, you big ox."

Lord Harcourt now stepped between everyone. "My apologies, Lord Winstone. My wife is not well, as you can plainly see," he said, shooting Lady Harcourt a quelling look.

To Syd's surprise, Lady Harcourt suddenly quieted, her expression turning completely blank. It was as though her soul had abandoned her, leaving nothing but the shell of a woman before them.

"I will take her home now," Lord Harcourt said, looking quite beaten down himself. "But Syd, my darling, precious girl..." He spoke with so much love in his voice. "I would like to introduce you to a very good friend of mine, His Grace, the Duke of Parkhurst."

Syd turned to the duke, absorbing every one of his features as she sought sign of any resemblance between her and him. "An honor, Your Grace."

The duke took her hand and bowed politely over it. "The honor is mine, Lady Thorne."

He then invited her and Octavian to meet him for luncheon the following day. "We would be delighted," Octavian responded for them both.

Lady Harcourt gasped. "You would honor this...this...by-blow? Has everyone turned against me? Am I to have no justice?"

"Lady Harcourt, in what possible way have you been hurt? There was no deception played on you. I have no idea what you seek, but it is not justice," Parkhurst intoned.

Lady Harcourt ran out in tears.

"Papa..." Syd turned to run after her, but Harcourt stopped her.

"No, child. This is my mess to clean up. Enjoy the ball. All will be well." He excused himself and took off after his wife.

Syd meant to follow, but Octavian gently held her back. "Syd, you cannot heal everyone's wounds. Harcourt will treat her gently."

She nodded. "He always has. Dear heaven, what a burden he's carried all these years."

Parkhurst eyed her as intently as she had eyed him moments ago. Was he looking for the same resemblance? "I will not take up more of your time now," he said, "but I very much look forward to seeing you tomorrow."

That said, he walked off to engage with others she assumed were friends he had not seen in a while.

She now turned to offer her apologies to Lord Winstone. "I am so truly sorry. If you wish me to leave, I–"

"No, Lady Thorne. You are welcome here. I am sorry that...I have no words for what we all just witnessed. Your mother, has she always been this unwell?"

Syd's expression turned pained.

Lord Winstone grunted. "Ah, Lady Thorne. That look says it all."

The remainder of the ball passed uneventfully, not even Clementine daring to cause more mischief for fear she would be equated with Lady Harcourt, a sad woman everyone now viewed as bordering on deranged.

Lady Winstone took Syd aside a moment. "My dear, please know how saddened we are by your mother's ill health. It happens to some women, you know. As we age and our looks fade. The children grow up and leave home. We are left all alone in a big, rambling house, wondering what use we are to anyone now? Most of us adjust, but it affects some ladies quite badly. Your marriage to Captain Thorne must have sent her over the edge. In her mind, how else was she to deal with the loss of a dear daughter than by pushing her away first? By her illogical thinking, it made sense to deny that you were ever hers."

Syd did not wish to disabuse Lady Winstone of her faulty conclusion. She meant it kindly, and Syd had no desire to invite more gossip by telling her the truth. "It is a sad turn of events," she merely agreed. "Thank you for the explanation. It is very kind of you to offer it."

Lady Winstone patted her hand. "You dear thing, I hope this helps you understand that you did nothing wrong. Now I shall send you back to your husband who seems eager to have you once more beside him. Oh, how I do adore a love match. There are so many marriages entered into for the sole purpose of increasing one's wealth or enhancing one's alliances. Is it any wonder there are so many unhappy couples? But it is a joy to see a marriage that is real."

Syd returned to her husband's side.

"What happened, Syd? What did she say to you?"

She placed her arm in his. "She said our marriage is not make-believe."

Octavian snorted. "I could have told her that. Care to dance? The orchestra is playing another waltz."

She nodded.

But he walked her away from the dance floor and toward the

terrace. "Where are you taking me?"

"Outdoors. Under the moonlight. In truth, Syd, I just wanted to be out of that ballroom and in the cooler air. Or we could give our apologies and leave now. I feel an extraordinary need to take you in my arms and hold you close."

"I feel the same." She cast him a wicked smile as she pointed toward some dense shrubbery along the stone wall running along the back of the garden. "Or you could just *take* me behind that row of bushes."

It took Octavian a moment to realize what she was offering.

He laughed softly once it sank into his mind. "I knew life with you would never be dull. Come on, love. I'll wrap my jacket around you so you don't get twigs poking your arse."

"Octavian! Oh, I did not think of that."

He grinned. "Because you've never been naughty like this before. But we are both tense and in need of a release. Trust me, you are going to enjoy this."

Was there ever a doubt?

CHAPTER 23

OCTAVIAN TOOK SYD'S hand as they sat in Parkhurst's magnificent parlor about to dine with the duke and Lord Harcourt. "Lady Thorne," the duke said once his footmen had served them and then left, closing the gilded double doors behind him. "It is long past time you were told the truth."

Octavian felt Syd's excitement shooting through her like bolts of lightning. "Yes, I wish to know. Who am I?"

Lord Harcourt, looking quite wan and beaten down, nodded.

"You are my brother's daughter," Parkhurst said, getting straight to the heart of the matter. "I said nothing while my wife was alive out of respect for her. You see, I loved Julia Crawford. That was her name, Lady Julia Crawford, daughter of the Earl of Crawford. But my brother was eldest, so he was meant to marry her. Our fathers had agreed upon it. Julia and my brother, Douglas, had no choice but to go along with the arrangement."

"But Douglas rebelled," Harcourt interjected. "He had fallen in love with Catriona Langley and would have no one else as his wife."

Parkhurst nodded. "Please know that I loved my brother and would never have done anything to interfere with his arranged marriage…even though Julia happened to be the woman I loved. This was all becoming a Shakespearean comedy. A Midsummer's Night Dream. Each of us pledged to the wrong people. Then suddenly, my brother and I saw how to make it right."

Octavian frowned. "What do you mean?"

"I helped my brother marry Catriona."

Syd gasped and almost spilled her wine. "What are you saying?"

"I was there at their wedding ceremony. I was his witness. You were born *in* wedlock, Lady Thorne. Not out of wedlock." He glanced from her to Octavian and then back to her. "It will, of course, cause some complication. If you and Captain Thorne were to have a son, he would have a superior claim to mine for the Parkhurst title. The terms of lineage are clearly set forth in the ducal grant of title."

Octavian stared at Syd's father. "Did you know this?"

"Not until a few days ago. Douglas...who is your true father, Syd...had rambled something about marrying Catriona on his deathbed. But he was delirious most of the time and I did not know whether to believe him."

"It wasn't Harcourt's fault," the duke interjected. "I lied to him when he asked me about it. Our father was in the process of amending the betrothal terms to replace me as the intended husband for Julia, the woman I loved. The *only* woman I would ever love. I did not want anything to jeopardize our happiness, especially any impediment to my claim on the title, for I knew by this time that she cared for me, too. So, when Harcourt told me what Douglas had confided to him about marrying Catriona, I denied it had ever happened."

The duke buried his face in his hands a moment before looking up at them again. "Fate had given me this opportunity, you see. I could not slam that door shut on my happiness. So I did the only thing that seemed logical at the time. Douglas was dead. Catriona had died in childbirth. Who was to know?"

"And I was desperate to have a child of my own," Harcourt said. "I knew my wife hated me and this would never happen for us. And there you were, Syd. This beautiful, green-eyed girl handed to me in answer to my prayers."

"Why did you wait until now to say anything?" Octavian asked, for he could see that Syd was too choked up to speak. "In truth, Parkhurst, why even say anything now when it might jeopardize your claim to the dukedom?"

"Because it was never about the dukedom for me. I would have been happy serving as the heir's spare for the rest of my days. But it was all for Julia. I would have lost her if her father believed I was not next in line to the title. I did it for love."

Octavian said nothing, for who was he to judge?

In his opinion, that marriage was based on a lie. Might he not have done the same if he and Syd were in those roles?

Had he not been willing to risk everything for Syd?

"Ours was a deep and abiding love," the duke continued. "I don't think two people were ever happier as husband and wife than we were. I lost her last year. We were never blessed with children, unfortunately. Perhaps I was being punished for taking advantage of my brother's death. Julia was innocent and completely blameless in all this. She never knew about you or Douglas's love for Catriona. We all kept it secret from her to her dying breath."

He now turned to Harcourt. "I'm glad you came to me and told me what your wife had done. This secret has lain buried too long."

Harcourt had tears in his eyes as he nodded. "I never meant to hurt you, Syd. You have always been my precious daughter. I tried my best, but I know I have been a miserable father. And now I shall lose you forever. There is no greater pain for me than to no longer have you, the greatest joy in my life."

Syd flung herself into his arms. "No! You are the only father I have ever had and all I want. You did the best you could. What child can ask for better?"

Octavian held his tongue.

Oh, lord.

The man was a weasel, an inveterate gambler, an idiot when it came to investments. However, Octavian quietly forgave him for all of it, even for attempting to marry Syd off to Sir Henry Maxwell. Well, that one required quite a bit of bile to swallow.

But Syd loved this man.

There was no denying he had done everything he could to protect Syd, in his own hapless way. He had stepped up when no one else would protect her. The man could have abandoned his wife and set up house with another woman. He could have found his happiness in one woman or a string of them if he wished, for he was an earl and women would have given themselves to him whether he was eligible or not.

But he had stayed with that cold witch in order to protect Syd's secret...or the secret he thought was true, that Syd was illegitimate. He had sacrificed everything to protect Syd, even given her the protection of his own name.

"Oh, my precious girl. How can you not hate me?" Her father was now blubbering as he hugged her and she hugged him back with fierce compassion. The two of them were shedding enough tears to drown them all.

Parkhurst was also sobbing.

Dear heaven.

Octavian set down his fork.

No one was going to eat a bite of this delicious meal.

After a moment, Harcourt looked over at him. "See, Thorne? Did I not tell you this girl was a golden charm?"

Octavian laughed. "Yes, you did."

Harcourt gave Syd another embrace. "I will admit, I was worried when I learned you had taken off for Gretna Green. I did my best to slow Sir Henry down in the hope we would not reach you in time. Still, I worried about your happiness, Syd. My stupid mistakes had forced your hand to find someone else to marry. I was so worried you would be leaping from one bad bargain straight into another."

Parkhurst grunted. "And I would have been as much to blame."

Syd turned to Octavian and smiled. "Octavian always loved me. He never wanted a make-believe marriage."

"And you, Syd?" her father asked.

"It was never make-believe for me, either. I have always loved him."

And this is what they admitted to their friends several days later during a dinner party hosted at the Hunstford townhouse. Ambrose and Adela were back from Devon. Julius had returned from York. The two dowagers were present, along with Marigold,

Leo, and Gory. Marigold's aunt and uncle, Sophie and John Farthingale, were also in attendance.

Harcourt, the man Syd refused to consider as anything less than her loving father, was not present. He had taken his wife to the seashore for a rest cure.

Octavian expected the hotel they were staying at was in actuality a hospital and Lady Harcourt would not be returning home. However, this was not a matter to be discussed at a dinner party. He would not raise it, and knew Syd did not wish to talk about it, either.

The conversation remained mostly light and jovial.

No one was surprised when he and Syd admitted they had loved each other all along.

"Good grief, you had it etched across your forehead, Octavian," Lady Withnall intoned. "And you, Syd. You were even more obvious. Haven't I always said so? In truth, I've never seen so much starlight spring into a girl's eyes whenever that big brute walked into a room. Well, he is a big, handsome brute, isn't he? I can understand why it was impossible for you to resist him."

Ambrose laughed and rose to his feet. "A man never had two better brothers. Nor a better wife." He toasted them all. "Nor a better sister-in-law. Syd, you have not only tamed my brother, but managed to make him father to a duke should you ever be blessed with a son. He will have no better protector than his father, or Julius and myself as his uncles. I raise my glass to the next little Duke of Parkhurst."

"To the next little duke," everyone said and joined in the toast.

After that round of cheer and jests on how quickly she and Octavian might produce him, Lady Withnall thucked on her cane and rose. "I would also like to propose a toast to Lady Gregoria."

Gory choked on her wine. "Me? Why me?"

Lady Withnall cast her a knowing smile. "Because you are next, my dear girl. There is no escaping the Marriage Mart. You shall have your Season and find your match. Nothing short of murder will have you escaping it."

At the time, no one expected the dowager's words to ring quite so true.

EPILOGUE

London, England
September, 1826

OCTAVIAN PACED ALONG the elegantly carpeted floor in the library of his and Syd's new townhouse. They had only moved onto the elegant square of houses three months ago. Octavian's heart had been in a roil even back then because Syd was already big as a house, and yet still scampering up and down stairs, bending down, sweeping, dusting, and doing all manner of chores he had hired an army of staff to attend to so that all she had to do was sit on her pert derriere and point.

But this was not in Syd's nature.

Not only had she refused to sit quietly and spend her days working on her needlepoint – something for which she had utterly no talent – or reading, but she was also running to the Huntsford Academy to help Gory in the forensic laboratory. Finally, the head curator, Mr. Smythe-Owen, one of the gentlest men Octavian had ever met, laid down the law and banned her. "You are alarming the entire staff. You shall not deliver a baby amid our dragon exhibits, or dear heaven, atop one of our forensic slabs."

So, she had been confined to their home and woke up this morning complaining of an upset stomach. Moments later, her water broke and completely soaked their elegant carpet. Octavian had never once lost his poise when facing enemy warships, or dodging bayonets and gunshots. But he was beside himself because this was a child about to come into the world.

His child.

And *his* wife was doing all the labor.

He had never felt so helpless in his life.

Or scared.

For this reason, he was not soothed by the presence of his brothers and Marigold's husband, Leo, who was here because *everyone* else was here. Those also present included the two dowagers, Lady Withnall and Lady Dayne. Of course, Marigold, Adela, Gory, and Sophie were here, too. Those were just the women. Along with his brothers and Leo were also Harcourt and Parkhurst.

They were all seated in the parlor, for no one dared approach him as he paced alone in his library and growled at anyone who attempted to draw near.

He was unapproachable, they knew.

He felt frustrated, and as restless as a lion in a cage.

Finally, Octavian's ears picked up the sound of a tiny wail.

Had he imagined it?

There.

He heard the tiny wail again.

Ambrose came running in. "Come on, you arse. That is the sound of your son...well, it could be your daughter. It's an awfully deep voice, though. I think it's a boy."

Octavian's heart shot into his throat. "How is Syd? Has the midwife come down?"

"Midwife's still upstairs. Syd must be exhausted, I'm sure. Go up and see for yourself."

Octavian tore up the stairs.

George Farthingale, the only doctor Octavian trusted to tend to his family, stood beside the midwife as she cleaned off a small bundle. George smiled at him. "You are just in time, Captain Thorne. Come meet your son."

Octavian was certain his heart would burst with happiness. "And Syd? Is she all right?"

George motioned toward the bed and nodded.

Since the midwife was still fussing with their son, Octavian spared only a moment to kiss the boy on his forehead, and went straight over to Syd. "Love, how are you doing? Can I get you anything? Are you in pain?"

"I feel like I just pushed an elephant out of me," she said, wincing as she laughed. "He sounds lusty."

Octavian nodded as he caressed her cheek. "Good set of lungs on the little fellow. He's all red and wrinkled."

"He did not have an easy time coming out of me, either. But he'll soon grow to be as big and handsome as his father."

Octavian kissed her on the lips with exquisite care.

The midwife set the newborn in Syd's arms. "We'll give you five minutes alone, just the three of you, then Lady Thorne must rest."

Octavian nodded.

He understood about chain of command and hierarchy.

The midwife ruled his home right now.

Of course, Syd would always rule his heart.

"Isn't he the most beautiful thing you've ever seen?" Syd remarked.

"Yes, love. He's perfect." The child was so tiny, he could fit in the cup of his hand. His little face was squashed and his eyes were squinted closed. Dark fuzz, as soft as velvet, covered his head. His ears stuck out and his head seemed awfully big for the size of his body. But who was he to contradict little Douglas's proud and doting mother? "No child has ever looked more perfect."

They had agreed to call him Douglas Sydney Thorne in honor of the father Syd never knew. As well, he and Syd had agreed on the name Catriona if they were to have a girl.

Perhaps next child.

However, Octavian was not going to rush things, for Syd would let him know when she was ready. "Have I mentioned how much I love you, sweetheart?"

"Not in minutes," she teased. "I love you, too. We are a family now, Octavian. Is this not a miracle?"

He nodded and kissed her again, careful not to lean on their new son, the soon to be acknowledged Duke of Parkhurst, as he pressed his lips to hers. A short while later, with Syd and the midwife's permission, Octavian brought Douglas downstairs to show him off to friends and family. "Just a quick look and then I must take him back upstairs."

Parkhurst and Harcourt immediately choked up and began to shed tears of joy.

Oh, lord.

"Come on, Harcourt. Step closer and have a good look at your grandson," Octavian said, for this is how Syd insisted he be referred to, as the child's grandfather.

Harcourt now wept openly.

Oh, lord, he thought to himself again. "Parkhurst, you too. He's your grandnephew."

Parkhurst nodded. "All's right with the world now, isn't it Thorne?"

Octavian nodded, pleased for Syd's sake that the truth had come out. He was even warming to Harcourt, who was trying hard to forsake his weasel ways and actually work on improving the Harcourt properties for the next heir in his blood lineage.

As for himself and Syd, they had come a long way since she'd tossed him off that roof.

That night, he held her in his arms and did not think anything could be sweeter. She was still sore and her breasts were magnificently big. But all he did was hold her because despite her protestations, she was tired and had to be aching. "Good night, minx. Sweet dreams," he whispered, certain she was already asleep.

"Good night, you big ox. I love you," she mumbled back. "Truly and forever."

Yes, this was so much better than a make-believe marriage.

THE END

Dear Reader

Thank you for reading *The Make-Believe Marriage*. Captain Octavian Thorne, the handsome brother of Ambrose, Duke of Huntsford, vowed to protect Lady Sydney Harcourt even if it killed him, which sometimes was a close thing because the hoyden did not know how to stay out of trouble. I hope you have been enjoying the latest in the Farthingale series, including *The Viscount And The Vicar's Daughter*, *A Duke For Adela*, and *Marigold And The Marquess*. Coming up next is the romance for Adela, Marigold, and Syd's friend, Lady Gregoria Easton. She'll find her match with Lord Julius Thorne, youngest of the Thorne brothers. You met the Duke of Huntsford (Adela's husband) in *A Duke For Adela*, and Octavian Thorne (Syd's husband) in *The Make-Believe Marriage*. I hope you now enjoy Julius Thorne, their very capable and confident younger brother as he helps Lady Gregoria Easton solve the mystery of who killed her uncle in *A Slight Problem With The Wedding*. They will have to work fast because Gregoria (Gory to her friends) is getting married in a week, but she's the prime suspect in her uncle's murder and the authorities are now on the hunt for her.

I welcome you to all the stories (including several novellas) in the FARTHINGALE SERIES, and if you are in need of even more Farthingales, then please try my Book of Love series where you will meet a host of Farthingale cousins, all of them sweet and innocent young ladies who cannot seem to keep out of trouble. In fact, they attract trouble wherever they turn, especially when it involves some very steamy, alpha heroes and that mysterious, red-leather bound Book of Love. Next release in the Farthingale Series is *A Slight Problem With The Wedding* because Gregoria (Gory to her friends) our Regency goth debutante is going to turn to Julius for help when someone murders her odious uncle and she is worried that she might be accused, or worse, that she might be the next victim on the list. Why did she turn to Julius instead of her intended bridegroom, you ask? Ah, therein lies the story. Read on for a sneak peek…

SNEAK PEEK OF THE UPCOMING BOOK:
A SLIGHT PROBLEM WITH THE WEDDING
CHAPTER 1

London, England
October 1826

LORD JULIUS THORNE felt a prickle run up his spine the moment he stepped into his elegant bedchamber in the Huntsford townhouse sometime after three o'clock in the morning. He was foxed, but not so deep in his cups that he could not sense something was amiss in here. It was dark…unusually dark, even for this late hour. "Who's there?"

Someone must have closed the drapes all the way so as not allow the smallest trickle of dawn's light to steal in. Whoever that someone was, he was still in here. Julius could feel the intruder's presence in the thickness of the air.

He slowly reached into the lip of his boot to grab his pistol, but had yet to withdraw it when a soft feminine voice called to him from behind those drawn curtains. "Julius?"

His heart shot into his throat upon recognizing who had called to him. "Gory?"

Was he more foxed than he realized?

There was no chance Lady Gregoria Easton, better known as

Gory to her friends, would ever be in his bedchamber. Especially not now that she had caught herself a viscount and would be married by the end of the week.

He did not like to think of her married to that pompous clot, Chandler Allendale. The man was completely wrong for her, but what right did he have to judge when he had never let on about his feelings for her?

Now, he feared it was too late. "Gory, I'm drunk. Am I imagining you?"

"No, Julius. It's really me," she said, little more than a slender shadow stepping out from behind her hiding spot. Her voice was so thin and shaky, he'd never heard her sound like this before. "I didn't know where else to turn?"

"So you came to me?" He hurriedly lit a lamp before rushing to her side.

That he was drunk and lovesick did not help the situation. Nor had his foolish agreement to escort Gory around London all week long because her betrothed was too busy to attend to it helped in the least, either. He had foolishly thought spending more time in each other's company might rid him of his feelings for Gory, but he was wrong.

She was stubborn, opinionated, independent, and determined to be the greatest forensic specialist in all of London. What other young lady would rather spend more time examining dead things than going to balls, musicales, and fashionable dinner parties?

Her quirky traits and stubborn disposition ought to have cured him of these unwanted feelings he had for her.

His stupid ploy had failed.

He was falling more deeply in love with her than ever.

He held the lamp up for a better view, and his heart immediately surged into his throat. "Dear heaven! What happened to you?"

She was wearing her wedding gown, a soft, pearl silk that he had seen when taking her to the fashionable modiste for a final fitting only yesterday. Not that he had wanted anything to do with enabling her to marry that dimwit viscount, Allendale. But she had needed a ride and he, like the clot he was, had volunteered to assist her as she went on this wedding errand to her modiste.

He blinked.

And blinked again.

The blood splattered all over her gown was still there.

It wasn't a drunken delusion.

Crimson trails of it seeped into the delicate silk, and dried splotches of crimson red stained her hands. "Never mind. You'll tell me later," he said gently, realizing she must be in shock when she did not immediately respond to his question. "Let me check you for injuries first."

He set the lamp on a nearby table, and then ran his hands along her body with aching care.

Once. Twice.

He was not surprised by the soft allure of her curves, for he'd gotten a good look at her yesterday, accidentally walking into the modiste's fitting room while she was still undressed. Why had the modiste's helper told him Gory was finished and needed assistance with her packages when she was still in there, standing in her chemise of sheerest fabric that hid nothing from his view?

Even though her back had been turned to him, there were several large mirrors in the room, so that in addition to her sweetly curved backside that was pointed at him as she bent slightly to retrieve something out of her reticule, he could make out her nicely shaped breasts in the mirror's reflection. Those ample mounds that were about to spill out of the bodice could fill the cup of his hand. He refused to dwell on what else he saw, but it was not an exaggeration to admit he would pay a king's ransom to explore her body.

He would have been sent straight to hell had he acted upon the possibilities then and there.

Instead, he had backed away before she noticed him.

But the sight of her delectable attributes was seared into his eyeballs as well as his heart.

Gory always hid her charming figure beneath the most hideous clothes. Who knew she had the body of an angel beneath all those layers of dark muslin? Well, he'd always suspected it because she was a very pretty girl.

He liked everything about her and should have said something when Allendale began to court her.

But he didn't.

By the time he realized his mistake, it was too late. Gory, the wonderfully eccentric, brilliant bluestocking who studied dead things, and was one of the foremost scholars in advancement of medical science, was now betrothed to Viscount Allendale.

They had made the announcement three months ago.

The wedding was to take place next week.

He and his brothers had been invited, of course.

His brothers were married to Gory's best friends, Adela and Syd. The wedding reception was to be held right here at the Huntsford townhouse immediately after the ceremony. His brother, Ambrose, Duke of Huntsford, had insisted upon it when Gory's uncle had cheapened out.

Her uncle was an unmitigated arse.

Had Gory accepted Allendale in order to escape the untenable situation in her own home? Julius had known she was unhappy there and ought to have done something about it, proposing to her himself.

He quickly shook off thoughts of Gory's wedding, an event that he was now determined to stop if Gory gave the slightest hint she might reciprocate his feelings. But none of it mattered now, for she was in a desperate way and trembling.

Gory never trembled.

She was afraid of nothing.

"Tell me what happened," he said, taking her cold hands into his warm ones, and having her sit in one of the cushioned chairs beside his hearth. "Let me fetch the ewer and basin. I need to clean you off while we speak. Gory, I can't find any wounds on you. Have I missed something?"

Blessed saints, his hands had skimmed over every luscious inch of her and found nothing obvious.

"I don't know. I feel dizzy," she said.

He frowned. "Perhaps you were hit on the head. Hold still while I take a look at your scalp."

She pushed his hand away. "No."

"Gory, I need to–"

She pushed his hand away again. "No!"

He sighed. "All right. Maybe later. How did you get all this blood on you? Where have you been? Was someone else hurt?" He stopped, for he was throwing too many questions at her all at once.

When she shivered again, he realized he ought to get something warm and liquid into her. But it was the middle of the night, too early for the Huntsford scullery maids to be stirring yet. In any event, he did not think it wise to alert anyone else to her presence, not until he got more information out of her.

The sky had been threatening rain all night and Julius now heard the first droplets striking against his window panes. He grabbed a fresh cloth from his dressing room table and dampened it in the water he had just poured from the ewer into the basin.

By the soft amber glow of the lamp, he rinsed her hands, and then washed the dabs of blood off her face and off a few tendrils of hair that framed her heart-shaped face. The pins had loosened from her hair and all those glorious chestnut tresses were about to spill onto her shoulders. After cleaning her face and neck, and wiping a few droplets of blood off the swell of one breast, he took the pins out and smoothed back her hair.

Big hazel eyes framed by dark lashes stared back at him.

Her mouth was pink and lush, although tightly pursed at the moment because she was so scared. "Gory, may I help you out of those clothes? The blood has soaked through all the layers, even to your chemise. I'll give you my robe to wrap around yourself for now. As soon as I hear the staff stirring, I'll have Adela's maid fetch you an outfit from her wardrobe."

"No!" She groaned. "No one can know I am here."

Julius was not certain what to do. "You cannot walk around in my clothes. They are too big for you and will never fit your slight frame. Besides, you won't fool anyone into thinking you are a boy."

She glanced down at her breasts and sighed. "When is Adela due back?"

"You know she and Ambrose are in Oxford for the next few days. They won't be back until the day after tomorrow."

She nodded. "They've been gone all week."

"Which is why I was enlisted to escort you around Town. But you needn't worry about the wedding breakfast, all is in readiness. Adela organized everything before she and Ambrose left. Will you allow me to help you out of your gown now?"

She nodded again.

He only meant to loosen the laces she could not reach on her own. But once he had done this, she still did not move. His brother, Octavian, now an admiral in the Royal Navy, had told him how some men, when strained to their breaking point, succumbed to battle shock. This is what Gory appeared to be suffering. "Gory, can you undress on your own?"

'No, Julius. Look at me. My hands are shaking too hard."

Dear heaven, what had scared this fearless girl so badly?

He groaned softly. "May I help you then? Would that be all right?"

The blood was so thick on her clothing, it surely had soaked through to her skin. He would need to wash everything off her as soon as possible.

"Yes, please," Gory said, obviously mimicking his thoughts. "I cannot bear to look at myself or touch anything I am wearing."

"All right." This was not how he ever dreamed of Gory shedding her clothes for him. He got the clothes off her with painstaking care, and looked his fill only for the purpose of examining her more thoroughly to determine if she had any significant wounds. Once again, he did not even find bruises or scrapes.

Her body was sweet perfection.

But her eyes looked a bit glazed.

She must have struck her head on something, but when he attempted to reach out again to inspect her scalp, she pushed his hand away. "No!"

And yet she made no protest when he cleaned the traces of blood off her stomach and breasts. He stifled a shudder because this girl was beyond perfect and he had lost her to another because of his own stupid procrastination.

Why did he wish to prolong his bachelor life when it was not all that enjoyable? He rarely drank to excess, although he had tonight. Of all the nights to be foxed when he needed to have his head clear! He was not one for gambling, and had not even touched another woman in months because his heart wanted only Gory.

He wrapped her in one of his robes, a black silk that fell only to his knees and had shortened sleeves. He thought she would not be completely drowned in it. His fingers grazed her soft shoulders as he tried to get her arms in the sleeves. "Gory, does it hurt to raise your arm?"

"No, Julius. My arm is fine."

But *she* clearly wasn't fine.

He sighed, silently debating whether to press her about her injuries. But she was too fragile at the moment, and did not appear hurt other than a blow to her head that she still would not allow him to examine. "All right."

She was so lovely, she made his heart ache. The robe was too big for her and she ought to have looked ridiculous in it.

She didn't.

When she shivered once more, he carried her to his bed. "Get under the covers, Gory. You'll be warmer that way. I'll pull up a stool beside the bed and we can talk."

She whimpered. "My uncle is dead."

Julius feared it was something serious like this that had brought her running here. Why had she fled here and not to her darling viscount? Well, he didn't care. All that mattered was that she was here and he was going to protect her. "We had better notify the authorities. But first tell me what–"

"No!" she cried softly. "You cannot let anyone know I am here."

He raked a hand through his hair. "Why should I keep you hidden? Others will worry when they realize you are missing. Worse, the authorities might think you are the one who did him in and are now on the run because of it. And what about your viscount? You are getting married in a week's time. Do you intend to hide out here until your wedding day?"

"May I? Do you mind?"

Did he mind Gory in his bed?

If it were up to him, he would want her there permanently. "I don't mind having you here, Gory. But is it not better to report the crime to the authorities before others find your uncle's body? Where is your aunt?"

Gory sat up, and then winced. "She's visiting her sister in Windsor."

The effort of sitting up must have pained her.

She put a hand to her forehead to give it a delicate rub.

Did this not confirm she had been struck on the head?

Why would she not allow him a better look? Not that he knew the first thing about proper treatment of a head wound. But he knew just the man to summon...Dr. George Farthingale. He was the best doctor in London and could be counted upon to be discreet.

However, Julius hesitated.

He did not want to embroil anyone else in this possible murder situation until he had more facts. "Gory, when is your aunt due back?"

"Later this afternoon."

"All right, this gives us several hours to attend to the problem. Tell me everything you know."

"Julius, you haven't asked me."

"Asked you what?"

She stopped rubbing her forehead and looked up at him with her hazel eyes wide. "Whether I killed my uncle."

He arched an eyebrow. "The thought never entered my mind...but, did you?"

GET A SLIGHT PROBLEM WITH THE WEDDING NOW!

Interested in learning more about the Farthingale series? Join me on Facebook! Additionally, we'll be giving away lots of Farthingale swag and prizes during the launches. If you would like to join the fun, you can subscribe to my newsletter and also connect with me on Twitter. You can find links to do all of this at my website: mearaplatt.com.

If you enjoyed this book, I would really appreciate it if you could post a review on the site where you purchased it. Also feel free to write one on Goodreads or other reader sites that you peruse. Even a few sentences on what you thought about the book would be most helpful! If you do leave a review, send me a message on Facebook because I would love to thank you personally. Please also consider telling your friends about the FARTHINGALE SERIES and recommending it to your book clubs.

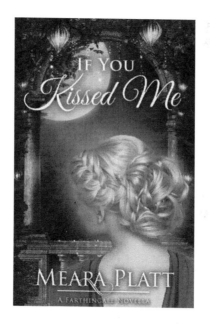

**Sign up for Meara Platt's newsletter
and you'll receive a free, exclusive copy**
of her Farthingale novella,
If You Kissed Me.

Visit her website
to grab your free copy:
mearaplatt.com

ALSO BY MEARA PLATT

FARTHINGALE SERIES
My Fair Lily
The Duke I'm Going To Marry
Rules For Reforming A Rake
A Midsummer's Kiss
The Viscount's Rose
Earl of Hearts
The Viscount and the Vicar's Daughter
A Duke For Adela
Marigold and the Marquess
The Make-Believe Marriage
A Slight Problem with the Wedding
If You Wished For Me (novella)
Never Dare A Duke
Capturing The Heart Of A Cameron

MOONSTONE LANDING SERIES
The Moonstone Duke
The Moonstone Marquess
The Moonstone Major
The Moonstone Governess
The Moonstone Hero
The Moonstone Pirate
Moonstone Landing (novella)
Moonstone Angel (novella)

BOOK OF LOVE SERIES

The Look of Love

The Touch of Love

The Taste of Love

The Song of Love

The Scent of Love

The Kiss of Love

The Chance of Love

The Gift of Love

The Heart of Love

The Hope of Love (novella)

The Promise of Love

The Wonder of Love

The Journey of Love

The Treasure of Love

The Dance of Love

The Miracle of Love

The Dream of Love (novella)

The Remembrance of Love (novella)

BOOK OF LOVE CONNECTED NOVELLAS
All I Want For Christmas (novella)
Tempting Taffy (novella)

DARK GARDENS SERIES
Garden of Shadows
Garden of Light
Garden of Dragons
Garden of Destiny
Garden of Angels

THE BRAYDENS
A Match Made In Duty
Earl of Westcliff

Fortune's Dragon
Earl of Kinross
Pearls of Fire
Aislin
Genalynn
A Rescued Heart
Earl of Alnwick

THE LYON'S DEN SERIES
The Lyon's Surprise
Kiss of the Lyon
Lyon in the Rough

DeWOLFE PACK ANGELS SERIES
Nobody's Angel
Kiss An Angel
Bhrodi's Angel

ABOUT THE AUTHOR

Meara Platt is an award winning, USA TODAY bestselling author and an Amazon UK All-Star. Her favorite place in all the world is England's Lake District, which may not come as a surprise since many of her stories are set in that idyllic landscape, including her paranormal romance Dark Gardens series. Learn more about the Dark Gardens and Meara's lighthearted and humorous Regency romances in her Farthingale series and Book of Love series, or her warmhearted Regency romances in her Moonstone Landing series or Braydens series by visiting her website at www.mearaplatt.com.

Printed in Great Britain
by Amazon